THAT'S
WHAT
SHE
SAID

THAT'S WHAT SHE SAID

A Novel

ELEANOR PILCHER

AVON

An Imprint of HarperCollinsPublishers

THAT'S WHAT SHE SAID. Copyright © 2025 by Eleanor Pilcher. All rights reserved. Printed in the United States of America. No part of this book may be used or reproduced in any manner whatsoever without written permission except in the case of brief quotations embodied in critical articles and reviews. For information, address HarperCollins Publishers, 195 Broadway, New York, NY 10007.

HarperCollins books may be purchased for educational, business, or sales promotional use. For information, please email the Special Markets Department at SPsales@harpercollins.com.

Avon, Avon & logo, and Avon Books & logo are registered trademarks of HarperCollins Publishers in the United States of America and other countries.

FIRST EDITION

Interior text design by Diahann Sturge-Campbell

Library of Congress Cataloging-in-Publication Data has been applied for.

ISBN 978-0-06-341210-1

25 26 27 28 29 LBC 5 4 3 2 1

For my dad, who probably won't read this book because in his mind I'm still only five years old. And for my mum, who will read every word. I love you both loads.

CHAPTER 1
BETH

I CAN'T BELIEVE I said yes to this. What was I thinking! And don't laugh!" I whispered forcefully. "I'm stuck in the toilets, hiding from eleven hens and a stripper called Don Carlos. How is this funny?"

"How is this not?" Serena continued to giggle. "Oh, babe. You knew what you were getting into when you RSVP'd. You can't back out now."

"I was trying to be a supportive friend to Bonnie, not a bean-bag for a stripper to bounce around on until they got comfortable."

"He *what*?" I imagined her lying on her bed in the flat we shared, drinking an Irish coffee and painting her toenails, leisurely enjoying her hangover-Saturday as was her weekly ritual.

I shuddered at the memory of Don Carlos—whose name was probably Robbie or Brett—gyrating against my shin.

"Why is it automatically assumed that if you're at a hen do, you've consented to be molested?!"

"Was it really bouncing or more of a graze? I know how these things work, typically strippers are quite hands off. They're quite disappointing in that regard."

"Well, I was hoping they'd be more hands off. But it's been less of an afternoon tease and more of an afternoon full-frontal so far. Stacey or Tracey or whatever her name is whipped his little waiter's apron right off the moment he walked in."

Serena snickered. "How little are we talking here?"

"Well, I'm not exactly the one to ask when it comes to size, Serena."

"I know, I know. Did you at least get a good look?"

I shuddered again. "Why do penises look blue?"

"Is it cold in there?"

"We're in a bar on the fourth floor of a Grade II listed building. I admit there's a draught."

"Poor man."

The door of the bathroom opened with a dramatic bang and a waft of perfume mixed with prosecco.

"Betty, are you in here?"

"Yes! Yes, I'm in here," I said, suddenly standing from the toilet—which thankfully I wasn't using—and waving my arm around like I was Kate Winslet calling for rescue from the *Titanic*.

"Bonnie wants to start the games and we need you. So *hurry up*!" She yelled the last instruction before promptly slamming the door.

"Wow, she sounds like a delight."

"I think that might have been Gale, Bonnie's sister? I don't know. I can't keep them all straight. Apart from Bonnie I don't know anyone else. None of the others from Elias are here. I know everyone loses touch when you change jobs, but I at least thought Rona or Grace would come. Both flaked and said they had family commitments. I wish I had that excuse."

"Ask your sister next time," Serena suggested wisely.

"Oh god, you're right." Penny might not have appreciated me using her as an excuse, but I could have gone to visit her and help take her mind off the stress that goes with fertility treatments. Particularly failed ones. But it was too late. I was here now.

"It still wouldn't get you out of the £200 deposit. The non-refundable one."

"Wait!" I said, snapping my fingers and hearing the sound echo in my head—a sound that can only be caused when you've drunk a bottle of prosecco too quickly in one sitting. "That's why I decided to come. I couldn't get my money back."

"That's it, babe. It's not to be a supportive friend to your ex-colleague."

"I like Bonnie, I *really* do," I began to hear my own telltale slur. "But not enough to have a penis in my face. Or what's next—that's why I called! Do you know what the first game is?"

"No, but I want you to tell me." I could hear Serena's smile through the phone.

"We have to write down an embarrassing sexual encounter and slip the note into his waiter's apron and guess what the pocket sits over?"

"Oh no, the horror," Serena teased. To her this would be a great game: she'd have a long and extensive rummage when it came to her turn to pull out a slip of paper. But for me, it was my worst nightmare.

"No, but think—what sexual encounter am I going to share? I'm twenty-eight and a vir—" I stopped short of saying "virgin" just in case Gale or Stacey or someone had slipped back into the bathroom without me hearing. The anxiety stage of my alcohol drinking had well and truly peaked.

"They won't care. You always worry about it and then no one ever does."

"No, no, Serena. *They'll* care."

The door slammed open again. Gale had returned, like the strong wind she had been named for.

"Would you get your well-rounded arse back upstairs! Bonnie is waiting! *You can't keep Bonnie waiting!*" Her screeches got louder with every sentence and echoed around the cisterns.

"I've got to go," I whispered hurriedly into the phone. "What should I do?"

"Oh, use one of my stories, I've got plenty," Serena said in a way that reminded me of when Penny would give in and let me borrow one of her dresses before a school disco when we were teenagers.

"Okay, thank you. Which one? The STD one?"

"No, that's not hen do safe—you'll get too many questions about symptoms from the naughty ones."

"What about sex with Zoey? You *love* talking about sex with Zoey! You *love* Zo—"

She cut me off as she always did when I mentioned her favorite person besides me. Zoey was special—though Serena often described her as her favorite fuck, in my mind, she was more than that. Not that Serena ever took any notice when I asked her if she thought so too. "Darling, you're not bisexual, how are you going to explain Zoey? No, how about . . ." She thought for a moment. "Ooh, what about that time I got caught having sex on that plane back from Japan and the flight attendant decided to separate us as punishment, so he put him—Toby, I think his name was—in coach and he upgraded me to first class. Where he then gave me his number."

"Like anyone would believe that was me!"

"Fine then, change it up and say you had sex on a plane, got caught, and the flight attendant separated you and the bloke."

"And if they ask about the bloke?" I quickly put her on speaker to access my notes app and write down the story.

"Tell them it was some guy you met on holiday in Marrakech. Then you won't have to explain to Bonnie when you had a nonexistent boyfriend. Ooh, speaking of—did she invite the good-looking guy from work you used to crush on, like she was threatening?"

"Evan? It's a hen do, and he most certainly is not a hen he is a . . . a cock?"

"A stag?"

"That's it, a stag! Yeah, he's not a cock. He's too nice to be a cock." I typed out Serena's story, with many glaring typos, and sighed. "I really have to go. One more minute and I think Gale will stab me with her stiletto."

"Well, don't forget to call Evan when you're six shots in."

"I am not going to drunk-call Evan!" I said, before hastily shouting "Thank you!" and hanging up.

In the distance I could hear not one but three sets of too-high high heels coming down the rickety Grade II building stairs. I was in for it now. But at least I had a story to share. And if worse came to worst I could always tell them I got the prosecco shits. Nothing bonds hens quicker than talking about toilet trips.

"You broke the seal, didn't you!"

"Have I got toilet roll in my arse crack?"

"Can you see my tampon string through this dress?"

All queries I had heard so far on Bonnie's hen do, and we were only on activity three, after nipple tassel and cocktail-making classes. We had clubbing before this evening was over. But before that, I had to face Don Carlos and his little apron.

The hinges of the bathroom door squeaked painfully.

"Bethany!" Only one person at this hen do actually used my full name.

"Bonnie, I'm coming now. I swear," I said, flushing and shoving my phone back in my bra.

She was outside my door in her all-white getup with her arms crossed.

"Seriously. It's been twenty minutes."

"I got the prosecco shits," I said nonchalantly, going over to the sink and being sure to double spritz with the cheap pink soap.

"I want to get the games started. Most of the girls have added their sexual encounters to Don Carlos's apron already."

"Yeah, come on, Betty, speed it up," Gale said, chucking a wad of hand towels at my face.

Bonnie sighed and looked back at her sister. "This is why she took so long. I knew I should have sent Amy; she has that calming tone."

Gale rolled her eyes. "That's why she puts us all to sleep when she opens her mouth."

"Gale . . ." Bonnie said warningly, and Gale shrugged.

"Sorry!" she said, clearly not sorry. (Thank god Penny and I weren't like this as sisters.) Barely a second later: "Oh hurry the fuck up, Betty!"

"For god's sake, her name is Bethany, and you know it!" Bonnie shouted. Bonnie was a stickler for full names—although god forbid you called her by her own: Bonita. Only my mother called me Bethany.

"Right," I said, using one of the hand towels to dry off quickly. "Let's do this. I've got my story ready; I just need a pen and paper."

Bonnie squealed and threw her arms in the air, already forgiving me as she shoved me out of the toilets and back up the stairs.

She was always the most dramatic coworker at Elias Recruitment, the agency where I'd been marketing assistant. I didn't have a choice whether I wanted to be her friend: on the first day she insisted we go out for lunch and then gave me a work orientation on what it was *really* like to work there, none of the

HR bullshit they had told me when I arrived. Thanks to her, I knew exactly where the best coffee machine was in the building, which toilet was quietest if I needed to have a sneaky shit, and the latest time I could make it in without my boss, Rona, causing a scene (9:20 a.m.).

We'd bonded—at one point Serena got quite jealous of how close Bonnie and I were. She went so far as trying to buy back my affection with an Amazon Prime subscription and a chocolate fountain for the flat—two things every twentysomething should have. But she needn't have bothered. My friendship with Bonnie was never going to be a ride-or-die friendship. She's too much of a gossip for that.

"We're all here!" she squealed again as we entered the hen do. Empty prosecco bottles lay strewn around the unmanned bar and the gluten-free snack table had been demolished. If you think children's parties are messy, check out a hen do.

Rounds of "finally" went around the long table, and I made apologetic noises as Celine—or Selina?—pushed some paper and a pencil into my hand.

"We need your story," she said, a glimmer of malicious anticipation in her eye.

I went to get my phone out of my bra but realized everyone was watching me. I was the last person to add their story to Don Carlos's apron. He, thankfully, was standing at the other end of the table with Bonnie, doing a little dance for her. I looked away immediately. His bow tie was coming loose from his neck, and it made me fear what else would be coming loose again soon.

Smiling at everyone, I leaned over my paper and began to scribble what I could remember about Serena's story on my piece of paper.

I was on a plane having sex with a guy and we got caught by the flight attendant.

Simple and to the point. That would do.

I folded the piece of paper over twice and waved it to get Don Carlos's attention. He stopped his windmill action to pop around the table.

"Milady," he said, pushing his groin forward. All the girls laughed, and I forced a smile as I slipped the piece of paper into the pocket. I felt nothing, thank god. "Right," Don Carlos shouted and clapped his hands together. "Let the games begin. Bonnie, my darling, you're up first. Reach into my pocket and pull out a story." He ran over to Bonnie, his arse cheeks flapping, and performed the same groin-shoving action as he had done to me.

Bonnie, utterly gleeful, thrust her hand into his pocket and swirled it around for a good few seconds before pulling out a piece of paper and reading.

"*I had anal sex on a first date!*" Everyone threw back their heads with laughter as Stacey or Tracey threw her hands up in pride.

"It was me!"

"Of course it was!" several chorused. Hopefully mutual friends and not just judgmental hens.

"My turn," she said flirtingly, calling over Don Carlos and rummaging in his pocket. She had one hand on his arse cheek as she searched, and Don Carlos pretended to blush.

"*My husband and I tried to spice up our love life by having sex in public, but the only changing rooms big enough were in Sainsbury's clothes section and we got caught and banned from shopping there.*"

"Melinda!" several women cried. It was obviously her—she was the only married hen. She held her head in her hands. For a minute I thought she was genuinely embarrassed, and then I saw she was beaming.

What was it with hens and their pride in embarrassing sex stories?

"Okay, okay," she said calmly, reaching into Don Carlos's pocket while maintaining the most severe eye contact with him. She pulled out a white piece of paper.

"*I was on a plane having sex with a guy and we got caught by the flight attendant.*" A round of "Oohs" went around the room as everyone looked at different hens expecting it to be one of them. I took a big breath and then raised my hand.

"Oh my god! Bethany!" Bonnie cried, standing up and slamming her hands on the table. All the other hens' eyes widened, and I felt a few of them were overselling their "oh wow, what a great story" reactions. None of them knew me, so they really didn't care about my escapades. Nonexistent as they were. "You little minx! And when was this?"

"A while ago," I said, wearily realizing that it was my turn to rummage.

"When, where, how? Tell us everything."

"There's nothing more to tell. It was on a plane, and we got caught." I looked to Melinda as a potential mature ally (she was married after all), but nope, she was digging into an egg and cress finger sandwich.

"Who was it, at least?"

"Just some bloke."

"Oh bullshit," Gale mocked. "Come on, give us some details. The mile-high club is impossible to join these days. The toilets are too small."

"Have you given it a go, then, Gale?" I asked jovially, trying desperately to move the conversation from me. I was so desperate, I even called Don Carlos to me so I could pull another story and move the attention away.

"Oh my god, was this with Evan?" Bonnie suddenly asked and my whole face changed.

"Who's Evan?" What is it with hens and gossip? It's like seagulls and seaside chips, they just descend on you.

"It wasn't Evan; he was my and Bonnie's old coworker." I really wanted Don Carlos to speed up and get over here.

"Bethany had such a thing for Evan. He worked in the project management department opposite her in the marketing department and he is like Michael B. Jordan, good-looking but super shy. I'm pretty sure he had a thing for her as well," Bonnie explained.

"He did not," I said.

"They kissed at the New Year's party," Bonnie carried on, like a runaway train. "Just before he left."

"It was on the cheek," I added, wanting to die on the spot. "At midnight. It barely counts." A kiss on the cheek is something cousins do, not potential partners. And besides, no guy as good-looking and as lovely as Evan would look twice at me in that way. Regardless, it could never happen. What guy would settle for a nonsexual—or potentially nonsexual—relationship? As a demisexual, I did on occasion feel sexual attraction, but I was twenty-eight and could still count all those instances on one hand, so I felt the sex ship had probably sailed, leaving me stranded on the equivalent of blue ball harbor.

"You had a New Year's party with your work?" one of the hens asked. I could have kissed her for changing the subject—and not just on the cheek!

"They didn't do a Christmas party, the office rebelled, so a load of the managers organized a New Year's one instead," Bonnie added. "It was a whole thing."

"Right, who's next?" I asked.

"I still want to know how she had sex on a plane," Gale said.

"Honestly, you can't get on your knees for a blow and unless he's The Rock, there's no way he could have lifted you up and held you there to screw you."

"It was a hand job," I said quickly, just to get her to shut up.

"Well that hardly counts as sex," Gale scoffed. "If we're counting hand jobs as sex then my number quadruples."

"We all know you're a slut, Gale," Bonnie said, slapping her sister on the arm. "Bethany is just more selective."

That's one way of putting it.

"But on a plane?" Gale said. "I wouldn't even bother going to the bathroom to give a hand job."

"Who said we were," I mumbled, but I forgot mumbles and whispers sound a lot like shouting when you're drunk.

"That's true," Melinda pointed out. "She never says bathroom in her note."

"So wait, what happened?" Bonnie asked, confusion across her face. It was like a cartoon, suddenly I felt all the hens' faces turn to me. Even Don Carlos was engrossed.

"Fine," I said, giving in. "It's not even my story, I borrowed it from a friend."

After a split second, a few of the hens threw their heads back in laughter, while the others turned to Bonnie to see if that was acceptable.

"I didn't have anything embarrassing to share," I said, lifting up my arms in helpless defeat.

"Was it Serena?" Bonnie asked after a second and then she also began to laugh, and the hens relaxed.

"There's always something embarrassing," one of the hens whose name I hadn't yet discovered said. "My embarrassing story is just about queefing."

"Hey! No spoilers!" Gale shouted across the table.

"And getting your period midway through."

"Well, that happens to every girl, doesn't it?" Melinda said coolly. I got the impression that as the married woman of the room she was also the matriarch. "Or your first time. Everyone's first time is embarrassing. My first time, my boyfriend asked me if we had recorded *Match of the Day* while we were midway. Clearly *he* wasn't into it."

"Oh god! Something like that happened to me," Stacey or Tracey said. "He was watching the Arsenal match on his phone while he was on top of me. The score was 2–1 to Arsenal, so at least he was in a good mood after."

Bonnie was cackling at the other end of the table, so much so she was at risk of falling off her chair. "Crikey, it's been a while since our first times, hey ladies?!" Everyone nodded in agreement all smiling about "those" days while I sat at the end of the table desperately holding it in that I hadn't had a first time, or any time at all.

"Go on then, Betty," someone said, still not getting my name right. "Pick another story."

"Okay," I said, relieved that we were at least moving away from me. Don Carlos appeared and shook his groin side to side; he was shaking it so much I was tempted to hold his arse cheek as Stacey or Tracey had, just to keep him still.

I reached in and pulled out my hand almost immediately, spilling three folded pieces of paper onto the floor in the process. Everyone laughed.

"God, you're such a prude!" Gale shouted. "You're acting like a virgin!" The cackling among the ladies grew the loudest it had been all day. I pushed through, clambering on all fours to gather the remaining stories. Only then did I look up and realize that I was now face height with Don Carlos's dick. This only made everyone laugh harder.

"The Prude and the Dick," Gale said unkindly as I climbed back to my seat. Great, I was officially the prude of the hen party.

A lump in my throat had formed so it was painful to speak, but I gulped it down and shouted: "*I queefed so loudly during sex that it caused me to laugh so hard I peed myself.*"

Immediately the girls started to point at the hen who had already claimed the story, while I dug into my bra for my phone. Under the table, almost to the level of predictive text, I messaged Serena.

> Please come!! I need help.

I felt the vibration almost immediately and glanced down at the screen.

> On my way. X

CHAPTER 2
SERENA

FOR ONCE, BONNIE was tolerant of my butting in. After some intense eye-rolling and some bribery with a round of prosecco, I was welcomed into the hen party.

"Well, if it will make Bethany happy," Bonnie said with a candyfloss voice that made me want to stab a fork into my gut. Or hers.

Obviously, Bonnie had noticed Beth's downturn in mood as much as I could sense it from across the room. She had been silent upon my arrival, barely standing when I had to defend myself to the forever–maids of honor at the door.

I reached her chair and balanced precariously on the arm, placing a reassuring hand on her shoulder. "You alright?" She smiled but looked like she wanted to cry.

"I kind of suck at hen parties."

"No, hen dos just suck in general," I returned, barely keeping my voice to a whisper and getting many glares from the bottom end of the table. I smiled and winked at the glaring hens with a "come and get it" attitude. They quickly turned away.

"Right, I'm thinking we need to get pissed," I said, grabbing my Amex, which was in for a heavy night. Thanks to my parental guilt account, I could afford it. "Proper wine for us, none of that piss I just got the others." I stood and offered Beth my hand. "We're just popping down for drinks," I said to the group, though no one acted like they even heard me.

"You okay, Bethany?" Bonnie asked from the top of the table. Behind her the stripper, Don Carlos, was preparing another game involving stickers. Definitely time to get Beth out of the room.

"Yeah, just hot." Beth smiled overly brightly. "Might go for a smoke." She pretended to gesture to a cigarette in her tiny purse—even though she didn't smoke—and followed me before any of the other hens could request to join.

"Honestly, all I do is lie at these fucking things," Beth said as we clambered down the rickety flight of stairs.

I laughed. Beth returned to her actual self more and more with each step we descended.

"Not having the night of your life, then," I said. "Not feeling like *one of the hens*."

"If I never see one of these girls again, it will be too soon." She glanced upward to make sure no hens were spying on us.

"Even Bonnie?" I asked hopefully. Beth knew my thoughts on Bonnie were not positive.

To me, Bonnie was the epitome of a wanker. She still wore her Glastonbury wristband six months after the festival ended, she shared Instagram photos of her Le Creuset collection just to prove she owned Le Creuset, and she refused to use they/them pronouns even when asked because "you're one or the other, not both."

"Two of your most expensive Sauvignon Blancs, please," I told the bartender, who looked me up and down as I flashed my Amex, the cheeky sod.

"I thought you were doing dry January?" Beth pointed out.

"Sauvignon Blanc is dry." I winked.

She laughed, relief at being away from the other hens loosening her up. "So how did you get here so quickly?" Beth asked, leaning against the sticky bar top.

"I'm a speedy dresser, and I did my makeup on the tube."

"Oh, teach me your ways!" We clinked our newly delivered glasses together.

"To us!"

"Not to Bonnie?" Beth queried, not waiting before taking a sip of the wine.

"I think Bonnie's had enough toasts in her honor for one day. Any more and she'll need to grow a second head to distribute the weight of the first one."

Beth laughed uneasily. The nervous energy in her was dissipating, although it was obvious by her shoulders—up by her earlobes—that the hens had hit her nerves.

"What's on the rest of the day's agenda?" I asked Beth, trying my wine. The alcohol made my nose tingle, but not unpleasantly.

"Once we're done here, we're heading back to the hotel for pre-drinks and outfit changes before heading off to this disco club in Shoreditch. Think tequila and glitter."

"My kind of night," I said mischievously.

"Sometimes I wish I had your confidence, Serena," she said, with sincerity that made my face tingle with pride.

"It's confidence and a fuck-it attitude—I have plenty to share. Take some of mine!" I placed my wine down and began wafting the air in front of me in Beth's direction. She stepped back and swiped the air to stop me as eyes turned to us in our odd play-acting scenario. At home this was a regular kind of occurrence, but I supposed it would look odd in public.

But the whole point of the fuck-it attitude was not to care, so I didn't. Beth, however, was blushing from collarbone to hairline.

"Stop it!" she giggled. "We've got a whole evening to get through."

"*Pft!*" I said, reclaiming my glass and my card from the bartender. "Easy. We've got this."

"We've got this," Beth repeated, with the intensity of a mantra. "We've got this."

I placed my spare hand on her shoulder again and pulled her into an awkward one-arm hug as we turned to head back up the stairs.

It was only one night out, after all. What could happen?

None of the hens were aware that it was TV Theme Night at the club of choice, not that it mattered to anyone but Gale. She spent the better part of twenty minutes shouting at a poor bartender, while the rest of us headed downstairs to the disco to dance it out to "I'll Be There for You."

After Gale left, I got the already exhausted bartender to make up a batch of Club Tropicana shots, paying him a huge tip as a way of apology. Life hack: always get the bartender onside before you get shit-faced, that way they'll be much more favorable when you're a mess at the end of the night. I was a pro at this.

And boy was I right about being shit-faced.

Thanks to my pro-partying life as a lifestyle and celebrity journalist, it typically took more than a bottle of prosecco to make me feel remotely tipsy, but I forgot how quickly Beth could get pissed. Not to mention the other hens were messy-as-fuck drunks.

I would need at least five shots before I felt anything, and then just a few more shots to get black-out drunk. My favorite kind. Most people hate it, but I love the surprise the following day—and by surprise, I usually mean waking up on the floor of my kitchen with my head in an unused saucepan and my hand in a glass of water. Deciphering that incident had reminded me just how deep my daddy issues go.

Later, I found myself screaming "If only I'd been a boy!" on the dance floor as "I Don't Want to Be" began to play.

Beth, wasted and lovable at this point, slapped her arms over my shoulder and screamed, "I'll always love you!" Before randomly starting to cry. The hens spotted her tears and instantly surmised that she was undone by the memories of *One Tree Hill* and joined the awkward hold. When the song finished moments later, we were all crying and dancing together in the middle of the floor like an American football team grappling for a ball.

"That's it, girls, let it out," the DJ said, his diamond earring glittering.

"Oh fuck off!" I shouted. He countered by putting on "Walking on Sunshine." No one can cry to that song, it's practically illegal. You have to sing and dance along like you're solo dancing in an elevator where no one can see.

Upon being released from the American football hold, I gestured to Beth that I was getting a drink and she sweatily clasped my hand to follow.

I left her at the end of the bar while I went to cajole my tipped-up bartender to let me skip the queue and get two shots of tequila. He was obliging, as I'd intended.

"My français is très mauvaise!" I heard down the bar as I placed the two limes in my mouth and clasped the two shots and saltshaker.

"Non non, très bon."

In the space of three minutes Beth had found a man. I almost dropped the tequila, or I would have if she wasn't attempting to talk to said man in another language.

"Voulez," she giggled, her foot slipping beneath her. "Vouz couchez avec . . ."

"Tequila!" I interjected, as loudly as I could over the drum solo. "Who wants tequila? I know you do." Effortlessly I slipped between the man, who was very clearly *not* French, and handed Beth her tequila. She was instantly gratified, having not yet realized that she was attempting to get with a man for the first time. Not that "get with a man" meant anything to her beyond kissing and some heavy petting.

That was one regret I, as a good—no, *best*—friend could halt in its tracks.

"We were gonna voulez together!" the bloke slurred, his spittle spraying on my cheek. Somehow my foot gave way beneath me as well and my tequila shot spilled down his shirt.

"Oh shit!" I said. "I'm so sorry. We're going to get cleaned up." Beth had just shot her tequila without the lime and was now sporting an agonized expression on her face, but she followed me.

"Yuck, yuck, yuck," she groaned, diving into the first available cubicle to spit into the cistern. She had a remarkable gag reflex when it came to drinking. I knew not to worry about her throwing up on a night out from drinking—she was much more of a hangover-vomit girl than an on-the-night one. As for me, it's a good thing I had the money to pay taxi fines.

I splashed water on my face, glancing in the mirror to spot that the hen-mandated glitter on my face had lasted surprisingly well. I was now sporting one red-glitter eyebrow and one blue. Stunning.

I bet I could still score looking like some Brexit-wanker.

Deciding to forget about it, I slipped around the corner to see Beth sitting on the floor of her cubicle. It looked comfortable, so I joined her, shutting the door behind me and shifting the lock into its sticky cavity.

I shut my eyes for a moment as the latest beat of a heavy

TV show theme rang through my head. When I opened them, looking at Beth, I realized that she was pulling the top of her jumpsuit to check inside.

"What . . . are you doing?"

"Just checkin' on my boobs."

Of course. That's totally logical. I shrugged and then did the same.

"Yep, still there," I told her, pulling one boob slightly up out of the bra to give them a boost.

"Mine too," Beth sighed, clearly relieved.

"Having fun?"

Beth nodded and smiled at me, her fringe falling into her eyes. The Tracy Turnblad hairstyle she had done expertly back at the hotel hadn't survived the night.

"I miss this."

"What?" I said. "Getting drunk?"

She nodded.

"We get drunk all the time." We tended to order more bottles of prosecco than varieties of vegetables when we did the weekly food shop.

"I mean going out, dancing . . ." She was reaching the peak of her evening. We would have to leave soon otherwise she was at high risk of falling asleep, and as much as I was a good friend, I would likely bundle her in a taxi and then return to the bar to get with the bartender. I must not do that!

Not least because I had been paying him tips all night; it would look like I was paying him for sex. But would it be rude to ask for the tips back?

"The girl group will be missing us."

Beth's eyes opened suddenly. She found my face and darted forward creepily fast. Her body was half-resting on mine and her fringe was tickling my forehead, swinging back and forth across my glittery eyebrows.

"That group is dangerous. They got me *so* pissed!"

Biting my lip in an attempt not to laugh, I nodded and forced a serious expression.

"It's true, they are dangerous. Let's come up with a game plan."

Beth lifted her finger to my nose and tapped it gently.

"Boop," she said, still serious. "Here's the plan . . ." I waited. "I forgot the plan."

Unable to contain my laugh, I pushed her back and gripped her arms. "The plan is . . . don't attack until you see the whites of their wines."

"BUT, LIKE . . ." BETH was saying to Bonnie while the other hens were all scattered about the bar as the bartenders were clearing up. Most of the other Saturday night clubbers and drunks had left since it was way past closing time. Yet we remained.

"One dick forever!" Beth screamed. She didn't need to shout; the DJ had long since packed up and left. But she hadn't yet recovered her hearing from the evening's blasting music anyway, so she hadn't quite noticed yet.

"Yeah, I know. It's sad but . . . I love him." Bonnie had been nonstop crying for hours. I was pretty sure her tears were made from vodka since that's all she had consumed at this point.

"What's that like?" Beth asked, leaning forward on her elbow unsteadily. "Are you happy with your choice? Like, don't you want to try poly—polyam—other dicks?"

Bonnie shook her head, borderline outraged.

"His dick is my dick now. Forever!"

"His dick is your dick."

"Babe," I said lightly, rubbing my forehead as I came down

from my buzz. "I think it's time we head home." The bartender looked across the bar and smiled at me, but even he was nodding. It was time for us to leave.

"How many dicks have you had? Before this one, I mean?" Beth continued to shout at Bonnie, who shrugged.

"Too many to count."

"Really?"

"Really," she nodded, wiping away her tears. "But this is the best one. It's so perfectly pink and long. Like a long rose."

"A rose?" I said, too quickly. Bonnie glared at me. No dick I had ever seen had looked like a rose. To me they all looked like naked mole rats. But that didn't mean I didn't like them.

"What was your favorite?"

"This one," Bonnie said, growing ever-serious as Beth grew ever-curious.

"What does it feel like?"

"Like . . . a dick?" Bonnie replied, starting to back away.

"When did you first have sex?" Beth pressed on.

"Why?"

"Curious."

"I've ordered an Uber," I said to Beth, standing to gather our nonexistent things. "Where's your coat?"

"You're so weird." Bonnie pushed off Beth's shoulder to move back toward the safety of her wider hen group, one of whom—probably Gale—lifted her head from the barstool it was resting on to shout, "*She's a bride!*" like a broken pull-toy.

"And your friends are robots," I shouted at Bonnie with her back turned. "At least mine's unique."

"Thanks, babe." Beth smiled, still oblivious to the fact she had freaked out Bonnie. Neither would remember it, probably—but if they did, I really hoped it meant the end of this friendship.

I know I shouldn't feel ownership of Beth, but by god I hated Bonnie.

"Come on, we're going home," I said. Beth swung an arm about my shoulders, and then attempted to swing her legs up too so I was cradling her. "Babe, I love you, but no." I patted her forehead and half-dragged her out of the club, back to the safety of our flat and the comfort of our own toilet.

It was as I pushed one of Beth's legs into the Uber that the bartender came hurrying out, holding his bag and saying he'd finished his shift.

I looked him up and down. With cocktail and tequila goggles on he was cute, and that was good enough for me.

"You should sit in the front, she might puke," I lied, and he grinned and did as he was told.

CHAPTER 3
BETH

SERENA'S SPOTIFY PLAYLIST was playing in the kitchen as I threw up in the bathroom.

Serena had been kind enough to give me full use of the bathroom while she resigned herself to the plastic sink bowl in her bedroom, not that she had needed it. The bitch.

"We should have ordered a kebab," I shouted from my position on the floor. When we'd got home at three a.m., she had insisted that I get into bed, fully dressed, and go to sleep. I had been desperate for food, and a kebab was all I could think about. Sweaty-scented meat and underdone chips. Hangover perfection.

However, she had been a bit busy with the bartender from the club. Not that I even registered he was there until that morning when I was awoken by a scream.

"And why did the bartender scream?" I asked Serena, who appeared at the bathroom door with two glasses of water with fizzing orange tablets inside.

She handed me one before swigging her own. "I caught him rifling through my knicker drawer. Not the end of the world—at first, I thought he wanted a memento, that would have been acceptable. But nope, he was stealing a pair to wear himself."

I grimaced and felt the last remnants of the prosecco making its way up my throat.

"I commend his hygiene; except the pair he went and chose were my bloody expensive period pants—pun intended."

I laughed and Serena smiled. "There was something rather funny about watching a man scream in horror at having his penis touch the lining of panties that frequently absorb my menstrual blood."

My stomach started to churn again, and I sipped my orange-flavored water and felt it turn to chalk in my mouth.

"He flung them off so quickly and kept screaming, which was when you walked in," Serena continued. "Where did you get the pepper spray and gas mask from?"

"It was a bandana and deodorant."

"Well, I applaud your creativity," she said, then, "Why did you ask him about his penis, though?"

She was referring to the moment that I stopped pointing the deodorant can in his face and asked him if his penis, which was on full display and not as blue as the one I'd seen the day before, was regular size or below average?

"Just curious."

"It was below average, by the way," Serena said matter of factly.

"Well, he didn't have to be so sensitive about it," I said, shutting the toilet lid and using it to push myself off the floor. Just rising four feet made me dizzy. "Screaming *you're insane* and barging past me wasn't very polite."

"It was fun to chase after him with my remaining period panties, though." And she really had. Serena was very protective of me, and the bartender calling me insane was simply unacceptable. She scrambled out of bed, completely naked herself, and pelted the bartender with period panties all the way down the flat stairs while he attempted to gather his things. "Lose my number!" she screamed as he ran out the door, trying to jump into a pair of jeans on Sydenham High Street.

Thank god it was six a.m. and no one was out walking with their dogs or children yet.

"How're you feeling?" Serena asked as I wobbled into the kitchen.

"Like I know what the temperature of hell is," I replied, stepping past the kitchen to the living room and falling gratefully onto the super-plump sofa.

This was a very typical morning for both of us; one of us hungover and the other playing the role of supportive adult. Usually, we described our roles as Glinda the Good Witch and the cyclone. I wasn't usually the cyclone though.

"One dick forever," I mused quietly, curling up. It wasn't long before Serena joined me, having made herself a cup of coffee. I gagged at the smell but recovered. "Could you do that?"

"Do what?"

"The one dick forever thing," I said, almost choking as I gulped down more water.

She snickered loudly. There was no need for an answer from her really.

"You're so curious right now about all this sex and relationship stuff, aren't you?"

I shrugged. "To be honest I've been thinking about sex for a while now. Not so much relationships, though. But I can't seem to stop. It's like a bad UTI, I just can't seem to shake it."

"Well, it's only natural," Serena said, leaning across to grab her laptop from its charging station. "You're twenty-eight and still a virgin. Of course you want to know what it's like. It's just like kissing or eating sushi."

"It's nothing like eating sushi," I argued. Her sudden look of *you'd be surprised* silenced me from arguing further.

Serena exhaled loudly. "You know, if you're interested in all this, I can just fill you in. After all, I've seen a fair share of penises and vaginas in my life."

I squinted, a little horrified at the idea of seeing *more*.

"That really wasn't the best example of a penis either," she continued, ignoring my revulsion. "I have some dick pics that you can look at if you'd like."

"I'm good," I said quickly, placing my hand over her laptop screen in case she was about to whip them out. "I'm just . . . I don't need to look at them, I just don't know much about penises; in fact, I don't know much about vaginas either. I feel kind of ignorant," I finished weakly, crossing my arms.

"Ignorant? It's just anatomy. And besides, you don't need to know anything besides the basics. And the basics are if you're heterosexual, a penis goes inside a vagina, and if you're not, then other things go inside of it like fingers, toys, vibrators, and speculums."

"I know that!" Heat crept up my neck. "Maybe I'm curious about the *feeling*. How does it all fit? What are the mechanics of it?"

"You're overthinking it," Serena proclaimed, shutting her laptop and smiling at my innocence. She knew how much I hated it when people patronized me for not having any sexual knowledge.

It's the fear of any virgin, even for one like me who's usually so blasé about my sexuality, to be called out for being inexperienced.

That and the pity that follows when people assume you'll always be alone in life. No sex, no marriage, no children, no one to put you in a nice nursing home and visit you before you die. That's the only life virgins can expect in the twenty-first century, apparently.

"If you want to know what a body part feels like inside of you, do this!" Serena said, putting her finger in her mouth and pushing out her cheek as if it had been caught by a fishhook. She kept smiling repeatedly, pulling her cheek taut so that the inside of her mouth pulsed around her finger, enveloping it.

Never one to comment on her strangeness, I followed suit and did the same thing.

"That's what it feels like to have a finger inside your vagina," Serena said, removing and wiping her finger on her leg. I carried on for a few more seconds and then sighed.

"All I can feel is my finger bashing against my gums."

"Pull your cheek out farther then." She watched me try again. "Push it in deeper," she muttered. "A little more."

"Anymore and I'll barf!" I said, still stretching out my cheek so my speech was garbled.

"Do you feel it yet?"

"I don't know!" I shouted. "I've never fingered anyone before, so I don't know what it feels like."

"Haven't you fingered yourself?" Serena twisted and attempted to correct my finger position, but I pulled it out before she could try.

"Only when I've had an itch, and even then, barely."

"So why do you want to know what it feels like again?" she asked, picking up my hand defiantly and separating my index finger from the rest. I rolled my eyes but let her carry on.

"Maybe it's because I was completely out of my depth at the hen do. Do you know the girls were so proud of their sexual fuckups? Like just fucking up was a means for a trophy in life."

Serena chuckled blithely. "I didn't realize it would be so sex-ually charged. Bonnie never struck me as that kind of girl."

"Aha, but the bride doesn't plan a hen do, the *hens* do! And none of them would take my suggestions to go axe-throwing or go-karting seriously."

"Well, normally you wouldn't be seen dead in those places, so we can forgive them for not taking them seriously."

I shrugged. "Also, I got *another* smear test letter yesterday. Apparently, I'm due as it's been three years since I "had" the last one, but I never even had it! The nurse just turned me away the second I said I was never, and had never been, sexually ac-tive. Apparently, sex is the cause of cervical cancer nowadays."

"That's bullshit!"

I agreed. "I spoke to Penny about it, seeing as she's had plenty of tests and ultrasounds up the wazoo given IVF and everything. She told me to complain and go back, it's not about sex. But as a non–medical professional, and a virgin, I have no idea what's true and what's not. So I didn't bother." Serena stretched her arms above her head, lips pursed. "Being a virgin is starting to make me feel like I'm lacking some-thing crucial. And I don't know, I'm just curious about every-thing at the moment. I'm twenty-eight and I know nothing. I am the Jon Snow of sex." I exhaled sharply. "Supposedly it's this massive part of life that results in impeachments of presidents, countries toppling, *life* even, yet it just completely skipped me and moved on to the next not-so-innocent girl in the neighborhood."

Serena smirked. "Well, let me teach you my ways."

Without warning she lifted my finger and put it inside of her mouth and told me to pull. I did as she told me to and hooked her so hard that she almost fell off the sofa. A moment later

Serena began to suck, pulsing her cheek against my fingertip and watching as my expression changed.

At first I was genuinely curious as it did feel different this way, a kind of pulse, but then I felt this sudden wave of repulsion. Is this what it's really like?

I didn't remove my finger, though.

"And you do this for *fun*?"

"Aha!" Serena yelled, smiling widely. Obviously, the sensations were always going to be hard to explain, what with my finger in her mouth, and the knowledge that mouths and fingers are lacking in some basic pleasure organs which makes the whole pulsing sensation much more enjoyable, I hoped. But at least I was getting the general gist.

"I should have been a sex-ed teacher."

"Thank god we don't have any other housemates," I replied, still considering the sensation. "No one would understand this scene if they walked in."

With her other hand Serena raised it in a high-five and I responded in turn. We liked our mad little ways. It made our friendship fun.

Serena quickly released me and wiped her mouth with the back of her hand. I used her dressing gown to wipe off my finger.

"That was a really gross way to start the day," I said. "First hangover vomiting and then a weird mouth-fingering session." I sighed. "We're bonkers, aren't we?"

"All the best people are." Serena grinned again.

My stomach gurgled. "I need food." I pushed myself off the sofa and back toward the kitchen. "Omelet?"

"Oh, go on, then," Serena said, nestling further and reopening her laptop. I began to pull out various implements, groaning whenever there was too loud a sound.

"You know you mentioned your smear test," Serena said, stretching out across my now-vacant seat.

"Ye-es," I said, elongating the word as I added three eggs to a bowl and began whisking.

"I got my letter a few months ago," she said, still stretching, "but I haven't got around to booking it yet."

"So?"

"So, what if we go together, since you said you got your letter as well."

I began chopping up some spinach leaves and onions on the kitchen counter, too hungover—and lazy—to search for a clean chopping board.

"Sure. If there's an appointment slot for the two of us and they accept me into the smear test club."

"What would you say about me turning it into an article idea?" she hedged.

I looked at her over my shoulder. "What kind of idea did you have in mind?"

She smiled innocently. "It's kind of genius. I could pitch it to Arnold as a feature for Cervical Cancer Prevention Week at the end of the month, but you can also get some answers about general anatomy and sexual organs while we're there. Win-win. I can reach out to our nearest gynecologist about a double-length appointment so we can both get it done and I can get an interview at the same time. What do you think?"

I paused, knife aloft. "Please tell me you're not going to tell Arnold—your *boss*—about my sudden anatomical curiosity in the process?"

"Bethany, focus. Smear test, yay or nay?"

I nodded, which I regretted instantly. Why does it feel like the alcohol is sitting in your head in the morning?

"Yay," I replied, thinking that that was the first time anyone had ever said that about a smear test.

Serena appeared in the doorway, resting her head against the doorframe as I fried her omelet. "It'll be fun. You can ask all the questions you want about your vagina and cervical health, and I can get a lead feature on the website."

"Plus we can avoid cervical cancer for another few years."

"Well, maybe. It's not a test for cancer, just a test for abnormal cells that could one day lead to cancer." I neatly lifted the omelet onto a paper plate—who wants to do the washing up hungover—and handed it to Serena, who reached for a fork. "You're a doll."

My phone started to buzz in my pocket. Penny was FaceTiming. Serena took a few bites of her omelet and her face started to turn as green as the spinach.

"S'cuse me." She raced to the toilet, the first evidence of a hangover hitting her. I inhaled steadily as I accepted my sister's call.

"What is that face?"

"Mornin'," I muttered. "Serena and I are hungover."

"Ooh, fun times! I miss them." Penny sighed dolefully.

I smiled sympathetically at her and loaded the next egg into the pan. "What can I do for you?"

There was a pointed silence, and I took a moment to properly look at my sister. She was sitting in her bathroom and her morning makeup was already wiped across her face. "Oh no, Penny," I said, knowing exactly what had happened.

"It didn't take," she said with finality, her voice choking up again.

"Oh, Penny," I repeated, feeling genuinely awful for her. This was the third round of IVF and potentially the last, according to her doctors. "Do you want me to come up?" I offered, though

I had no idea how I was going to afford train fare to her in the Cotswolds.

But she shook her head. "No, I'm just feeling sorry for myself. And delaying having to tell Patrick. Not that it won't be easy to guess when he sees my face," she said, pointing to the mess of mascara on her cheeks.

"Is there anything I can do?" I asked, feeling utterly useless from my spot in the kitchen.

"Distract me?" she suggested after a beat. "What's going on with you? Why are you hungover?"

My omelet was burning. I groaned as I took it off the heat.

"It was Bonnie's hen do." I hoped she wouldn't ask for details, not wanting to describe Bonnie. I felt too hungover to be kind. "Ooh, you'd be proud, I flirted with someone in French last night!"

"But you can't speak French?"

"Mais oui," I joked, which made her smile. "Oh, and I'm getting a smear test!" I announced, with perhaps a bit too much enthusiasm to cover my terror.

CHAPTER 4
BETH

THE FOLLOWING MORNING, Serena headed off to her office in Holborn while I set up shop at home. The benefits of being self-employed are great at first, but after a while, the need to get up for core hours of working—in my case between ten a.m. and four p.m.—becomes increasingly difficult. Especially when you're struggling to find any meaningful work and you're still feeling the effects of a major hangover.

But I managed it, eventually. By eleven I'd done all my emails. Mostly this consisted of me sending people my rate-card on request, knowing I'd likely never hear back from them. And unsubscribing from clothing-store subscriptions from 2008, which I was pretty sure were in breach of the General Data Protection Restrictions.

Then I looked at prospective marketing jobs, because the freelance lifestyle was punching me in the tits on the daily. My bank account had a permanent minus symbol attached; I had phone calls from the bank I ignored as expertly as I ignored the emails from the gym telling me they missed me.

And I was not enjoying myself.

If anyone were to ask, I was *loving* the freedom of freelancing, but really, I was a stay-at-home companion for Serena. She paid all the bills in return for me keeping the place habitable and occasionally cooking her dinner.

At noon I left the flat with my societally inappropriate sticker-covered laptop—I love a "Fuck the Patriarchy" moment—for a nearby café.

Edith's Café. It was not owned by an Edith, but apparently named after one. I always went there for their seafood sandwich special and a Diet Coke at lunch. Nothing like routine to make the day go faster. Even when you could hardly afford it.

I liked Edith's; it was an old-timey, adults-only café, which meant it was always quiet. The manager, Delphi, always sat at one of the many empty tables doing the previous day's *Evening Standard* crossword or scrolling through Instagram suffering from chronic comparison syndrome.

"Alright, love," she said without looking up when I entered. "The usual?"

"Yes, please."

"Michel!" Delphi screamed, gaze still on her phone. "Beth's here."

"The usual?" a high-pitched man's voice echoed from behind the plastic kitchen curtain.

"Yes, please, Michel," I shouted back.

"How's business?" Delphi asked as I opened my laptop and plugged it into one of their sockets.

"Could be better, could be worse," I parroted the usual response I gave anyone—except Serena—who asked how my business was going.

Part of choosing to go freelance was so that people would stop checking up on my work and leave me to my own devices. Sadly, this was not the case.

"I've just managed to book a client for a one-on-one coaching session on TikTok, and a start-up has asked for some help with programmatic advertising."

"What's the start-up do?" she asked in her most disinterested tone. Instagram stories were clearly more exciting than I was.

"They produce an app that helps antiques dealers find suitable auction houses to sell their goods."

"Sounds . . ." She didn't finish her sentence, but it was easy to finish on her behalf. Dull.

"It's alright. Marketing is marketing, after all."

"Aren't there any fun businesses out there that you could market, though?"

"I could market this place," I said, looking around at the chintzy-decorated café with its threadbare armchairs, aged rugs, and flower paintings in secondhand frames. "But you'd have to pay me."

"With what? Shirt buttons?" Delphi scoffed. "The owner has a hard enough time paying me and Michel, add on a freelance marketer and the whole place would go under."

"Maybe they could provide my lunch for free?" I suggested in what I imagined was a suave voice.

Delphi finally looked up. "You're pretty much the only regular customer. If we start giving you free food we'd close in a week."

"I doubt that my £6.99 seafood sandwich is keeping the business afloat, Delphi," I joked. Actually, what was keeping this place going was the owner's drug dealing business on the side. I had never met them, but I was pretty sure that they only kept this place as a front. Delphi was the manager because the owner was her aunt's second husband.

To anyone else she would be an underqualified and lazy employee, but to me she was a great sounding board for ideas and even better for keeping me motivated to work on my business into the afternoons when the appeal of the television or a nap was strong in the flat.

"Why did you go freelance again?" she asked. "It sounds like all work, no fun. No gossip, no support, no free fruit basket in the office to pilfer food or free tampons in the toilets." Her bluntness was as refreshing as ever.

I felt like I should return the favor and be honest and say, *I thought I'd earn more money freelancing after hearing from one of my old university friends that they earned three times their yearly salary in three months after going freelance.* But I had barely earned three months' salary in a year.

It wasn't just the financials that motivated me to leave, though—I also never fit in at Elias Recruitment in my two years as a marketing assistant. Apart from Bonnie, who moved into hybrid working and was hardly ever in the office, I never really connected with my colleagues. It's hard to fit in when you don't have dating stories to tell on Monday morning, or when you don't care about their sex lives, or the fact that there is a sale on at Lovehoney. It's frustrating, particularly when they look at you with either pity or confusion when you admit you don't go on dates. It removes you from future conversations, then moves into alienation at lunchtime so you end up eating £2 falafel balls alone in the cafeteria waiting for someone to invite you to their table like you're thirteen again.

It was just like the hen do, but also incredibly boring and barely paying the London Living Wage.

When I thought I could make more money and completely rid myself of the shame my colleagues made me feel—intentionally or otherwise—for being romantically and sexually inactive, I jumped at the chance.

But to Delphi, instead of admitting that, I simply replied,

"I didn't like being told what to do by people I didn't trust or respect."

"You anarchist!" Delphi grinned.

I laughed as my phone began to buzz, and I pulled it out as Michel hit the bell and Delphi stood to get my lunch.

"Hey Serena," I answered. "Did you forget your phone charger or something?"

"No, I'm fully charged. But Arnold has approved the smear test story! We're a go! I was thinking I could book us in for some time this week. How about it?"

My stomach dropped. "Okay, sure. Sounds like a plan." Even though I raged against the system that seemed to think that cancerous cells only grew on the promiscuous like it was the eighteenth century, I had been quite relieved that my smear test hadn't gone ahead. But now I had to put on my big girl panties—or maybe my newest briefs, what does one wear to a smear test?—and do it.

"Hey Serena!" Delphi called down the phone before I could stop her.

"Is that Delphi?"

"Yep, she says hi."

"Hello!" Delphi screamed again. The two of them weren't friends as they'd never met, but they knew a lot about each other through me. And Delphi was a part of the very small collective who knew I was a virgin. She had a knack for getting to the bottom of things and she wheedled it out of me in a way that I can't even remember how we got onto the topic in the first place. If it wasn't for the slight issue regarding her dodgy employer, I'd say she would make a fantastic detective.

"Say hey back so it sounds like I'm polite," Serena returned.

"Serena says hey." Delphi nodded in acknowledgment and picked up her phone again. "So, when are you thinking? For the . . ." I didn't finish. I didn't want Delphi to know what we were discussing—although by the way her eyebrows rose, I was pretty sure she was thinking *challenge accepted*.

"I mean, I think we could go as early as tomorrow."

"Tomorrow?" I said, in a much higher-pitched voice than usual. "I could make that work." I coughed to clear my throat.

"It will be fine," Serena said in her most comforting voice. "I'll be there the whole time and I'll go first, so it's no bother. Remember what we said before the night out?"

"We've got this," I said, rolling my eyes at the cheesiness. "I know, I know."

"We do! It'll be easy, you'll see."

"Okay, you're the boss." I scratched my face and looked at Delphi who was trying her best to appear not to be listening. "Speaking of bosses, what did Arnold think about you taking another morning off work?" Serena was becoming the expert "flexible" worker. She hardly ever seemed to be in the office anymore, and when she was, she was often finding ways not to be there.

"Arnold is so obsessed with wedding planning at the moment he doesn't even seem to notice if I'm in the office or not. Besides, he doesn't usually care where I am so long as I produce a good story."

"Sounds like we're going to need to get a bigger desk in the living room. We can't both work from the coffee table or sit on the sofa. It's bad for our backs."

Delphi had dropped her phone and was listening intently now, dropping all pretense of giving me privacy.

"Listen, my lunch is here; I'll catch up with you when you get home."

"Toodle-oo!" Serena finished, hanging up on me before I could do so on her. She always did like to have the last word.

I placed my phone face down on the greasy Formica and opened my can of Diet Coke, waiting for Delphi's inquisition.

She was very patient today. "You still have to pay for that sandwich, you know," she said eventually. I pulled my battered debit card from my pocket and handed it to her; she grabbed it but didn't move.

"So, what day did you and Serena agree for the . . ." she paused, waiting for me to finish.

I gave in immediately. I had never had any fight in me. "Smear test, Delphi. I'm getting a smear test."

"With Serena?" She looked appalled at the idea, and for some reason that made me pleased. It felt good to shock Delphi.

"Yep. We're going together and holding each other's hands," I said, forking a piece of lettuce and waving it briefly in her face. She grimaced.

"I don't want anyone but the nurse to ever witness me having one of those. Last time I had to sing 'Bohemian Rhapsody' to distract myself. Got through the first five minutes in soprano before she managed to expand the speculum. But we got there in the end. Want some salad dressing with that?" She rose before I could shake my head.

I had suddenly lost all my appetite.

CHAPTER 5
BETH

SO, CERVICAL SCREENINGS shouldn't hurt?" Serena asked Jane, the homely looking nurse sitting patiently in her plastic chair as Serena gathered up her knickers from around her ankles.

"Hopefully not. You can feel a little discomfort but it's different for everybody. It hurts some people more than others."

"Discomfort? I barely felt a thing," Serena said proudly, smiling at me encouragingly from behind the privacy curtain.

There was an available appointment the following morning, before the rest of the clinic officially opened. Only Serena and I, and the two weaselly looking receptionists, occupied the waiting room until Jane arrived and whisked us away into one of the larger examination rooms.

"As a nurse, does having more information about the procedure help you, or do you find that knowing too much can be an impediment?" Serena pressed on, with a wink to me as Jane turned her back.

"Not really. I didn't become a nurse until I was in my thirties, so by that time, I had had many of these tests already and knew what shape my body was and how best to find my cervix."

"Is that knowledge beneficial?" I ventured, sheepishly.

"Well, I mean, the more you know about your body the easier it is to give directions." She laughed lightly. "Unfortunately, cervixes don't operate under GPS, and they can occasionally be shy. This is what causes the most discomfort because the nurse will have to search for slightly longer. But often it just takes a twist or a slight change of position and you're fine."

I crossed my legs awkwardly. "Does that mean, since it's my first time, that you're going to have to jiggle the speculum about a bit before you can find my cervix?"

"It will depend on your body," Jane said in her most reassuring voice, as she finished clearing up all the paraphernalia from Serena's smear test.

The swab she had used for gathering the cells of Serena's cervix was sitting in a pot on the side of a trolley. There was blood on it, and she didn't seem to think that was worth mentioning.

Serena pulled back at the curtain and Jane stood up immediately to replace the protective sheet on the bed and get ready for my test.

"I'll only need a minute," she said, and began to gather all the items she needed from a clinical trolley behind the bed and an obnoxiously large lamp.

Serena appeared at my side, balancing on one leg as she tied up the shoelaces of her Doc Martens.

Jane was removing a speculum from its sanitary plastic bag. It made a lovely crackling sound as she removed it.

"Ooh, I feel like this would make a fantastic ASMR video," Serena said overenthusiastically.

"You should pitch that to your boss after you finish this piece," I suggested. "How to use ASMR to relax yourself during a smear test."

"It only works for fifty percent of people who try it. Do you use it?"

I ignored her as Jane had turned to me with a well-practiced grin.

"Right, ready?"

I gave an involuntary "yeah" and stood. Jane pulled the curtain around to give me some privacy.

"You can stay with me; I don't care what you see," I said to Serena, grabbing her wrist and forcing her to follow. She did so without hesitation.

Nudity in front of Serena wasn't a problem. We had seen each other naked on numerous occasions. Skinny dipping was a lead activity during our time at university—this was before my metabolism caught up with me and I developed hips and a wobbly bum practically overnight—before that, I was perfectly capable of prancing around a beach with my body on show with Serena there. Until the police turned up, anyway, then we had to run. And running barefoot on pebbles is a bitch.

As she joined me in the little protective alcove, she pulled the curtain a little farther out to protect my privacy, but there was no need. With a sharp inhalation I dragged down my best knickers from under my skirt and put them on the chair beside the table.

Serena smirked and jokily whipped up my knickers and swung them around above her head to try and lighten the mood.

"Come on, then, up you get," Serena said encouragingly. "Only a true friend holds the other's panties for her during a smear test." She gave me a wink for reassurance as I swung myself onto the stupidly thin protective sheet. It ripped the moment I attempted to shuffle my bottom down to the end of the bed.

"Did you shave?" Serena asked as I adjusted myself on the bed.

"Yes, didn't you?"

"I trimmed with the nail scissors in the shower this morning but didn't shave. I bet they've seen it all."

I was a woman who had the luxury of being able to grow a full bush and not have to worry about other people's thoughts on the aesthetics. But when you work from home and need something to quell the boredom, strangely enough neatening up a landing strip becomes a fun activity.

"It's now or never," I said, exhaling. I called to Jane: "I'm ready!" She appeared immediately, ripping back the curtain with a speculum in hand.

"Use this sheet," she said, offering me a separate piece of tissue paper, "to cover yourself." She started humming to herself as she pulled up a metal stool and put on some latex gloves. "Right, before I begin, Bethany, I just need to ask you the same questions as I did Serena here."

"Sure," I replied, still sitting up with my sheet covering most of my legs.

"When was your last period?"

"Two weeks ago."

"Okay, and you said you're not sexually active?"

"Nope."

"Have you ever been sexually active?"

"Nope."

"Ever?" She looked up from her drawer of medical toys to watch my expression as if to catch me out.

"Nope. I'm demisexual, and I don't find sex appealing."

"Never?"

"Well, no, it's *possible* for me to find sex appealing but I have to have a really, *really* strong emotional connection with a person to stir those feelings up. And that's yet to happen."

"Interesting," she said, returning to the drawer and dropping the speculum she had in her hand as she began searching at the back for another one. "How do you know if you're demisexual, then? If you don't mind me asking."

"Because I occasionally get horny while watching films and TV."

"How does that work?" Jane asked, finding a new speculum that was about half the size of Serena's and placing it on her tray.

"Because when an actor is doing their job really well then they're able to create an emotional connection with the audience, therefore I can get aroused by them."

"She's great when it comes to betting on the Academy Awards," Serena said, smirking as we both watched Jane's reaction. Seeing the difference between Serena's laissez-faire attitude toward my sexuality and Jane's slightly uptight confusion was rather funny. I appreciated having Serena there with me at that moment, as on my own this would have been another awkward situation of me having to defend my "decision" not to have sex.

"Will my being a virgin affect my smear test?"

"Well, it shouldn't," Jane said, her tone changing from bright to slightly more serious. "To be honest, we sometimes recommend that virgins don't bother having the smear test at all."

"Does being a virgin mean you're less likely to get cervical cancer?" Serena queried as if she and I hadn't already discussed and researched the same question after my last attempt at a smear test.

"There are some studies to suggest so. Nuns rarely get cervical cancer, which suggests that virginity can be beneficial in the case of prevention. Also, sexual intercourse increases your chance of getting HPV. However, new research suggests that virgins can contract it from infected surfaces. Either way, I would say it is sensible to still get a smear test, even if you're not sexually active."

"But I could say I didn't want one just because I'm a virgin."

Jane nodded.

"Yet I still might have abnormal cells anyway?"

She nodded again, ripping open the plastic bag containing the speculum rather than gently easing it out with the previous pleasant crinkling we discussed.

"Isn't that a little unfair to virgins to potentially say *don't bother? Hey, you haven't had sex so you don't need this test even though you still might have abnormal cells! But you're a virgin so who cares?*"

"That's not what they're saying."

"Sounds like it."

"Right!" Jane said, brightening her voice again. "Are you ready?"

"Sure. Do you want me to do the same as Serena?"

"Yep, lay back with your bottom at the edge and your feet together. That's it."

I let my legs drop to the side and watched Jane for a reaction to my vagina. There wasn't one. I was hoping she would be more impressed by my pubic grooming skills.

"I'm going to insert the speculum," she said, lubing it up a lot more than I had seen her do with Serena's speculum. "Deep breath."

I did as she said and waited. To be honest, it wasn't a problem. For someone who had never really fingered herself before, having a plastic object shoved up inside me for the first time wasn't that bad.

I stared at the yellowing ceiling and waited for Jane to twist the speculum inside of me. Unlike Serena's test, she seemed to be taking things incredibly slowly with me. "Will this break my hymen?"

"It may do. But normally in women your age, sexually active

or not, your hymen will have broken doing some other activity like using a tampon or even driving."

Serena was watching Jane interestedly. Clearly, having had her smear test done from the cheap seats, she was looking forward to watching the show from the orchestra.

"Okay, I'm just going to twist."

"Ah!" I said, feeling that a lot. "Jeez."

"Sorry," she said quickly, but she didn't say anything else.

"Did you feel that?" Serena asked me. "I barely felt a thing!"

"Yes," I said, screwing up my face a little as I felt the pull of the speculum against my labia.

"Relax your bottom," Jane said in her most soothing voice. "And take a deep breath."

I did as she said, but before the breath had even reached my diaphragm I was squirming and saying "ah!" again.

"Sorry," she repeated, quieter this time.

"Oof! What are you doing now?"

"Now I'm just moving the speculum around a bit. You're quite tight down there, which is to be expected, but that doesn't leave me much room to open the spec. If I can just get your vagina to relax a little, then I'll have better luck getting it open. Okay? Are you alright?"

"Mmhm," I said, sucking in my bottom lip as she continued to jiggle around, and my legs began to shake. It wasn't painful as such, just bizarre, and not something you would want to repeat.

"Is this what sex feels like?"

Serena put her hand atop my arm comfortingly as she peered around my knee to get a better look at Jane continuing to move the speculum inside of me.

"Maybe, if you're using a toy. But normally you'd be a lot

more aroused before you did that. Ooh! Maybe you should think of an emotional performance you like."

"What, like when all three Spider-Men hug in *Spider-Man: No Way Home*?"

"Hey, if that gets you going." She smirked. I laughed but it came out more like a repressed squawk as Jane plunged the speculum farther into me. "Ow."

"Sorry," she repeated, not looking up as she continued to mess with my insides in deep concentration.

"It was emotional, not arousing."

"Ooh, why not think about Ev—" Serena began to suggest but I gripped her arm so tightly that she didn't say his full name. I really didn't think this was the time to start fantasizing about my old watercooler crush and she took my viselike grip on her arm as a clear "shut up" message.

A few seconds later I took another deep breath, but still the jiggling of the speculum didn't get any better and it was about ten seconds away from being painful. And Jane hadn't even opened the damn thing yet.

"Any luck?" I prompted.

"Why don't you try putting your hands beneath your pelvis for me. Just put them into two fists and rest them underneath your back."

"What does that do?" Serena asked as I did what Jane suggested.

"It can help tilt the pelvis down and make it easier for me to find your cervix."

"Oh, is that what you're looking for?" I said sarcastically.

"You have a shy cervix."

"I do?"

"It does not want to come out to play today."

"Have you got the speculum open yet?" My teeth were gritted now.

"Barely. When I can see more of the cervix, I'll open it wider to get the sample. For now, though, it wouldn't be the most comfortable thing for you, so best wait until I catch sight of it."

"You make it sound like a sniper mission." I flinched as the speculum hit a particularly painful part of my vaginal wall. "I'm hoping to god that wasn't my G-spot."

"It will be over soon," Serena tried to say calmly.

"You can say that! We could have got through three more of your smear tests in this time. Oh—jeez!"

"Sorry."

"Think on the bright side, you have a tight vagina. Do you know how many porn stars would kill for that?" Serena joked to distract me. "Half of their vaginas are hanging out of their labia for the world to see."

"Oh, poor them! I'd have surgery for that option right now. Any closer?" I squinted at Jane.

"Not yet, I'm sorry. I can try a different speculum?" I felt the gentle tug as Jane went to remove the speculum.

"Don't you dare!" I shouted. "We've come this far."

Jane paused but then pushed the speculum back in and tried again.

"Relax your bottom."

"You relax," I muttered tightly. I could see sweat droplets appearing at Jane's hairline as she sat ever closer to the bright yellow light trying to get a good view inside me.

"What happens if you can't find it?" Serena asked, after a few more minutes of Jane searching and me yelping before reminding myself to take a deep breath and relax my bloody bottom.

"Well, I recommend that you book another appointment for a month's time and try again. Sometimes it can just be—aha! Wait, I've found it. I've found it."

"My cervix!" I shouted, almost sitting up in surprise but then remembering that I currently had a tool inside of me and wondering if I might snap it in two if I sat up too quickly.

"Yep. I've got it." The satisfaction in Jane's voice was contagious.

"Thank fuck for that," Serena said, letting out a large breath.

"You're telling me."

"Right, now I'm going to swab the cervix. I'll be as quick as possible, but I do need at least five rotations."

"Oh, swab away!" I said, slightly euphoric with relief. "My cervix is like Atlantis, who knows when it will rise again."

AFTER ALL OF that, neither of us had abnormal cells.

"Thank god," Serena said a few weeks later as we both lay on her double bed with our feet against her headboard staring at our letters. "Imagine if you had to go back to get the cells scraped off. You'd need to be knocked out or to have someone holding you down."

"It wasn't that bad," I told her. Although one look from her and a subconscious pinch of my cervix later I realized that she was right. "Well, at least I've lost my plastic virginity. Do you think that will count when Delphi next asks me if I've *done it* yet?"

"If she asks that, then Dephi's a dick," Serena said compassionately.

"No," I said. "She's just had one inside of her."

CHAPTER 6
SERENA

LOVED THE PIECE on smear tests, Serena. Did your mate really say her cervix was like *Atlantis*?" Hermione, a fellow features writer and my biggest competition, came rushing over to me in all her Oliver Bonas glory.

I finished applying my Taylor Swift–red lipstick and smiled. "She sure did."

"Seems like yours was easy to find," Hermione smirked, attempting passive-aggressive humor, but it bounced off me due to my strong self-awareness of my sexual proclivity.

"Yep. I'm perfectly symmetrical inside and out." Thank you, model mother! That's model as in *supermodel mother*, not model as in *mother of the year*. She was probably closer to *best financier of the year* than actual mother, since the only times she ever spoke to me was on Christmas Day when the whole world reminded her that holidays were, supposedly, for family. And on Mother's Day when she called to berate me for not paying her more attention.

The rest of the time she emailed to let me know about her life, never once asking about mine, and that I should be grateful that she had had the bank set up a standing order to send me

£1,500 a month for basic life expenses, which was more than the £1,000 that Dad sent me each month as she liked to remind me. The bitter divorce proceedings and "emotional damage" claims still lingered despite eighteen years having passed since the papers were signed. That £1,500 was still less than half of what she earned for one day's work as a model for a Japanese skincare brand. But I'm not bitter . . . much.

"Good to know. Well, look, Arnold has asked me to write up a piece on the best sex toys for Valentine's Day and I was wondering if you had any suggestions?"

I paused; having failed in her first attempt, this was Hermione's shot at a slut-shame. I would have bet my yearly salary that she hadn't even bothered to Google sex toys for the piece, she was just trying to get some stupid revenge for my getting with James—the cute receptionist—at New Year's. How was I supposed to know she had been flirting with him for three months beforehand? You snooze, you lose.

But a conversation about sex toys wasn't going to shame me.

"How many do you want?" I asked, mentally cataloging the pleasure chest of toys beneath my bed. "And how are you separating them? Do you want couple's toys, solo toys, travel toys—they're always fun! Or do you want penetrative, anal, or role play? What's your vice?"

I leaned back in my chair, rapping my fingers together like a sexualized Mr. Burns from *The Simpsons*.

"Uh well, I guess . . . partner toys because it's Valentine's Day?"

"Great." I sat back up and made a note on my ever-growing to-do list. "I'll send over some links later this afternoon. I have a lunch meeting with Arnold first."

"You're having lunch with Arnold?" she asked, clearly perplexed as to why she had the briefest of one-on-ones with him but I got to go out to lunch with him. Hermione craved attention, particularly from Arnold, and she was very upset that I got way more than she did. But what can I say? I was his favorite and most productive writer. Also, I'd set him up with his soon-to-be third husband, Gareth, so he owed me.

We had been at a magazine awards show in Soho and we hadn't won, so of course we were all drunk. In a fit of humility, I decided to spend the evening cheering Arnold up by getting him laid, rather than going on the prowl myself.

Gareth was nearly sober, sitting on his own at the end of the bar but ever-so-often flitting his eyes over at Arnold, who was wearing a particularly garish suit of green and pink. They clearly both had a love for tailored suits and white sneakers, even at formal events, so I sent over a drink to Gareth—pretending it was from Arnold—and then I told Arnold that a man was looking at him, so I'd done half the job. Presto. They moved in together practically a fortnight later. The wedding is set for spring.

ARNOLD AND I met at Rocco's, a pizzeria about half a mile from the office.

"I'm having a day!" Arnold announced upon entering with his usual campy flourish. "Also, what do you think of this outfit? Is it too much for the board meeting later?" It was a vibrant orange pantsuit.

"Yes. But wear it anyway."

"I will," he said, giving me a kiss on the cheek. "I need to distract the buggers from talking about the bloody rebrand."

"Same as usual?" A waiter with a geographically inaccurate French mustache asked as Arnold removed his outer jacket and placed his phone face up on the table.

"Yes, please, and a bottle of sparkling water. Thanks." I handed back our unopened menus.

"So what's new with you?" Arnold asked, glancing every few seconds at his screensaver as notifications popped up. I didn't envy the demanding life of an editor in chief.

"Not much. I was thinking of taking my housemate speed dating next week."

"What do you need to speed date for? Don't you have a million people's numbers in your phone?"

"Yes, but I've shagged all of them and you know me, I don't do seconds. Often."

"It's how you stay so fit, you gorgeous bitch."

I smiled coquettishly. Honestly, the number of calories you can burn through sex is incredible. It's no wonder I always crave McDonald's afterward.

"I'm not after a Peloton-like threesome, the speed dating is for my friend—no, seriously!" Arnold had begun to laugh in disbelief. "She's stuck in a bit of a funk at the moment, so I've made it my mission to get her out of it."

"Is this the same friend you had the smear test with?"

"The very same."

"The virgin?" he whispered, leaning forward like he was asking me about the destination of the Holy Grail.

"She's not an alien, Arnold," I said calmly. "She's demisexual."

"I know, I know. But I find it all so interesting. I mean, imagine possibly never having another horny thought or feeling in your life. It would be so dull." You couldn't argue there. If I didn't have sex, the only hobbies I'd have would be my creation of popular Pinterest boards on home interiors and an ability to write hour-long trivia quizzes on *RuPaul's Drag Race*.

"You can't miss what you've never had."

"But isn't she curious?"

"Well, she wasn't until recently. I don't know if she's hit a quarter-life crisis or maybe it's the biological clock ticking, but for the last few weeks, she's been quizzing me and my various houseguests on our sex lives. It's like she's studying it."

"Oh, babe. Sex is not like an exam. She needs to get out there and try it for herself. In fact, why don't you make that your next case study."

"What?"

"Help her lose her virginity as a demisexual. You're sexually active and very sexually aware. Babe, you're basically a sex magnet. You're flipping Olivia Wilde in *House* when she goes through her self-destructive phase."

"Thank you?"

"Wouldn't that be a fun piece, though? And so inspirational to others going through the same thing. You know that Gen Z are waiting longer than ever to have sex. Because of social media, they're not creating meaningful physical connections anymore. Soon they'll be having sex like the Sims. Woohoo!"

"More like boo-hoo."

Arnold nodded as our French waiter returned with our sparkling water and bread and oil.

"I'd have to ask her first. I can't just write about her behind her back."

"No, good heavens no. That wouldn't pass legal."

I was thinking more along the lines of friendship and the girl code. But nevertheless, it was true. Legal would have a field day if they thought I was writing about someone else's sex life without their permission. *The List* was all about self-empowerment, after all, but that basically meant we didn't have the money to shell out on lawsuits like the trashy gossip magazines did.

"See what she says and then let me know. We could make it an investigative piece, a full-on case study. Do you think she would be willing to try some things?"

"Things? Like what?" I dipped my ciabatta into the deliciously smooth olive oil.

"A psychosexual therapist, a Gwyneth Paltrow goop practitioner, a sex worker? I don't know. People who work in the sex trade who can answer her questions or offer her advice on sexuality. You know, I was looking up demisexuality and it's quite rare. Less than one percent of the world's population identify as demisexual."

"But until forty years ago, most gay people didn't identify as gay," I countered. "People probably don't even realize that they're demisexual, they probably just think that they're not turned on enough, or whatever feelings they do get is what allosexuality must feel like."

Arnold shuddered. "God forbid."

CHAPTER 7
BETH

SO WHAT DO you think?"

We were on the floor watching an episode of *The Crown* (that we had seen multiple times before).

"And your boss came up with this idea?"

"Yeah, he was pretty keen, he did a whole load of research into demisexuality beforehand and everything."

"The same boss you set up on a date?"

She nodded as I began chewing on a particularly wooden piece of pineapple. I'm all for fruit on pizza, so long as it's not vacuum-sealed first. It removes all the moisture.

"The wedding's in April. You can be my date if you like."

"Why are there suddenly so many weddings to go to?" When did our lives turn from silly themed house parties to wedding receptions and hen dos? Every other month there was a bridal shower or an engagement party invite. One joy of being freelance was that those significantly reduced when you no longer had colleagues who invited you to make up the numbers. "I'm so relieved Bonnie has chosen to do her ceremony abroad, so I don't have to go. There's no way I'd have the cash to get to the Amalfi Coast for a weekend."

"Well, there are no wedding invites coming from me. Ever." Serena stressed the last word.

"And here I was banking on being your maid of honor!" I wiped away a fake tear of disappointment.

Serena clicked her tongue, ignoring me. "So what do you think about the pitch? Honestly?"

"Honestly," I repeated, slowly picking at the rest of my pizza topping, "if the magazine will pay me for it, then sure, I'm all for it."

"Really?" Clearly, that was not the reaction Serena was expecting. "You want to do it?"

I screwed up my eyes a little as I finished chewing another piece of pineapple. Maybe my last slice. "I've been thinking about it a lot lately. I just can't seem to get it out of my head. Why haven't I tried to have sex before now? I know I'm not naturally inclined toward it, but if I don't try, am I ever going to have a relationship with someone?" I paused, a little embarrassed to admit that I might want to have sex when I'd never been bothered before.

Lately, it wasn't so much that I wanted to *try* sex, so much as I wondered if I would ever be able to have a relationship, or even date, if I wasn't necessarily willing to have sex.

There is no dating app for the ace community, at least as far as I was aware, so using Tinder or Hinge to find dates often meant I was walking into a lion's den of people who refused to even match with me if I put "demisexual" in my profile. And those who did usually did so because they didn't believe me, respect me, or bother to look up its meaning. Maybe having more understanding of my sexuality, and pushing the boundaries of it willingly, would help make dating more normal. Or at least dating *me* more normal.

I would no longer be seen as a challenge to overcome, or a

woman with low self-esteem issues. I would just be a normal, sexually active woman.

After all, feeling confident enough to have sex would make dating easier. And if I wanted to have a long-term and stable relationship, I would surely have to have sex at some point?

But before I could do that, I needed to learn more about my sexuality and how to be sexual in general.

"To have a relationship with someone, I kind of feel like I have to get to know myself a bit better," I told Serena. "And right now, I don't know what I want down *there*. I don't even understand what sex is, not really. Do you get what I mean?"

"Sort of . . ." she said. "I mean I'm in a different boat as you as I have had relationships aplenty, but they're all short-term and on *my* terms."

Oh, to be so confident!

"Do you think those of us who are sexually active get a longer shelf life?" she continued. "Because we know that we can do it, we don't rush it or even bother thinking about it until we decide we want to. But for someone like you, someone who's not sexually inclined, or that confident in themselves—not saying *you're not*, just other people—" she added quickly, "maybe you feel like you and others in the ace community have to start sooner rather than later, or you think you're going to have a harder time finding someone."

I started nodding. "Well that pretty much sums up my feelings," I laughed. "Do you remember that date I went on, with that bloke from Le Cordon Bleu who shut things down after half an hour just because I told him I wouldn't feel comfortable sleeping with him?"

"That's a Tinder date, though, that's a whole different arena of dating. Tinder dates are just for sex, not relationships. Usually, anyway."

"Yeah, but it sucked to hear!" I said, pushing my tray of pizza off my lap, remembering the gut punch feeling of having some guy tell me that I was worthless because I wouldn't have sex. "I remember thinking that if that's the kind of reaction I'm going to get from men when I tell them I'm not interested in sex . . ." I didn't even finish the sentence as I began to feel a lump form in my throat. "I don't want to be rejected because I don't want a penis inside of me."

Serena pushed her tray of uneaten pizza away as well and wrapped an arm around my shoulder.

"Babe, if any guy, or girl—"

"Guy," I interjected. "I know enough about myself to know I'm into guys, not girls."

"Fine, but if either ever rejects you for that reason alone, then they are truly not worth a single thought over. They are trash that should be kicked to the curb. Their reason for being an arsehole is a reason that's no fault of your own, so it's only them who's at fault. I mean, look at me! When I get rejected, I rarely ever know the real reason behind it."

"You're *too* sexual?" I joked.

"Maybe." She laughed. "Maybe I do come across too strong sometimes, or perhaps I'm too confident. Some guys like meek girls. I bet you that most of the rom-coms on Netflix are about men and women who meet in stupid one-off circumstances, where he looked across a room and chose *her*. Out of all the hot, sexual, and confident women in the room he'll choose the meek, quiet one who wishes that she was home doing her homework or writing love letters she'll never send."

I scoffed. "I sometimes worry my relationship apathy is rubbing off on you."

"It's true, though!" Serena laughed her twinkly, effervescent laugh. "What guy in a club has ever ignored the woman who's grinding up against him on the dance floor for the woman in a turtleneck sitting on her own in a booth with a glass of water? No one! It's messed up. Films want you to think that all women have a shot, even when they're putting out *stay away from me* vibes. But, like you said, if you're going to have a relationship with someone, you need to put yourself out there. So, let's do this!"

She pounded the carpeted floor with her fist, which the downstairs neighbor, Mr. Kilmeckiz, returned with a thump of the end of his broomstick.

"Loving the can-do attitude, babe," I replied, pushing myself up from our awkward hold and reaching for my half-finished glass of rosé. This was going to happen; we were going to explore the topic of sex and develop my sexual—or rather nonsexual— experience, and Serena was going to be my personal sex doula.

"Let's do it. I'm ready for a sexual odyssey!"

Serena offered up her hand for a high-five and I gently pressed my glass against her palm.

CHAPTER 8
BETH

WHEN SERENA GETS a project, it's all go.

The following day, she worked from home with me. The two of us sat across from each other at our secondhand dining table, with a folded water bill under one leg to stop it rocking. Me in my pajamas, sitting cross-legged with my belly rolls rubbing together, and her looking far more put together in an off-the-shoulder "I just threw this on" Ted Baker ensemble that I could never afford.

Serena worked on gathering research and making a general timeline for the piece, while I slipped into some LinkedIn DMs to scrounge up some clients to at least make my monthly goal of two grand.

The freelancing pool was dry, and my search for a full-time office job was proving fruitless. My CV probably didn't help; I doubt many advertising agencies are looking for someone with a wealth of experience in writing SEO posts on maintaining golfing greens or ad strategies for carpeting companies.

"Okay, how do you feel about an online yoga session to improve your sexual muscles?"

I shrugged. How did I feel about any of this? Honestly, bemused. How was I to know what I wanted to do? I hadn't given much thought to sex until a few weeks ago.

"We can do it together!" Serena beamed.

"Oh, are you doing this too?" I teased. But of course she was, and if she had said she wasn't I would have made her do it. I wasn't about to go through this embarrassment alone.

"Duh! Like I'd miss out on some pelvic exercises."

"Seriously, though," I stressed, feeling a sudden flare of nervousness. "I'm going to need support if I'm really going to do all of this."

"I will be your sexual doula," she swore dramatically, lifting her hand to her heart so that her laptop almost toppled onto the floor. We grabbed it simultaneously, just in time, and mine almost went flying as a result. The dangers of working on the sofa. "I will be your ergonomic desk chair," she continued, laughing as we both corrected ourselves. "I'll be your bespoke Samaritan, your phone PopSocket, your shapewear."

"I get it! You'll support me."

"I'll be your compression socks, your memory foam inserts, your travel pillow . . ." she continued, evidently on a roll. "Your spider catcher, your makeup setting spray, your underwire, your bobby pins . . ." Finally she ran out of breath. "I will support you through it all."

"You'd better," I mumbled under my breath, returning to my LinkedIn searches. "Can we try goat yoga next?" I added.

"How is that going to help you lose your virginity?" Serena helped herself to my cup of tea, then grimaced when she tasted it. "God, you're bad at making tea."

That made me laugh after all her blather about being supportive. But she wasn't wrong.

"It's not going to help me, I just want to try goat yoga," I said, spell-checking my latest sales pitch to a start-up bra company called Bust and Beauty.

Don't be a lady, be a legend! Specialized marketing to help propel your business into the shopping carts of an enraptured feminist audience.

It wasn't one of my best, but it would have to do.

"Okay, so that's a therapist, yoga, the smear test, and maybe some more porn? What else can we do . . ." She was clicking her tongue against her teeth as she scrolled down various Google pages on sex therapy. "Ooh. How about dilation?"

"If that's another procedure, think again." No way in hell was I letting another nurse near my vagina with a speculum until I had to.

"It's not a procedure. It's a home dilation kit. You get a set of four varying-size dildos—for want of a better name—and practice penetration. They recommend it to women who've got vaginismus, or undergone hysterectomies or radiotherapy for cervical cancer."

"I've got or had none of those."

Serena deflated a little.

Well, what was the harm, actually? Now I had had a speculum inside of me, surely some plastic dildo wouldn't be difficult.

"Okay, fine," I agreed, suddenly curious to know what it would feel like and suddenly being eager to try.

"Yay!" Serena clapped gently and added the set of dilators to her Amazon cart.

"Any other devices you want me to try?"

"Well, I was going to go onto Lovehoney and see what they had on offer."

"Please tell me that this is not coming out of my rent money?"

"Nope. I'm charging it to the magazine."

"Does that mean that *The List* will technically own my dildo? Isn't that a little odd? What if they want it back?"

She didn't even bother to look at me. Instead she picked at her nail bed. "They're not going to ask for it back. It's for a case study, they'll be fine."

"Can we just charge any more stuff to my credit card?"

"As if. If anything, we'll put it on mine," Serena said nonchalantly. "Aren't you short again this month?"

"I can do the rent but not the bills," I admitted guiltily. It had been a slow month.

"I got you." Serena didn't even blink. Wouldn't it be lovely not to have to worry about money and be able to spend your savings on sex toys willy-nilly? Speaking of willy-nilly . . .

"Can I at least choose which toys I use?"

Clearly Serena had been waiting for me to ask. She sidled around the table, dragging her laptop with her. On her screen was the largest variety of vibrators and dildos I had ever seen.

"Right, what takes your fancy?"

"I've no idea. None of it."

"Not helpful," Serena said, butting me aside as she clicked onto the sale page. "Right, let's start with the basics. Vibrators. These are mostly for outer clitoral stimulation but can also be used for penetration or as a fun toy during intercourse."

"Are you helping me choose a sex toy or explaining the history of vibrators?"

Serena said nothing but clicked on a vibrator. It was a small remote-like toy that had a vibrating head on a spring.

"You can get the best angles that way," Serena explained when I queried.

"It looks like the female robot from *WALL-E*."

"Don't ruin *WALL-E* for me, Beth—don't do it."

Too late.

Serena moved onto the dildos page. This was where I felt the most threatened.

"Are penises usually this size?" I asked as she clicked on a ridged and veined dildo that was being modeled as if for a shopping channel.

"No, these are above average. But good fun on your own." She pointed to an option below the video of the woman now vibrating the dildo inside a fish tank. "This is the one I would recommend for you. It has a base, so you don't have to always hold it. It's good for getting used to the bouncing action."

"Okay, you do know the whole point of this exercise is not for me to go out and lose my virginity immediately. I just want to learn more about sex and the experience in general, to get more comfortable with my body and *eventually* have sex. It'll take time."

"Babe," Serena said softly. "I'm sorry, but you're going to have to bounce."

"That sounds a lot like exercise. No wonder I've never felt inclined to try it."

"Fine," Serena said hastily, shutting down the page with the bounceable dildo. "How about this? For now we stick with the vibrator and the dilators and later we'll move on to the more penetrative sex toys. It might be better to get used to the dilators first; walk before you can run."

"You mean glide before you bounce?"

"Exactly."

Beth's Sexual Odyssey

- ☐ Meet with a sex therapist
- ☐ Do yoga to strengthen pelvic floor

- ☑ Have a smear test to confirm cervical health
- ☐ Try dilation
- ☐ Experiment with solo-play sex toys

THE FOLLOWING DAY I was on the sofa chatting with Penny over FaceTime and eating a chili leftover from the night before.

Penny was at her desk in her home office, looking effortlessly busy while I willed someone to email me with some work.

"The more emails I send out the less work I seem to get," I told Penny as she added some papers to color-coded files behind her desk.

"It's hard out there at the moment, the economy . . ."

"Don't start talking to me about the economy." I banged my head (lightly) against the coffee table. She laughed.

"Well, it's sucky right now. Even Patrick and I noted the lowered viewings the other day." She and her husband ran their own real estate agency, inherited from Patrick's family, catering to the rich looking for five-bedroom country homes.

"Yeah, but even with one viewing you'll likely make a profit as you work with mega millionaires, while I deal with independent digital start-ups who don't like to pay for anything."

"You'll get there, you're just experiencing ups and downs. Have you thought about passive incomes?"

Here we go, my big sister giving me business tips as always.

"Let's face it, you're the businesswoman of the family. I'm the lazy one who hates taking orders and getting out of bed for a nine a.m. meeting."

Penny said nothing, but the disapproval plastered over her face was as obvious as her thick sixties eyeliner.

"I'm just saying . . ."

"So, Serena and I are working on this new project together," I interrupted before she could get preachy. I only called her to check on her after the latest IVF disappointment. But, as expected, she didn't want to talk about it and was throwing herself back into work to distract herself. I didn't press her—it was her personal business after all. And as much as I was happy to tell her I was working on a "project" with Serena, I was hardly about to tell her all the details.

"What kind of project?"

"Just some ideas for her magazine. Sometimes we do these little experiments together, so she has something to write about."

Penny nodded. "Like when you followed the advice from your horoscope for a week?"

I scoffed. "That was pointless." Never again will I follow mindless instructions about money from a random newspaper. I bought a £10 scratch card because I was supposed to be lucky that afternoon, and the horoscope lied. It was a sad day.

"Or the time that you watched a new movie every day for a month."

I smiled. "That was great. I can now say I have seen every Godfather and Matrix movie, but I bloody hated *Lawrence of Arabia*. That is four hours of my life I'm not getting back."

"It's a great movie!" Penny said, aghast.

"It's Peter O'Toole riding a camel for four hours. Not my idea of fun."

"You have no taste," Penny said simply. "So, what's this project about?"

"About sexualities and the like. I'm just a test subject." I flicked my hair jokily. Penny wasn't aware what my sexuality was, but she had never asked.

Penny pursed her lips, slightly intrigued, and I wondered

if today was the day, until she asked, "Are you getting paid for it?"

I had another mouthful of chili, wiping my lips afterward with the tea towel I had draped on my shoulder like Gordon Ramsay.

Swallowing, I replied, "Serena said she would get me a freelancer fee, but I mean that's only going to be about two hundred pounds, and that's only if the piece gets published."

Penny crossed her arms on her desk, putting down her papers and staring at me through the phone screen.

"You know if you just applied yourself . . ."

"I do apply myself!" I said, noting how my voice raised in pitch. I probably didn't *always*, but who could blame me. We were living in the middle of one of the worst economic situations—now here *I* go—and the world wasn't always kind to those who weren't suited to office work. "Or at least, I try to."

"You never finish a project," Penny pointed out, returning to her paperwork again.

"I do! I got a degree, didn't I?"

"Barely," Penny muttered.

"A second-class degree in marketing is not the end of the world, it was a hard course, and I got a job straight out of university, so no harm done."

"You interview well, I give you that."

"And I know what I'm doing. I just wasn't a fan of writing up all the theory behind it." It's not like I'm often asked to do that in the real world.

"Well, everything I learned getting my real estate agent license I still use, so don't knock education."

"When did this turn into a lecture?" I asked her, smirking. "I only called to . . ." her eyes flickered and I changed tack, "chat with my big sister, not my guidance counselor."

"Same thing." She winked.

"And I *will* finish this project with Serena," I said pointedly.

"I'll believe it when I see it," Penny muttered again, before sighing her usual *I've-got-a-ton-of-work-to-do* sigh.

"I'll do it!" I told her, before saying a quick goodbye. And I was going to be right. As much as I had had the same feeling about going freelance—and look how *that* was going—this article was much more short term. I hoped.

Determined, I pushed away my chili and forced myself from the living room floor to go to my bedroom. It was the smallest room in the flat, which was only fair since I hardly contributed to the rent. It consisted of one double bed, which barely fit within the walls, and a chest of drawers at the end with one drawer of ephemera and makeup and the rest purely for my un-ironed clothes.

Serena once told me that I was an easy housemate to live with, because it only took me one trip up the stairs with an overflowing Ikea bag of clothes and a suitcase of toiletries and I was moved in. I didn't even have cutlery for the kitchen, not unless you count my bamboo chopsticks that I once got from a Secret Santa at Elias.

I pulled a box from my chest of drawers.

The dilators Serena had ordered had come in the post a few days before, delivered while I was out at lunch and so had been deposited with one of our odd neighbors whose name I hadn't bothered to ask. Truthfully, the only reason we knew Mr. Kilmeckiz's name downstairs was because our mail landed on the same welcome mat as his. *Welcome* being such an ironic thing to have on a doormat in London.

I had gone to collect them from the neighbor, an older man who opened the door in just his shirt—*only* his shirt—but he had opened the parcel "by mistake." It was one of the most humiliating experiences of my life having to argue with a neighbor over who rightly owned my vaginal dilators.

I was about two sentences away from telling him exactly where to shove the plastic dildos when he threw them at my head and slammed the door. Only then I had to retrieve them from the pavement, where a relatively good-looking construction worker was walking by with a plank of wood. Not a euphemism.

All in all, the whole experience had put me off trying them for a few days.

But maybe Penny was right. I needed to apply myself completely. Grab life by the horns—or the dildo in this case—and actually finish a project.

I lay on my back, attempting the same position that Jane the Nurse had instructed me to sit in while she searched for my cervix, and I held the smallest dilator—a 3-millimeter-wide pink tube—at an angle. I had lubricated it up beforehand with some of Serena's products, but the lube made the whole experience much less appealing because I could barely keep the tube steady in my now slippery hand.

Serena's only instruction had been *get naked, cover yourself in lube, and see what happens*, so I didn't know that there was a wrong way to do things.

"God, I'm stupid," I said aloud, breathing in deeply before taking the plunge. A literal plunge in this case.

The dilator surprisingly went in very smoothly and I recognized the feeling from the smear test, so I didn't tense up. What was different however was that unlike a speculum, the first dilator had a much smaller girth so didn't really dilate anything.

I pushed it in as far as it would go without hurting. I must have a very long vagina as I almost lost the handle. No wonder Jane the Nurse couldn't find my cervix. Forget Atlantis, my vagina was more like the TARDIS.

I let it go and waited for a strange feeling to overtake me but there was none. Honestly, I could barely feel a thing, and this made me wonder about the quality of these dilation tools.

Was I meant to be feeling something? Isn't that what sex was all about?

I reached for the instruction pack and read over them.

"*Hold the dilator firm upon insertion. Patients are advised to insert, remove, and reinsert, repeating the process several times,*" I read aloud, holding the instruction pamphlet above my head.

I exhaled loudly and so powerfully that half of the dilator popped out of me.

"Whoops." I pushed it back in and heard the disgusting squelching noise of the lubricant. This whole penetrative business was not working for me. I couldn't see myself seeking the experience again. But if I wanted to know what my body could do, I needed to keep going.

CHAPTER 9
SERENA

THURSDAYS WERE ALWAYS rubbish days in the office. Freelance journalists rush to get their best (or semi-best) pitches to you before the end of the day because they know that none of our journalists are commissioning on Friday. We're all too busy finishing off our own pieces, or in meetings we'd pushed back all week to deal with the onslaught of emails from contacts, printers, and sources.

I'd spent the better part of the afternoon sending nice rejection after nice rejection to journalists who pitched two or three times a week, never getting a piece selected because it was so clear that their ideas were being shipped off to every magazine out there.

I had a contact at nearly all the other magazines, my favorite being Zoey from *Eve*, a smallish Liverpool-based print magazine that had a wide circulation due to an investment from a famous director. Reese Witherspoon had her production company and Gwyneth Paltrow had goop. This director just wanted a little slice of the side-hustle pie, and thank god she did, as Zoey was one of the best journalists I'd ever slept with. And *Eve* was a great magazine.

As I walked up the path toward the flat, I texted her.

> Received a pitch on the mental health effects of ghosting today. Did you get it?

She replied as I shut the door and walked upstairs.

> Yep. Was intrigued until I realized they meant actual ghosts.

> I thought their psychoanalysis of Virginia Woolf's opinion of the modern day was quite fascinating.

> Shame she's not around to comment though . . . or is she?

I laughed out loud and sent back a line of ghost emojis, to which she replied with a line of hearts.

> Down in London for a panel next week. Drinks?

I stopped on the landing and folded my lips over each other, trying to contain my smile.

Uhh, yes!

I was feeling a bit out of character of late, and spending time with Zoey—or rather going down on her—seemed like the perfect remedy. Zoey was confident and ebullient, while also having the rare talent of being able to hold an intelligent conversation for longer than a minute after sex.

Everyone I had brought home recently had been very disappointing choices on my part, and what with work being so dull and my parents only just realizing that it would be parental—no, *polite*—to say Happy New Year to their only daughter (nearly a month late!) I could do with the lift. Seeing Zoey would be like getting a scalp massage at the hairdresser, the best bit of the day.

Want to crash here? I texted back, holding my breath in unexpected anticipation.

> Would love to! I'll send over the dates.
> Will your housemate mind?

As if! But I knew it was polite to ask, particularly as I was hoping to have rather kinky sex.

I walked across the landing toward Beth's bedroom.

"Hey, Beth, are you in there?"

"What do you want?" she asked, more high-pitched than usual.

"Remember Zoey?"

"Of course I remember Zoey!" The volume of her voice rose with the pitch.

The last time we had properly spoken about Zoey, besides the hen party, was after I returned early from a trip to Liverpool to see Imagine Dragons in concert for a review. The concert was fun, but Zoey going down on me during "Demons" in the women's bathroom was transcendent. It was like a movie, I had a score to my orgasm.

During Zoey's turn—we missed most of the actual concert but when you can hear the music did you really *miss* it?—I was doing some of my best work to "Walking the Wire" when she muttered "I love you." I didn't think she meant it, and I didn't admit I heard it, but just in case I didn't stay for the weekend like I had planned either.

It was surely a heat of the moment thing. She didn't really have feelings for me. We were friends, occasional fuck buddies, text pals. We were not dating material. We lived in completely different cities, miles away from each other, and I am not the sort of person you "date." You fuck me, you screw me, you pleasure me, you do not date me. Something Beth wholeheartedly disagreed with me on, trying for weeks to convince me otherwise. But I'm sure. Zoey was just a good friend with great benefits. Nothing more.

"She's coming to London next week and wants to know if she can crash here? I said she could if you're cool with that?" There was no reply. "Can I come in?"

"Sure," Beth replied, and I opened the door.

She was lying on her back, legs akimbo with a tube sticking out of her vagina. She had attempted to throw a blanket over her legs to cover herself up, but it wasn't quite covering everything. Thankfully, having witnessed her smear test, this scene barely made me blink.

"Yeah, of course she can stay," she said, attempting a nonchalant tone. "Is this going to be a fun date-night thing for you?"

I almost choked. "No. It might be a sex-night thing, but nothing else. You know that Zoey and I aren't in, or ever going to be in, a relationship."

"You say that." Beth rolled her eyes.

"I mean that," I insisted. "Besides, before you fix my dating life, I don't see *you* trying hard to date. Have you messaged Evan yet, like Bonnie and I and everyone else on this planet keep telling you?" I had never seen her light up so much about a person until she came home every night raving about Evan.

Her face flushed. "He's old news. We haven't seen or spoken

to each other in months, not since he left Elias last year. I'm moving on."

"Yeah, sure you are . . ." I said, crossing my arms and smirking at her. But she said nothing else. "So, what are *you* doing?" I asked, nodding toward her bizarre posture.

"I'm dilating," she said, deadpan. "I don't think it's working."

"How?" I cleared my throat. "How do you mean?"

"Nothing's happening. I don't feel anything."

"Well, are you dilated?"

Beth glared at me. "How am I meant to know?!" she shouted, throwing a pamphlet of instructions at my head. I caught it and smoothed out the pages.

"Okay," I said, in my best can-do voice. "You've inserted the dilator—that's the toughest bit, so well done."

"Don't be patronizing." She crossed her arms over her chest.

"I'm not, I promise! I think, looking at this," I said, referencing the instructions and the various diagrams of how to insert the dilator, "it's more of a pelvic exercise. It's a practice tool, like those handwriting pens we used to get at school. They're kind of crap for anything else, but for practicing calligraphy they're not bad."

Clearly she did not appreciate my metaphorical explanation.

"Please tell me I haven't been lying here for over an hour with a lubricated dick-stick inside of me for no goddamn reason."

I shut the pamphlet carefully and placed it on her chest of drawers.

"Well, at least you're prepared for your incontinence years."

I knew this comment wasn't helpful to her. But I didn't expect to have the lubricated dick-stick removed and thrown at my head. It would have been okay if I had just ducked, but my years as the captain of the cricket team at my boarding school had instilled in me an instinct to catch.

"Thank you for including me in this," I told her.

I left Beth to clean up and went to the living room, texting Zoey that she had successfully secured a bed for the night.

I didn't clarify exactly which bed. I'd never presume anyone coming to stay was coming purely to sleep with me. But god I hoped so when it came to Zoey.

I couldn't put into words how I felt about Zoey, and I had never tried to. It had been about eight months since we'd last seen each other in person, but she was such an energetic woman it was impossible not to be pulled into her orbit and spend more than just time in bed together. Something I never did with my other friends with benefits.

The morning after our last tryst I had woken up to discover her completing a full round of yoga—more like contortion—on my bedroom floor before she instigated having sex again. She had the stamina of an Olympic gymnast. Afterward she barely took a breath before inviting me into the shower for a further round that I would have continued long after the water went cold, but she insisted we have breakfast in town before we went to an exhibition her friend had curated at the Tate. At the gallery she proved to have so much knowledge about photographic art that I was turned on looking at a portrait of an upsidedown gorilla being handed a camera by someone out of focus.

And to top it all off she is stunning, like Kristen Stewart edginess meets Anya Chalotra's stunning physique in *The Witcher*.

When we first met at a writer's seminar, I could hardly take my eyes off her. We didn't sleep together at first, we were just work friends, relationships that apart from Arnold were not something I usually put much energy into. But we talked all the time over WhatsApp, and she always hooked me with a witty aside or a genuinely interesting comment on our life in journalism.

It was only the second time we met in person that we did sleep together, and it lasted hours. Probably my longest sex marathon, purely because I didn't want it to end. And clearly neither did she.

But neither of us ever broached the subject of a different type of relationship. Particularly me. Why would I? We live so far apart, and our jobs take up most of our lives. Zoey is the only person I've ever met (apart from Arnold) who finds work genuinely enjoyable. Even Beth, who works for herself, hates her job.

"Okay, I'm done with that. Can we tick dilation off the list and never discuss it again?" Beth appeared in the kitchen and flicked the switch on the kettle with unusual aggressiveness.

"You need to persevere!" I said, shaking images of Zoey in the shower out of my mind. "This kind of attitude will get you nowhere."

Feeling sudden motivation on Beth's behalf I fetched my bag from the hall and pulled out my laptop. I returned to the living room and opened up the screen to Google.

"What are you looking for?" Beth asked, placing the hot chocolate she'd made down on one of our mismatched coasters.

"As your sex doula, I think it's time for step two of this little sexual awakening of yours."

"It's a sexual odyssey, not a sexual awakening," she said scornfully. "I have had an orgasm, and now I've even experienced penetration. Twice!"

"Getting an orgasm from a massage chair when you were fifteen and penetration from a speculum does not a sexual odyssey make," I quipped. "You have had orgasms since, right?"

She nodded. "From other massage chairs and shit," she joked.

I shook my head and continued to type, while Beth returned to the kitchen in search of snacks.

"There are some Pringles in the top right-hand cupboard."

"Bingo! Although they're salt and vinegar, bleurgh," she muttered, returning with the tube hugged close to her chest.

"Okay," I said as I found the online page I was searching for. "Round two. What do you think? Psychotherapist or regular therapist?"

"Is there a difference?" She collapsed on the floor with her Pringles and hot chocolate.

"Psychotherapist it is," I decided. "Feels like it's more targeted."

"They'll still likely bring it all back to my mother." Beth made duck lips with her Pringles. "You know there's no way we'll get to see a therapist in a few weeks, though," she said through her new beak, before crunching. "The NHS has waitlists for people with more pressing concerns."

"I've found one that offers short-period trials on a private basis."

"Private?" Beth's head shot up. "I still can't pay—"

I blew a raspberry at her. This was my answer for anything money related.

"You know, if I didn't know your parental history," Beth said, "you would be easy to resent for being so darn rich."

I shrugged; money was not my priority. Yes, my parents kept me funded enough with guilt money, but I could live easily on my salary from *The List* if I really wanted to. Sure, I'd have to budget more. But why should I turn their money down when they put me through so much shit in my childhood? I was closer to the flight attendants on the back-and-forth flights between Dubai, Japan, and London than I was with my own parents.

"Have you heard from them recently?"

I scoffed and opened my email. Sitting unopened at the top was the latest from my father. Alongside the belated "Happy

New Year" subject line there was a code to book myself flights to Dubai. Beth pulled the screen to face her.

"Are you going to go?" she asked, in the kind of tone you use when asking someone on the tube if they're okay when they look like they're about to faint.

I chuckled darkly. "Not likely," I said, returning the screen to face me. There was no other "look forward to seeing you" or even a "hope you're well" message. "He probably didn't even send it himself. He has assistants that do this type of stuff. You know, summoning me to come and charm some upper-class bankers and their sons for a weekend." I sighed, feeling a rush of emotion in my chest that made me want to simultaneously punch a wall but also cry.

My dad was a through-and-through businessman who was in love with himself first, and other women second. His daughter could never be his equal—as she wasn't a man—and she could never be a sexual conquest—as she was his child—so to him I was basically worthless. But as a banker he knew the value of paying me off as it meant I occasionally felt obligated to help him in his traditional (otherwise known as sexist) business ventures.

"I'm due a guilt-trip call from my mother right about now as well," I said, making sure my voice was light-hearted as I closed the message.

"When was the last time you heard from her?" Beth asked, curling her hands around her mug. I thought back, beyond the stupidly late New Year text. I couldn't really remember the last time I'd spoken to my mother. Unlike my dad she did usually use her phone to text or call every now and then, but only when she wanted something. Never out of interest or concern.

The two of them had been bad at communication ever since I was a child. Sticky notes and messages via the maid were how they usually spoke unless they were fighting, in which case it was always face to face.

When the fighting finally ended around my eleventh birthday and the two of them were indifferent but amicable in each other's presence I thought that finally their marriage was working. We were going to be a proper family.

I found out, weeks later from the maid, that it was because Mum had finally filed for divorce.

Family was not the priority for either of my parents growing up. Neither was marriage, if the rumors about their many extramarital affairs were true, and I know they were.

When I was a teenager, a few months after their divorce was finalized, I found a box of photos in Mum's attic of the three of us together when I was a newborn. My parents looked relatively happy in all of them, grinning and relaxed in each other's company. I cherished the photos for months, carrying them with me everywhere, until my Mum found me looking at them one day and pointed out that they were all posed and not candid. After that I could only see the insults and jabs being prepared in their minds as they waited for the flash to go off.

They had their moments as parents. Before the divorce Mum would take great care to lay out my clothes for me each morning, explaining why she had picked each piece to suit my coloring or my heart-shaped face. Dad always worked late because of meetings with clients in various time zones. But on occasion, he'd wake me up when he got home to do something silly, like a living room dance party on the Wii, or to make chocolate and vanilla milkshakes at midnight. These moments were few and far between, and after the divorce the gap widened until they stopped completely. Later, I rebelled, and they gave in, giving me whatever I wanted, except attention.

"It's been a while," I said simply, pushing my frustrations from my mind.

"Well, you're very welcome to join my family," Beth said, nudging me with her foot as she leaned back into the sofa and offered me a crisp.

I smiled. Sometimes I really wished I had a sister to keep me company through the crap of my childhood. Surely then it would have been less lonely and maybe I would have had someone on my side. But luckily I had Beth now.

"Thanks, babe," I said, and inhaled deeply. "Right, the psychosexual therapist can do Wednesday at six p.m. in Catford. Up for that?"

"Sure. And she'll want to talk about my experiences, anxieties, and sexuality? All that bullshit."

"Yep." I nodded again. "And it's a man."

"What?" Beth shouted. Ah. I had not foreseen this.

"Just because he's a man shouldn't mean he'll treat you any differently than a woman therapist," I tried to explain.

"It's not so much that . . . Whenever I talk to men about demisexuality—like on dates and things—they're always the ones that say things like *demisexuality sounds just like hanging out before sex*. It's the most frustrating response any demisexual can get. And I've never had that response from a woman before, only men. Why would a therapist be any different?"

"Well, his name's Thomas and he's a licensed psychosexual therapist and relationships counselor. The fact that he specializes in sex and sexuality makes me think he won't say anything like that. Also, according to his bio he's in his fifties. But we must not call him a perv—he's a licensed professional." That last note was for me, not her.

Beth gulped audibly.

CHAPTER 10
SERENA

I HAD BEEN hoping that Zoey would come to London on Monday and stay the whole week, but she said she would be getting in on Tuesday evening, doing the panel on Wednesday, and then leaving on Thursday.

There was no logistical way I could have multiple orgasmic shags with her in that time. I had work! (Maybe I should call in sick?)

The only time we would have together was when we were both at home, and then there was Beth to think about.

She didn't care if I had a woman in my room, but we had to be conscious of having loud, overly gymnastic sex.

"Forget it. I'll ask Delphi if I can crash at hers," Beth said when I brought it up.

"Are you two at that stage yet?"

Beth considered. "I'm just going to ask to crash on her sofa for a night, we're friends enough for that, I think."

I leant over the side of the sofa, where she was lying with her laptop propped against her knees, and kissed her exposed forehead.

"You're the best."

"If she's staying over from Tuesday, does that mean you won't be free to meet this sex therapist with me on Wednesday afternoon?"

I groaned. "Ah, shit." I had totally flaked on the date. "I can make it work," I offered, flapping a bit as my selfish insides screamed "No!" while the friend in me reminded me that I was supposed to be supporting Beth through her sexual odyssey. "I, erm, could just leave it as an overnighter. She wouldn't mind, it's still about eight hours together. That's not bad." I reluctantly reached for my phone to text her.

After not seeing her for months, now I'd have to rush her out the door. Usually that wouldn't be a problem—in fact it would be my preference—but I wanted to spend time with Zoey for as long as I could in the two days she was down. That would be a multi-orgasmic day. I could skip the gym for three weeks after that workout. And it would be good to chat with her. About work, of course, we were work friends with benefits after all.

"It's fiiiine." Beth craned her neck awkwardly to look at me. "I can go on my own and report back."

"Really!" I tried to control my relief. "Are you sure?"

"Yes," she acquiesced, smiling knowingly. "It's just a chat; it'll be pretty interesting to hear what they have to say."

"Oh my god, amazing. And do you think you could record the session on your phone?" I wondered if that was a step too far as soon as I asked. Therapy is usually so private, but what's the difference between me being there and me listening to it back for the article? Unless she said things about me while I wasn't there to moderate it?

I didn't have time to consider what she would say about me before Beth nodded.

"Fab!" I leaned forward and kissed her again, making a show of smooching my wet lips across her forehead.

"Gerroff!" she cried, flinging one arm back to hit my flank. I knew that although she was quietly interested in what the therapist would have to say, she wasn't so keen on the whole idea of talking to a male sex therapist about it, particularly given her lack of experience with men in general. Now she had to go speak to a male expert, I mean talk about mansplaining a situation. But I really, really wanted to spend some time with Zoey. Sometimes your clitoris just makes the decision for you.

It had been ages since we had last seen each other. But I still remembered the hours we spent together. The sex had been amazing, and I mean *amazing*. I had never felt so aroused in all my life.

I WAS AN excitable mess when I entered the office. Only ten hours until I would meet Zoey at London Euston Station and cab it back to the flat. I was going to go all out and splurge on a real London taxi, not an Uber.

Clearly my excitement was exhibited by my colorful outfit and wide grin, as the moment I entered the office Arnold appeared and paused in front of me.

"You're in heat. I can smell it."

I winked. "That's just my perfume."

"Who's the guy?"

"Girl, this time." I walked around him toward my desk, while everyone else in the office—already in and hard at work as I'd sauntered in at quarter to ten—returned to staring zombielike at their screens.

"Aha, you're wearing orange lipstick. You only wear orange lipstick when you're meeting a lesbian."

"No, I don't." I laughed. I was pretty sure this orange lipstick was new and barely used. "We've met up before. I'm looking forward to catching up."

"Or going down."

I slapped Arnold around the arm, and he winced dramatically. But it was true, after all.

"Will I meet this one?" he asked as I opened my laptop and pressed the on button. Instantly, the computer woke from sleep mode onto Lovehoney and its variety of strings of pearls—not the wearing-around-the-neck kind. Arnold took one look and said, "That one would suit you."

"I don't think *suit* is the right verb, but okay." Not one to ignore my boss's advice, I added that string of pearls to my cart and clicked onto my work tabs.

"But seriously, will I meet this one?"

"You might already know her." Arnold had met Zoey as many times as I had. Obviously without taking her to bed, but enough to comment that her writing style is "annihilating in a positive way." She could get to the heart of an issue, particularly in interviews, without making anyone out as the bad guy. Quite a feat for someone working in the British press.

Arnold made little "ooh" sound and tapped me affectionately on the shoulder. "So, any pitches for me this morning?"

"I was going to perfect some before the eleven o'clock pitch meeting."

He *pft*'d me and sat on my desk. He was so short his legs swung under it like a metronome.

"Pitch me now. I might cancel the pitch meeting, it's all Harry Styles this or Meghan and Harry that."

"Well, since I'm doing that piece with Beth on her sexual odyssey, I thought I would keep it to listicles and interviews this week."

"Hit me!"

"Okay, how about a shots game for when you're single and attending a wedding. Take a shot for every time someone asks you about your love life or says, *not found the right one yet?*, or starts telling you about their wedding with loved-up eyes at their partner."

Arnold was nodding. "This wouldn't happen to be based on any of my weddings, would it?"

"It's all weddings," I clarified, lying through my teeth. "Although, maybe I should add something about finding a single gay person to introduce as your partner?"

Arnold shook his head. "It's not worthy of a shot. Stick with the awkward conversations and embarrassing taxi-for-one moment."

"Got it."

"What else have you got?"

I pushed back from my desk and opened my drawer to gather my basic office stationery. I jotted down all my ideas throughout the week in it, including my to-do lists, shopping lists, and updates to my wank bank (currently Chris Hemsworth and Tom Hiddleston were my number one hits, particularly together. And there was plenty of fan art to accommodate me on that.)

"Uh, how about a piece on fifteen things Gen Z aren't buying anymore," I said, reading off the top idea. "Business suits for work, life insurance, cruises, irons, etc."

"Make it fifteen things Gen Z refuse to buy anymore. Makes it more inflammatory."

"Sure." I scribbled it down. "Do you want any more?"

"You could do this week's best sex piece?" He jabbed me with his elbow as he jumped off my table.

"I did one only three weeks ago."

"So? I get the feeling that tonight's activities are going to be better than three weeks ago."

I rolled my eyes, although I suspected that he might be right.

I'm not one to put pressure on myself or have high expectations, but there was something so dependable about sex with Zoey. Tonight was going to be an experience worth writing about no matter what happened.

ZOEY WAS WAITING for me when I got to Euston. She had texted me to say that she had managed to get on an earlier train and would be in at five thirty.

I left the office at five to make sure I was there to meet her on time, but I got distracted by a fight that broke out on the Piccadilly platform. I only watched for a little while, engrossed in the madness like a rubbernecker drawn to a car crash, but then I saw that one of the assailants on the floor was wearing espadrilles, so I knew it wasn't serious.

Then I spotted Zoey. She was sitting on a bench next to a larger man laughing loudly at a program he was watching on his phone.

"Hey!" I trilled. Why was my voice so high-pitched?

"Hey!" she returned, greeting me with a super warm hug. "It's been ages."

"I've been really looking forward to seeing you."

"Me too," she replied. She was so statuesque, and I could wrap my arms entirely around her. She fit perfectly. Tiptoeing to hug her, my cheek rested against her soft ears, and her ornate marble stud earrings imprinted against my skin.

It was a long minute before she released me, wafting her jasmine perfume toward me as she did so.

Her red hair was up in an artfully designed French plait, and she was wearing her black jeans, a loose white V-neck, and a chunky statement necklace. Minimalist, but stunning.

"Have you got any bags?" I asked, looking around. She had only brought an overnight rucksack and a small Michael Kors handbag, so there was no need for me to act as her personal bellhop.

"What's the plan?" she asked, after hiking her bag onto her back, wafting yet more of her addictive scent my way. Arnold was right, I was in heat.

"I thought we could just head back to my place and order in. Save you lugging all your stuff around the city."

"Sounds perfect." Her voice was low and tipped with a soft Merseyside twang. It was my version of ASMR: hearing her say anything made my skin start to go all tingly and made me long for my bed. Although I suspected the longing for my bed was for a different reason.

I shook my head a little. Regardless of her hotness, I needed to be thinking of Zoey as a friend and a guest. She wasn't coming over just to sleep with me, she wasn't a sex worker, and neither was I. We may well have sex—and it may well be the best bloody sex I ever have in my life—but she is also a woman with thoughts and feelings that deserve respect and appreciation . . .

She fisted me in the hallway the moment we entered the house.

It was glorious.

CHAPTER 11
BETH

PETE'S GONNA MAKE some carbonara, do you want some?" Delphi asked, sticking her head around the door of her and her boyfriend's tiny box room.

I was sitting on the blow-up mattress on the floor, replying to an interesting-looking email in my freelance account.

"Yeah, sure, sounds lovely." I lifted my head to give her a quick appreciative smile.

"Pete!" Delphi shouted from the door. "She said she'll try and stomach it."

"Ha bloody ha!" an extremely low male voice called back. Pete was a tattoo artist with his own studio in Camden. He made buckets of money from tourists, hipsters, and the occasional big-name A-lister from the US looking for an authentic London tattoo.

He was the poster child for his business: he was covered from forehead to pinkie in ink ranging from religious crosses, dangerous looking teardrops, and ridiculously cute Pikachus that he could make dance on his arm muscles.

Underneath the extremely hard exterior was an utter Italian

softie. Delphi loved to take the piss out of him, and as such, a fruitful relationship with a tiny spare room was born.

"Thanks for letting me crash here tonight."

She shrugged, still hovering by the door. "It's not often we get visitors. It's a change of pace. What are you working on?"

"Some company has just reached out for a marketing services quote."

"Ooh, that's exciting." And for once Delphi did sound excited. "What's the company?"

"It's called WOW or *War on Waste*. It's a zero-waste franchise. They've got pop up stores all over the country."

"And they want you to do their marketing?"

"They're asking for more details about what I can do for three grand," I explained. "I mean, this could be a big client for me. My first *big* big client."

"What kind of thing are they after?" she asked, stepping in to join me on the blow-up mattress like two preteens at a sleepover. My side of the mattress went up as she sat down, although she weighed about as much as an empty suitcase.

"General social advertising, some design work, social media management, looking for brand partnerships, all that jazz."

"Sounds like a lot."

I shrugged. It wasn't like I had anything else to do.

"But still," Delphi said, overly jolly. "It's big news!"

The shock of having well-paid work after so long was such that I was barely able to talk properly.

"We need a drink. Oi, Pete!" she shouted. A big bushy beard appeared moments later. "Do we have that bottle of cava your mum left here?"

"Sure. It's the cheap stuff, though."

"Well, it's not like we have any expensive stuff, is it?"

Pete shrugged and disappeared again.

"It's alright," I said. "Water would taste expensive to me right now."

"Yeah, I'm bloody Jesus, I can turn water to wine." Delphi laughed. "Are you gonna text that flatmate of yours? That's usually the first thing you do when you get some success."

Success? She could only be referring to the time I won a fiver on a scratch card, that or the moment my mother went into a dead zone while berating me over the phone for forgetting Father's Day. "Serena's busy." I had been honest with her as to why I needed a place to crash, it was the sort of tidbit that Delphi loved to hear about my personal life. And I didn't mind sharing it as it wasn't really anything to do with my personal life at all. In the case of asking to crash for the night, though, she had returned my honesty with equal bluntness.

"I'm on my period right now, so I guarantee you Pete and I won't be having sex. I don't really mind, but Pete hates it. He says the bed looks like a murder scene afterward, and his dick is the weapon. Typically, though, the idea that his dick is a weapon makes him rock-hard. Men and their godforsaken egos. I think sex on my period just leads to the bedsheets turning into the Japanese flag." I let her have a moment as I tried not to let my expression betray my secondhand embarrassment.

"So who is this *Zoey* person?" she asked me as Pete returned with two mugs of cava. Clearly they didn't own wine glasses either. Fair do's to them.

I shut my laptop and moved to get comfy.

"Zoey is another journalist. They met a few times at panels and conferences over the last year or so, and according to Serena, Zoey is the best shag of her life."

"Ooh, lucky for some."

"I heard that," Pete replied from the kitchen. Delphi gestured for me to continue.

"There's no big romance or anything, Serena is the antithesis of that, but I think Zoey is the only lay that has ever meant something to her."

"Like a first love, you mean. How you never forget a first love, you never forget your best lay." Delphi sighed wistfully.

I nodded. "And for someone so emotionally unavailable as Serena, I think that's a big deal for her. And frightening as well, which is why I wanted to leave them to it."

"Damn," Delphi said, swigging back her cava like it was juice. "That's some deep lesbian shit. Here I was, thinking Tinder was deep."

How had she ever come to that conclusion? I didn't even want to know.

"Are they dating then?"

I scoffed so hard I sucked the cava up my nose.

"No!" I gasped, feeling the bubbles gliding down the back of my throat. Gross. "More like arranged fucking."

"Very Jane Austen meets *Fleabag*." Delphi nodded appreciatively.

"Yeah, kinda." Not sure if it was the best example. "To be honest, I sort of want them to get together. As much as Serena says she only cares for her sexually, it's obvious that it's more than that. She's never asked me to leave her alone with a fuck buddy before."

"Maybe she just wants to do it all over the house?" Delphi suggested.

"She's a proud sex positive woman and I'm happy for her to bring home whomever she chooses to the flat, but we do have boundaries," I said. "Sex nowhere but her bedroom and the shower—that one I can make allowances for because she cleans up. And as for having company when I'm home, she's usually very good at communicating beforehand and keeping things quiet-ish in her room. But to want the flat to herself, that means she wants to go all in and give her best performance. And that means she's looking to impress both before and after." Something Serena had never done in the ten years I had been living with her.

CHAPTER 12
SERENA

SO THIS WAS what it was like to wake up in bed next to someone and *not* want to get them to leave immediately.

I woke first and denied the urge to stretch and find a cool spot in the sheets, as the heat radiating from Zoey's side reminded me that I was not alone. Normally, if someone had overslept their welcome, I would wake them and warn them that as soon as I had finished peeing, I wanted them to have gone. But not Zoey. Zoey could stay until I got back from work, and then some.

As carefully as I could, trying not to make any noise or dip her end of the mattress, I moved onto my side and stared at her.

She was sleeping on her back, one arm draped above her head with her little finger sitting atop her forehead while her other dexterous fingers relaxed on the pillow. Her lips were slightly parted and there was a crusty line of drool down one side. I itched to wipe it away for her, to save her the potential embarrassment—but she wasn't the type to get embarrassed.

Zoey sighed a little in her sleep and shuffled her head across the pillow, her hand remaining exactly as it was. I froze, wondering if she was about to wake and see me staring at her. Was that weird? Of course it was weird! But still I couldn't stop.

Her scent was a strange mix of sweat from her exposed armpit and the lingering jasmine perfume from last night. Her lips had tasted of cherries from her lip balm and running my tongue over the layer still residing on my lips from last night, I could taste her again.

She snuffled. One leg lay atop the duvet while the other poked at mine, her leg hairs tickling my smooth skin.

I smiled at the memory of me rubbing my cheeks across her legs as I climbed her the night before. She had been on top at first, but we decided to switch halfway through. We were ambidextrous lovers; we didn't have a preference.

I lay back down next to her, so I wasn't resting my elbows on the memory foam. I didn't want my bed to remember me that way. Though it was unlikely my bed had any idea of my body shape since it was so often full of bodies, it was practically a shelter.

Zoey snuffled again and I knew instinctively that she was about to wake. Her whole body shuddered with an internal stretch and her hand balled into a fist. The heat radiating off her was incredible. No wonder she had to lay with one leg out from under the duvet all the time. If she didn't, she would likely spontaneously combust.

"What are you thinking?" I heard her say. I was staring at her exposed leg, the blond hairs standing to attention in the early morning sunlight that streamed through the top of the curtains.

"That you're hot." I smiled, looking up directly into her green eyes.

"That's nice," she replied, turning over to face me but shutting her eyes again as she wrapped her arms around my pillow.

My phone buzzed on the side table. Instinctively I reached for it, but I was berating myself mentally for not turning it off.

I didn't want to be disturbed right now. Who knew when I was next going to have Zoey in my bed? I wanted to savor it.

That was a new thought.

I swung my legs out of the duvet in surprise. That was the first time that had ever happened. It couldn't happen. I wasn't the committed, or even vaguely repetitive type.

I paused. My phone continued to buzz. I snatched it up.

"Hello?" I said, without looking at the caller ID.

"Hey, it's Beth. If I'm messing up the vibe, hang up," she spoke quickly, excitedly almost.

"No," I laughed, grateful it wasn't Arnold calling to ask me to get in early for once. "No, it's fine. Hold on." I turned on the spot and looked down at Zoey, but she was already back asleep.

Standing carefully, I took my dressing gown off the back of the door, draped it around myself, and headed toward the living room.

"I'm back, just needed to get out of bed."

"Figures." I could hear traffic coming through the speakers; she must be outside.

"Has Delphi kicked you out already?"

"No," she said. "But I couldn't spend one more minute on that bloody air mattress. Honestly, I have bruises in places I didn't know you could get bruises." She groaned dramatically to prove her point. "Please tell me I can come home tonight."

"Course. Zoey's here tonight as well, but we won't be as vigorous as we were last night."

"I'll believe that when I *don't* hear it."

"She's got to head back to Liverpool tomorrow morning for an afternoon meeting. She needs her rest."

"But you don't want her to leave?"

I hesitated. "Does anyone want the greatest fuck of their life to leave? I think not."

"Well, I can't answer that question now, can I?" Beth's laugh crackled down the line.

"Are you heading back here?"

"God no!" she shouted over the din of a roaring vehicle. "No, I'm heading into central. Thought I would get some work done at the British Library."

"Good luck getting Wi-Fi."

"No but actually, guess what!" She didn't wait for me to guess. "I've got a new client! A proper client. One that can pay actual money, and full price too."

"Get you!" I smiled. "You go, girl." The platitudes from *The List* Instagram account spurted out of me before I could stop. "That's great news."

"Isn't it?" She sounded relieved. "It's been ages since I've had a proper client so I'm excited to get started."

"Aha." I nodded into the window frame. The condensation was cool on my skin after the heat of Zoey's. "So you've got the get-up-and-go bug for once."

"I think I have." It had been a while since I had heard Beth sound excited about anything work-related. "What about you? Have you got the get-up-and-get-out-of-bed bug, or do you have the stay-here-and-never-let-go bug?"

I laughed without meaning to. "You're making this sound more and more like an infection."

"Well, it's an infection waiting to happen. Remember to have a good piss, by the way. We've run out of cystitis medication."

"I'll be fine," I protested weakly.

"Regardless, piss anyway," Beth said in her most motherly tone.

"I will piss. And you need to piss off, I want to get back to bed."

"Ooh! You've got *that* bug."

"I do," I whimpered, closing my eyes against the window. This was new for me, and I didn't quite know what to do, or how it made me feel. Every emotion inside of me was jumbled together like a heavy load of washing. "I really do."

"Aww. Can you take the day off?"

I shook my head, knowing that Beth couldn't see, but she took my silence as the answer.

"Not even a morning off?"

"I can't. I'm already the world's worst employee, and I can't keep flaking like this. Even Arnold has limits. And besides, he knew that I had a date last night. It would be impossible to make up a good enough excuse to get the day off now."

"Sex accident that led to A&E?"

"He'd make me write about it."

"You know you don't have to write about every detail of your sex life. Just use mine!"

"I will never write again," I deadpanned.

"Ouch. Remember, I've got the sex therapist this afternoon as well."

"Oh hell, yeah. Let me know how it goes!"

"Damn you for making me go alone," Beth said dramatically.

"I know. I'm sorry. If I could schedule it during work hours I would, but I really need to file my Vaginal Valentine's Day story so that the artist can get to work and then I have that interview with Saoirse Ronan."

"I can't believe Saoirse is more important than my psycho-sexual health." I smiled at her sarcasm. "Okay, bugger off. But you owe me one!"

"I'll tell you what, I'll pay the rent next month. How about that?"

"Deal! Although I may be able to contribute for once, now I have an actual client."

"Get you." I made a smiley face with my finger on the condensation of the window.

"Right, go back to bed and give Zoey a big kiss from me."

"Why would I kiss her for you?" They'd never even met before.

"Because any woman my best mate's in love with is worthy of a kiss from me."

"I'm not in *love*," I retorted. "What does it matter anyway? She's going home tomorrow."

"Then tell her you have feelings for her tonight!"

"As if, I'm not thirteen, and I'm not in love." I wiped the smile off the glass. "Right, go away."

"I'm going, I'm going. Love you!"

"Love you too, babe." Replacing the phone in the pocket of my dressing gown, I turned slightly, only to hear the shuffling of feet moving away but then pausing.

Had Zoey been standing outside the room listening?

"Hey," she said, appearing around the corner after another moment of shuffled footsteps. She leaned against the doorframe, only wearing a pair of knickers. "So, what's for breakfast?"

I smiled and tried to shrug off the intense fear that Zoey had just heard me discount my feelings for her over the phone to my best friend.

CHAPTER 13
BETH

I LOVED THE hustle of the city, not so much the bustle. Getting jolted from side to side on buses and being made to stand for an early-morning shopper with a trolley ground my gears. I knew it was my youthful duty to offer my seat to pregnant women and the elderly, but quite honestly, I wanted to refuse and tell them that I was on my period and in pain. But indoctrinated etiquette forbade me.

As I hopped off the bus outside Kings Cross, I headed toward the British Library. I always liked the massive metal gate with words inscribed across it. Going through it made me feel fancy.

The courtyard was mostly empty, with only a few PhD-looking students and the occasional ancient researcher stumbling over the fire vents and past the sculptures.

The reading room was occupied by two other people: a man in a hoodie bent over an artist's pad with a pen, his music turned up about two decibels too high. And another man, in a black pinstripe suit, reading a dictionary in another language.

I sat down and spread out my work detritus and took a moment to soak in the sensation that I was about to work properly for the first time in about three months.

But then my phone buzzed.

"Shit." Oops. "I'm so sorry," I mouthed to the suited man, who looked up disapprovingly as I fumbled for my phone. I pointed to the exit and then back at my laptop and mouthed, "Will you watch that for me?" He nodded once but then shook his head. Weird, but I had to trust him for now.

"Hello?" I whispered harshly when I was out of earshot of the reading room. In my haste I hadn't bothered to look who was calling.

"Hey, is this Beth?" A man. Damn, had I answered a scam call?

"Speaking, who's this?"

"Hey, it's Evan Cartwright."

Holy fuck.

Evan Cartwright, my old colleague at Elias Recruitment. My old colleague who I had the biggest crush on and never said anything about it to. *The* Evan Cartwright. The one that got away—or the closest I'd had to the one that got away.

"Oh my god," I said without thinking and quickly screwed my eyes together mouthing "fuck" as this was already weird. "It's been a while!" I laughed breathily, and I heard him do the same.

"I know, I know," he said, "I meant to give you a call ages ago, or at least WhatsApp." Yes, and why was he calling me and not WhatsApping? He must know that phone calls are not usually appreciated.

Although I couldn't help but warm up at the sound of his voice.

"That's okay, how have you been? How's the new job?" I never really knew why he left Elias. Both of us left around the same time, about a year ago, but we were dealing with two different areas of recruitment; him as a project manager working on securing senior clients and me in marketing attempting to help the business develop its reach. We never found much time to catch up except for weekly watercooler moments in the joint kitchen of the office and the occasional walk from the coffee shop near the office building when we happened to bump into each other on our morning commutes.

"Really good, it's actually why I'm calling. I never really told you, but when I left Elias I left to start my own business."

"Oh wow." He and I were growing more compatible by the minute! "That's amazing."

"Yeah." I could hear his smile down the phone. "And it is literally WOW, it's a zero-waste company called *War on Waste*."

"Wait, WOW? As in WOW, WOW? I got an email from that company yesterday."

"Yeah, that was us! My cofounder David found your details on LinkedIn and reached out. When I saw your email this morning, I thought I should call. Or rather, I wanted to."

Were the planets intervening? This was some spooky serendipitous shit in motion.

"And WOW is *your* company?"

"Yeah, I know! It's so odd to say I have a company now." I imagined him ruffling his hair and rolling on his ankles like he used to in the kitchen when he would be waiting for me to fill my mug at the coffee machine. The picture was clear as day in my mind. "David's an old friend from school and he and I are both really into sustainable living, so we started the business together. We have pop-ups all over the country."

"It sounds incredible, and I was really excited to get the email last night," I said honestly. "I'm guessing since you saw my reply, that you also saw I sent over my rate-card, but now I know it's *you*, mates-rates apply." Screw my freelance bottom line: it's Evan. *The* Evan. Serena would collapse when I told her he'd called me.

"That's so kind, but truthfully your rate-card works for us, and I think this would be great. I mean, I already know you're talented and you're great at what you do—you're the only one who ever got any work done at Elias. They massively underappreciated you—and I would love to work with you again."

My cheeks flushed as a door opened and another library patron walked in. They looked startled to see me hovering in the corridor, probably looking like a demented version of the Cheshire Cat.

"It sounds like a fantastic opportunity," I said, just spewing words that felt compulsory to say in work conversations like these. But this was *more* than a work call. If Serena were here she'd be coaching me to ask for more and give it my all. And probably to flirt with Evan too.

So I channeled my inner Serena and went for it.

"Actually, it would be great if we could meet up to discuss the role in person so I can figure out exactly what it is you're looking for. We can hash out some objectives, and all those wonderful marketing shenanigans. And just catch up . . . since it's been a while."

"Nearly a year," Evan said. "But I would really love that. It will be great to see you again."

YES! My heart was thumping so hard it was like I had just plugged my body into the library's electric mains.

"Amazing—erm, how about lunch? Do you remember Coffee Office in Camden?"

Anywhere but Edith's Cafe. There was no way I was bringing Evan to meet Delphi—she'd crucify him, and that's if she were on her best behavior.

"Blast from the not-so-distant past," he said. I could hear the smile in his voice. "Absolutely, let's meet there." We exchanged a date and time—a couple of weeks' time so I could do all the necessary prep work.

"It's been really great to chat to you again," Evan said eventually after promising to send over some initial marketing material.

"I agree, and I'm really looking forward to coffee . . . and discussing WOW," I said quickly. This was a work call, I hadn't just arranged a date, no matter how much it felt like it.

"Great, I'll see you soon," Evan said.

I smiled and nodded as if he could see me. "I'll see you then," I parroted before clicking off.

The moment I heard the click my mind became aflame with anxieties. Had I spoken too quickly? Did I mumble? Did I sound impressive? Was I unprofessional? Or too professional?

And most importantly, was he aware that I had a crush on him?

We had our kitchen chats from time to time, but we never really hung out. When we had gone to lunch together, we went with other colleagues, and it was always for work reasons, never socially.

Bonnie always joked that he had a thing for me, but he never acted differently with me than he did with her or anyone else.

Maybe the flirtation was simply in my head?

It was his cofounder who had approached me about the WOW job first over email, not him; he hadn't even realized I'd gone freelance. But then I didn't know he had started a business either. Could you really be that interested in someone and not cyberstalk them?

He didn't have Instagram or TikTok, and I hadn't even thought to look at LinkedIn for fear that he would see me snooping. But what if he had reviewed my socials?

He would have seen the various photos I shared on Instagram of Serena and me at home, selfies with pizza boxes and murky wine glasses. Or the silly TikToks I occasionally did lip-syncing to scenes from *Schitt's Creek*.

My face was burning from the heat emanating off my ancient phone and the embarrassment that had flooded through me.

It was just one work call. Why was I overthinking this?

But it was *Evan*. Of course I was going to overthink it. He just had to enter a room at Elias and my heart would start fluttering.

And now he needed me—or better still, wanted me.

CHAPTER 14
SERENA

ARNOLD, I'VE FILED those stories you asked for. Do you want me to start on anything else?"

Arnold was sitting at his desk on a bouncy yoga ball reading something on his phone. He didn't look up but shook his head with a frown.

"You alright?" I stepped in and pulled the door closed.

"Yeah, fine. Gareth's just messaging me about flowers."

"For the wedding?"

"Is having flowers at your third wedding a bit pretentious?" he asked, completely serious, leaning over his desk. "I mean, I've done this twice now. Do I really need the flowers?"

I smiled softly. "You can have what you want; it's your wedding."

"That's the point. I've had two already. I can't really say it's *my wedding* as that makes it sound like it's my only chance to plan. I've done this before—badly. Besides, I've already done white roses and pink tulips. What's next? Marigolds?"

"You've got wedding guilt, haven't you?"

Arnold sighed and placed his phone down, pushing his hair away from his face with a strained groan.

Poor Arnold, he loved to be in love, but he really shouldn't bother with the wedding bit. It was all ceremonial anyway, not worth all the money in my opinion.

"One in three marriages end in divorce," I told him, speaking quickly as he scowled at me. "Maybe for you it's the opposite. One in three marriages succeed. Maybe this is that marriage!"

"To be honest I don't care about marriage . . . I mean, I do, it's just this bloody wedding. I've already planned two and I really don't want to have to plan a third. But it's Gareth's first and he wants the whole shebang and who can blame him? But he's sick of me just saying yes to everything. And to be honest I must stop that—the things I've agreed to!" He shuddered.

"It can't be as bad as the doves at your last wedding." Two turtle doves had flown the rings to Arnold and his ex at the altar. Or they were supposed to—one of them flew off and the other, momentarily confused, perched on Arnold's shoulder, shat down his suit, and then flew off before he could unlace the ring.

"There are swans."

"Right . . ." I said, cautiously, not sure how helpful I would be in this conversation. "Well, those stories you asked for are done and I was going to get to work on Beth's sexual odyssey piece, unless you had anything else for me."

"Oh, distract me for a minute. How's that going? Have you got her in the sack yet?"

"Not personally." I laughed.

"No, not you, but with someone else. I don't want you two to shag, it will ruin your whole BFF storyline. So, what have you done?"

"Would you believe it if I told you she's off to see a sex therapist in a couple of hours?"

"Is she?!" Arnold's face lit up and he leaned back on his ball.

He wobbled for a moment before regaining his balance. "I can't wait to hear about that."

His phone buzzed again. And then again. And then again.

Clearly Gareth wanted an answer on the flowers.

"I'll let you know," I told him, opening the door as he growled at his phone. "Just tell Gareth that you want something simple, maybe even silk flowers. Less hassle than real flowers."

"Ooh, silk flowers are a good shout. We can go to the garden center this weekend."

I left him to his plans, shutting the door as he dictated his text message to Gareth out loud.

"How . . . do . . . you . . . feel . . . about . . . silk . . . flowers?"

Bless him. I returned to my desk. My inbox had lit up with the flurry of post-lunch pitches from freelancers and replies from interviewees. My interview with Saoirse Ronan had been canceled due to a change in her filming schedule, which meant the interview was going to be conducted via Zoom the following week. It gave me most of my morning back and had been the perfect excuse for why I had to leave early after Zoey caught the tail end of my conversation with Beth. She hadn't mentioned it, but it felt like something had changed between us.

I opened WhatsApp online and sent her a quick message remembering her panel was at lunchtime. *Go and smash it!*

She replied with a GIF of the Incredible Hulk in *Avengers Assemble* smiling at Captain America's instruction to smash.

"Love it!" I went to write. But somehow it autocorrected to "Love you."

Thankfully I didn't send it, and my heart raced as I pummeled the delete key.

Phew. I hadn't sent it. I had stopped it.

But . . . would it be so bad if I had sent it?

I hadn't sent it, though, right?

I rushed to the bathroom and locked myself in the first cubicle, my breathing coming thick and fast. I felt my stomach collapse inside of me and my pulse slamming into my neck. Why was I reacting like this?

It was just a harmless message that I hadn't even sent.

I checked again.

The only thing in our thread was the Incredible Hulk grinning at me. It no longer seemed funny but mocking.

That was close.

I said "love you" to Beth all the time. But that was Beth. She was like my sister, my mother, and my wife all in one. "Love you" was platonic between us.

But saying "love you" to Zoey could never be like that. There was only one interpretation of "love you." Now our friendship had developed from casual texting to hours-long sex to going to galleries and having breakfast together. Saying "love you" was opening the door to a road I wasn't sure I would ever want to walk down.

Suddenly my mind was ablaze with all the things I could say to her that could be interpretational. "Fuck you" could be both instructional and full of anger, "liar" could be as a joke or confrontational. But saying "love you" to her was strictly a declaration.

And I'd only just screwed her again after nearly a year. I couldn't love her. It's not possible to love someone so quickly. Particularly when you've never loved anyone in a romantic sense. I don't go in for all that anyway. Love is not something that creeps up on you, you have to put effort into it. Otherwise, I'd love my parents or Hermione or all the people I've ever brought home for an evening's fun.

I sighed and leaned heavily against the back of the toilet.

I had to get Zoey out of my system. This was such an over-reaction, and I wasn't here for it. This wasn't *me*.

Closing WhatsApp, I flicked onto Tinder. I had hundreds of matches and about twenty messages I had yet to reply to. Usually, I just went for whoever was at the top, and if we hadn't got around to sharing our addresses by the third or fourth text I moved on.

There was a guy called Terry and another man called Sarge beneath him. I messaged them both *I want to fuck* and waited for the first to reply. I had just finally got my breathing back to normal levels when my phone buzzed again.

I'm free. It was from Sarge.

He sent me his address and I texted Arnold to tell him I wasn't feeling well, pocketed my phone, left the bathroom, and hurriedly returned to my desk to get my things. All the while a voice in the back of my head berated me like one of my old nannies, telling me I was going to regret this.

Putting on my headphones I played T. Rex's "Get It On" at full-volume and rushed toward the exit to head to Wembley to fuck Sarge and get Zoey out of my head.

CHAPTER 15
BETH

THE THERAPIST'S OFFICE seemed to match my imagined view of a private practice. There were automatic sliding doors, and a reception area bedecked with hand sanitizer and bowls of communal sweets, defeating the point of the hand sanitizer. The receptionist was wearing a full-length cardigan and had a long weave, which draped over the back of her chair and was all that was visible as I hovered by the appointment windowpane.

I cleared my throat. But she didn't turn.

"Excuse me?" I asked quietly. And then again, a little louder.

"Hang on," she replied, turning in her chair to reveal that she was finishing off the *Evening Standard* crossword. Fair do's, I thought. I would do the same.

I peered down at the last clue she was on, reading it upside down.

Afternoon snooze (6), six across.

The receptionist was flicking the bottom of her chewed-up pen against the paper. The only clue for the word being an E in the middle.

"Siesta."

"Ah, bloody hell," the woman said, writing it in frustration.

Oh no, was she going to be one of those people who gets really upset when other people complete their puzzles for them? I backed away, forgetting that there was a glass pane about the width of a two-pound coin between us. "I won't be called upon as a codebreaker anytime soon." She dropped her pen and smiled at me.

"You got all the rest."

"Oh no, the doctors did that. I just picked it up from the staff room on my break. I've got no head for that sort of thing. Too much stuff in there already." She jabbed her forehead with her finger so hard she left a red imprint above one of her eyebrows.

"Erm, I'm here to see . . ." My tongue had begun to feel heavy in my mouth. I shook my head. "I think it's Thomas Bates?"

"Aha, Mr. Bates. Sit down, I'll let him know you're here and he'll come get you when he's ready. Can you fill this out in the meantime?" She handed me a clipboard with a yellow piece of paper asking for my medical details. I hovered at the reception while filling it out, only shuffling to the seat farthest from the receptionist, behind a pillar, when I got to the box at the bottom of the page, asking me to disclose what I wanted to discuss today.

Tick boxes offered topics of conversation including:

- ☐ Erectile dysfunction
- ☐ Loss of desire or libido
- ☐ Difficulties with orgasm or involuntary ejaculation
- ☐ Arousal difficulties
- ☐ Out of control sexual behavior
- ☐ Concerns about porn consumption
- ☐ Fear of sex, avoidance, or sexual phobias
- ☐ Sexual shame
- ☐ Sexual trauma

I went over the list several times and flicked between ticking fear of sex and arousal difficulties. I was demisexual, not *afraid* of sex per se, just not interested most of the time. It was hard to explain and there was no box to tick for that, there wasn't even a box to tick regarding queries about sexuality, or lack thereof.

People on the asexual spectrum—such as myself—didn't exist apparently.

You don't have sex, therefore you don't have a say. You don't contribute to the procreation of the planet, therefore you're invisible. That's what it felt like half the time, even at a sexologist appointment.

I ticked *arousal difficulties.*

"Bethany?" A soft voice called from in front of the pillar I was hiding behind. I jutted my head out and waited for his reaction, but it didn't come. I was the only one in the small waiting room. Clearly sex appointments happened in the mornings, not the afternoons. I understand that. Who has the energy after work? I gathered my things and went to greet the short middle-aged man.

He was bald and slightly hunched but kind-looking. He had a spot of something from his lunch on his shirt and wore jeans with his shirt tucked in, like some haggard schoolteacher.

"Hi," I said. He twisted and smiled in my general direction, but still didn't look directly at me.

"Ah, Bethany Mitchell?"

I nodded, but then said "yes" as well.

"You'll have to come toward me a bit more," he said, pointing to his deep blue eyes. "Afraid I've got terrible eyesight, I can only see things about six feet in front of me, otherwise it's all a blur."

"Oh," I said, stepping forward immediately.

"Ah, there you are." He smiled and offered me his hand,

which I took gingerly, shuffling the clipboard beneath my arm. "My office is just through here, have you got everything?"

Even though I knew I did, I still looked around my feet and back at my chair just to check.

"Absolutely. Lead the way, if you can. I mean . . . I don't . . ." I fumbled over my words, but Mr. Bates just laughed and turned on the spot, leading me to a door that he opened with his extendable access card. He held it open, and I flushed, walking with my head down like a school child caught passing love notes to a crush.

"Have you come from work?" he asked politely, leading me down a tunnel of corridors that I doubted I would find my way out of.

"No. Well, sort of. I'm freelance."

"Ah, so your days are your own."

I shrugged, not that he could see. This was a common misconception of freelancing, which I was too embarrassed to correct right now.

"I worked in the city today, so I came in from there."

"Not too bad getting in from Central. I live in North London and that's a right pain. My wife keeps telling me I should find a new practice, but I've been here for nearly fifteen years, and I'm set in my ways. What about you? How long have you been freelancing?"

"Oh, about a year, I think."

Mr. Bates nodded before stopping suddenly outside a small kitchen and leading me inside.

Were we having our session in the kitchen? Ah, no: he was just collecting two mugs from a communal mug tree and filling them with hot water from a giant urn on the side.

"Tea or coffee? Or would you prefer a cold drink?"

"Uh, coffee would be great. Milk, no sugar."

"I'll have tea."

To fill the silence I blurted the first thing that came into my head. "This is a very strange kind of doctor's office?" I needed an icebreaker.

"Well, it's not a doctor's office. We're more like a private counseling center, but I don't think of myself as a counselor," Mr. Bates said.

"What would you call yourself?" Oh god, please don't say *love guru*.

"Probably a teaching assistant." Well, my scholarly first impression was dead on.

"Not a teacher?"

He laughed and shook his head as he added a healthy, or rather unhealthy, spoonful of sugar into his tea.

"No. I don't instruct anyone on how to do anything, and I certainly don't grade anyone on it either. A teaching assistant seems more suitable: they know what's going on and at what point in their learning their charges are in, but they're mostly there to make sure students are comfortable and understand what it is they're doing. Does that make sense?" He screwed up his face as he looked toward me, as if for approval. I pursed my lips and nodded.

"Sounds pretty decent to me," I said, taking the coffee Mr. Bates offered me and following him into the far cozier room opposite.

I hadn't had any kind of therapy before, so I wasn't sure if Mr. Bates's office was normal. There were two deep armchairs facing opposite each other with a cheap Ikea table between them, decorated with a fake cactus and several coasters.

His desk was cluttered with his lunch box, unwashed utensils in a plastic bag and a yellow lamp, also undoubtedly from Ikea. Clearly, the private counseling world didn't pay as much as I thought.

"Do you have your clipboard?" Mr. Bates asked, taking a sip of his tea before shutting the door and sitting opposite.

"Yes, here you go." I handed it to him.

"Right, then." He held the clipboard about two inches from his nose and read quickly. "Would you say you're in good health right now? Both physically and mentally?"

With his face hidden behind the clipboard it was easier to answer.

"Yeah, I'd say so."

"Not on any medication? The pill or anything?"

I shook my head and laughed, not realizing he was looking at me.

"Is that funny?"

"Well, to me it is. You'll get to that bit."

"Will I?" he asked, putting the clipboard down on the coffee table and picking up his tea again, before leaning back comfortably. I took this as my cue to start talking.

"Yeah, well, I . . . I guess I should explain why I'm here. Oh!" Jumping, I remembered to get my phone out of my pocket. "Hang on, do you mind if I record this?"

"It's up to you. I don't record anything."

"Oh, it's not for me, it's for a friend."

"A friend?" His brow furrowed again, though I imagined with his job he had seen it all, or at least heard more than most.

"Yeah, she's doing a story on me and my 'sexual odyssey.' She's a journalist and was meant to come with me today but was busy so I promised I would record it." I started the recording, sitting back and feeling suddenly hot.

"Sexual odyssey? Do you want to start there?"

"I suppose that would be easiest."

He nodded. "Start with whatever you like; I'm just here to listen."

"Well, actually, before we jump straight into that, could you just explain to me how this all works and what I'm supposed to get out of this? Because honestly, I don't know. My friend Serena—she's the one I'm recording this for. Hi Serena!" I shouted into my phone and waved, stupidly. "She booked it for me as she thought seeing a sexologist would be imperative to, like I said, my *sexual odyssey*."

Mr. Bates considered this for a moment. "Well, it's pretty simple, although I imagine it seems quite foreign to some people. But I'm a trained sexologist of over fifteen years. As a sexologist I work with individuals, couples, and groups on tackling issues regarding sex that can be one of many things, from performance issues to pain, trauma, shame, or trust."

I smiled briefly to prove that I understood. It didn't sound scary. Yet.

"This session is just a getting-to-know-you session. I'll start by asking some questions about your sexual background and your sexual understanding—for example, how much sex education you received growing up, and if you have any sexual concerns. Ultimately, though, the show is run by you, I'm merely a conductor." He bowed his head like a showman, but then looked serious. "There is absolutely nothing physical about this type of counseling. Sometimes my clients come in expecting to receive a seminar on how to masturbate or a physical demonstration, but that's nothing to do with sexology."

"No, that's porn." I laughed, but I knew I was blushing more than a nun at a *Magic Mike* show. "I wasn't expecting a live sex show, thankfully."

Mr. Bates laughed and then drank some tea. "You'd be

surprised how many people make that mistake. This is just another form of talk therapy, like cognitive behavioral therapy or grief counseling."

"But how will talking help physical problems? I mean, *I'm* not here to discuss physical problems like erectile dysfunction, obviously, but can talking really cure a flaccid penis?"

"A flaccid penis?" Mr. Bates smirked.

"Well, a limp dick, then?" I said quickly, wanting to prove that I was sexually aware and confident, even as a virgin.

"Normally, a lot of sexual issues come from an underlying cause that's not been dealt with. I'm not just talking about sexual abuse, although that is sometimes the case, but merely a lack of understanding due to inept sexual education at school or an uncomfortable first-time experience. By understanding sex and sexuality, a lot can be cured physically and emotionally, which benefits a person's sex life."

"Why did you get into this field of study?" This was actually really interesting.

"Same reason as most. I thought it would make me the most money."

"I don't believe you," I said, smirking right back at him. That was a cop-out answer if ever I heard one.

He shrugged, and I knew that that was the best answer I was going to get. We were here to discuss me, after all, not him.

"So, shall we start by discussing what it is that you've decided to come here for. What's troubling you?"

I inhaled and looked around the room for a moment, preparing myself. I was usually very comfortable with admitting I was a virgin to anyone who asked (hen parties notwithstanding) but there was something about admitting it within a therapy session like it was a problem that I didn't like. It wasn't something I considered a negative: I was honestly indifferent.

"I guess I'm here to talk about my virginity and my sudden desire to learn more about sex."

"Learn more, or experience sex?" he asked casually, without a hint of judgement.

"Either, really. I'm not sure. I mean, I know how to have sex and that it's entirely normal and can be fun, but I've never had the urge to have it because I'm demisexual."

Mr. Bates nodded again.

"Do you know what demisexuality is?" I asked, feeling my forehead tighten as I waited for yet another person to tell me that my sexuality was an overreaction to a simple dislike of sex.

"Yes. As a demisexual you only have sexual feelings for someone when you're in a committed relationship or you have a strong emotional connection."

Huh. "Exactly," I stammered. I was always surprised whenever I didn't need to explain my sexuality or argue about its validity. "But, as you can imagine, finding someone to be in a committed relationship with without having sex is nigh on impossible. At least in my experience."

"Is your worry that you'll never have sex, therefore? Or that you'll never have a relationship?"

"Maybe. Right now, it feels like an impossibility and a possibility." I struggled to explain how it felt. "I know that I could just go on Tinder, find a guy, and ask them to come around and sleep with me. And I could probably force myself to do it. After all, all I would need to do is lie down and let them put their dick inside of me. Sorry, *penis*."

"Call it what you will. John Thomas, disco stick, I've heard them all. Dick is fine with me."

I laughed and sat back in my chair, relaxing a little as Mr. Bates put me at ease.

"Sex sounds so easy, but when you've never done it or rarely had the inkling to even try, it feels like jumping out of a plane without a parachute. But unlike skydiving, I often get looks of horror or pity when I admit that I've yet to sleep with someone. And that really pisses me off."

"Do you think your frustration could get in the way of your experiences? Does it hold you back from trying, or do you find it motivates you?"

"Neither. I'm confident enough to say that I'm happy not having sex. But then when I try to explain that to people like my sister, friends, or even just acquaintances they all just think I'm only saying that because I've never done it and therefore can *only* think that way. Life without sex is normal when you've not done it before, just like life without putting on makeup every day is completely fine and you don't feel underdressed when you've never done it before. But once you have sex or you put on makeup for the first time, suddenly a life without it is missing something, even when you might not want to have sex, or put on makeup every day. Do you understand what I mean?"

My face was getting hotter and hotter, and my speech quickened as I continued. I had the sudden urge to stand up and leave, even though Mr. Bates hadn't even said anything back yet.

"It sounds to me like you think of sex as a milestone which you haven't yet reached. Even though you've freely admitted that you've rarely wanted to even try it."

"Yeah. It feels like a level I must pass to get to the next stage of living. And the treatment I get for being a virgin at twenty-eight, it really . . . I hate it." I actually felt tears pricking my eyes.

Jesus Christ, what was it with this therapy malarkey?

"Would it help to change your perspective on sex, or even to ignore it for a moment? Tell me, when was the last time you went on a date?"

"Like a Tinder date?" I scratched my nose to make sure no tears had escaped out of the corner of my eyes.

"Any kind of date. Specifically, a date that you had hopes to progress into a relationship."

I thought back to my limited catalog of dates and honestly couldn't find one that I had hoped would progress any further than the first date.

"None to be honest. Most of the guys I've dated have ghosted me the moment I told them I was demisexual and wouldn't sleep with them. It became easier just to tell them over chat and then wait for them to stop replying instead of lugging it to central London for an overpriced drink and an awkward conversation."

"How many second dates have you had?"

"None," I said immediately. "I did once have a relationship with this bloke at university, but we never had sex."

"A friend? Or did you classify as boyfriend and girlfriend?"

"The latter. But we weren't really, we just had a lot of classes together and were being peer pressured to couple up, so we did for a little while, but it never went anywhere. I don't think I really fancied him. He was just a friend."

"But you felt comfortable doing that? Do you think being in the same vicinity was helpful in allowing you to feel comfortable enough with him to start dating, even without a sexual component?"

"That sounds lazy." I forced a laugh and nodded. It sounded exactly why and how I developed feelings for Evan. Was I just projecting feelings onto people because I saw them often? "Let's just say I wouldn't have actively pursued him in a bar if it wasn't for the fact we sat next to each other nearly every day." My mind wandered back to Evan. If he hadn't called me about WOW, I'd never have called him. I would never have been brave enough to make the first move for anything.

"And would you feel comfortable approaching someone at a bar?"

I went to speak but then stopped.

"What?" Mr. Bates asked. "What were you going to say?"

"I was going to say yes, but then . . ." I paused again and looked at the yellowing ceiling of his office. "Then I thought, why bother when he'll leave as soon as I tell him I don't want to have sex."

Mr. Bates peered at me without really looking at me. I must have looked like nothing more than a collection of shadowy specks in his eyes.

"So basically," I began, "I'm not allowing myself the opportunity to develop a relationship with someone because I'm afraid they'll reject me because I don't want to have sex."

"What if it's the opposite?"

"What do you mean?" I asked. "I'm afraid that they *won't* reject me?"

"Yes. Maybe the idea of someone willing to wait until you're ready is scary. Because then maybe, you will want to have sex, and you're not ready for that yet."

"So all this comes down to a fear of sex?"

Mr. Bates sat back. "Possibly," he said. "It sounds to me like you're struggling with an overwhelming sense of peer pressure regarding sex, and that you struggle to commit to someone long enough to develop an emotional connection with them, which may well lead to sex."

I swallowed. Did he think something was *wrong* with me? I felt totally and utterly fine with my sexuality and sexual status.

But maybe my sexuality and status weren't the problem. It simply *was* a fear of sex.

Oh for lack-of-fuck's sake.

CHAPTER 16
SERENA

HEY!" I SHOUTED up the stairs, slamming the door for extra awareness of my return home. Zoey had texted to say she was getting drinks with her fellow panelists, and I was welcome to join, but I fobbed her off, saying I had a headache. She had texted me while I was cleaning myself up at Sarge's beige flat. The guilt punched me with more force than he had produced in the thirty minutes we spent in bed together. I couldn't go and see her now. That wasn't fair. Sleeping in bed with Zoey that evening—and just sleeping—was going to be torment enough.

"I'm cooking dinner," Beth replied, slightly dejectedly, from inside the kitchen. "You're back late. Where's Zoey?"

I wanted to talk about anything else but Zoey, myself, or what I had done with Sarge.

"At drinks. It's a work thing I didn't want to intrude." I cleared my throat. "What are you making?"

"Well, we didn't have much in," she said, opening one of the bare kitchen cabinets for show. "So I decided to use up that penis pasta we got from Ann Summers last year. Thus, in answer to your question: we're having spaghetti bollocknaise for dinner."

"Perfect!" I went into my bedroom to change into my ugliest long-length pajamas to make myself as unsexy as possible for Zoey's return.

"Please tell me you didn't put bloody baked beans in the sauce again?" I returned to the kitchen, pulling on my hooded pajama top, and looked at the steaming casserole dish. "Oh, Beth!" I whimpered at the sight of extra-large baked beans, and even a few pork sausages.

"What? It tastes delicious." She grinned.

"There is sausage in my bollocknaise," I teased, stepping behind her to fill a glass with red wine.

Beth didn't reply but began plating up.

"Do you want a spoon?"

"No, I'll slurp," I told her, sitting down and getting cozy. She handed me the chipped plate. "How was therapy?"

"Fine," she replied, turning her back on me to fetch her own. "I recorded it on my phone. I'll send you the file later."

"Ah, great. Although it feels kind of voyeuristic, listening in on your therapy session. Anything you want to warn me about?"

Beth shrugged, still with her back to me. The fact that she was yet to look me in the eye gave her away.

"Oh, I'm sorry, babe. Was it awkward?" I dropped my fork onto my plate, waiting for her answer. "Don't worry, then, I won't listen if you don't want me to. I can always just call him, or another sexologist, and ask for a definition of the job or something. That's all I really need it for."

"He thinks I'm afraid of sex," Beth said, finally shifting so I could see her face. She didn't look sad or frustrated—just confused.

Spaghetti bollocknaise was probably not a great choice for dinner after all.

"Or at least," she added, "afraid of relationships that will *lead* to sex."

"Is that an official diagnosis or something you just discussed?" I tried to eat my pasta nonchalantly.

"Mostly a discussion. We discussed a lot of things." She sighed, grabbing her plate to come and sit down too. "Peer pressure, my beliefs about sex, family. All that fun stuff."

"And you concluded that fear of sex was the problem."

She shrugged and began cutting up the dicks on her plate into tiny pieces.

"He seems to think I have commitment issues, which is probably a given since I hate dating and can't be bothered these days because the men I've dated just eff off the moment I tell them I don't want to screw them."

"They're just twats, though. Thirsty, good-for-nothing arse-holes."

"I know that!" She shoveled a forkful of pasta into her mouth. "But still, it surprisingly made a lot of sense. Being demisexual, it's like I need the planets to be aligned before I can actually feel horny. I need to be physically aroused and emotionally connected, and for some reason that has never happened."

"God, when it fits into place, though, you'll legitimately have found *the one*," I told her, acting gobsmacked, like we had uncovered the definitive theory of love in our grotty two-bedroom flat in Sydenham.

She gasped sarcastically. "We should write a book." But then corrected herself. "However, first, let's maybe write this article."

I heaped more spaghetti into my mouth to stop myself speaking. "This is really good, by the way." I waited for Beth to fill the pause, but she didn't. "So, what are you pulling out of this therapy session? No sexual pun intended."

"With you there's always a sexual pun intended."

She had me there.

"I think I'm going to go back and see him again," Beth said, shrugging like this was just a casual thing when I got the sense that this was in fact much more.

"Great. Good to know that sexology is a legitimate path of mental and emotional health."

"Surprisingly, I would say it is. Mr. Bates just seemed to get me, straight—"

"Hang on, Mr. Bates?"

"Mr. Bates," Beth confirmed.

"Wicked. Carry on," I said, reaching over to grab my phone to make a few notes.

"He just seemed to understand and didn't think I was crazy, which was quite refreshing actually," she laughed. "You know, I think therapy is becoming my new favorite hobby."

"And what about *Mr. Bates*, then? If he diagnosed a fear of sex . . ."

"More like *suggested*. I don't think therapists usually diagnose anything in the first session."

"Fair do's." I adjusted my notes. "Since he suggested you had a fear of sex, did he give you any inkling of what your sessions will cover in the future in order to help you get over it?"

"Well, I have homework."

"Oh yeah?" I sat up straight, hoping for something dirty.

"I have to go on a date."

"Oh." I slumped back down, disappointed.

"Apparently I have to go on a date, preferably not via Tinder, and actually give the bloke a chance. Maybe even go on a second date."

"Surely that's got to be optional?"

"Well, to be honest, the homework was to go on a *second* date—not a first—so I have to get through a first date to do that and I don't want to go on more than one."

"Where do you want to look, then? If not Tinder, do you want to try Hinge?"

"God, there's so many questions on that thing."

"Then try Jigsaw or Match.com."

"Match.com?"

I slapped her on the shoulder. "I don't know many, apart from Tinder. I'm old-fashioned and actually like to pick people up in bars."

"Or at traffic stops, Richard Gere style?"

"Don't put a downer on *Pretty Woman* for me."

"Such a god-awful film," Beth said, forking some more penis pasta into her mouth.

"Do you even want to go on a date? It's not really your thing, is it?"

She shook her head, not looking at me. "No. God, I hate it. I never feel worse about myself than when I'm on a date, wanting to be myself but ultimately just pretending so that the guy won't run away or try to kiss me."

"Dating sucks for everyone, though," I began, but then paused. "Although I suppose I wouldn't know. I don't date as such, do I? I just sleep with people. Is that dating?"

"I'd say it's a form of dating. Casual dating at least. Or maybe it isn't? Maybe you have a fear of dating, and I have a fear of sex." Beth laughed for a moment before suggestively asking: "Speaking of dating, is Zoey not coming back tonight?"

"She is." I could hear my voice getting all breathy and high-pitched. I quickly spooned more pasta into my mouth. That pestering feeling of guilt rose again.

"Are you already at the slob stage of your relationship?"

Relationship? I chewed for a lot longer than necessary, all the while avoiding Beth's eyes.

"Oh, you didn't?" she whispered, her shoulders dropping in disappointment. "You screwed her over."

"What?" I snapped.

"You screwed someone else, didn't you?" Beth made it sound like this was a regular thing, as if I leapfrogged from one bed to another without thinking about it. I slept with people when I wanted to sleep with them, what does it matter if it was only a few days after another sexual escapade? It wasn't like I was getting under someone to get over someone. I was just fucking around, scratching an itch. At least that was normally my reason. With Zoey I had never jumped into a bed with someone quite so soon. In fact, sleeping with Zoey usually led to a sexual drought. But not this time. "Who was it? That receptionist again?"

"No!" I said, affronted that she'd think I'd go back for seconds with a colleague—one-offs are socially acceptable, two times and you run the risk of getting a hard-to-shift office reputation. I sighed. "It was just a random fuck on Tinder."

"Tinder?" She slammed her spoon down, but after the clattering she took a breath and placed her plate down calmly on the table and put her arm around the back of the sofa. "What happened?"

"Nothing happened," I told her. "I just wanted sex."

"You slept with a random stranger less than, what, *twelve* hours after having sex with a woman you quite clearly have feelings for, and you think that's nothing?"

"You're spending too much time at the therapist's office."

"And you need to spend more time there."

"Hardly!" I said incredulously. One session in and suddenly she's an expert? But Beth wasn't finished.

"You never try to figure things out, I mean look at you and Zoey." She inhaled sharply but didn't give me a chance to change the subject. "You won't even consider the idea, even when you've got a girl who might just be perfect for you."

"How do you know? You've only ever met her, like, once. And on FaceTime!"

Beth grinned manically, as if the answer was obvious and written across her forehead. "But I've met *you*, Serena. I know what you're like, and this is the first time you've been anything other than sexually interested in a person. For god's sake, you kicked me out to have a night in with her. *And* told me you had feelings for her."

"That's hardly a big deal."

"For anyone else? No, it wouldn't be a big deal. But Serena—" Beth placed both her hands on my shoulders. "If I haven't had a relationship with anyone since what's-his-face you've not had any relationship, ever. And if I'm going to try this bloody dating thing again, I dare you to try it with me."

For a moment I considered it, or tried to at least. The thought of asking Zoey out on a date made my stomach churn.

Did I want her to leave and go back to Liverpool? Not really. But I didn't want her to come back here tonight either. I didn't know what I wanted; all I knew was that I needed time. A lot more time.

"I can't," I told Beth honestly. "Not now. Not tonight." I shook my head, feeling an unfamiliar prickling sensation across my eyeballs, like sudden onset pins and needles. I realized it must be the formation of unwelcome tears and I inhaled deeply, looking away from Beth. "I fucked up."

"She doesn't know that."

"Yeah, but I do. I can't ask her on a date now. Not after I went and fucked a stupid stranger just to try and . . . I don't know, feel something else."

Beth sighed and rested her head against the back cushions, still looking at me.

"How did your work go today, by the way?" I asked, hoping to move the conversation away from Zoey and relationships for just a little bit. I needed a moment to calm down.

"Ah." Beth, bless her, didn't press. "So I got a call from this company called WOW. . . . It was a really good call."

"Fantastic! So does that mean you've got some solid work for a while?"

She nodded, slightly flushing with what I could only guess was excitement.

"Why are you not jumping around like a flipping four-year-old on SunnyD right now?"

She flung her arms half-heartedly in the air, and I grabbed them and began to wave them for her, whooping as I did so.

"It's official," Beth laughed. "I can officially pay my portion of the rent this month."

"Holy crap!" I exclaimed, dropping her arms and hugging her awkwardly around the shoulders. "This news calls for prosecco."

"Aka bougie pre-drinks."

"Let's do it." I shuffled over to her and the coffee table to fetch the alcohol with no holding back.

THAT EVENING WE drank so much, mostly from my insistence that we play a Lord of the Rings (extended editions) drink-ing game, combining Beth's favorite movies with my favorite drinking activity. It was a toxic mix and we both passed out on the sofa before Frodo had even reached Rivendell.

The next morning when Beth stretched and her big toe came threateningly close to entering my nostril, we shuddered awake and exchanged looks of surprise at the blanket tucked around us. The empty bottles and half-filled glasses were nowhere to be seen and there was a note perched in front of two mugs with tea bags waiting in them.

I unfurled myself from the sofa and Beth's numb limbs and went to read the note.

> *You two looked so cute! Left you some of my herbal tea—blueberry flavored—to help with the hangovers. Had to leave early. Will catch-up with you soon. Zoey x*

"What is it?" Beth asked groggily, turning onto her stomach.

"Zoey's gone."

"Gone to work?"

"No. It's Thursday. She's gone back to Liverpool."

"Ah, shit."

"Yeah," I said, closing my eyes as tears threatened to spill again. "Shit."

CHAPTER 17
BETH

SENSING THAT SERENA needed a distraction after Zoey's departure, I left it to her to set up my dating profiles for me. I knew that Mr. Bates would undoubtedly criticize me for not attempting this myself, but whatever. I was never the kind of person to ignore help when offered. Particularly when it came to something I didn't really want to do.

I instead focused on my new project with WOW, and Evan.

For some reason when the moment came to tell Serena about the job and about Evan, something stopped me. Embarrassment? Fear? Either way, I didn't want to share it with her right now. I seemed to be sharing everything else. This was just for me.

Evan had emailed me the materials and data I had requested to create a marketing deck based on their clientele, demographics, and competition. And not long after that he texted me.

Just checking in. How's it all going? Did everything I send make sense? And when I hadn't replied instantly—mostly because I was crafting the perfect response in my notes app—he texted me again. Hope you don't think I'm chasing! I promise I'm not a micromanager and then:

> Although that's exactly what a micromanager would say.

> And now I can't stop texting you which only starts to suggest I am a micromanager.

I had to stop him so I replied:

> It's okay! Everything makes perfect sense. And for the record, I don't think you're a micromanager. We both know what those were like and you're nothing compared to Elias.

> Oh phew! Got myself in a tizzy there for a second.

Tizzy! I replied with a stick-out-tongue emoji. His response was a simple wink.

Was this flirting? No: surely this was just banter between two colleagues—old friends and colleagues. That was it.

But I liked it.

With my workdays now surprisingly full, I could often be found sitting in Edith's, eating a cold salad that Michel threw together from limp leaves and cut vegetables, researching SEO strings and audience demographics for zero-waste living.

"I don't think I've ever seen you working," Delphi told me. She was frustrated I had ignored her social media ramblings. There are only so many times she'll believe me when I tell her she looks great in a photo that I don't even look up to see.

"Ha bloody ha," I said, adding in yet more keyword searches to Google analytics.

"No, seriously!"

"Have you ever tried this zero-waste life?" I asked her, sensing that she was getting needy for conversation. "It seems like the sort of thing that you and Pete might try."

"We kind of tried it, but not really. I just went down to the nearest shop with some empty jam jars and filled them with couscous and peanut butter, but we don't eat that stuff that much and I don't feel like trekking half an hour away every time I need a top-up when I could just get it cheaper in the corner shop."

"But it's better for the planet," I said, trying to sound concerned, as was my generation's duty. "Do you know that if Anne Boleyn had used tampons, those tampons would still be floating in the ocean today?"

"Well, that's gross." Delphi pulled a face.

"It's only as gross as some of those stuffed animals and skeletons they have at the Natural History Museum."

"Yeah, but still. They've been cleaned!"

"And what do you think the ocean would have been doing to that tampon for five hundred years if not cleaning it? It couldn't have broken it down."

Delphi recoiled.

"Are you seriously *just* working?" she asked again, a few minutes later.

I sighed and finally looked up.

"Yes, seriously. I'm working. I wasn't lying when I said I was freelance and looking for work, you know."

"I know, I know," she said, holding her hands up in defeat. "But I haven't seen you this focused before. It's like you're trying not to focus on anything else at all. Are you pissed off about something?"

"What?"

"Well, whenever I concentrate as hard as you it's because I'm trying not to think about something else. Like the results of a mammogram or whether or not Pete is doing gang tattoos again."

"He does gang tattoos?"

"Did," she said sternly, and that was the end of that interrogation. "What are you trying not to think about?"

"Dating." Both finding someone to go on a second date with, and not being able to date Evan.

"Is that it?" she said, smiling and leaving her table to join me at mine. "Got a date tonight? Is he a minger?"

"Who says *minger* these days?"

"Well, me, apparently." Delphi held out her hand palm up on the table and I unlocked my phone and gave it to her. Within seconds she was scrolling through Hinge, swiping yes or no (mostly no, thankfully) trying to find me a date. "You trying to find a fella?"

"Not really." I sucked my teeth and returned to work now that Delphi was distracted by my phone.

"Why the sudden anxiety about it, then?"

I shrugged. It wasn't *sudden* anxiety for me, this was a never-ending anxiety that was pushed on me from the age of eighteen, when the world suddenly stopped telling me not to talk to strangers and started telling me to go home with them instead.

"Just thought it was time to get back on the horse."

"I never knew you even entered the stable."

I bristled. "I have been on dates before, Delphi. It's just not something I enjoy."

She shrugged and continued swiping. "I never enjoyed them much either."

"Well then, how did you meet Pete if not by dating?"

"We met at one of those events—you know, the ones where the women sit at the table and the men circulate every seven minutes. At the end, you tick a box if you want to see them again and if you both tick each other's names then you get each other's number."

"So you and Pete went speed dating?" I sat back, surprised that that would have been Pete or Delphi's scene. Delphi seemed more like your typical Tinderella, and Pete was a hopeless romantic underneath the gruff exterior. I could see them meeting at the pub, but not at a speed-dating circuit.

"Yep. I didn't give him a choice about dating me though. As soon as the event was up, I went up to him and asked him on a date, without even giving my scores in. We went to the nearby pub, then a club, then back to his place, then back to mine, and then to his work. It was like five dates in twenty-four hours."

"And from that you knew he was the one?" I teased, impressed that she and Pete had managed to fit so much romance into such a short space of time.

She scoffed loudly. "No, but when I moved into his flat two weeks later that changed things. I was kind of trying to live like a nomad before, which basically meant I was couch-surfing, and he had a memory foam mattress and an air fryer so that sealed the deal. Within a few months we had sorted out life insurance, prepared our wills, and arranged for a civil service."

"You're married?" I suddenly spluttered.

"No!" she said, horrified. "We're just officially each other's next of kin. Marriage. *Pft!* It's archaic. And *weddings*," she groaned loudly, and pretended to stab herself with a fork. "It's like *The Hunger Games*. I can just hear Caesar Flickerman now: Congratulations, you've survived planning a wedding, now go forth with tons of debt, the knowledge that getting out of this relationship will cause you even more debt, and enjoy being related-in-law to each other's families. Bleurgh, nope."

Well, that stumped me.

Delphi sighed and put her makeshift shank/fork down on the table. "You know, you and Serena could probably have a civil service if you wanted to. You act like a married couple anyway."

"We're good, thanks." It wasn't the first time we'd been mistaken for a couple. "Although if it were for an article, I'm sure Serena would convince me somehow." I was surprised by the bitterness of my tone.

It wasn't like Serena *always* came home with projects or activities that were completely mad. There were the occasional outings to wreck rooms, Shrek raves, and silent discos in crypts, but it was rare for her to ask me to help her with articles on sex positions or getting nipple piercings. Both of which she had written, though . . .

Serena just liked to involve me and get me out of the house. And occasionally she did listen to my pitches or proofread a presentation, but admittedly never as often as I helped her with her articles.

But I liked to help her. And now she was helping me to explore my sexuality and learn more about my body.

Although it had been her idea to turn it into an article, not mine.

"I never thought I'd end up with someone like Pete," Delphi said with a yawn. "He smoked when I met him. I fixed that after a few weeks. I was sick of everything I owned smelling like an ashtray."

"Good for you."

"It was awful, and it made his teeth yellow. I mean, he may still have really bad morning breath and listens to way too much Eminem for a thirty-eight-year-old, but he's a soppy git who cooks me dinner and pays the rent whenever I'm short. So, I love him really."

"So I just need to find a person I like as much as you like him."

Delphi patted me on the hand and grinned. "No, you need to find a person you love as much as Serena."

"A 100 percent sex-positive confidante? Do you think that's really my type?"

"No, a *leader*." Delphi held her hands up innocently. "There's always a dominant one and submissive one in a relationship. I'm definitely the dominant one, but that doesn't mean that Pete can't be dominant when the mood takes him. We just prefer to stick to the roles we like to play."

I sighed and rubbed the bridge of my nose. I wasn't sure being called submissive was going to do wonders for either my Hinge profile or my sexual confidence, but I was willing to take advice from anyone at this point.

"I think you should try speed dating," Delphi said, returning to her phone and Instagram. "Just get through a load of frogs in one go. It will help with the anxiety as well."

"Speed dating?" I pondered the idea. Maybe speed dating would be more my style? It sounded a lot better than going on dates one at a time, and the meetings even had a deadline to them.

It might even be possible to class the "second date" as the meet-up after the first speed-dating session. Would that count for Mr. Bates?

I knew that technically it would, but really it wasn't a second date at all as a few minutes was hardly going to be enough time to get to know a person. But as every career adviser at school has said at some point, we typically judge a person after thirty seconds, so maybe speed dating was the way to go after all.

"Delphi, has anyone ever told you that you're a genius?"

"Many times," she said. Modestly.

CHAPTER 18
SERENA

I LIKE THE sound of this one," Beth said as I lay in bed, wiping off my makeup regretfully. All day sitting at my desk, I had been unable to concentrate. All I could think about was my night with Zoey and my stupid day-fuck with Sarge.

What had I been thinking?

Beth was trying her best to distract me. She was holding her phone to show one of the many links that Delphi had sent her that afternoon, for a straight speed-dating event the following evening at a member's club in Piccadilly. Apparently, Tuesday was a very popular day for speed-dating: no pressure of Friday-night drinks and no backing out after a weekend to think about it either.

"It's at the place opposite Wasabi, so I can always get dinner on the way home."

"I think your priority should be about the event, not where you're getting dinner after," I said, grabbing her phone in order to scroll through the details of the event.

"I know," Beth began, "but I'm a pessimist. I'd at least like to know I've got something to look forward to, even if it is just takeaway sushi."

"Well, it looks as good as any of the others," I said, not finding any red flags in my brief scroll and handing her back the phone.

"What, no interrogation of the location of the club? No brainstorming on the kind of men who go to these things, or even a request to join?" Beth gasped falsely and winked. "Although if you did join you would be a bit of a distraction."

"Have fun," I muttered, throwing my spent makeup wipes across the room, but they didn't even make it one yard before falling to the floor, inches from the bin. Beth watched the descent of the wipe.

"Okay, what's up, missy?" she asked, edging toward me on the bed. I had already pushed my legs beneath her body, so she straddled them over the covers. "You've been glum all weekend. Is it Zoey?"

I didn't deny it—how could I when it was obvious—but I did sigh and stare out the window to avoid her pitying look.

"You can't beat yourself up about it, babe," she told me, rubbing my arm comfortingly. "You'll get another chance to see her, put things right."

"She left thinking there was nothing wrong though, and she was right. It was perfect."

"You haven't been in a proper relationship before; it's bound to be difficult to get on that bandwagon." Beth didn't add that the only relationships I had properly witnessed growing up had been my parents' tumultuous affairs and never-ending breakups on international flights. Emotions were never going to be my strong suit—but I didn't need Beth to tell me that. And she never would, not unless we were both two bottles deep in chardonnay to help soothe the unprocessed trauma from it all.

"Is it, though?" I asked after a little while, turning back to face Beth and falling farther into my piled-up pillows that enveloped me like a hug. "I always thought getting into a relationship was the easy part, it was maintaining it that was hard."

Beth *pft*'d loudly at me.

"You and I are not your typical leading ladies," Beth explained. "I'm not into sex or dating. And you are great at both, but not so great on the commitment side of things."

"We've always been more pride than prejudice, though," I interjected. "We've got that going for us."

"We do!" Beth cackled. "But today, I need a man, so . . ." She picked up her phone again and without hesitating pressed *pay now* on her tickets to the speed-dating event the following day.

"If I'm going to try new things and fail, you can try new things and fail too. We have to pick ourselves back up. And tonight's pick-me-up is takeaway on me."

"Ooh, get you," I teased, nestling farther into my covers. "You get one paycheck and it's all takeouts and speed-dating events."

"And I wonder why I'm always broke," Beth said.

CHAPTER 19
BETH

NOT ONLY WAS I the first to arrive at the speed-dating event on Tuesday—even before the host—I was wildly underdressed compared to the other attendees who had come in their best cocktail dresses and suits.

I reread the instructions, but yes, the dress code was casual-smart. I guessed that artistically ripped jeans and an ill-fitting yet comfy halter neck were perhaps not what they had in mind. I hadn't even put on lipstick, just an extra spritz of Serena's most expensive perfume.

"Bethany?" A woman asked from behind as I hovered by a tiny bar nursing a glass of awful pinot grigio.

"Yes," I said tentatively. At this point I was almost tempted to put on a fake accent and pretend I was called Anita Grande, cousin of Ariana, and fake it until I made it.

"It's lovely to meet you. I'm Bella." Bella extended a French-manicured hand, and I took it, hoping that she wouldn't mistake the condensation from my wine as nervous sweat. "Is this your first time?"

I suppressed the urge to say the clichéd *how can you tell?*

and just nodded. She directed me toward a small table and bench.

"Women are going to sit on the benches and the men are to circulate on the chairs," she explained. "You'll have about eight minutes with each suitor before a bell chimes to signal them to move on. Have you got your name badge?" I had, but I hadn't put it on. I never knew where to put name badges on my clothes and because I was wearing a halter neck, I had few options. I could really only put it in the center of my chest, giving the *suitors* (vom!) clear instructions to stare at my boobs from the moment they sat down, or on my belly, which was the portion of my body I had the least confidence about.

However. I needed to do this. I held up the badge to Bella and decided that for the sake of the game I would pin the badge to my boobs.

"How many people are you expecting?" I said, after clearing my throat and praying that my face wasn't as red as her lipstick.

"Oh, about twelve, so six women and six men. We try to keep it as even as possible so that we don't have tables of women waiting for men to come to them." I just *loved* the not-so-subtle hint that it was more often women who came to these things than men, that gave me *bundles* of confidence. "You've come on a good night."

"Oh?" I said. "Any reason in particular?"

"A lot of our regulars come on this night. Excuse me." She hustled off to the door to greet two gray-suited men.

Regulars, I repeated in my head. As in people who went speed dating often. Surely if they were regulars and there were more than one, then they were just serial daters dating the same people over and over again if only for just eight minutes. Surely at that point you're just a nonexclusive dater with epic laziness?

I was still pondering, when the bench next to me began to sag and more women joined. Most of them ignored me, talking to others who they were obviously friends with or at least knew as another fellow *regular*.

"First time?" A woman with startlingly white hair said as she slipped across the bench to the table next to me.

"Uh, yeah. First time. You?"

"Oh, I've done this loads. Not this one so much, just once or twice over the last year."

"Yeah, Bella said that this session was quite popular." I stopped myself from questioning her about the regularity of her attendance. I didn't want to make it sound like she was some sort of speed-dating obsessive.

"It's pretty decent. Not too expensive, but not too cheap. It means you get the right sort of men coming to these. The ones that are slightly more serious about dating but not so serious that they're after settling down with the *one*."

I grinned harder than Emilia Clarke, trying to give off the impression that that was exactly what I was after, and surprisingly I think it was. Had I unknowingly found my dating scene?

"Be careful of that one, though," she said, gesturing to a blond-haired, athletic-looking guy currently laughing with his whole body at the hostess station. "He's quite handsy. Best to make sure your coat is on your lap when he comes over."

"Oh," I said, a little shocked but pleased with the warning. I immediately stood to fetch my coat from the coat rack by the door to use as protection when the dating began.

"Smart." The white-haired woman winked as I returned.

"Right, everyone," Bella called from the bar, clapping a hand against her metal clipboard. "I think we're ready to begin. Has everyone got their name badge on and their scorecard in front of them?"

I looked around for the card and found it already on the table with my name on it, a small yellow pencil laying on the top.

"Fabulous. You'll have eight minutes to get to know the person sitting opposite; there are questions on the back of your scorecards if you need any conversation starters. When the bell goes, *men*, you will need to move to the next table. The time will begin again after fifteen seconds to ensure that everyone gets their full eight minutes. At the end of the session, please place a cross in the box next to the name of the men or women that you would like to see again and hand your scorecards back to me. If each partner puts a cross next to the other's name on the scorecard, we will send them each an email with the other's contact details by the end of the night to facilitate a date. From there it's in your hands. Does that all make sense?"

There was a general murmuring of understanding. I couldn't help but notice that the men were already bristling and eyeing each woman up expectantly as they waited to be allocated to their first positions. The women nearest to me were finishing off their final primps, smoothing out their hair and licking their front teeth clean of any smears of lipstick.

I readjusted my name badge so that it didn't turn vertical and slip into the crevice of my cleavage.

"Right, men. Follow me." Bella quickly placed all six of the men behind the chairs and hit the bell. "Sit down and begin your dates."

My first date was Tom, nice enough and appeared to be just as nervous as I was. After a minute or two of exchanging details about our jobs and ages we both got stage fright and ran out of things to say.

We didn't talk for the remainder of the eight minutes, instead we fiddled with the stems of our wine glasses and looked at everything in the room except each other.

He had left his seat before the bell rang and I made a mental note *not* to go on a second date with him. Surely Mr. Bates wouldn't mind that.

I didn't think he'd mind me not choosing to put a cross next to the names of the following three dates either.

Kylo, whose genuine name was Kylo, had never seen Star Wars and didn't understand why I kept asking him if that was really his name. He was also constantly checking out the woman he would sit opposite after me, without caring if I noticed.

Sidney was sweet but about thirty years too old for me. At one point his dentures slipped out of place, and he had to push them back in, but not before a little dribble escaped down the side of his chin.

Harry seemed quite promising. He sat down and immediately asked if I was enjoying my evening. It was difficult to say no when the guy I had just gone on a date with was sitting less than a yard away from me, so I gave an overly reassuring nod that I think Harry interpreted quite well.

"Same!" he said, in a sort of sing-song voice that I used whenever I told my mother how many vegetables I was eating in London.

"I'm a doctor," he told me at the beginning of the date, but by the end he was a mechanic with his own business. He healed "cars" apparently, when I called him out on it, except when I asked him what kind of cars he said, "Big ones." Bye-bye, Harry.

I was now mentally repeating *just two more, just two more* in my head when the handsy athletic bloke appeared, sauntering over like he was dancing to a beat that no one else could hear.

"Hey, I'm Joey," he said, offering me his hand. I stupidly took it to shake, and he pulled my hand forward in order to plant a sloppy, extra-wet kiss on it. There was not enough hand sanitizer in the world that would make me feel clean again.

"Beth." I made a point of crossing my arms after that so he couldn't spend the next eight minutes staring at my boobs.

How could Delphi have said that speed dating was decent for meeting people? That was clearly a lie. I wanted my money back—and not just because I hadn't met *the one* but because no money was worth this level of discomfort.

"So, what are you?"

"Job-wise?" I queried, and he shrugged, as if he didn't really have an opinion either way. "I'm a freelance marketing professional."

"Oh, cool cool," he said, without the slightest sincerity. "I'm a footballer."

For fuck's sake.

"Yeah, I play reserve for Charlton."

"Wow," I said, blinking heavily.

"Yeah, it's pretty exciting right now." He stretched and pushed his hair back out of his face, undoubtedly, to show off a bicep, which was about as impressive to me as a Tesco's multibuy display. "I'm also a Cancer. What's your sign?"

"Sign?"

"Yeah, like astronomy?" This was just getting better and better.

"I'm not really into *astrology*," I said, picking up my glass to finish off the last of my now warm wine in a large gulp.

"Hang on, hang on," he said, leaning forward against the table. "Let me guess. I'd say you're a . . ." he paused for dramatic effect, and I rolled my eyes as I went to gulp the last of my wine. "Vagitarrius."

My coat had slipped onto the floor without me noticing and his hand was firmly pushed up against the inside of my crotch, a single finger wiggling ferociously against the inner seams of my jeans as if to rub them open.

In my shock and horror I released my large gulp of wine in a spit take worthy of a 1950s comedy that went all over his prideful smirking face before I shoved the table against him so hard that he face-planted against it under the force.

I heard the smash of my glass and the general gasp of the other attendees as I stood and grabbed my coat off the floor.

Hyperventilating and at a complete loss for words, I stared at Bella, who stood horrified by the bar with her clipboard, and turned quickly to leave.

"Wait!" Bella shouted, as I got to the door and shoved it open. "I need your scorecard!"

CHAPTER 20
BETH

I CALLED PENNY as I reached Trafalgar Square. Not Serena.

Penny was my sister, she had a blood requirement to pick up the phone when I called, and she would know what to do and how to calm me down. And I was very aware of the fact that I needed to calm down. My mascara was running down my chin and the lump in my throat was choking me. It was an overreaction, or at least that was what I was trying to tell myself.

Sure, being touched inappropriately by a stranger in a bar was terrible, but I was on a date, and it was only over my jeans. But: I hadn't given him permission. I hadn't invited it, and I definitely didn't desire anything of the sort. The very act of a man touching my crotch, even covered by denim, was more than a massive violation for me: it was utterly repulsive. Surely it would be for anyone, even if they weren't demisexual and a virgin like me? Honestly, I would rather he had wanked off in his chair than touch me.

"Hey?" Penny said, sounding confused. "Are you alright?"

I gulped.

"Are you okay? What's wrong?" I heard the switch in her tone that she had inherited from Mum. Mum always started calls brightly and would quickly assume the worst and ask "what's wrong" in a tone about two octaves deeper, even if the only "issue" was that I couldn't find her preferred brand of hummus in the supermarket.

"I had a date," I told her, stifling a sob. It was almost a ridiculous laugh, but I felt so gross that it turned into another wet sob.

"Oh no," she said, kindly.

"Yeah," I sniffed, forcing the lump in my throat back down. "It went badly. Very badly."

"What happened?" There was the sound of rustling. I checked my phone clock quickly; it was only half past eight.

"Are you in bed?"

"Yeah, but I was only reading. Patrick's gone to some birthday drinks, but I thought I'd chill for once."

"Oh, sorry."

"No worries, you can still call me and I can chill."

"Even if all I want to talk about is a godawful date?"

"Well, you sound pretty upset, so as your big sister it's my duty to put down my toys and listen."

"Or book, now that we're older."

"Thank you for the reminder," she joked, and I laughed. This was the real reason why I called Penny. She was easy to talk to and got to the heart of the matter, but not without some light touches and airy comments to partially distract me along the way. Plus, she didn't know the extenuating circumstances of my experiment. She wouldn't judge me for falling apart over being groped, whereas I wasn't sure Serena would be able to hold off on making a judgmental comment, since sex was more of her wheelhouse, and she'd want to dissect the action before condemning the man. Although, in my case, she would probably offer to kill him either way. "So what happened then?"

"Well, it was a speed-dating event. I'd never tried it before so I thought I would give it a go." She didn't need the full details.

"Right, and?"

"And it was terrible." I sniffed again and felt more tears fall down my cheeks. "There wasn't a single guy there I liked. . . . And then to top it all off there was this one guy who decided that personal boundaries didn't apply to him, and he could just grab my crotch where I was sitting and try to chat me up with a stupid line about being a *vagittarius*."

"Oh, god!" I heard Penny say in a tone of disgust. "He grabbed your crotch?"

"Finger wagging and all." She couldn't see but I was doing the finger movement action as I walked past the statue commemorating Edith Cavell.

"That's disgusting."

"It wasn't just that, though, it was the whole thing. I really *hate* dating, and I mean *hate* it. This isn't just something that sucks for a time, and then you find the one and everything's fine. I don't get it, Penny. How do you find one person in a city of nine million via Hinge or a chance encounter, and decide during a drink in a crummy bar that they're *the one*? How is that possible?"

"Well, it's not always. I think a lot of people marry people they knew in school or uni, or who were siblings of their mates, that sort of thing. Maybe you're one of those people. You need to know a person before you can date them."

"That kind of makes dating in a city I wasn't born in quite difficult then."

"Maybe you need to stop dating and try something else, like joining a club or a society or something? You don't meet people at work, so you can't build those platonic relationships that can blossom. You always did have personal space issues growing up—and before you yell at me, I don't mean that as a bad thing. I'm just saying that you never wanted to go to friends' houses or hang out."

"I'm an introvert. I like my own space."

"But then do you still want to find a person to spend your life with? Are you sure that's for you? It's not for everyone. There are plenty of ways to live a full life without a partner. Heck, you can even have kids without a partner these days. And if biologically conceiving or carrying isn't your thing, then you can adopt or foster. I mean, that might be something that Patrick and I look into one day, so I don't know why you couldn't do the same if you wanted to start a family on your own. I wouldn't judge."

"But everyone else would."

Penny scoffed. "Beth, if we worried about everyone judging us, we would end up on a carousel of anxiety. You just can't worry about other people. I don't."

"Penny, there's something else," I said, deciding suddenly that I wanted her to know what I'm going through. "I'm a virgin. And not because I'm saving myself for marriage or anything, but because I'm demisexual. I actually find sex, or the idea of it anyway, quite disgusting most of the time."

"Oh, it is disgusting," she said, not missing a beat, or appearing the slightest bit surprised by my revelation. "Sex is something that you get used to with time, but it's not initially great until you've worked out your personal preference. I never really understood what the fuss was all about, honestly. I mean, I've had fun and enjoyed it from time to time but now, with the babies and the IVF, sex is a means to an end and it's not enjoyable in the slightest. Even Patrick says he's done it so much he's bored of it."

"Okay, now you're babbling."

"No, seriously." She laughed. "I'm trying to reassure you

that you're not missing much and if you don't want to do it, now or ever, that's fine."

"But I want to know what the fuss is all about!" I whined, sitting on one of the fountain edges of Trafalgar Square, pigeons cooing around me.

"You just had your crotch touched by a stranger and you called me in tears . . . Are you sure you really want to know?"

I groaned. "I don't knowww." I wiped the last of my tears away. I was calmer now but I still felt gross. "Is there really a moment that you just decide that you want to have sex and that's it? Is that what happened to you?"

"Sort of. It's kind of hard to put into words," she said as I heard her opening the door of her fridge. I could picture her, dressed in her extra-fluffy pink dressing gown she's had for over a decade, reaching for a can of kombucha or some sort of disgusting smoothie concoction. She never drank normal drinks like tea or Coca-Cola. I smiled as I listened to her nighttime routine play out. The canned drink fizzed into life in the background.

"Try?"

"Okay, so, I was dating Sean, my first proper boyfriend. We had been dating for about four months and I was putting all this pressure on myself to have sex because otherwise it wouldn't be a *real* relationship. But the more pressure I put on myself the less I wanted to do it. Until finally, I was at a party with him— some stupid party on the green outside school—and we were wrestling. We were being childish but by wrestling we were the closest we had ever been to each other and I realized afterward, when we were just lying there and snogging, that I really wanted to have sex with him. Later, like a few weeks later, we were in his bedroom, and I stole his phone, and we were wrestling again and within seconds I had the same feeling and was peeling off my clothes. He followed suit and it was messy and a bit weird, but at the same time both of us enjoyed it because we had wanted to do it in the moment."

"So I should start wrestling," I said dryly.

"It wasn't the *wrestling* that turned me on, it was the fact that if I could put my hands on every part of his body and wrap my legs around him on a hill outside school in front of all my mates, surely doing practically the same, but without clothes on, in the privacy of our bedrooms wouldn't be so scary. And it wasn't, not really. Not after you get over the first few seconds. Then you realize it's just mechanics and biology."

"Wrestling. Mechanics. Biology," I repeated.

Perhaps all I needed to do was to think of it more logistically.

"Sean was pretty decent to have sex with, to be honest," Penny said with a slight giggle. "We both were virgins, so we went on the learning curve together." She had a sip of her drink and cleared her throat. "Maybe, if you stop thinking about it, it will help you get into the moment? And stop forcing yourself to do stuff you hate."

I wasn't sure what she meant? How could I not think about sex when I'm trying to learn more about sex? And if I truly wanted to have normal, healthy, and happy relationships, surely I had to think about it?

As much as I loved her and appreciated her advice, I knew I would ignore it.

I just wanted to feel normal in my own body as I approached my thirties, and the ticking clock of life began to beat faster and louder in my head. Was it so odd to suddenly start thinking about sex when you've never experienced it before? I just wanted to know what the fuss was all about. It might have taken me ten more years than the average person, but I wanted to get it over with.

"It's just wrestling, mechanics, and biology," I repeated.

"If that's how you want to see it. I see it as a pain in my backside, and not just because of the increasing number of hormones I have to inject back there."

"Too much information," I grumbled, shaking my head.

"What, it's just wrestling—"

"Oh, shut up!" I interrupted, making her laugh.

"What are you going to do with the rest of your evening? The night's still young, you could go and see a movie or go out with Serena. Or you could go home, get into bed and marathon-watch a favorite TV show, like me. I'm truly living the dream." She clinked her can of kombucha against the phone.

Although those all sounded like good ideas, I had a task I needed to do. I was sick of being afraid.

I needed to have sex, and I had the perfect idea how.

CHAPTER 21
SERENA

I SAT ON my bed going through my WhatsApp messages to see who I had screwed from Tinder since the year had begun.

How could so little time have passed and yet I had got through so many men. And one woman.

Sleeping around had never been complicated to me, or something to be anything but aroused by. Other people wanted sex, I wanted sex, and we verbally consented before acting on our desires. What's so wrong with that?

But I had never experienced the sensation of guilt of having multiple sexual partners before. Not even when I went from one man to the next in the space of a day. I might sleep with a man in the morning before going to a work event that evening and shacking up with the guy working at the coat check.

In a city as wide and as horny as London you could always rely on one person in the city to be up for it at the same time as you.

I could scroll through Instagram and determine whether they would be down through their reels or stories. Reading people and their tells was like reading a novel for me.

But I wasn't feeling anything that evening. I was just doom-scrolling, my eyes not keeping contact with anyone's content. Until suddenly I had scrolled across all my most frequent stories and accidentally entered my dad's feed.

He hardly ever used Instagram, but clearly someone had taken his phone and recorded a video of him on the balcony of his hotel room a few hours ago.

"Are you recording?" he was saying, his shirt buttons undone to an unsightly low level, a tooth-fang necklace around his neck. Nothing screamed midlife crisis more than a tooth-fang necklace. "Are you going to give it to me?" He was laughing, trying to get the phone back while he held a glass of prosecco—sorry, Dom Pérignon—in his hand and a woman giggled behind the camera. I wondered who she was for a moment before I saw it.

What the *hell*?

The London Eye.

He was in fucking London, and he hadn't told me.

"What the actual . . ." I screamed as I threw my phone against the wall.

I ran my hands through my greasy hair with a frustrated sigh. The absolute arsehole hadn't even told his daughter he was in the same city.

Groaning, I propelled myself off my bed and rushed to the wall to find my phone again.

I opened the app again, just to make sure I wasn't completely going insane. No, it was definitely the London Eye. That mother—I denied the urge to throw my phone again and instead took a long deep breath, leaning my head against the cool—now dented—wall and exhaled for a few seconds.

With one hand I found his name in my phone contacts and pressed dial.

"Hello?" someone answered after two rings, but it wasn't my dad. It was a woman's voice, slightly muffled as if they'd leaned away from the phone to have a drink. "Hello?"

"Could you put my dad on the phone?" I said darkly. There was a lot of background noise, it sounded like they were in a bar or a busy restaurant.

"Who is this?" the woman asked, suddenly irate.

"It's Serena." I sucked my teeth, trying not to lose my cool.

"Someone called Serena?" the woman said distantly, as if she were telling someone else.

"Ah," I heard him say. His rich, low voice was unmistakable. "Serena," he said. No endearments or dad jokes, he was straight to business. "What can I do for you?"

"You could have told me you were in London."

"I thought you would have gone to Dubai by now. Did the tickets expire?"

"I have work! I can't just drop everything. And why would I go to Dubai if you're not there? Was that your plan? Invite me there while you weren't home so you didn't have to bother to entertain me?" I felt like my throat was swelling with anger.

"Not at all," he said, dismissively. "Business called me to London unexpectedly. There was no time to arrange anything. After all, you have work, you can't just drop everything." I could hear the smugness in his voice.

Where was the dad who used to have dance parties with me in the living room? Or make milkshakes at midnight?

"You could have just let me know," I said quietly. "It wouldn't have been hard. A text, an email, a phone call?"

"Oh," he said, but nothing else. He had been caught, but he didn't care enough to find an excuse. Nor did he try and remedy the situation by planning to see me now.

I waited for another few seconds, hoping the awkward silence would be enough for him to invite me to tea. But no offers were made. This was not a negotiation.

"Look, I have company . . ."

"I heard," I muttered. "I hope you're paying her well for her time. Your daily fees are quite substantial, and I would know." I didn't let him speak after that—I just hung up. What was the point of staying on the line with someone who had so little interest in me as a person?

The woman hadn't known who I was when she answered his phone for him. Did he even have my number? And why did she answer his phone for him? Was that sexy, to let your companion answer your calls? If he were truly here for business reasons, surely he wouldn't let her do that?

Everything I knew about my father, which I realized was very little, was baffling.

He wasn't terrible as a dad when he tried when I was younger, but he never tried now. He hadn't in years. And now it appeared he had forgotten that he had a daughter entirely.

Was that what he always wanted?

I threw my phone lightly onto my bed and sank down onto the floor.

I couldn't let this one stupid call break me, not after I had put up with his and my mother's apathy my whole life. This was nothing new.

For a few moments I comforted myself with the dark thought that one day he would need me to help him when he was elderly or dying, and I could refuse. I took pleasure in the daydream of my ignoring his calls or refusing to arrange—or even attend— his funeral. Why should I care when neither he, nor my mother, ever cared about me?

Sniffing loudly and wiping my eyes with the back of my arm, I forced myself up from the floor and into the shower.

It was only when the water was cold, and I had done all my sobbing under the protection of the noisy showerhead, that I got out, but I didn't want to get dressed. Instead, I moved to the living room, drip-drying under a towel, and began to play a Christmas playlist, thinking it would cheer me up.

It didn't. There's nothing quite as depressing as playing Christmas songs in February.

But still, it was more appealing than lying on my bed and thinking about my parents or Zoey.

So I lay on the floor of the living room, still wrapped in the damp towel from my shower an hour ago, playing the role of a woman in a quarter-life crisis.

MY MOPING WAS only—but finally—disturbed by the return of Beth screaming up the stairs about needing a stripper.

If anything was going to get me out of my low mood, it was going to be that. "You what?!"

"I need a stripper! Speed dating was a disas—why are you on the floor?"

"Being dramatic."

"Makes sense." She stepped over me, removing her jacket and shoes and chucking them onto the sofa before she began pacing. I returned to lying down and watching her, upside-down in my eyeline.

"Please return to your sudden desire for a stripper?"

"I need to get sex over with. I'm done with therapy and dilation. It's just sex. It's just wrestling, mechanics, and biology. I want to have sex, now, and get it over with." She continued to pace, her hands on her hips. "It's a bloody catch-22 situation, I want to get sex over with, but my sexuality is making me feel like I can't. But to have sex I need to *not* be thinking about having it. I can't deal with this bullshit anymore. I just want it done!"

Wow. She'd lost it.

Out of the two of us, I thought I would have been the one crying out for a stripper and rampaging mindlessly, not the far more stoic, Ophelia-drowning-in-a-lake one.

That's madness for you, though, it's the opposite of everything you think you are.

"I don't think a stripper is actually what you mean," I said, still lying perilously close to her quickening footsteps. "You mean an escort, or a sex worker. Escorts tend to be more high-end, though."

"An escort, then." She stopped pacing for a moment. "I always thought that was a car?" Before she began retracing her steps. It was a miracle we still had carpet in our flat.

"Do you remember that student at university, called himself *Guy*."

"Who?"

"Guy. He lived a few floors up from me in the dorms and he used to go around telling everyone he would have sex for money. I have his number if you want it."

"Don't you have a more recent option?" Beth said, *finally* taking a seat at the dining table. She was starting to pant.

"I'm not a pimp," I laughed, twisting my head awkwardly to look at her.

"Sorry, sorry. That's not what I meant," she said, holding up her hands. "You kept Guy's number after all this time?"

"I never shagged him, and I can have men's numbers and not be interested in them. I may enjoy sex, but I don't shag everything that moves."

"I know that, but it seems odd to have him in your contacts."

I pushed myself up off the floor. "Do you want Guy's number or not? He still lives in London, I think. At least he did from what I last saw on Instagram."

I could see the tell-tale hesitation pass across Beth's face, but she shook it off and nodded furiously. "Yes, call him for me. See if he's up for it."

"I'll text him," I corrected. My phone was in my bedroom, still laying on the covers from where I had thrown it down after my call with my dad. For a second I wondered if there would be a message of apology, but there wasn't. Not from him anyway.

Sorry I had to leave so suddenly the other week, Zoey had texted over an hour ago. It was so great to see you. My stomach twitched inside of me, and I paused for a moment wondering how to answer. But I couldn't do that right now.

"Right," I called, more brightly than I felt. "I've texted him." I returned to the living room and chucked my phone at Beth, who grabbed it midair.

"What did you say?"

"Just the basics, you know, the *how are you* and *are you still sleeping around for money? I'm in South London and I've got a friend who might be interested*, blah blah."

Beth looked aghast.

"Don't worry! I am your sex doula. I'm here to talk you through this."

This didn't seem to help. "Wrestling. Mechanics. Biology," she whispered to herself, repeatedly. The phone buzzed in her hands.

"Ah!" she shouted, throwing it back to me. I caught it and checked the screen.

> Hey! I'm good thanks. Still available for business. Do you want me to come round?

"Well, that was easy," I said. Pleasantly surprising too.

"It's for my friend Beth," I said aloud as I typed, feeling Beth's eyes burning into me as she forced herself not to protest in her nervousness. "Here's our address. How long will you be?" I pressed send.

Beth grabbed a pillow and shoved her face into it. I remembered the fear of my first time as a fifteen-year-old with limited sex education and a worryingly vivid imagination. I crept over to sit next to her.

"You don't have—" I began.

"Stop!" She held up a hand in front of the pillow, still smushing her face. "Don't give me an excuse. Just . . . help me." She lowered the pillow in a defeatist way that only made me pity her more.

I rested my head against the back of the sofa and stared at her for a moment, wondering what I could say that would help.

"Do you still have those knock-off AirPods?" I asked.

CHAPTER 22
BETH

FORTY-FIVE MINUTES LATER, the doorbell rang.

Serena had dressed and was hiding in her bedroom, the door shut, but on a call to me. I'd loosened my hair from my high ponytail to hide the earbuds.

"Oh shit, shit, shit." What the hell was I doing?

"Just open it," Serena said calmly. "Nothing behind that door can hurt you. You're in a safe place and entirely in control. Just open the door."

"For fuck's sake!" I hissed in return, forcing myself to take a few steps forward at least. "Am I out of my mind?" I whispered, more to myself than to Serena.

"Just open the door," she repeated as I walked down the stairs, breathing deeply to try and steady myself. This was a normal act between two consenting adults. Completely normal. Asking your friend to call an escort she knew from university just so you can lose your virginity is completely normal . . . right?

"Open the door!"

I took another breath and reminded myself this was what I *wanted*. And then I opened the door.

The familiar sound of the aged lock twisting and the door being dragged across the carpet was strangely calming and I smiled at Guy like a model hostess.

"Hi," I said, slightly more brightly than Serena and I had discussed. She wanted me to be sultry, but that just wasn't in my ability. Instead, I sounded like I was greeting children collecting for charity. Guy, who was taller than I expected with red hair, smiled at me. "Come on in." I took a step back and waved my arm forward as if Guy needed direction up the stairs.

"Thanks," he said, taking off his jacket as he ascended the staircase.

Well, that wasn't so awful, I thought as I shut the door behind him. But then I felt panic spread through my head like a wave. I had drunk two glasses of prosecco in very quick succession before getting dressed in my favorite jeans and a basic T-shirt and upping the quantity of my mascara for good measure. Serena had offered to lend me something *sexy* to wear, but I wanted to feel like me as much as possible. I wasn't acting, I was just going to have sex.

At least, that was the plan.

I didn't see the need to go all out and change into fancy lingerie—which I didn't own—or to shave my legs with extra care—particularly when all our razors were likely blunt and rusty. Besides, he was an escort. I didn't need to impress him; I just had to use him—with his consent.

I followed Guy up the staircase, quietly observing him from behind. I could hear Serena breathing in my ears.

Was he exuding confidence? Was he attractive? Had he made an effort?

He was good looking, in a Jack Quaid or Rafferty Law kind of way. He was slim and not too muscly, which hopefully meant

I wouldn't get freaked out by his jacked-up body before I showed him my own. He didn't have a beard, which would have been a big no-no for me, and honestly, he had a really good butt.

I was wholly objectifying him—but what else are you meant to be thinking about when asking a stranger around purely to have sex with them?

"Do you want to go to your bedroom?" He paused at the top of the stairs and reached for the doorknob to Serena's bedroom. The room where she was currently hiding.

"No!" I shouted, almost falling on top of him as I reached out to block him. He looked at me in surprise. "That's my housemate's bedroom. She'd freak out if we went in there." I recovered.

"Do you mean Serena?" he asked, turning a little as I stepped back and straightened my shirt.

"Yeah, Serena. She's a great housemate, but we have rules," I said, tensing my forehead a little as I thought *what rules*.

"You're doing great," Serena whispered into the phone as I led Guy away from her room.

"So . . . this is the living room," I said, for Serena's benefit.

"It's great," Guy said, clearing his throat and placing his hands in his pockets. "Much cleaner than mine. My housemates are Neanderthals, still living it up uni-style so it's more shot glasses and cheap posters."

I hesitated for a moment but then chuckled lightly. Was he nervous too?

"No shot glasses here, I'm afraid. Just . . . just candles," I finished weakly. Serena had done a quick job setting the mood, putting the lights on a dimmer, lighting every candle we had in the house and arranging them on every available surface of the living room. Guy was going to think I had set up the room for some sort of sacrifice at this rate. A pumpkin spice latte–scented sacrifice.

There was a painfully long pause as I froze up and waited for instruction.

"Ask him to sit down!" Serena nudged.

"Should we . . ." I gestured to the sofa awkwardly.

"Yeah," Guy said, moving swiftly to the sofa. "Ooh. Springy," he said, lightly bouncing as if testing the elasticity.

"Yeah," I replied, still standing in front of him.

"Now kiss him!"

It was now or never I supposed. I inhaled deeply and then moved to sit next to him. I was a little too forceful in my movement, though, and fell into his lap, almost placing my hand on his crotch to balance myself.

"Sorry!" I shouted as I attempted to correct myself. I was acting like a landed sea mammal.

"It's okay," Guy said immediately, holding back a laugh. "We don't need to rush."

"No," I replied, some panic evident in my voice. But this was what I wanted. I just needed to get back in control of the moment. "No, just let me get—*condom*!"

I heard Serena suppress a giggle. Had I really just shouted *condom*? It sounded so odd coming out of my mouth that it had lost all meaning.

"I mean *bathroom*!" I attempted to correct myself, standing again and rubbing my forehead, not looking at Guy as I walked around the coffee table. "I'll just be one minute. Bear with me." I quickly stumbled into the bathroom and slammed the door unintentionally hard.

"Are you alright?" Serena asked immediately.

"It's happening," I said simply, panting a little bit as my pacing resumed in the tiny room.

"What's happening? You're just talking to me right now," Serena pointed out.

"You told me to kiss him!"

"I thought it would be best to fill the space."

"Oh god!"

"Okay, okay, relax. It's alright. Nothing's happened, you're all good. You're in control," she said, attempting to sound soothing.

"Wrestling. Mechanics. Biology," I chanted. The mantra had helped me calm down earlier, maybe it would help me once more.

"Alpha, beta, omega," Serena repeated over the phone, teasing me. "Whatever gets you through."

"Don't make fun of me," I hissed, reminding myself that Guy was only one room over and he might be able to hear us.

"Sorry," Serena said. "You've got this. Remember, he's just a boy, he's harmless and chose to be here. He's just attached to one of your dick-sticks, nothing more."

"I can't believe I talked you into letting me do this."

"Me?!"

Fair point. It was mostly my crazy plan.

"I should have just slept with you," I said pointedly. "I trust you more than anyone."

"Oh, honey, I'm flattered. But we're in a sexless relationship—we're practically married."

"I know, I know. It would be even weirder."

"You're not even bisexual."

"I know, okay? I just want this over with." *This* being sex, but also this stupid plan. Honestly, what was I thinking?!

"Okay then. Just get back in there. Talk to him, go with the flow."

"None of this is actually helping, you know," I said, opening the door to the bathroom and heading out again.

"I could always put on a sexy playlist from my end so it's more like the movies; sex with an accompanying score."

"Oh, shut up!" I replied in a tight whisper as I headed back toward the living room. She began humming "Sexy and I Know It" regardless and then issued my next instructions. "Enter the room confidently. You're super sexy, Beth."

She's right. I'm sexy. I've got a good body, working genitalia—as far as I was aware—and I could have sex. It's so easy that billions of people did it every year. I could do this.

Once again, for just a moment, I believed my own mind and I entered the room with a stomp and a slam of my hand against the door.

But then I lost my footing and fell into the standing lamp.

"Whoa!" Guy exclaimed in surprise upon my reentry.

"Sorry," I said immediately. Damn prosecco.

"Why are you sorry?" Serena asked.

"Nothing," I replied.

"What? Are you alright?" Guy said, standing from the living room, and I realized I had just spoken aloud to Serena.

"I'm fine, fine. Sorry," I said again, standing up straight and straining my lips into a smile.

"Stop saying sorry!" Serena instructed loudly in my ears. "Own it. You mean everything you're doing. Now get over there."

I breathed in and began to walk toward him, placing both my hands over his shoulders. He tensed a little.

"Is this okay?" I asked him, surprised that he seemed a little nervous. Did escorts get nervous? "We can stop. . . ." My heart leapt with relief before he replied.

"No, I'm good." He placed his hands over my arms and gently rubbed them, pushing himself slightly closer to me so that I could feel his breath on my chin.

"Now . . . say something sexy," Serena commanded.

"Your clothes . . ." I began, thinking off the top of my head. "They bother me. Take them off."

Guy laughed, slightly nervously but also—I thought—genuinely pleased.

"Perfect!" Serena said passionately, and I felt a surge of confidence. "Now help him. Help him take his clothes off—is he wearing a jumper? Take his jumper off."

"He's not wearing a jumper," I whispered out of the corner of my mouth.

"Huh?" Guy said, looking up from where he was previously focusing on unbuckling his belt. "I'm not wearing a jumper. It's surprisingly warm out for March."

"Yeah . . . I know. I'm just surprised," I recovered, awkwardly. "No jumper," I repeated for Serena's benefit.

"Sorry, I'm just trying to picture it."

"Well, stop," I whispered to her.

"What?" Guy said, his brow furrowing as he paused on his belt. "Do you want me to stop?"

"No!" Serena and I said in unison.

"Oh, okay then." He returned to his belt and pulled down his zipper. Before going any further he looked up again, a cheeky smile sprouting on his face. "Do you want to take any of your clothes off?"

"Erm . . ." I said, dropping my arms from where they still rested on his shoulders and thinking for a moment. What could I take off that would show the least amount of skin?

"Yes. Take something off; your top or your jeans," Serena agreed.

"Okay," I replied to both of them, and I began to unzip my own jeans.

"Funny that you go straight for the bottoms rather than the top," Serena said, having heard my zipper.

Was it funny? I had had no problem taking off my jeans for a smear test or to go skinny dipping before. Also, my top hung fairly low and would cover most of my thighs, so really I was just showing him my knees.

"Help him take his clothes off."

"Here . . ." I began, stepping forward with a breath and moving his hands out of the way to remove his belt. "Let me." I thought it would be easy, it looked like your standard issue belt you'd get for a fiver in Primark, but I couldn't get the buckle loose. "I'm shaking."

"Be confident. You want this," Serena reminded me.

"It's okay," Guy said, taking my hands away from his belt and bringing them to his lips instead. Was this meant to be sexy? It was weird, not sexy. Who actually kisses people's hands outside of a regency romance?

"Oh," I said, unable to hide my slight confusion at the gesture.

"I'll just . . ." I began, removing my hand from his and pointing back to the belt that would not win this fight. I was going to remove it and that was that. I felt strangely passionate about the issue.

"What's going on?" Serena whispered after a moment.

"This is a bit fiddly." I laughed, ignoring her questioning.

"I guess now we're getting somewhere," she teased.

"No, the belt," I said aloud.

"It's a bit, hold on, let me—" Guy said, and he tried to move my hands out of the way again but I batted them aside.

"No, I got it," I reassured him, a bit too determinedly.

"Yeah, you tell him who's boss!" Serena joked.

"I can't," I whispered, beads of sweat forming on my brow.

"You can!" Serena returned, really getting into her Coach Carter–esque role. I could envision her pumping her fist in the air.

"I thought the bra would be the fiddly bit," Guy mumbled.

"This is a bit tougher than I thought."

"We'll get there," Guy returned with a smile, clearly finding this whole situation amusing.

"As soon as it opens . . ."

"Ask him for help to open it . . ." Serena suggested. Clearly she thought this struggle to undress him had gone on long enough.

"Can you help me?" I sighed defeatedly, dropping the buckle like it was a kettlebell.

"Sure," Guy said, amusement still present in his voice as he swiftly and with one hand undid the buckle and pulled it out from his waistband.

"I want your hands all over me," Serena said, forgetting, it seemed, that she needed to give it as an instruction and not a personal suggestion.

"What!" I exclaimed loudly—so loudly that I heard Serena knock something over in surprise in her bedroom.

"What?" Guy said, also surprised at my sudden exclamation.

"Say it!" Serena corrected herself, but it was too late.

"No, I can't," I said. I was done with this.

"Can't what?" Guy asked, very clearly confused as his hands hovered over the edge of his jeans.

"Just say it. Say it like you mean it!" Serena whispered.

Oh fuck it. "*I-want-your-hands-all-over-me*," I shouted, very quickly. Too quickly. I slapped my forehead. I wasn't ready for this.

"Uh . . . okay," Guy said, now dropping his hands from his waistband and placing them on his hips. He was looking more puzzled by the second. "But I thought you wanted to take it slow."

"I did! I-I-I do," I stuttered.

"Do you want to go to the bedroom?"

"Here's just fine." But here wasn't fine.

"Is he wearing pants?" Serena asked cautiously over my earbuds, and I just wanted to rip them out, but to do so would alert Guy about them being in there in the first place.

"Do you want to take off your pants?" I asked him. Did he want this? Maybe if he did then I could feed off his desire, but as it was, I couldn't feel less desirable even if I smothered myself in butter, rolled around in cornflakes and stepped into the street and shouted *eat me!*

"Only if *you're* ready?"

"To see his dick?" Serena asked. "God, just tell him yes."

"Y-yes," I stuttered again, trying to keep my nerves under control. I heard Serena sigh. Was she frustrated?

"Push him against the sofa. Get it over with!"

Just get it over with. I took a deep breath and shoved Guy back onto the sofa. He let out a surprising high pitched "*Whoa!*" as he placed his hand down to stop him from toppling from the floor.

"Now . . . straddle him!" Serena said, sounding like an emergency line operator giving vital advice.

I did as she said. "Oh-my-god," Guy said again. He apparently wasn't the calmest of escorts.

"Now . . . fondle him!"

"Fondle?" I repeated, my voice somewhat frantic.

"*Fondle?*" Guy's voice broke.

"Should I?" I said, ignoring him.

"Yes, or give him head."

"What! How did we get from fondle to head?" I shouted; all pretense forgotten in the horrifying moment.

"Wha—we didn't?" Guy said, still holding himself up on the sofa with one hand. He gave a little shrug and said, "If you want to, though . . ."

"No!" I shouted, with sudden confidence in my conviction. Head was a complete no-no.

"You could try?" Serena suggested, playing the devil on my shoulder.

"No!" I shouted again. This wasn't right.

"No?" Guy repeated.

"I'm not doing that."

"Oh, okay . . ." he said, deflating a little but nodding with assent. He wasn't going to force me into anything.

"Well, grab it, then. Touch it."

"Eww," I groaned.

"It's not that bad . . ." Guy was trying to comfort me, without knowing that there was a whole other conversation he was not part of.

"I could never do it," I told him with a slight apologetic smile.

"Ever?" Both Guy and Serena asked at the same time.

"It's not for me," I whispered, my cheeks flooding with heat in sudden embarrassment.

"You don't know until you try," Serena said in my ears.

"It's okay," Guy said at the same time, correcting his posture slightly. "Would you prefer it if I went down on you?"

"Definitely not!" I shouted.

"It's quite fun actually," Serena added.

"Nope. Not happening," I replied forcefully.

"Do something!" Serena said harshly. Didn't she realize that this was going nowhere?

"Urgh!" I leaned down to Guy just as he pushed himself up and our heads collided midair with a crack. I'm surprised Serena didn't hear over the earbuds.

"What happened?"

"He headbutted me," I said, rubbing my forehead with my spare hand.

"It was an accident and why—why are you talking about me as 'he'?" Guy rubbed his own forehead.

"Urgh, that hurt," I replied, completely ignoring him. "Fuck me."

"I'm trying!" Guy deadpanned. And suddenly the tension broke.

I snorted and rolled back on my legs. Poor Guy was still under me, half-dressed but also trying not to laugh at this disastrous interaction. What other reaction was there?

The sex was never going to happen, who was I kidding? Penny was right, you can't plan for things like this. Particularly not when you're demisexual; you're meant to have a strong emotional bond with someone before you're attracted enough to have sex with them. Why did I think I was going to be able to just put it all behind me and shag a stranger?

And why did Serena or I think she could coach me through it? We were two totally different sexual beings.

This was a failed experiment. It was utterly foolish to think that this was the way for me to finally experience sex. We weren't in the 1800s, arranging marriages and being forced to sleep with a stranger-for-a-husband the night of the nuptials with family and a priest watching for confirmation. There was no need for unnecessary pressure or a secondary to help you through it, not unless you *really* desired it. And I didn't.

It had nothing to do with fear, I just didn't want to have sex with this man.

I heard the click of an ended phone call over my earbuds and then a door opening with Serena calling out:

"Anyone want a cup of tea?"

CHAPTER 23
SERENA

IT TURNED OUT *Guy* wasn't even his name. He was called Rupert.

Once I came out of my room and explained the whole odd scenario, he just laughed—he didn't even ask questions. I actually think he was quite glad not to have to sell himself for a night. Although we did offer to pay him still. He rejected our offer in return for a cup of tea before I called him an Uber.

Beth had scarpered into the shower and into her comfiest pajamas before Guy—or Rupert—had even put his shirt back on.

"I'm not really into the whole escort business these days," he clarified as the two of us waited for his Uber. "I only did it at uni for a bit of extra cash and bragging rights. Now it's once in a blue moon."

"It must have been a good gig at university," I said.

"It was fun," he admitted, clearly remembering the good times. "But these days it's just a little past the weird mark, and it's a bit embarrassing. I don't tend to do it so much unless I know the people or they're friends of friends."

"Well, thanks for trying."

"What do you do, then?" he asked as we headed down the stairs. The Uber was just around the corner. He briefly pointed to the bathroom door as if asking my permission to say goodbye to Beth or not, but I shook my head. She was embarrassed. Best to leave her alone.

"I work at a magazine, *The List*. I'm a senior features writer."

"That's cool."

"Yeah, it's not bad. Means I meet a lot of cool people and get to spend my days doing whatever I want to write about. There are worse things." I opened the door to let him out.

"Being an escort, for instance?" Rupert asked, smiling mischievously. I smirked.

"Well, thanks for the tea. Goodnight," he called, and I waved him off to the approaching lights of a Prius, before stepping back into the flat and shutting the door.

"I'm mortified," Beth said. She was now standing at the top of the stairs, her forehead slammed against the banister.

"Don't worry about it," I laughed. "He wasn't fussed." I patted her shoulders as I went past her. "Do you want a drink?"

"I want to drown."

"No drownings allowed, but how about a mimosa? A classy drink for a classy lady."

"Drown my sorrows?"

"You have nothing to be embarrassed about," I assured her. "Tomorrow it will just be a great anecdote. Something for your next hen do!"

Beth narrowed her eyes. "Why did I let you coach me? Why did I think having an audience would be a good idea?"

"I would have hung up and put earplugs in the moment it got really steamy," I promised her. I had no intention of being a voyeur. That kink wasn't for me.

"God, even just the start of that . . . *attempt* was like a raunchy version of *First Dates*. I just feel . . . urgh!" She jammed her palms against her eyes as if she could erase the memory from her mind's eye.

I poured two glasses of our remaining prosecco and some orange juice. "You'll look back and laugh about it soon. Definitely before the article comes out."

"No!" she shouted suddenly, her head shooting up. "This isn't going in the article."

Well, that wasn't happening. "Babe, we have to add it. It's great copy and a big part of your journey."

"This fucking journey," she said. "I don't want this escapade in print, it was just some desperate, impulsive, and utterly stupid idea that no one needs to know about."

"But Beth . . ." I began, but she put her hand up to silence me.

"No! No '*but Beth*'—this is my life, Serena, or have you forgotten whose *journey* this is?"

"You're just embarrassed, give it . . ."

"Because this is fucking embarrassing, Serena! And you don't even seem to care," she shouted.

"It was your idea, Beth!" I reminded her, taking a large mouthful of mimosa. Being constantly interrupted was starting to annoy me. "Although you do have a habit of making decisions that aren't always good for you—and then being too stubborn to admit it—I was just trying to be supportive."

It wasn't meant to be an unkind comment, mostly because we both knew it was true, but I could tell I had hurt her. But honestly, after my dad too—I was sick of people not facing the truth.

"If I'm so predictable and make so many wrong decisions, then why did you go along with my decision to lose my virginity? Surely that was one bad decision that you shouldn't have let me make. Or are you just waiting for me to fail?" Beth slumped against the wall and began rubbing her eyes again in frustration. "You should have talked me out of this."

"Oh, so now this is *my* fault," I returned, my voice louder than I had anticipated. We heard the familiar sound of Mr. Kilmeckiz's broomstick against the floor.

"It's not your *fault*. But Serena, this is humiliating for me. I wish you got that instead of acting like all of this was some joke." She was breathing heavily like she might cry. But it didn't make me feel any less exasperated. "I don't want to fight, I'm just pissed off . . . with myself, mostly."

"Well, I'm going to bed," I said finally, grabbing my drink and leaving hers on the side. "I won't write about it if you don't want me to, but I thought you wanted this. I was just trying to help."

Beth said nothing as I passed her, but I could tell she blamed me for her pride being hurt. I got it. We all act out and try to blame others when we're embarrassed.

A few days peace and quiet and she'd be fine and back in the proverbial saddle, I thought. That was always the way of it before.

But it wasn't this time.

FOR DAYS AFTER the evening with Rupert, Beth remained distant and quiet. When I came home from work, I would find her in her bedroom, with the door closed, playing loud music, dinner already made. None for me.

It was the unspoken rule of the flat that if one of us was hanging out alone in our bedrooms with the door closed then we wanted to have proper alone time, and therefore I left her to do it. But after two weeks of coming home to find her still camped out in her bedroom I started to worry that things were seriously souring between us.

Maybe it was the loneliness of not having Beth to speak to when I got home, or the anxiety that something was seriously wrong, but I decided to message Zoey.

We jumped back into our flirty WhatsApp routine without issue. I don't know why I had avoided it for so long.

She asked me about my day, checked in when I got home, made me laugh with anecdotes from her recent interviews. It was only when she asked me how Beth's sexual odyssey was going that my anxiety would flare up again.

It's fine, I lied. We're pressing pause for a few weeks, to give Beth a breather and I've got a ton of work at the moment. Did you hear the board of The List wants to make some budget cuts? We've been running around like headless chickens. Well, Hermione and the rest had, I was just putting my head down and making myself indispensable. Budget cuts were nothing new.

I didn't tell her I was dealing with some family drama; I didn't want to dive into that, even with Zoey.

Everything with my dad still sat heavy in the forefront of my mind, though I was trying not to think about it.

There had been no further communication from him about his stay in London, but he had deposited a lump sum of £3,000 into my bank account a few days after the call. No message, of course.

If I thought he felt guilty I would call it guilt money, but instead it felt more like a payoff to keep quiet about his shocking behavior as a parent.

I hadn't touched it. I didn't need it and I didn't want it. But I also hadn't sent it back. Every time I went to open my banking app to return it, I found myself thinking, *actually, I deserve it.*

After everything my parents put me through, why shouldn't I have a little—or, in this case, a rather big—luxury? A single woman in London, particularly in the uncertainty of the world of journalism, couldn't be stupid about money. And here were my parents throwing it at me, even if it was just to keep me out of their lives.

This money was all that tethered us. If I let it go, then I had to let them go. But then I would truly be on my own. And with Beth not talking to me, Arnold distracted by his wedding, and Zoey and I being . . . whatever we were or were not as the case may be, I didn't want to feel more alone than I already felt.

CHAPTER 24
BETH

AH," MR. BATES SAID. "Aha," he muttered again a few seconds later. I could tell he was trying not to laugh and was only just succeeding.

"You can laugh," I told him, knowing full well that the story of my evening with Guy—sorry, *Rupert*—the escort was funny in hindsight. Even if it did still make my stomach clench with dropkick-level embarrassment.

"I will never laugh at you," he promised, leaning forward for his glass of water and clearing his throat. "The situation is a unique one, though, I will admit that."

"You've not heard of asexual people hiring escorts before?" I offered.

"No, that I've heard before. It's the earbuds." He smiled pleasantly before sipping his water. "It's also"—he cleared his throat—"you and Serena again."

"Again?"

"It's never just you who pushes ahead with these experiments, it's always you *and* Serena."

"Well, I needed her help," I pointed out. "I wouldn't have

the first clue how to hire an escort, and Google isn't likely to turn up a decent one."

Mr. Bates said nothing for a moment.

"Aren't you going to ask me how it all made me feel?"

"How did it make you feel?" he parroted back to me.

I bit my lip in frustration, grateful he couldn't see how irritable I was.

"Bad," I admitted eventually. "Like a failure. Gross. I felt objectified. Embarrassed. Inexperienced. This is not just with Rupert, this is also with the guy at speed dating."

Mr. Bates nodded profusely. "I'm sorry that happened to you. That was completely inappropriate."

"It was so random, there was no need for it, and it was like the other women knew and accepted it. I mean, that woman gave me the warning about the coat."

"That doesn't mean it was acceptable. The fact that the other women *potentially* knew and had not made the hostess aware is not your fault."

"I didn't make her aware either," I admitted awkwardly.

"You could follow up over email, if you want to," he suggested.

"I will." I pulled out my phone from my pocket and set a calendar reminder to do just that. Maybe I would write a Yelp review about the whole event while I was at it; I could accept my fate as the poster child for what not to do as an demisexual woman. I imagined that was how Serena would paint me in her article for *The List*, particularly after these two terrible experiences. Not that she knew about speed dating yet. I still hadn't told her what had happened—and she hadn't even tried to ask. I didn't want to bring it up until I spoke to Mr. Bates.

I thought perhaps it was all in my head. That I had overre-acted, despite what Penny said. That it was just a normal part of dating I was unaware of. But Mr. Bates's reassurance was a relief. If that was what dating was truly like, I wasn't going to carry on this experiment any longer.

"I really don't want Serena to write about what happened," I told Mr. Bates, putting my phone back in my bag noisily.

"Why not?"

"It's humiliating, for starters," I said, twirling a piece of hair around my finger for something to do. "Not to mention Serena would control the narrative, not me."

"Hmm . . ." He held the sound for a long time. "Did you feel supported by Serena?"

"With the earbuds?"

"And afterward. Even during."

"Well, she didn't really follow my pace," I admitted, feeling like Serena should have recognized that everything was moving too quickly, even over earbuds. "But we didn't have any sort of safe word or a signal for that."

"You spoke to her in the bathroom."

"Barely. And I was so panicked, I should have just ended it there."

"Why didn't you?"

I paused and licked my lips. "I just wanted to get it over with."

"Is that why you started this . . . what did you call it?"

"We were calling it my *sexual odyssey*," I told him, kissing my teeth after saying it aloud. I realized I had come to resent that term.

"What do you want to call it now?"

"An experiment?" I suggested. "Or a learning curve."

"Okay, so why did you start this experiment, for want of a better term?" he asked kindly, and I smiled. Mr. Bates had a great handle on reassuring me with just the tone of his voice. He recognized my discomfort before I even admitted it.

"I wanted to feel less inexperienced and learn more about how sex and my body works. I've never experimented before, and I thought learning about what makes my body tick would help."

"Did you register that that would require stepping out of your comfort zone?" he inquired, and I nodded.

"Definitely. But I thought it would involve a bit of porn here and some attempts at dating there," I offered, before thinking about what had actually happened so far. "I hadn't imagined escorts, dick-sticks, and humiliating articles."

Neither of us said anything for a minute. The silence was palpable. I could hear the whirring of the heating system throughout the building.

Mr. Bates cleared his throat again.

"Can I ask," he began. "From the list you mentioned in our first session, the one you and Serena put together, how many of those things do you actually want to try? And how many of your recent experiences were on there?"

I produced my phone again to go back over the list we created. It seemed like years ago since we had sat together and brainstormed it. But really it had only been a few weeks.

- ☐ Meet with a sex therapist
- ☐ Do yoga to strengthen pelvic floor
- ☑ Have a smear test to confirm cervical health
- ☐ Try dilation
- ☐ Experiment with solo play sex toys

"I mean, I've tried three of the five," I said after reading the list aloud. "And I was happy to do all of them. Even though they felt uncomfortable to do at first."

"Of course." Mr. Bates smiled. "I asked you to try to have a second date as part of your work with me," he added. "And that wasn't on the list."

"No, but if I want to have a relationship—which I suppose is partly why I want to increase my knowledge now and not later—I'm going to have to try going on second dates at some point. Just not with guys that borderline sexually assault me."

"Oh, it wasn't borderline," Mr. Bates said seriously, but nothing else.

"I suppose the escort was my idea," I added. "But it was a bad one. I wish Serena had stopped me."

"Would she usually?"

"No," I said, almost too quickly. "Not when she thinks it's a good or a fun idea."

"Were the earbuds your idea as well?"

"No!" I exclaimed. "No, that was all Serena."

"And the article?"

"Definitely Serena."

"Hmm," Mr. Bates added, then went quiet for a second. I didn't fill the gap with a question like I usually would. I waited for him to ask me a question. He gave in after a few minutes pause. "Do you really want to do this experiment at all?" he asked eventually.

"Yes," I said.

"Really?"

"Yes."

"Even now?"

I said nothing, staring at my feet.

"Do you want to continue with the list?" he asked again, quietly this time.

"I don't feel like I can stop," I admitted.

"Why not?"

We both knew why not, but I didn't say it. Serena had a whole article planned, there was an arc to follow, a list to complete, and I had barely scratched the surface of learning more about my body and my sexuality. I just had a list of experiences I hadn't enjoyed or hadn't offered me much in the way of knowledge.

The only thing that had helped so far was the therapy, and that was partially only because Serena wasn't involved.

I gasped.

"Are you okay?" Mr. Bates asked.

"Y-yes," I said, stuttering slightly. I didn't know how to say what I was thinking without coming across like a bad friend. But, as ever, Mr. Bates seemed to be able to read my mind.

"How has Serena supported you throughout this experiment?"

"She tries, in her own way," I mumbled, rubbing the calluses that had formed between my fingers from years of holding a pen too tightly.

"Earbuds?" Mr. Bates suggested, the tiniest bit amused as he said it. I stifled a doleful smile.

"Earbuds," I agreed.

"Do you feel she would support you if you decided to stop with the experiment and return to how things used to be?"

"I don't know." Probably not what I truly wanted to say. "I think she would try to get me to finish the list, or try and alter it somehow, in a way that would still be helpful."

"Helpful to you, or to her?"

I cracked my knuckles painfully.

"Her," I said finally. Mr. Bates said nothing else for a moment. "But I *do* want to experiment." I strove to keep my voice even. "For years I've been the girl with no follow-through—ever since university, in fact. I've never gotten a promotion or gone on a proper second date, I've never really changed anything or even chased a dream. I've never experimented in any areas of my life. I just sort of float by, starting things that I never finish."

"That's not just because you're demisexual, though," Mr. Bates reminded me. "You're still young."

"I'm nearly thirty."

"You're still young," Mr. Bates repeated seriously. "You'll be experimenting your whole life and you won't even realize it half the time. And most of those experiments mean going outside your comfort zone."

"I suppose I went freelance," I suggested, trying to join the dots. "But I haven't made a success of it. Serena bails me out half the time."

"And is that what you're feeling is happening with your experiment? She's bailing you out?"

"Sort of?"

"In return for an article?"

"Well, the job thing isn't in return for anything."

"Really? I thought you said you did the cooking and cleaning?"

"Well . . ." I didn't have an argument for that.

"Would you say Serena depends on you?"

"Maybe a little less than I depend on her."

"Why a little less?" Mr. Bates shuffled in his seat, getting comfortable.

"She's fiery and independent; she doesn't *need* me for anything. She could quite easily clean the flat and cook something for herself if she needed to, but I'm better at it and I'm around more. Honestly, I'm usually the hot mess in our duo."

Mr. Bates had some more of his water as he considered for a moment. I really wanted him to say that, in his considerably well-educated opinion, I wasn't a hot mess at all, that I was being too hard on myself. But I suppose, despite the fact he was being paid—by Serena—he couldn't tell me what I wanted to hear.

"Interesting," he said eventually, which was infuriating.

"What is? My relationship with Serena?" I asked. "It's just your regular kind of friendship. We're just very close."

"How long have you known her?"

"Since university. We met in the first year and lived together in our second and third, and then just carried on living together when we moved to London."

"And how did you meet at university? Were you in the same class, the same group of friends?"

"No, not really. We met on a night out at a club during freshers' week. I was in the smoking garden—not that I ever smoked, but I'm not really a fan of clubbing. It's hot and loud and expensive, and unless you're drunk it's hard to enjoy."

"So you were sober," he clarified.

"Before uni, I didn't drink, didn't smoke, and didn't take drugs. If I hadn't gone, I would likely still be the purest person to walk the planet. At least now I've lost my alcohol and drug virginity." I laughed, although Mr. Bates just stared. "Serena was in the garden surrounded by a group of men, all of them drunk, and she saw me alone and came to sit with me. She sent the boys packing and offered me a cigarette."

"Did you take it?"

I nodded.

"And did you smoke it?" he asked. I nodded again. "But you said you didn't smoke?"

"Not before university. And not since. But it was freshers', and I wanted to fit in. We sat outside for ages, chain-smoking a pack of cigarettes."

"Quite impressive since you hadn't smoked before." Mr. Bates raised his eyebrows at me.

"It was a total mistake. Within minutes I was nauseous and running to the toilet to throw up. Serena followed me and held my hair back while I threw up in a sink. All the toilets were taken."

"Pleasant."

I shrugged. That was just clubbing.

"I wasn't drunk, but she made me get a taxi home. I was broke, still without my student loan due to a screw up, and she said she'd pay. We ended up going back to hers and she made me my first cocktail. It was delicious."

"And this whole time you were talking?"

"Oh yeah. Talking about classes, where we were from, what we studied at A-level, where we were living. We were both in dorms, although Serena was at a much fancier version than mine. I was in the cheapest building you could get. Her dorm was more like a flat shared between three, while mine was more like ten prison cells connected by a long corridor and a tiny kitchen." With the ever-present smell of rotting rubbish from the kitchen; the mountain of washing always sitting in the sink; the grime across the never-cleaned cooker; and the never-ending clutter of hair ties, paper clips, and receipts that littered the corridor that led to all the bedrooms. As a rule, you never walked barefoot to the kitchen, not unless you wanted a tetanus shot.

Serena's flat was nothing like that. For one thing it had a living room, or a "common room," fitted with cable TV and brand-new furniture. Her kitchen was cleaned every other day by a cleaner and she had an ensuite with a bathtub.

Sitting in her common room that first evening, drinking cocktails and watching *Strictly Come Dancing* was how it all started. In fact, it was like that was when my adult life started.

Up until the point I met Serena, I was just a shy teenage girl. Apart from picking fights with Penny—mostly out of jealousy for what I perceived as her unreachable perfection—I barely interacted with anybody. I used social media to stay in the loop at school, without making actual connections with any of my classmates, and played simulation PC games for conversation. Serena was the first person who wanted to hang out with me in person—not just be a follower on my Instagram feed but a real-life friend.

"She was very easy to talk to and one of those people with whom the conversation never gets dull or awkward." I cleared my throat and wondered if I should share that Serena offered to let me share her bed that evening, or not. It's the sort of tidbit I could tell Mr. Bates would want to break down, but it felt important to explain.

"Was she trying to instigate sex?" Mr. Bates asked, either for confirmation or to get me to say it aloud.

"Yes." Oh, it was awkward. "She put her hand on my inner thigh as she said it, but it wasn't forceful and somehow it wasn't uncomfortable either. That was the first time that had ever happened to me. Even now someone puts their hand on me without warning and I freak—I mean look at that bloke at the speed-dating event. He touched me and I all but fled the city."

Mr. Bates nodded, but I wondered if he was thinking what I was thinking—that a hand on an inner thigh and a fist and finger in the crotch area were different levels of inappropriate touching.

But *was* a hand on an inner thigh inappropriate in circumstances like mine and Serena's? We were clearly getting on really well, there was a definite vibe between us, but it wasn't sexual, at least not to me. With me it never is.

"I told her I wasn't into girls, and she immediately withdrew but was not embarrassed or awkward. She didn't seem upset in the slightest, although she apologized just in case she had offended me. Which she hadn't. She still offered to share her bed, strictly platonically, but I said I'd prefer the sofa."

Mr. Bates rested his head on his hand, obviously contemplating what I had said.

"Theoretically—and I *mean* theoretically as we'll never know for sure—do you think if you were interested in women, you would have felt comfortable enough to have sex, or any form of sexual intimacy, with Serena then?"

I didn't really know. I'd considered it, of course—Serena and I were so close that sometimes I referred to her as my girlfriend. Jokingly.

But just because our relationship was sexless and I wasn't sexually or romantically interested in women, that didn't mean that there wasn't intimacy between Serena and me. We had seen each other naked—and more. The dick-stick incident may have been the most physically intimate for me, but we had been known to get into the same bath while drunk, both with and without clothes. She had felt my breast when I told her I thought I had found a lump, which was merely the world's largest zit, and she had asked me for help to inject thrush medicine into her vagina when she was too sensitive to do it herself.

"Sometimes I think we know too much about each other," I said eventually. "I think my relationship with Serena has surpassed that of friendship or sisterhood into something else. But that something isn't sexual or romantic, it's complicated. It's also quite trapping." I crossed my arms.

"That's an interesting choice of words. How so?" he asked softly.

I barreled forward before I could second-guess myself.

"I just mean that no matter what happens we could never stop being in each other's lives, even just mentally. She knows too much about me and I about her. Even if I were to flee to one end of the world and her to the other, we would never truly be apart."

"This sounds like a very intimate relationship to me," Mr. Bates said. "You ticked wanting to work on arousal and intimacy issues when you first arrived for these sessions."

"I didn't know what to put on that thing," I told him honestly. "I don't know what's wrong with me."

"Firstly, there's nothing wrong with you. There are things you simply want to work on, to develop and to understand. Secondly"—he leaned forward, his eyes jolting from side to side as he struggled to solidify me in his sight—"sexual intimacy and general intimacy are two sides of the same coin. It seems to me that while you may find sexual intimacy a challenge due to your sexuality, you do not struggle with intimacy entirely. Therefore, why should you fear that you'll never find a person to be sexually intimate with when all you might need to do is develop general intimacy with a person, in your case preferably a man, like the intimacy you already share with Serena?"

I shut my eyes for a moment and a flash of memory stirred: something I had once said to Serena. It was her last birthday at university, and we had decided to throw a house party. Nearly all the students in our neighborhood showed up. It had been a great night.

We were all rip-roaringly drunk, and many memories were made that night. From Serena's decision to piss on the doorstep when the queue for the loo got too long, to all our plates being broken when some fool decided to lay them all out on the floor and use them as drums. (Yes, several people needed stitches.)

But the clearest memory I had was of Serena and me sitting on the doorstep (pre-piss). I had rested my head on her shoulder as I could feel the world spinning on its axis and only she seemed to steady me. I said, "When I look for a man, I look for you with a penis."

Looking back from the safety of Mr. Bates's underfurnished therapy room, perhaps that was the defining moment in my and Serena's friendship.

That was the night before she and I agreed to find a flat together in the city after graduation. It was also the night that she first told me about her mum and dad. Their growing indifference and failure to see past their grievances as exes and just to see the daughter that they shared as something other than a commodity that they had distributed in their divorce proceedings. After she told me, I felt so much admiration for her, for bringing herself up with such self-centered parents, but I also felt slightly responsible for her from then on. *I* had good parents.

"I suppose it's possible I could have a relationship with a man that's like mine and Serena's. The only difficulty is that Serena and I are both women and there's this sort of unspoken safety between women that draws us to each other and makes it somehow easier to be comfortable with one another. I've never felt comfortable around men, not in the same way."

Mr. Bates was nodding again, still leaning forward, presumably to view me and my reactions better.

"I know that your first attempt to go on a second date didn't go so well," he began, and I scoffed.

"Not really."

"I think you should try it again. And then again if it doesn't work that time. And just keep trying. I know that might seem like the worst advice I could possibly give you, just to keep dating—but I really think the more you open yourself up to the experiences you have, even the bad ones, the more comfortable you'll feel when finally a good one comes along."

Hmm. "Really?"

"Really. And I give you full permission to leave the moment a date is terrible if it is *truly* terrible. But, for the most part, dates are often awkward, not terrible. And awkwardness solves itself with time. Or it's never there to begin with, like with you and Serena."

"So, what you're saying is, if I can have an intimate relationship with Serena, I can have an intimate relationship with a man."

"I think it's entirely possible." He smiled, but then he repeated one of his previous questions: "Could you stop the experiment?"

I considered him for a moment, thoughts whirring in my head as I thought about all the things that Serena and I had discussed over the last few weeks. The way she had been ramping up the activity from the original list with a can-do flair that was bordering on dictatorship. Was I really running the experiment, or was she? And for what reasons?

"Maybe."

"Maybe," Mr. Bates repeated. "Maybe if you asked Serena nicely?"

I groaned. "When you put it like that."

"Like what?"

"My friendship with Serena doesn't work like that," I argued. "She's very involved but she doesn't run my life."

"I'm glad to hear it, but why would she need to be involved at all? Couldn't you just stop?"

I rolled my lips together, letting a gap of silence form between us. "I've never been very good at telling Serena no," I admitted eventually.

"Why?" Mr. Bates was not stopping. "Why can't you tell Serena no?" he repeated after another silence.

"Because . . ." I began, stuttering again. I felt like my mouth was full of spit that I didn't have time to swallow. "Because what if it ruins our friendship?"

"You're worried saying no would ruin your friendship?" he parroted again.

"I don't want her to see me as a flake."

"Don't you think that your own sexual understanding should be something that you derive for yourself when you're comfortable and when you want to? Not when someone else wants you to?"

"She's helping me," I reminded him.

"Is she?" He let that hang there for a moment.

Was she helping me? Sure, the experiment had been my idea, spurred on by embarrassment at Bonnie's hen do, but I had never intended it to grow to the level that it had. If I had known it would eventually lead to straddling an escort half-naked and completely clueless a few weeks later I would never have brought it up.

But Mr. Bates had been helpful. The smear test had been successful and to an extent informative. Even the dick-stick hadn't been the worst experience; I now knew I was capable of being penetrated and it wasn't the worst thing to ever happen to me. That was progress.

But the rest?

"You challenge me," I said, pointing to Mr. Bates despite knowing he couldn't see me. "My sister, even Delphi to an extent, encourage me. But Serena demands me," I told him. "I think that's what is really annoying me at the moment."

"So, it is annoying you?"

"Yes," I admitted, feeling a warm sense of relief to admit it safely. "She's annoying me. The article and the demands, the earbuds, are annoying me. Even when they're not demands per se, they feel like demands."

"Because you feel like you can't say no," he reminded me, and I nod.

"Exactly," I added for his benefit.

"Do you think it's time for you to create some space between yourself and Serena? I don't mean push her away, but perhaps talk to her about pressing pause on this experiment for a while and talk to her about how it's making you feel."

Easier said than done, I thought. Serena had never been one for talking through her feelings or taking constructive feedback. I could tell her that her haircut looked awful or that her thong was showing under her dress with ease, but telling her she was frustrating me or hurting my feelings felt nigh on impossible.

I couldn't remember the first time we had fought, excluding the tense few moments in the kitchen after Rupert the escort left. And even then, after I returned to my room, I felt like I was going to throw up with the anxiety that everything was ruined.

The moment my door hit the lock I regretted snapping at her. I wondered if I had pushed her too far, if she would forgive me for being frustrated even when really I was still angry with her for making it all about her.

Serena was such a flight risk, even after the ten years I had been her best friend. I saw how she treated Zoey, pushing her away despite clearly having deep feelings for her. What's to say she wouldn't push me away like that? And then where would I be? Forget my job and the flat, who would I have left? Delphi? Bonnie?

"Is this your challenge for the week?" I asked Mr. Bates, my throat stinging from an anxious lump that had formed.

"I think it would be good for you to give yourself a break," he suggested calmly. "And perhaps having some space from Serena for a short period. To reset and think about what you really want to do. And whether or not you want to carry on with this experiment."

It wasn't really a big ask. He wasn't telling me to dump her and run for the hills. It was just time to revisit what I actually wanted. And was that this experiment—or *sexual odyssey* as she continued to call it—or was it something else?

"I'll give it a go," I promised him.

CHAPTER 25
SERENA

EVEN THOUGH THINGS were quiet in the flat, with Beth recharging her social batteries, I had a lot of work to do to keep me occupied. Both Zoey and I were preparing our batch of summer articles, joking as we journalists usually did about the weather reports of snow while we were planning photoshoots for beachwear accessories and writing articles on experimental ice cream flavors and the benefits of SPF 50 foundation.

One evening, while sitting alone in the living room, braless and exhausted, which felt like my new permanent state of living, Zoey FaceTimed me.

I'd had a long day; the board members of *The List* were calling for a potential rebrand, and we were all required to complete forms and answer questions about what we thought *The List* truly meant to readers. I had been quiet on WhatsApp all day, so I assumed Zoey was just checking in. I pressed accept and as soon as I saw Zoey's smiling face my exhaustion seemed to fade.

She was sitting at a desk, her hair up in a messy bun and wearing the thickest black-framed glasses I had ever seen.

"Hey!" I said in a sing-song voice. "What's up?"

"Hey." She smiled down the camera at me. "Just wanted to see you."

My heart did a little leap in my chest.

"Aww, did you miss my gorgeous face?" I teased, striking an angelic pose.

"Always," she said. "Thought we could catch up, face to face for once. How's life?"

"Same old, same old. Finishing up some projects and working on this rebrand. Aside from that, I've just been marathon-watching Netflix and eating too much cheese." And freaking out about all my relationships.

"Not going out at the moment?"

"It's too cold." I shivered dramatically for her benefit, rubbing my bare arms up and down.

"Same here. If it's not snowing, it's raining, and if it's not doing either of those then it's simply freezing! Half the time I think my nipples are about to crack off."

"Oh, my skin's been awful," I said, touching the dry skin on my face.

"Well, I was talking more about the lack of sex, but sure, my skin's dry too."

"I should have known! You and your nipples."

Zoey had particularly sensitive areolas—in fact, she swore that she would never achieve orgasm without her nipples. And strangely enough, in an experiment I did when I touched every part of her but her nipples she *didn't* orgasm. It was the first and only time that ever happened. I made sure never to miss that erogenous zone again.

She could tell my mind had wandered to her body and for a brief moment she seemed to lean into the camera, smirking in a very telling way.

I licked my lips and inhaled deeply, pushing myself away

from that glorious daydream. But it was a mistake. Suddenly my mind pulled me back to that afternoon in Wembley, having bad sex with a guy whose name, I was pretty sure, was fake. Who calls a child *Sarge*?

I had an impulsive urge to tell Zoey, to explain why I was so weird with her during her visit. Why I hadn't stayed up for her on Wednesday night. Surely she must have known something was up—otherwise she wouldn't have left without saying goodbye, no matter how sweet Beth and I looked curled up on the sofa together. And it couldn't have looked that sweet because we both had hangovers from hell the following morning.

"Listen," I began, but so had she. In the awkwardness we both laughed, but it was Zoey who spoke first.

"I was thinking of coming back down to London soon—"

Oh fuck. Everything in me seemed to swell.

"—*Eve* is doing great, but we're interested in expanding. There's even some discussion of working with *The List* more formally. And London is always the best place to get interviews."

"Well, that's true," I told her. My voice wobbled traitorously. "London is the best. No offense to Liverpool, of course."

"None taken," she said. "I love it here, we've got some great nightlife, but you hardly ever get the kind of news or celebs we need to survive coming to Liverpool, and there's only so many times I can have a conversation with a publicist about how to operate Zoom or use FaceTime!"

Preach. Half of those interviews are spent trying to find strong enough Wi-Fi so we can hear each other. I kept swallowing as the strange weight inside me seemed to have reached my throat and was closing it off.

"I talked to the board and the editor in chief, and we're discussing the possibility of me relocating to London to be the main celebrity editor."

"Really?" She was going to be within taxi distance of me!

But oh no . . . she was going to be within taxi distance of me.

"But—but I thought you preferred features over interviews?"

"I do, but I have the most experience on the team," she said dismissively. "And I can throw in the odd feature here and there when staffers are on holiday or we're out of freelance budget."

"Hmm," was all I could manage to get out. I always thought of Zoey in Liverpool, never living anywhere *but* Liverpool. Whenever she was down in London, she waxed lyrical about her magical city, its culture, the liver birds, and bloody Kim Cattrall. Her family had lived on the Wirral for nearly nine generations. She had drawn a diagram of her family tree on a pub napkin once to prove it. So why would she move to London? Just for a job?

Or was it for me?

The night in the toilets of the Imagine Dragons concert came flooding back into my mind. The soft "I love you" to the score of "Walking the Wire." We had never discussed it. Not on the phone or even when she next came to London.

She didn't mean it. She couldn't have.

We were just friends with benefits. Anything else would be ridiculous and would end badly. Better to be avoided at all costs.

Despite the joy hearing her say "I love you" might have brought for the second before the terror hit in that stall. That jolt of lightning that seems to burn from the inside out, just from three little words, is not enough to make a relationship worthwhile.

They're just words, and I knew well enough from observing my parents' marriage growing up, that words mean nothing when they're sweet and everything when they're painful.

I gulped. "So you're seriously thinking of moving down here?" I asked, trying to remain supportive while getting enough air in my body.

"I am!" She beamed. "I'm thinking of coming down soon. I need to go flat-hunting."

"Wow!" I exclaimed, my eyes popping. "So it's really serious, then."

"It will be on a trial basis to begin with, to see how well it works. I mean if we can't get the interviews or the premiere slots then there's not much point and I'll go back. But still, a six-month stint in London doesn't sound too bad, does it?"

She was asking me. I was playing a role in this. It wasn't just her telling me that she was going to be around to hang out and sleep with, she was asking if that was okay.

My heart was screaming at me to tell her how excited I was that I would be able to see her more than a few times a year. But I could barely expand my lungs from the sudden terror flowing through me, let alone declare that this was something I had only ever daydreamed about.

And it had been. However much I denied it.

But along with the daydreams were the nightmares. I was going to fuck this up if she moved to London. I already fucked it up when she was here for just a few days.

I'd never seen relationships work out. Neither Beth nor I had ever really been in one, and my parents' relationship could be the basis of a textbook on what not to do.

I could do sex, that was easy enough, but everything else? Trust, care, love? I'd just mess it up. "It will be so much fun!" I exclaimed, the air bursting from me like an escaped balloon at a party. "I can take you to all the hotspots and give you all the right contacts. It would so cool if we could do something

together, you know, *Eve* and *The List*. Some sort of partnership piece or competition. That would be great. I'll talk to Arnold and see what he can do. This is going to be so much fun!"
I repeated, clapping my hands together like a child who's been
told they're going to Disneyland. "You'll have a great time in
London."

There was a flicker of disappointment. I could see her
deflating—but she maintained her happiness at my forced joy
even as I was talking about all the things we could do together,
which were clearly platonic and work-related activities.

I strayed heavily away from the topic of dating and sex, not
mentioning my love life or indeed her own. And not once did I
offer my room for her to stay when she came down to initially
flat-hunt. I couldn't do that now, not when my stomach was by
my knees with nerves at the thought of her moving to London
permanently.

What if she asked to stay with me permanently? What if I
asked her to?

"Maybe we could have a best hits of *RuPaul's Drag Race*
evening?" she suggested as she gave me the dates for her next
trip down. In just over a week.

"I might not be here that week," I told her.

"What?" she asked. "Why didn't you say?"

I took a short breath. "Yeah, I know I told you Beth and I
were taking a break from her sexual odyssey but it's back in
full swing now," I lied.

"Oh?" she said, the disappointment more evident now than
before. I ignored it, acting as if I couldn't tell that anything was
wrong in the slightest.

"Yeah, we've got back into it and that week I'm taking her
on an excursion to get a new angle."

"An excursion?" she repeated. "To do what?"

"Kind of like a retreat, except it focuses more on your body and comfort levels." I was talking out of my arse, of course. I hadn't booked or planned anything of the sort. "We're trying to progress things a little further now. She's done a lot of talking and thinking in the process, but it's time to actually dive right into the heart of the matter."

"I suppose so. It would make for interesting reading."

"Don't go stealing my pitch ideas!" I joked.

"Hey, listen, I've got to go," she said quickly. "I've got an edit that's due tomorrow that's going to need a lot of work. I'll confirm the dates I'm down next week and we can find time to chat then. Alright?"

"Yeah of course!" I said, smiling widely. "It'll be good to hang out."

"Yeah," she said softly. "Right, then. Speak to you later."

"Speak to you later. Bye!" Hanging up, I fell back against the cushions and exhaled heavily.

Oh shit.

So I needed to book a tantra retreat asap.

I was lucky: there was a tantra workshop in Devon the week that Zoey said she would be down. It came to just under £3,000 for both Beth and me to attend all week. And luckily, I had that £3,000 from my dad. It was practically a sign.

I added in my bank details and paid for the tickets without asking Beth.

If worse came to worst I could ask Hermione or someone from work and call it research for an article I could make up on the spot.

But I hoped Beth would come along. I know she'd been feeling uncertain about everything we were doing but she *had* wanted to do this. It was her idea, and this tantra workshop was more about self-sensuality than anything else we'd done.

The workshop was about confidence and self-love and that's what she needed more than anything else. The confidence to believe she was worthy of love: romantically and maybe also sexually.

This would be good for her, and a great little mini break to get our friendship back on track.

It was the perfect plan.

I would tell Beth tomorrow, when Zoey confirmed the dates of her visit, and then there would be no going back.

CHAPTER 26
BETH

AND IS A tantra workshop something you *want* to do?" Mr. Bates asked during our third session.

I had booked the session with him almost immediately after Serena's announcement that she had booked us two tickets to a weeklong tantra workshop in a few days' time.

"It wasn't something I'd even considered," I admitted. "I mean, when we started planning out things I could do I think she mentioned a workshop, but I hadn't even heard of tantra, and we never properly discussed it or put it on the list."

"But what about now? Now that the option *is* there, do you want to do it?"

I considered his question a moment longer than was necessary. "Not particularly."

"Then why are you going ahead with it?" he asked, smiling in a slightly frustrated way. The whole conclusion of my second session with him had been about saying no to Serena, putting some space between her, me, and the experiment. But I had fallen at the first proper hurdle.

The break on the experiment over the last few weeks had been good. I finally felt like I had a chance to focus on my work with WOW, and Evan. I got to catch up on a series I wanted to watch that I knew Serena would hate and to speak to Penny about stupid stuff to keep her mind off the IVF and the latest bad news.

It was nice to think about something other than my sexuality for a while, to return to feeling a little more like me and not just a demisexual woman on a half-hearted mission.

Serena respected my space, even if it was begrudgingly. We barely spoke and I could practically feel my social batteries beginning to burst after the break, but in truth I was beginning to miss her.

And then this tantra workshop came into the picture.

Two months ago, when my mind had suddenly sparked the idea of getting to know my body and sexuality more, I had not expected it to lead me to a bloody tantra workshop in a manor. I was thinking that I would watch more porn than I had before—having watched porn in the past, mostly out of curiosity as opposed to sexual stimulation—maybe try to go a little further with a date than just a drink.

But *this*, this was unexpected. But it was also what you get from being friends with Serena Hamilton-Jones.

Things were not simple and homemade, they were big, story-worthy experiences. It came with the territory of her being a journalist, but also with her being *her*.

She wasn't asking me to pay, or even telling me I had to go. Instead, she said that she thought it was a good idea, that it would boost my self-confidence and body awareness, which was more like what I wanted the experiment originally to be about.

I cleared my throat. "You were right the other week," I admitted. "I'm going because Serena asked me to, not because I want to." It was the truth, however much it hurt.

"Did it feel like a demand?" Mr. Bates asked, gently, slightly prodding the prideful wound.

"Not really," I said, feeling like it was not not a demand either. "She had already booked it, though."

Mr. Bates's eyes widened, but he didn't say anything else.

The fact that she had booked it without asking me first was frustrating, but that was typical Serena: buy first, regret later.

The workshop felt like her white flag of apology. The two of us had been weird around each other since the incident with Rupert. Partially because I was trying to put some distance between myself and the experiment, and her, for a little while, but also because we hadn't addressed anything. As much as I knew Mr. Bates wanted me to confront her, I couldn't find the courage to do so. And Serena never asked me if anything was wrong. So really I just dodged the issue.

But the workshop was a potential opportunity to clear the air.

The pamphlet for the workshop was harmless enough, with a pretty picture of a country estate and a group of faceless patrons having a gong bath—whatever that is!—in a *Saltburn*-esque dining room. I could do that. Yoga had been on the list, and if meditation was involved, then that would give me plenty of time to think about what I wanted and whether the experiment was worth finishing. Or if it was even possible to finish it.

"Did Serena give a reason for booking the workshop?" Mr. Bates asked. "Beyond the experiment?"

I shook my head and added, "No. Do you think she should have?"

He smiled at my attempt to get him to answer a question for a change.

"I wonder about the timing. Was there a reason for doing it now? Booking it without consulting you first?"

"She was worried it would be overbooked and there's not another one like it for months."

"I see." Mr. Bates cleared his throat. "Is she keen for you to restart the experiment for her article, or is she trying to reinvigorate your interest in it?"

It was a question that had played on my mind ever since she'd told me it was booked.

"I didn't ask for the specifics."

"Do you think you could clarify that with her beforehand?"

Why did I suddenly feel like a teacher was telling me off?

"I could say no."

"But you've already admitted that you don't want to go, but that you're still going anyway."

Straight for the jugular.

"When you put it like that . . ." I let my voice drift off and exhaled heavily.

Mr. Bates picked me up. "I think, before you go, you should confirm what the workshop is about. Make it clear what you want out of it, and set some boundaries."

"Boundaries like?"

"What don't you want to happen?" he asked, spinning the question back to me, as always. Sometimes I really wished he would just tell me what to do. But then, I suppose I have Serena for that.

"I don't want to be embarrassed," I said hesitantly. "If I'm uncomfortable—more than just out of my comfort zone, but *uncomfortable*, uncomfortable—I want to be able to leave."

"Good idea," he said, nodding. "The ultimate goal of any tantra workshop, from my limited experience, is that by the end of the workshop you'll be more comfortable than you were when you first started the workshop. That doesn't mean you'll be ready to rip off your clothes and shag anything that moves, but maybe it will mean you'll feel better prepared to embrace intimacy when it's offered."

"I hope so." I sighed. "It would be pretty pointless otherwise."

"Push yourself, but don't force yourself." I immediately wanted to get that tattooed on my body.

Push myself, don't force myself. I could do that. But could Serena?

"Also," I added quickly. "I want Serena to be involved," I gulped. "I want her to support me, but also go through it with me. She hasn't really done anything with me since the smear test and I think it would be fun to experience something together."

"Do you think it will help her to understand how you're feeling?" he clarified.

"Exactly!" I said. "Maybe that will help her help me."

Mr. Bates nodded slightly. "I think those are very good ideas."

I beamed at him, relaxing like I just got away with not doing my homework with a typical "my dog ate it" excuse.

Mr. Bates didn't ask me anything else but relaxed into his chair with his lukewarm cup of coffee.

"Do you think I'll get a date at this tantra workshop?" I asked him to fill the silence. He smiled at my playful question. "Seems the sort of place where I might meet a like-minded guy."

He made an "mmm" sound, before slurping his tea noisily. "Maybe if you have an open mind you'll make a connection with someone. But I wouldn't make that your intention."

"Do I need an intention?"

Mr. Bates smirked but didn't reply. What did he know that he wasn't telling me?

"I guess I'm going to a tantra workshop, then," I said finally, not with excitement, but neither with dread.

CHAPTER 27
SERENA

A TANTRA WORKSHOP is a brilliant idea!" Arnold had squealed when I told him my reason for needing some sudden time off. "Although I need you back here as soon as possible to help me put the final touches on the wedding."

"Of course!" I swore, taking his hand over the table at Rocco's. We had decided to catch up properly, having missed our lunches recently due to the rebrand and my own flaky work schedule. "Whatever you need from me, you let me know," I told him, stuffing in my last mouthful of gnocchi as the waiter approached to clear the table.

"I have a list," Arnold said solemnly. As I well knew. But it was going to be easy enough to handle the things that I was supposed to oversee: tying together the packages for the wedding favors, ordering the calligraphy seating chart, and getting to the venue the morning of the wedding to help the decorators with covering the chairs in satin fabric.

I was sure I could persuade Beth to help me with all the final touches, since she was going to be my plus-one.

"The workshop finishes on Friday, and we'll be back in London well in time for the wedding on Sunday."

"A Sunday wedding. Good god, what must people think of me?" Arnold said dramatically, putting his head in his hands as the waiter whisked his plate from under him.

"Thank you," I mouthed to the waiter as he walked away. I rubbed Arnold's arms supportively with the joking affection he needed.

"And a wedding on top of a rebrand," he said, reaching for his wine glass, which I placed in his hand. "Why do rebrands always come at the worst time?"

Truthfully, the rebrand wasn't a surprise.

For the last few years—at least since I joined the team four years beforehand—*The List* had been struggling to get by, just like most print and digital magazines of the noughties. People may have been online more, but that didn't mean they were searching the internet to read puff pieces on celebrities or the cost of being single. All they wanted was hard-hitting news, porn, or cheats for Animal Crossing, and *The List* was only supplying one of those.

What worked before would not work now. Our readership didn't know whether to come to *The List* for fashion ideas or hard-hitting pieces about the catastrophic running of the British government.

"I think the board would love some fresh blood in the group," Arnold said dejectedly, picking up his second glass of wine. I followed suit. I wasn't desperate to return to the office, not with all the hubbub and Hermione's constant badgering about whether there were going to be voluntary layoffs.

"How's Zoey?" he asked. Oh no. This was worse than Hermione's questioning. "Don't think I didn't know who you were meeting a few weeks ago." Arnold laughed. But as soon as he looked at me, he frowned. "Have you two fallen out?"

"No, no," I reassured him quickly. "I'm just being stupid. She's coming down in a week or so."

"I know. She emailed me to set up a meeting."

"She emailed you?" That pricked up my ears.

He shrugged as if it was unimportant. "Yes, she wanted to schedule a meeting to discuss a few crossover ideas. You know, a potential partnership. And to get the general lay of the land now that *Eve* is considering expanding."

"I didn't expect that to be the sort of thing you'd agree to," I said. "To talk to one of our competitors," I clarified. Not wanting to admit that I had thoroughly overexerted myself, recommending Zoey do so in the first place.

He cleared his throat. "No offense to Zoey, but *Eve* is hardly a groundbreaking publication. Its turnover may be good on-line and up in Liverpool, but it doesn't even catch a whiff of the stories we write until after we've published them. I'm not threatened by them."

"But even still."

"Call it a mentorship," he suggested blithely, sensing my distaste for the idea. "She's going to be new to the city, at least in the work-sense, the least I can do is help her get settled. I thought you'd be pleased."

"Why? Because she's my friend?"

He took a long sip of his drink. "I thought she was more than that."

It was my turn to drink.

"It would be confusing to have Zoey in my professional life as well as my personal life," I said, not meeting his eye as I added to myself, *I would have to choose.* What if I got it wrong and I lost her as a friend and got stuck working with her for months? It would be agonizing. For both of us.

"If you don't want me to do it, I won't. I'll just say I'm too busy with the rebrand or something." He seemed reluctant. "It would hardly be a lie."

"No, don't do that," I said, softening. "It's not like it can hurt." Arnold watched me for a moment. I felt my cheeks blush.

"There's definitely trouble in paradise," he said under his breath, with full hopes that I'd hear.

"We were not in paradise. It was just sex," I lied.

"And what? The sex was bad?"

"No, of course not."

"What then?" Arnold was smiling now, his need for gossip overriding his sensitivity as he clamored for the full story like the journalist he was trained as.

"It's . . ." I stopped for a beat. "Zoey's suggested that we could be more than friends, or more than just friends with benefits."

"And?"

I couldn't look at Arnold and instead focused on watching the few passersby on the street outside as they walked leisurely back to their offices from their lunch breaks.

"It's not something I've ever done before," I finished quietly. "I'm not a relationship kind of girl."

"Well, why don't you just tell her that?" He twirled his glass gently. "Although I think what you really want to do is actually give it a go."

"I do not," I said quickly.

"Yes, you do. You wouldn't be acting like a loved one waiting for bad news if you weren't considering it. Even internally." He smiled in an I-told-you-so kind of way that was both irritating and endearing at the same time. Only people who care about you can give you that look.

"How do you know what I'm thinking?" I said, trying to laugh it off and pretend like this was part of our typically light and airy lunch conversations, but it was getting harder and harder to act in front of him. Particularly as I had no wine left in my glass and there was no food to move aimlessly around a plate to pass the time.

"Oh darling," Arnold said sweetly, placing his free hand over mine on the tablecloth. "When you've been married as many times as I have you can tell when someone is hankering after a little stability, or even just a change. It's why I'm so bad at marriage and so great at divorce."

"You will work on it with Gareth though. If things go wrong, I mean," I said, reverting the conversation back to him and his future husband. The change didn't go unnoticed by Arnold, who smiled softly before returning to berating himself for his pessimism about his upcoming nuptials.

"Honestly, they should make getting married harder and divorce easier," he bemoaned. "If that were the case, I would really have to perfect myself before I even considered walking down the aisle."

"Well, lucky for me, the only aisle I ever dream about walking down is the candle aisle of TK Maxx," I teased, smiling on the surface yet feeling an uncomfortable tug within my midriff that reminded me I was lying.

CHAPTER 28
BETH

MY WHOLE WORK calendar had been turned upside down when Serena booked the tantra workshop. Normally I wouldn't have to worry about work being affected, and neither would Serena, which is why I imagined she booked it without consulting me. But for the first time in months, I actually had a project and meetings lined up, and now I was spending most of my days staring at my screen in the living room or at Edith's with Delphi.

"You've gotten boring," Delphi said one afternoon after I barely registered she had said hello, twice.

"Sorry," I said, still not looking up from my screen. "I just have so much to do before we go," I told her as she slipped into the booth opposite me.

"Well, don't mind me, I'm working on a project of my own."

"Uh-huh."

"Yeah, Pete and I are looking at taking his tattoos on tour."

"Oh yeah."

"I might get him to tattoo the name on my face as an advert for Instagram."

"Sounds good."

"No, it doesn't!" she snapped. "That sounds fucking awful. And painful."

I stopped typing and sighed apologetically. "I'm sorry."

"It's okay," she said, never one to hold a grudge. "Although I am being honest about the tattoos on tour idea. Do you think I could manage the freelance life?" Her eyebrows flickered across her face in a Jack Black–style wave.

"Well, you know my opinion on freelancing isn't great, even when I'm busy." I laughed, gesturing back to my screen.

"Don't let me distract you," she said, opening her Instagram app again.

"I won't. But thanks for the company," I said, and she kicked me under the table. "Ouch!"

"Sorry," she said. "That was my attempt at friendship footsie."

"Oh," I said, rubbing my shin.

DUE TO THE change in plans I had to ask Evan to meet with me a whole week earlier than we had initially discussed.

Luckily he was fine with it, and rearranged to meet at a coffee shop in Camden on Monday.

It was just after midday when I arrived, slightly early and more than a little flustered. I was going to see Evan after all. My heart had been hammering in my chest since the Overground doors had slammed shut at Sydenham station.

I ordered two coffees when I arrived, initially thinking that one would be for him and the other for me. I in fact drank both within quick succession simply for something to do, and to stop me from spiraling.

I had worked so hard on the deck. It had taken me days of research and data mining to get it looking as professional as possible. Penny had worked her Excel magic to make my tables of data look more professional than just streams of numbers. And she had been my mirror when I was practicing my pitch.

Seeing that she and her husband owned their own business I thought that she would be the perfect person to get advice on how to come across as confident and charismatic in Evan's presence. And not so much of the bumbling fool that he remembered from the kitchen at Elias Recruitment.

"Make sure you don't speak too quickly; you tend to mumble if you do that," Penny instructed.

"It's a nervous tic," I argued. "Remember when we were in school plays? I was always a bloody sheep or a cow, so the teachers could have an excuse for me not to speak. I was a frickin' elephant at the birth of Jesus!"

"Proof that teachers don't always do the reading," she quipped as I breathed a final sigh of relief on my practice run. I had done what I could and all there was left to do now was pitch it to Evan.

Sitting in the coffee shop, my hands were shaking. Not only from the nerves but from the amount of coffee I had consumed.

I opened my laptop to prepare my screen and a WhatsApp message came up in the right-hand corner. My phone lit up beside me with the same message. It was from Serena.

> Upgraded us to first class on the train! My treat. Also, what underwear do you think I should pack? What does one wear to a tantra workshop?

She could have wished me good luck in my meeting, I thought darkly.

I opened the message box to reply.

> Not sure. Go with the ones that aren't
> holey. And cheers for first class. Shall
> I pick up some cans of gin on the way
> home? I'm in Camden right now.

Minutes passed as I waited for her reply and a waitress came over to clear my empty cups.

"Do you want another?" she asked.

"Oh no, just a glass of water." She began to walk away. "Actually, can I get a pitcher and a second glass? I've got someone joining me in a minute." The waitress nodded but I thought I caught a weird look at the request for a pitcher of water. It wasn't like I hadn't already paid for my seat; I had gotten two coffees, hadn't I?

> Oh yeah. Good plan on the non-holey
> panties. Also, do you want to watch a
> movie tonight? They've added a ton of
> new films on Netflix. And yes, please!
> Can I get a strawberry flavored one if
> they have it? Thanks!!

I replied with a bland smiley face emoji. Enough said.

"Bethany?" A voice said nearby. I looked up to see Evan walking toward me hesitantly.

Everything around me seemed to go into slow motion. It reminded me of the feeling you get right before you faint. But I couldn't faint. I wouldn't. This was a business meeting and I was a professional.

But my god, he was good looking.

At least six foot three, with a slim chest and waist, looking effortlessly dapper in a white shirt and jeans.

I waited a second too long before smiling and getting up from my seat to shake his hand. As I went in for a handshake he went in for a hug and I ultimately ended up punching him in the stomach as he gave me an awkward shoulder squeeze.

Oh fuck me.

He laughed and stepped back, removing his over-the-shoulder bag and dropping it to the floor.

"It's really good to see you," he said brightly. "It's been ages."

My tongue felt like it had swollen two sizes in a second.

"Y-yeah, it is," I stuttered, shaking my head a little and sitting down opposite him. "But you don't need to call me Bethany—whenever someone calls me Bethany, I think of my mother telling me off."

He laughed and I blushed, regretting the overshare immediately.

"Not a problem, Beth," he corrected himself. "I remember you telling me before. I don't know why I called you Bethany, I always call you Beth." He cleared his throat. "Must be having a moment."

"I've asked for some water, but do you want anything else? A coffee? A scone?"

"Oh, don't tempt me," he teased, rubbing his belly. "It's there one minute and *scone* the next." I laughed politely at the overused British pun. Perhaps he was nervous as well.

That bolstered me.

"Thank you for coming down a week early. I'm afraid my friend has sort of disrupted my plans by booking a trip for us without asking me about the dates." I minimized her message on my screen before I got angry about it again.

"A holiday?" he asked, genuinely interested. The waitress came over to our table at that moment with two glasses and the pitcher of water and I waited for her to leave, hinting for her to hurry up with many "thank you, that's lovely" comments as she insisted on laying out our table perfectly.

"Well it's . . . it's not really a holiday. More of a work trip, but not for *my* business. My friend's a journalist and . . ." I didn't want to tell him about the sexual experiment. It made me feel too much like a science specimen. "We're going to a tantra workshop together."

He paused from pouring each of our glasses. "Oh," he said clearly confused. "A tantra workshop?"

"Thank you," I muttered, taking my glass, my cheeks reddening. "It's, erm, hard to explain and a bit risqué."

"Well, now I'm highly intrigued." Evan smiled, sipping his water.

I hadn't forgotten how nice his smile was. It was reassuring and kind. I could already feel the awkwardness between us dissipating as we sat together.

"Well, it's a sort of body confidence and sex workshop," I said, quickly but without mumbling, as Penny had instructed. "But not like an orgy or swingers or anything like that!" I reassured him, raising my hand just in case I gave him the wrong impression.

My cheeks were so red I must have resembled Pikachu, but I couldn't help but laugh at the absurdity of it all. And Evan reacted similarly. Smiling like a clown—a gorgeous, Alfred Enoch look-alike clown.

"Well, I guess that's life in the city for you. Far more exciting than life in Hertfordshire." He leaned forward on his elbows. "You must let me know what you think of tantra when you experience it."

"I will do. Or my friend will at least, seeing as it's for her publication." I laughed again, my nerves returning.

But he didn't seem to mind, in fact he was smiling more broadly than before.

"I wish I had the confidence to try experiences—maybe not tantra," Evan said. "But not just a boys' trip to Dublin or Croatia. I feel like I never actually do anything unique. I'm too nerdy, too focused on work."

"Hey! Nerdy's good," I exclaimed. "Look at Henry Cavill—everyone loved him even more once he revealed his *World of Warcraft* hobby." I mean, he was also objectively hot.

"Speaking of Henry Cavill, how betrayed did you feel by *The Witcher* recast? I remember you used to really like that show."

He remembered! To be fair, I had been *drooling* over Geralt of Rivia—the Legolas and Aragorn combination character I never knew I needed.

God, it was embarrassing. But still. He remembered.

"I can't believe you remember that." I flushed, and he grinned.

"Of course I do, I remember quite a lot."

"Oh really?" I wondered just how much he kept locked in that big brain of his. "Now I'm intrigued. I want to quiz you."

"Go on then. Although I want to preface this by saying I'm not a complete stalker, I just have strangely good recall."

"That's what all my stalkers say," I joked, before asking him about my typical lunch (a Tesco meal deal that was all I could afford), my go-to drink (Mountain Dew if I could find it, otherwise a straightforward hot chocolate from the machine), and my favorite lipstick (red). He got them all right. "Wow, that's creepy good."

"I know." He blushed. "It is a bit creepy. I bet you don't remember anything about me."

"No, I do! I remember you used to have that Caesar chicken salad a lot, and you always had your earphones in listening to some podcast or an audiobook, never music."

"I still don't listen to much music." He shuddered. "Nothing good has been released since Fleetwood Mac wrote *Rumours*."

"You philistine! You weren't even alive then!"

The two of us were in the tantalizing throes of reminiscence for a while longer, until eventually Evan cleared his throat in a "should we get down to business" kind of way. "What do you think of this project that we're working on then. At WOW?"

"Subtle maneuver toward work," I teased, reopening my laptop screen, and immediately shutting down my messages to get to my well-prepared deck. He pulled his chair around the table so he was no longer sitting opposite me but next to me. He had some great-smelling cologne on, and I'm not ashamed to admit I took a big breath—covering it with a pretend stretch of my back—just to breathe it in a bit more.

"Right, this is what I've come up with over the last few weeks."

"Aha," Evan said, eyes darting over the screenshots and prettily designed tables. Thank god for Penny and her strong Excel skills. I can barely draw a table, yet with a few bits of data and a few clicks she had created 3D-looking pie charts and color-coordinated bar graphs to jazz up my presentation. Evan seemed very impressed—only on a few occasions did he ask me to clarify some details, otherwise he just nodded and smiled.

"Wow," he said, as the presentation finished and I prepared to email it to him. "Very impressive."

He didn't move away as I pulled the computer farther from his gaze. Instead, he continued to sit next to me, leaning on his arms as he drank his water.

"It's amazing work and so helpful. I feel very inspired right now." He laughed gently, and I did the same, relief flooding through me. "I should add you to the roster full time."

I chuckled without planning to and he picked up on it.

"Freelance life not everything you hoped?"

I inhaled and sat back in my chair. "Projects like yours are rare," I admitted. "And freelancing can be quite . . ." I paused, plucking at a loose thread on my sleeve randomly.

"Lonely?" Evan finished for me. I said nothing, but I smiled. "I know what you mean," he agreed sympathetically. "David and I started WOW, but it wasn't until we hired our colleague Kate and rented some office space that we felt like a business. Before that it was mostly me in my bedroom making calls and watching Skillshare videos on how to be an entrepreneur."

"I recognize that feeling. I don't miss Elias, not the work anyway, but the camaraderie wasn't all bad."

"You had me," Evan said softly, pausing for the briefest moment that felt strangely like a minute, before adding, "and Bonnie. She was always around." He cleared his throat. "I heard she got married."

"Yeah, she did." I smirked. "I went to the hen do." My stomach flipped in fear at having to discuss the disastrous event with him, so I quickly added, "The wedding was abroad so I didn't get to go, but yeah, she's married now."

"Amazing." He smiled. "It's so weird hearing how everyone's moving on with their lives."

"Well, look at you," I pointed out cheerfully. "You've got your own successful business and you're expanding. It's very impressive, but you were always a force to be reckoned with."

Evan shifted in his seat, rubbing the back of his neck.

"I always thought so at least," I added quickly, inhaling so loudly to cover my awkward compliment that I sounded like a blender.

Evan snickered but not unkindly. "Ah, thanks. I promise my life's not glamorous or anything, I mean I'm still living with three housemates in a run-down flat."

"Hey, housemates aren't all bad. I've lived with mine for nearly ten years," I said.

"Boyfriend?" he asked quietly. I almost choked on my water.

"God no, just Serena. My friend, the journalist." I laughed. "I've been single for . . ." I didn't want to say "forever," that sounded depressing. "For a while," I finished, hiding my face behind my glass of water. I was going to burst or drown myself at this rate. I put the glass down and sighed. "The cost of rent is extortionate right now," I added for good measure, and Evan took the bait gratefully.

"Isn't it! I'm still in a commuter city, so costs are brutal. It's a little easier with housemates, but not great."

"Exactly," I agreed, smiling at him as we both relaxed again. "This has been a very productive meeting," I said, segueing back to WOW and the reason we had met today.

"It all looks perfect to me," he said. "And I think we're actually ahead of schedule because you've been so productive over the last few weeks."

"Well, I didn't want the tantra workshop to impact WOW," I said honestly. "That's hardly something that would help you to recommend me to future clients."

Evan shook his head and chuckled. "No, I understand. But honestly, this is great work. I'm really, *really* impressed."

"Thank you." I blushed again, but this time it was the nice kind.

"When I get back to the office later, I'll sign it off with the guys, but I think we can transfer the full marketing budget over to the new bank account and I'm happy for you to let rip and do your thing. Everything you've shown me looks spot-on, and I trust that you'll keep me up to date." It wasn't a question, more like a statement of his confidence in me, but I reassured him that I would.

"If you want, I can get the next round of digital advertising out this evening so that they're running while I'm away, and I'll send you the first batch of results when I'm back."

"Yes, that would be fantastic," Evan said. "Although," he began tentatively, "I know we were only looking at the website and digital advertising initially, but I've been meaning to ask if you had the capacity to look into some brand partnerships and media options as well, if you're able to do that? For an additional fee?" he added quickly.

More money! And more time with Evan. . . .

I almost went to say no, that I would do it for free. But I heard Penny's voice in the back of my head squealing *Are you mad! Do you always want to be poor and unable to pay the rent?*

"Sure, I'd love to," I said, gleefully grinning from ear to ear. "It's been such a fun project to work on, I would be happy to be involved even more."

"Fantastic," Evan said, reaching into his back jeans pocket to get his suitably battered phone. "I'm just going to Whats-App David and Kate to let them know. They're both great, but they're not marketing people at all. And as you can see from me, I like to talk but I'm not the best at *doing* anything."

"That's not true, you're managing people just like you managed at Elias. Honestly, that's something I would be terrified of doing."

"It's a lot of fun really." He looked at me out of the corner of his eye. "Particularly in a start-up with friends, it's just like hanging out all day."

"Right. I've not had that for a while; the friend-colleagues type of things. Being freelance you don't always get that opportunity to mingle and actually work *with* people, as opposed to *for* them."

Evan nodded and finished his text to the others. "I should introduce you to them in person; we mostly work from home, but we do have office premises we use once or twice a week. Half the time it's just me. If you ever fancy a day out of London and want to get that oh-so-fun office vibe just let me know. I'll buzz you in."

Being buzzed into an office by Evan was one of the most tempting offers I had ever received in my life.

"I'd really like that, actually," I said, feeling a surge of confidence I hadn't felt in years. This was so easy, and so comfortable.

"I'll give you my personal number—you've already got my work number—so you can just text me when you fancy it," he said, gesturing to his phone.

"It would be easier if I just popped my personal number into your phone, since yours is already out."

"I think I've already got it. It's the same as it was when we were at Elias?"

"Oh." He raised his eyebrows. "And here was me thinking you had lost it."

"Do you still have mine?"

"Guilty!"

I shoved him playfully.

"So now neither of us has an excuse not to talk to each other."

I bit my lip to stop myself from grinning ear to ear. Butterflies fluttered in my midriff.

"Text me when you're back from that workshop of yours," Evan said. "I've got to admit, I'm pretty curious about what that's going to be like."

"You and me both," I said. "I'll give you a sneak peek of Serena's article. Should give you a laugh." I handed him back his phone.

"I'd like that."

The pause between us widened, but both of us sat there smiling like fools, clearly not wanting the meeting to end although it had come to its natural close.

"Are you going back to Kings Cross?" I asked, making the first move as I began to gather up my things.

"Yeah," he said, following my lead by moving his chair back and pocketing his phone. "I was thinking of walking. I'm not a massive fan of the tube, and it's not too far."

"I'll walk with you," I said without thinking about it. "If you don't mind?" I added, just in case. "I'm not a massive fan of the tube either." Honestly, I didn't care about the tube in the slightest; I just didn't want to let him go yet.

"Great," Evan said, tucking his chair in and lifting a hand to the waitress who was hovering nearby to clear our table. "I hoped you would say that."

I had to remind myself again not to faint.

CHAPTER 29
SERENA

BETH WAS IN her room on the phone to her parents when I came home. It was late, as I had decided to go out for Friday night drinks with the team, giving Hermione one too many cocktails as revenge for her dragging us all to a karaoke bar. Needless to say, my plans to watch Netflix with Beth were scrapped.

I went to the kitchen to get a lozenge for my overused throat and rested on the kitchen counter for a minute, listening to Beth's conversation from up the hall.

"Yeah, yeah. Serena and I have got an Airbnb and we're just going to go chill for a week . . . hmm . . . yeah. I don't know. Read a book or two, go to a local museum . . . We're in Devon, mum, that's Cornwall. *Poldark* finished filming ages ago . . . No, I won't be going to see the sets, that's in Cornwall, Mum. We're going to Dev—Dad, tell her we're going to Devon and they're two different places."

I stifled my laugh. I had only ever met her parents a handful of times, but I always got the sense that they were kind and involved, while also respectful of giving their daughters space to live their lives without parental guidance if preferred. The first time I met them was when Beth and I moved into a flat together in our second year at university. We occupied the two rooms on the top floor and hardly ever saw the other two students living with us. Beth's parents had insisted on helping to move her in— although her dad was the one who did all the moving, while her mum sat on the third-hand leather sofa taking pictures in case the landlord tried to screw us out of our security deposit.

The second time I met her parents was at graduation.

Her mum wore such a large hat that it cast its own shadow, and when a summer storm began we all gathered outside of the cathedral where the ceremony took place and I spotted several parents sneakily trying to get close to Beth's mum to shield themselves from the rain. In the final photo of our graduating class, you can just spot me and Beth in the corner, laughing so hard our eyes are crinkled, with me pointing off into the distance at the group of parents under her mother's hat, like a spectator tourist.

I kind of loved her mum though. She was certainly a bit scattered, and sometimes overly harsh, but she was a proper embarrassing over-the-top mother. I didn't know how desperately I wanted one of those until I was standing at graduation on my own waiting behind the official photographer as he snapped a picture of Beth in her gown, with her mum and dad beaming on either side of her.

I didn't even get so much as a "well done" card when I sent my parents an obligatory photo of me in my hat and gown holding my fake diploma.

Later, when I was staying at Dad's Dubai house in the spring, I found the photo still in its brown paper packaging in a filing cabinet when I was looking for takeout leaflets. Nothing says pride and joy more than that.

"I'll send you a text when we get there," Beth said, her frustration obvious. I heard the springs of her bed move underneath her signaling the near end of the call.

I jumped off the side of the kitchen cabinet, still sucking on my lozenge, and wandered over to her bedroom door.

Tapping it gently, I pushed it open.

She smiled at me briefly, as she was lying on her front before returning her expression to a barely-holding-it-in look of annoyance.

"Parents?" I mouthed, already knowing the answer of course. She nodded. "Tell them I send my love."

"Yeah . . . yeah . . ." Beth was saying. "And Serena is here, she sends her love." She smiled up at me. "Mum sends her love too." There was a pause and Beth rolled her eyes dramatically. "She wants to know if you've settled down yet?"

I scoffed and immediately started to laugh, placing my hand over my mouth in an attempt to stifle the sound. Beth was doing the same.

"She hasn't, no," Beth said. Only her mother could be so tactlessly blunt. I loved it! There was no one else in my life like that, not even Arnold. He at least had learned the art of dancing around a subject before going in for the kill. Beth's mum just came right out with it. "Yes . . . yes . . . I will tell her. Okay. I *will*. Okay. Love to Dad. I'll call you later. Okay then . . . yeah. Love you. Bye." She hung up and immediately released a large exhalation as she flattened her face into her duvet.

"Why is it," she said, upon surfacing, "that when I talk to my mother, I feel like I've just run a cross-country sprint?" She rolled onto her back to sit up.

"What did she want you to tell me?"

"Oh god," Beth said, looking over at me apologetically. "Only that it's about time you stop being so picky and just pick one." Once again, she buried her head in her hands. "The worst thing is, she *genuinely* expects me to pass on messages like that. Not just to you—although I know you can take it—but to everyone, even my clients! I can't introduce her to or tell her about anyone."

Beth got up and walked past me into the kitchen.

"Do you want something to eat? I was thinking of making a late-night toastie before going to sleep."

"Have you packed?" I asked, leaning against the doorway as she got cheese and ham out of the fridge.

"Not yet. But it's not like I'll take much. Just some clothes, toiletries, a few books, and maybe my laptop. Toastie?" she asked again, holding up the frying pan.

"No, thanks," I said, clinking the lozenge against my teeth. "Cheese toasties and lemon lozenges doesn't sound particularly appetizing."

"Singing or shouting?" she asked nonchalantly as she got to work buttering the slightly stale bread on the counter.

"Singing. Hermione's brainchild, of course. It's the only bar she knows in London. I think for the good of the company I'll have to take her out one of these days, as there are only so many times I can humiliate myself singing "Mamma Mia" in front of the same bartender every other Friday."

Beth snorted, knowing full well that me singing ABBA was torture for all those within a fifty-foot radius of me. I may be good at many things—and humble to boot—but singing was not one of them.

"Fair do's," she said, cutting her cheese.

"I'm going to go pack."

"Not your holey panties," Beth reminded me, although her tone wasn't as teasing as I thought it should be since I was joking when I initially made the comment.

"Yep. I'll pack my in-between panties. Not my best but not my worst either."

She nodded, seemingly indifferent to my delineation of underwear.

Although we had got through most of the tension that had been caused by the escort escapade, there was still something between us that I hadn't quite cut through yet. But I was hopeful that our little mini break to Devon would be the perfect solution to all the tension in the flat, and we'd be back to our usual selves before the week was out.

I turned toward my bedroom to get packing.

"Actually," Beth began, and I turned back to see her leaning awkwardly against her doorframe, fiddling with the edge of the catch. "Before this workshop, can I just ask you a favor? Well, actually, not a favor," she began rambling and shuffling her feet. "More like a request. Maybe even a demand."

"What is it?" I asked, cutting through her awkwardness.

She inhaled. "Will you promise me that if I don't like it, we can leave?"

"Of course!" I began, but she lifted her hand to signal she wasn't finished.

"*And* that you'll take part. It won't just be me making a tit of herself meditating and touching her boobs, or talking about an embarrassing sexual experience or whatever it is they'll ask us to do."

"Sure, I've got no problem touching my boobs," I teased, beginning to offer her a demonstration, which was awkward for both of us. "Sorry," I said, stopping as Beth rolled her lips together. "I promise to take it seriously. It will be fun."

"I'm not sure about fun." Beth laughed nervously.

"We'll make it fun," I swore, placing my hands on either side of her shoulders and nodding. "Really. We'll have fun. And if we don't, we'll leave."

"That's all I ask," she said softly, and I nodded again. "Right. Go pack."

"Yes, to packing!" I sung, marching to my room loudly and hopefully.

IT STARTED OFF well.

Our afternoon train trip to Devon was uneventful. After trekking the full hour it took to get from Sydenham to Paddington to finally begin our journey, Beth and I relaxed into our first-class seats and automatically fell into holiday mode.

Beth was particularly organized as we got into our carriage and settled into our comfortable seats. She pulled out a shopping bag weighed down with cans of gin and tonic. "Not all for the journey," she told me. "Some are for me to drink pre-tantra sessions."

Understandable preplanning.

She had also splurged on a bag of Percy Pigs, a tub of brownie bites, and even some strawberry laces.

"I feel like I'm off to the beach!" I said joyfully.

"Don't eat them all at once," Beth said sensibly. "We need to save some for the journey back."

"Yes, *Mum*," I teased, ripping a packet open and helping myself to the strawberry laces. Immediately I held them up to Beth's face, wafting the synthetic strawberry scent her way to entice her into a strawberry lace-tying contest with our tongues. (I was by far the best, but that was a given. My tongue was the more athletic of the two.)

We filled the carriage with our childish squeals of "cheat!"

and unembarrassed laughter, drawing disapproving gazes from the other first-class passengers. Oh well.

"Sorry," Beth would say, raising her hand in supplication, before swiftly falling back into giggles.

I didn't look at my phone the entire journey. Beth did reach for hers a few times but didn't let it distract her. She was careful not to show me the screen, though. Maybe work stuff.

Eventually, she put her phone down and we watched a few pre-downloaded Netflix series on the final leg of our journey. Beth offered me the earbud, wiping it against her sleeve first lest there was any earwax on it. She was always so thoughtful like that. By this point I was three gins down, and the only thing lining my stomach were double-knotted lumps of strawberry laces, Percy Pig heads, and the odd brownie. Not the best mix; I was feeling quite heady.

She had downloaded a few episodes of *Merlin*, the BBC series that both of us had admitted to enjoying a little too much when it was airing in our early teens. I was a Gwaine fan, but she was ever dedicated to Arthur.

"I like the name *Gwaine*," I told her, overpronouncing it with a tangible Welsh accent. "*Ger-waine*," I said again as the train began to pull into our station, and Beth and I started gathering our things. There was an audible sigh of relief from the bald man sitting behind us. Clearly our conversations hadn't riveted him during the three-hour journey from London.

"It's a nice name," Beth agreed, to humor me more than anything. She had only drunk one can of gin and had taken charge of the shopping bag when she noticed me opening my third can and already eyeing up a fourth. The bag was now stowed safely out of my reach in her rucksack, which was otherwise full to the brim with books and even a bottle of sunscreen.

I knew I hadn't given her much information when it came

to tantra workshops and what could be expected of our week ahead, but I had hoped she would have gleaned that it was in fact a *workshop* and not a spa week.

We were here to realign our chakras and have conversations with our yonis. We were not going to be lounging outside by a pool in bikinis reading *Heatstroke* and *Doctor Zhivago*.

But as we clambered awkwardly onto the platform and down the slippery cobblestone slopes leading to the taxi rank, I didn't think it best to remind her of the week's agenda. Particularly since the journey had been such a refreshing return to our usual carefree silliness. I wanted that to last as long as possible.

CHAPTER 30
BETH

THE WORKSHOP LOCATION was remarkably grand. The manor house sat behind a long gravel drive, and there were *grounds*. Already, there were people milling about together, sitting on benches under giant oak trees and gathering in huddles by French doors with mugs of tea and polite conversation. The official start was the following day, but it seemed people were getting to know one another already.

Despite the bucolic setting (her being such a city girl), Serena beamed at me as she got her rucksack out of the boot and tipped our driver too much. Clearly the gin was still coursing through her system. I made a mental note to get her a cup of coffee and a sandwich as soon as possible.

There was a small reception area at the entrance, manned by an older woman wearing oversized and bedazzled spectacles and a long flowing caftan. She fitted the tantra theme perfectly, and even spoke like she had drifted out of an ecstasy cloud and was just coming down to earth again.

"Good evening, ladies," she whispered, to which our responding "Hi!s" sounded overexcited.

"We're the Hamilton-Jones party," Serena told her as the lady scanned her clipboard.

"Welcome. I'm Alice. Yes, I see you here. I'll just get your keys and take you upstairs."

"We're sharing a room," Serena reminded me as we waited to be escorted.

The hall was striking and very wide, smelling faintly of incense and that old musty scent that never leaves posh houses. Photos hung of the family who had once owned the premises, all of them looking stringently Edwardian with their bushy mustaches and lack of teeth.

"I wonder what they think of the place now," Serena whispered—or attempted to—in my ear. Her voice echoed around the cavernous hall, but Alice, who had just returned with our keys, merely smiled.

"I'd like to think they'd be pleased," she told her. "The Richardsons were a very modern family for their day, and full of scandal too."

"Great! My kind of party," Serena said, following Alice, who had begun to gather up the material of her caftan so she didn't trip as she walked up the stairs. "I would definitely bang that guy in the photo. I love a mustache in my nether regions."

"Serena!" I said, slightly appalled.

Alice paused for a moment, turning her head as if to make a comment but deciding against it. I couldn't tell from behind her if she was horrified like myself, or maybe agreeing with Serena? From the way she walked a little faster and farther away from us though, I guessed the former.

Serena gave me a confused look, as if to say, *what's wrong with thinking that?*

I shook my head at her but said nothing. This didn't help.

Serena sped up to match Alice's pace and said: "Beth's never experienced oral sex so she's not going to understand," she said in an undertone to Alice as if I wouldn't hear. But I did.

With an embarrassed moan, I scurried behind them like an obedient dog. I just had to ignore her and hope there were no other expletive moments during our stay.

She was definitely being weird, even with the alcohol in her system, though Serena was notorious for being able to handle her drink better than anyone. I couldn't understand how three cans of gin and tonic could affect her.

"How long have you been running tantra workshops here?" I asked Alice, to disrupt Serena before she could carry on.

"Oh, about six years. The space is split between several organizations and charities. We also run silent retreats, meditation, and yoga—but tantra is our most popular."

"I'm not surprised." Serena grinned widely.

"Here you are," Alice said finally, barely out of breath. I had taken a moment's rest against one of the faded wallpapered walls.

"There's a bathroom down the hall and it's just you up here so it's all yours. Fresh towels can be requested, okay?" She opened the door to our room, and we found it flooded with light as the sun set just over the driveway. It cast a gorgeous shade over the plain room.

Two double beds sat pushed up against the wall. There was a small TV on a desk, with some complimentary tea and sugars, and the world's smallest travel kettle.

"A hairdryer and the safe are in this wardrobe," Alice said. "There's a phone in the bedside cabinet, although there is a charge for any calls made outside of the house. In the bathroom you'll find all the usual items for washing, plus some complimentary lubrication from one of our partners."

Lubrication?!

"If you need anything else at all just let me or one of the other workshop leaders know. You'll meet Doug, Beatrice, and Lanni later. Dinner is at seven p.m. this evening and we have three options available: one meat, one vegetarian, and one vegan. Lanni, our team leader, will be doing a greeting during dinner, and your first workshop begins promptly at ten tomorrow morning in the sunroom. There's a map and full list of workshop activities on the dresser."

Serena and I bobbed our heads in unison like ventriloquist's dummies. Both of us just wanted Alice to leave now so that we could unpack and explore and discuss the upcoming activities.

"Are there any rules we need to follow?" Serena asked, slightly more serious than she had been before.

"Not particularly. We encourage free space and free thinking. The front doors are locked at ten in the evening, but open again at five in the morning if you desire an early morning walk. The grounds here are very lovely, particularly at dawn. The front desk is also unmanned during those hours, but we practitioners stay here during the course of the workshop so we're on hand in any emergencies. Okay?"

"Brilliant," I told her, before Serena could start pestering her for more information. I wanted to get settled and be alone before dinner. (Serena not counting.) "Thank you, Alice."

"Of course," she said. "I'll see you in the dining room at seven." She shut the door behind her.

I immediately flung myself back onto the sheets, which released a scent of flowery washing powder. Serena laughed and copied me.

"Well, this is plush!"

"I didn't skimp on the luxuries. Only the best for my best friend on her sexual odyssey."

I bit my lip to stop from retorting that this experience wasn't really for me. I hadn't asked to book a weeklong trip to a tantra workshop, and I certainly hadn't suggested we go to a fancy—likely very expensive—retreat either. But Serena *had* paid.

"What are these workshops, then?" Serena bolted up from the bed like she had a rocket up her arse and reached for the paper on the dresser. A smile crept onto her face as she read.

"Did you hear what she said, by the way? About free lubrication?" I asked.

"This *is* a tantra workshop," Serena repeated, still scanning the sheet. "It seems appropriate that we might want to wank off at some point. We're meant to be connecting with our sexual energies after all."

Suddenly I didn't want to lie on my bed anymore. How many people before me had wanked off on this bed? Or done god knows what else?

Serena seemingly read my mind and began to laugh heartily.

"Oh, come on! We slept on worse during university."

That was true. How many times were mattresses changed at student houses? Not often I'd expect.

But we weren't eighteen anymore.

"What's on the agenda?" I asked, crossing my arms and walking over to Serena. She tried to conceal her amusement as she handed me the sheet, clearly watching my face for a reaction of horror. I refused to give her the satisfaction, although I couldn't lie and say that I *wasn't* horrified.

"'Walk the Earth. Banish your self-consciousness as you return to the earth in this revitalizing workshop, in which we encourage participants to channel their divine energies in ritual touch, movement, and affirmations. Clothing is optional.' Right," I said. The next line included reassurances that all workshops highly prized consent and comfort, but all attendees must embrace nudity with compassion, sacredness, and courage. "What the hell have you gotten me into?"

She couldn't contain her cackle of glee at this.

"What am I going to tell people?" I looked over the agenda once more. I wasn't *not* panicking. "That's not even the worst one! It looks like they build up to *devotions* and *ritual touching* throughout the week. Ritual touching. Look! On Thursday we have the *Divine Devotion*, aka the *Puja*, and on Friday we have an initiation! When we take what we've learned about ourselves, our bodies, and our spirits throughout the week and channel it for self-pleasure among the group. It's a genuine orgy."

"It's not an orgy," Serena said, continuing to laugh. "It's not! I promise. I looked it up. It's more like a body confidence ceremony. You choose what you want to do and how much skin you want to show, and if you want others to participate."

"Others!" My voice broke as I sat back on my bed. A mattress that had been humped on innumerable times was clearly the least of my worries this week.

"Only if you want them to! I looked at the comments for this workshop. Some people chose to just sit in the room in just their underwear, others choose to masturbate or just touch themselves. Only a few actually have penetrative sex."

"What? And this is like a team-building exercise?"

"It's more like a confidence-building exercise. You take what you've learned throughout the week and channel it. I mean, after four days of being touched by strangers, talking about our yonis, and stripping off when we want to, you won't be as self-conscious as you feel right now."

"What are you going to do?" I demanded. Serena shrugged.

"I don't know. We'll just have to wait and see what we learn, I suppose."

"And we can say no if we want to?" I had the sudden desire to grab my rucksack and run.

"No one is going to force you to do anything. It's all optional. Remember, you only have to do what you're comfortable doing and if you don't want to do it, we leave." Serena smiled amiably at me and then winked as she took the brochure out of my hands.

I sighed and pulled myself further onto the white sheets of the bed, crossing my legs beneath me.

Watching Serena skip around the room unpacking like she had just moved in, I had a sense of foreboding deep in my stomach.

Yet despite Serena's laissez-faire attitude, I didn't want to upset her or make her angry by blowing up at her. What if she felt I was being a stick-in-the-mud about something as trivial—to her—as tantra?

She already knew my misgivings about the workshop, and the fact that I wasn't keen on coming in the first place with my initial response of "why?" when she told me she had bought us tickets. But as with all elements of our relationship, I wanted her to be impressed with my stoicism and ability to try new things. I didn't want her to see me as boring, because if she did, I didn't know if our friendship would continue. And I didn't know who I would be without her.

"Why can I hear the voice of the Tesco self-service machine saying *unexpected item in shagging area*?" I purposely joked, flinging myself backward across my pillows to make Serena laugh. It worked. Foreboding be damned.

CHAPTER 31
SERENA

IT WAS LIKE being on a school trip, except the students were thirty years older and the curfew was two hours later. Shit food still: a standard bulk-baked shepherd's pie, macaroni and cheese, and a chicken-less salad with browning avocado.

I stocked up on the mac and cheese, helping myself to more than was technically polite, but I was starving and eager to line my stomach. Beth was much more cautious, spooning tiny amounts of carrots and peas onto her plate, alongside her shepherd's pie, as if making up for my greediness by taking less. The way I saw it, for £1,495 per person, the least the workshop could provide was an all-you-can-eat buffet.

We chose to sit at a table for two, rather than join one of the congregating groups in the midsection of the food hall. We weren't the only people to have signed up for the workshop as a pair, but we were clearly the only noncouple of these prematched duos. At the other two-person tables we eyed several couples already glowy-eyed and buzzing with attraction for each other.

"There are less people than I thought there'd be," Beth said, adding salt to her plate like others add gravy.

"Want some shepherd's pie with that salt?" I commented sarcastically, but Beth didn't react. "Well, don't come crying to me when you get hypertension. And people probably haven't come down yet."

"Was there a limit on how many people could take part?"

I shrugged, spooning the first forkful of mac and cheese into my mouth. It was rubbery and overly peppered. Not as good as Zoey's.

"So what do you think so far?" I asked. "Any bangable patrons?"

Beth knew I was teasing. There was no one bangable here. The odd twentysomething was scattered around here or there, nervous-looking or already paired up with someone. There were quite a few in their thirties and forties, by the look of them at least, all approaching middle-age faster than they'd like and preparing for a midlife crisis or an "adventure." And then, confidently sitting in extravagant bohemian wear and beaming smiles, were the fifty-plus patrons. They looked friendly at least, but not the kind of people I would be comfortable with touching my yoni in the more revealing rituals.

"Will they separate us into age groups?" Beth leaned over to whisper, not wanting to insult anyone sitting nearby. It wasn't like I was any wiser than her, but I thought it would be best to appear happy either way.

"I guess we'll find out. I doubt it, though, there are only about twenty of us here so we'd be in pretty tiny groups if they did split us up."

Beth's expression made it clear that the latter idea would be preferable—but that was the whole point of tantra, to leave your head and enter your heart. To remove your inhibitions and self-consciousness through devotions and spiritual rituals.

At least, that's what the *About Page* said on the website when I booked the tickets.

"Where's your phone?" Beth asked out of the blue.

"Hm?" I said, acting as if I hadn't heard her while I stabbed more macaroni onto my fork. "There's definitely more mac than cheese in this recipe."

"Your phone?" Beth repeated. "I haven't seen it all day. I would have thought you'd be attached to it in case Arnold called with a work or wedding catastrophe. Or Zoey?"

I shuffled in my seat, trying to remain nonchalant as I chewed my food incredibly slowly. I wasn't going to talk about Zoey; I'd slip up if I did. Instead I said: "This week is about you. I'm supporting you and focused on you, so the last thing you need is for me to be constantly on my phone answering emails and playing *Zen Koi.*"

Beth narrowed her eyes. I needed to change the subject.

Thankfully, I was saved by the appearance of Alice and another slender woman who I assumed was Lanni, the workshop leader.

"Good evening, everybody," Lanni said in a calm voice, with the edge of a fading Scandinavian accent. "Welcome to our Tantra Sensation workshop. I hope you have all had a chance to settle in and familiarize yourself with the grounds and talk to some of your fellow workshoppers. I just wanted to take a quick moment to introduce myself and the rest of the team who will be supporting you through your journey this week."

I glanced at Beth and both of us rolled our eyes.

"I am Lanni, I shall be running the devotions, or Puja, workshops with you. This is Alice, who I believe most of you have met. Alice is our Shakti practitioner with many years of experience of tantra massage and touch guidance to share."

"I bet she does," I whispered out of the corner of my mouth to Beth, who coughed to stifle a sudden laugh.

"Behind you, you'll find Doug." All heads turned to the back of the room where a paunchy man wearing an open Hawaiian shirt and khaki jean shorts was standing confidently against the wall with a clear cup of herbal tea. He raised his hand in a friendly greeting. "He will be running our movement and innocence sessions. And to your right you'll find Beatrice, who is also a tantra massage practitioner who will be running our sessions on the power of yoni and vajra."

No need to translate those two words, I noticed guests either sit up straighter or recoil at the mention of the Sanskrit for female and male genitalia.

"Consent and comfort are two of the foremost aspects of this week's workshop. While clothing is optional within any of our daily workshops, we ask that patrons remain clothed on the grounds and within the halls in between workshops and during mealtimes. We also remind all our attendees that at no point will you be asked to do anything you don't want to do." I noticed Beth shuffling in her seat, her shoulders dropping with relief.

Lanni placed her hands atop her flat chest and closed her eyes as if in prayer. "What I will ask is that you dig deep into *why* you feel uncomfortable with any of the tantra rituals, and to sit within your discomfort for a moment or two before deciding whether you are unable to partake in an activity. We will start your journey slowly into the realms of ritual awakening, with compassion and spiritual guidance."

She opened her eyes and smiled softly to each corner of the room, capturing the gaze of every one of the workshoppers. I refused to look away in case she thought I was one such "nervous" patron who would flinch at the idea of being touched or taking part in a massage class.

However, Beth took a moment to feverishly concentrate on picking a hangnail she noticed on her finger.

"There are no incorrect ways to experience tantra. This is a journey of pure self-development, filled with intimate connections between spirit and heart, which at the end of the week we hope will lead to a divine experience that will allow you to leave this place and live your life from a place of pleasure."

I glanced around the room. It seemed like the others were becoming enraptured by the pure confidence of Lanni and her belief in what she preached.

"Why does she remind me of Charles Manson?" Beth whispered. I snorted and instantly covered my nose as if I had sneezed.

"Excuse me," I said aloud; several eyes had broken from Lanni to look at me.

"We will begin our first session at ten tomorrow morning, in the sunroom. Please leave all electronics and extraneous items in your rooms, unless you have brought a totem that can remain on your person."

"A totem?" Beth mouthed to me. "Like a safety blanket?"

I refused to snort again. It was clear that Lanni's speech was supposed to be the kick-off whistle that announced how serious and wonderful this experience was about to be. I imagined for a more confident or experienced person this would be the equivalent of signing into a spa and receiving your complimentary gown and flip-flops before entering the steamy dressing rooms that smell like eucalyptus. I could simply smell chlorine.

"Well, that was enlightening." I turned to Beth after Lanni finished off her speech and invited all of us to return to our meals.

"God, I need water," Beth said without listening to me. I wasn't surprised with all the sodium on her plate.

THE FOLLOWING DAY Beth and I slept in and had to rush down to the canteen to get the last dregs of breakfast. Already the kitchen staff were clearing away tureens of leftover egg whites and the odd vegetarian sausage. Beth and I scrambled to ladle the last of the baked beans and fried tomatoes onto our plates before they took those too and returned to our table with a pitiful breakfast and two cups of tea.

"Good morning, ladies." The tantra massage practitioner approached us out of nowhere. "I didn't get a chance to properly introduce myself last night. I'm Beatrice." She didn't hold out her hand like I expected but placed a hand on each of our shoulders. I suppose in tantra there is no such thing as personal space.

"Hi, I'm Beth," Beth said with a polite smile, and I mirrored her expression.

"And I'm Serena."

"I'm so pleased you could join us this week. Is this your first time with Tantra Sensations?"

"First time with tantra anything," Beth said, feigning confidence.

"Oh, how wonderful," Beatrice beamed. She had pastel pink hair bundled into three small buns around the top of her head so that she unintentionally resembled a satellite, and she wore long empty chains around her neck that swung precariously close to my bean juice as she leaned forward over our table. "It's a wonderful path to follow when you begin. A true warrior's path." She inhaled deeply with her eyes closed.

I had been hoping that this wouldn't be such a hippie experience—for Beth's sake as well as my own—but clearly, I was mistaken.

"You will walk through the troubles to the light," she began, opening her eyes to look at Beth with a warm and open gaze. "You will laugh, you will cry, and you will question."

"That's . . . good," Beth said, looking back from me to Beatrice to me again. "That's exactly what we're after."

"It's so wonderful," Beatrice said, removing her hand from me and placing it atop her hand already on Beth. Clearly, she didn't feel the need to connect with my energy any longer. Grateful to be without the hold on my fork arm though, I began to tuck in.

She hovered a little while longer but eventually moved on to some other *divine* soul to express her pleasure at seeing them returning for another workshop. The patron in question held out her arms to Beatrice but the two of them didn't embrace, merely clasped each other's arms and shut their eyes.

"I feel like I need 3D glasses to see this energy these people keep referring to," I said.

"*This energy* is tantra, I believe," Beth said sarcastically. "I hope there's a big lunch, I'm going to be starving later if this is all we get." She cut her tomato into quarters. Smart. It would last longer.

"WELCOME FRIENDS, WELCOME. Please find a space within the room, wherever is comfortable to you." Beth and I stuck tightly together.

Lanni was leading the opening session, wearing a short batwing cheesecloth dress and black underwear that was clearly visible whenever she stretched out her arms in front of the floor-to-ceiling windows.

"Welcome. Today's opening session is titled *Walk the Earth*. It is a simple and calming ritual we like to open the week with which encourages each of you to throw off any inhibitions that may have gathered outside of these walls. This is a safe space, a spiritual space. There is no judgement here." She began to walk slowly about the room, her accent emerging more as she became more swept up. "No one is too old or too young, no one is too thin or too fat, no one is too ugly or too beautiful. You are genderless, ageless, bodyless."

Patrons began closing their eyes and gently swayed on the spot, some leaning back to direct their faces to the ceiling. I knew I should be doing the same, listening to Lanni's words as instructions and not merely dismissing them. But my focus wasn't on releasing my inhibitions but on Beth, and—helpless to my own heart—Zoey.

She will be arriving in London today.

I would have met her at Euston and traveled with her to the flat viewings she had booked. They were spread out across the city from a studio in Finchley to a house share in Kennington. She wanted to stay near a tube line that could take her into Euston, to make it as easy as possible to make trips to and from Liverpool when she needed to.

I hadn't replied to any of her texts since the day before we left to catch our train to Devon. But last night I had taken a sneak peek at my messages when Beth had fallen asleep. Two cans of gin and three episodes of *The Walking Dead* had finally subdued her.

Zoey had sent me updates about her planned journey, some messages about her Airbnb not being a total shitshow and how she was heading to four viewings on her first day in the city. I refused to break my own rule and reply to her. I couldn't chat to her like nothing was different—she was moving to London. Things *were* different.

"Here goes nothing," Beth said to me out of the corner of her mouth as Lanni passed us. I looked at her to see what she meant and found her emulating the other patrons around her, head back, eyes closed, and gently swaying. I followed suit.

"Dissolve the negative imprints of past sexual experiences.

Dissolve the criticisms and the concerns; they are meaningless. Connect with your inner energy. Inhale deeply, feel it growing inside you like a bubble of light fit to burst. Inhale again."

A loud gasp of breath was taken by the group, almost harmonized, while we all swayed on the spot.

"You're here to have a relationship with yourself. Forget all the nonsense we carry around about our bodies, it doesn't matter. You are a ball of light. A powerful energy: find it, use it. Now"—Lanni's voice dropped in pitch—"speak your intention to the universe. What is it you are here to do? Speak it aloud, no one is listening but the universe. Speak your intentions."

People began to whisper and mutter reasons for their coming to the workshop. A woman's voice next to me said: "To be comfortable with enacting my sexual fantasies." Over and over again she repeated it. "Sexual fantasies. Sexual fantasies."

"Enjoy sex with my wife," one male voice rang out.

"To feel confident as someone living with HIV," another voice cried.

"Find a way to orgasm without watching pornography."

I glanced over at Beth as each workshopper revealed their aims, but she hadn't reacted at all. She was still swaying on the spot with her eyes closed, clearly getting into this. Her mouth moved a miniscule amount, whispering whatever her intentions were to the universe. I guessed that they were "to lose my virginity." I edged closer to hear.

Out of the corner of my eye I noticed Lanni had spotted me glancing around, without speaking an intention. I quickly resumed the position and began muttering, "To help Beth lose her virginity. To help Beth lose her virginity."

"Now," Lanni's voice called out over the hubbub of intentions. "Walk the Earth!" she cried, like a warrior sending her troops off to battle. "Continue sharing your intentions with the universe but walk Mother Earth and tell one another. Share your hopes and your dreams, speak the truth to one another."

All around people began to bump in and out of my contact zone. Shoulders grazed mine and I found myself ducking between two patrons as they almost collided with me. It was like PE class all over again.

"To help Beth lose her virginity," I repeated in between dodging. I had lost Beth somewhere in all the noise and movement. But I knew that this was how it was supposed to go. This wasn't a vacation, after all, we were here to work. Otherwise, why call it a workshop?

CHAPTER 32
BETH

TANTRA WORKSHOPS WERE oddly domestic experiences.

From sleeping on memory-foam mattresses, to *EastEnders* always being on TV in the common room.

You wouldn't know you had stumbled upon a tantra workshop if you walked up the drive, unless you happened to peer through one of the windows at the back of the house and saw several nude people sitting on cushions in a circle and touching one another's shoulders.

The first workshop had been fairly easy, much like a drama class taught by an overzealous teacher just returned from a sabbatical in Thailand. Lanni was incredibly passionate, but her voice had an ASMR quality that was surprisingly soothing. I found myself hypnotized enough to feel comfortable walking around the floor, grazing my hands across the other patrons' bodies, all the while whispering my intention for the week.

"To not be afraid of sexual intimacy. To not be afraid of sexual intimacy."

I lost Serena in the crowd, and I realized I didn't mind. Having her out of my sight meant that the tense charge between us and our friendship was lost, and I could connect with whatever energy Lanni was saying was within my body.

Whether I *did* connect with such energy was another thing, but I didn't mind the attempt.

The second workshop was to take place at two p.m. after a light lunch and a two-hour break in which we were encouraged to go out and enjoy the grounds.

"I'm going to take a nap," Serena said after we finished our Greek salads and another cup of tea in the common room.

"Okay," I said, not interested in joining her. "I think I'll go walk the grounds for a bit. Like Lanni said." She nodded but didn't say anything else as she pushed her plate away and got up to leave.

"Do we still have some of those chocolate brownies?"

"Yep, they're in a bag in the wardrobe."

"Oh great."

"Don't eat them all. We need some for the journey home."

"I won't, I won't," she said, smiling her usual charming smile, and walked away. She wouldn't eat them all, she'd leave just *one* for the journey home, that we would have to share. As if that were considerate. But what was the point in hiding them from her?

I took my mug with me, cupping it between my fingers as I stepped out onto the veranda and gazed across the long widening field behind it.

It was a true vista of land, with the coast just visible if you squinted. It's the sort of place that someone famous would have enjoyed painting, back in the heyday of pastoral landscapes.

I would have liked to have taken a photo and perhaps sent it to Evan. We had been texting for days now, ever since our meeting. But I still hadn't told Serena about him. It was the sort of thing I'd normally be bursting to share with her. But I resented that she hadn't even deigned to ask about my life, beyond discussing my sexual odyssey. We used to talk about things, but now it seemed we only ever talked about her life or this bloody experiment. I was beginning to feel less like her friend and more like her test subject.

"Hi," a voice called out to my left, pulling me out of my thoughts. I looked over and saw a group of workshoppers sitting at an old picnic bench under a lamp heater. "Come and join us. It's much warmer under here."

"Sure," I said, sitting down at the end as two fiftysomething women scooched up a little for me.

"I'm Tony," said the man who had invited me over.

"I'm Beth."

"Hi Beth," the two women next to me chorused and giggled. "We don't usually talk in unison," said the one closest to me. "I'm Eileen, and this is Beryl." She gestured to the woman who was clearly her friend. "We're club members, so we're used to seeing each other all the time."

"Club members?" I asked, looking at the two men across from me who had laughed.

"We just mean that we attend a lot of these sessions together," Beryl explained. "We met here three years ago."

"Oh, I see." I smiled. They seemed sweet and very open.

"Is this your first time?" The gentleman opposite me asked. He was the only one of the group who made me slightly uncomfortable, probably due to the fact that he was a man nearly double my age. It's a bit like running into a teacher at Glastonbury a few years after school.

"Yes. How can you tell?" I joked weakly, but they all laughed.

"It gets easier the more sessions you do," Beryl said.

"Don't skip any, that's crucial," Eileen continued for her. "You'll find yourself regaining your inhibitions if you don't do the whole thing in order."

"That's why the workshops are laid out the way they are," Tony explained. "So that you build on each achievement until you finally get to the initiation." God, it sounded like a cult when he put it like that.

"Can I ask what you all are here to achieve?" I asked, slightly nervously. "Is that allowed?"

Beryl laughed, and Eileen answered: "Oh yes dear, it's not like prison. We can share what we're here for." They all laughed roaringly.

"I'm here to work on my orgasms," Beryl said, not a blush in sight.

"And I want to be better at helping my husband to orgasm," Eileen said, looking to Tony as if this was pass the parcel.

"I'm not her husband, just to clarify," Tony said. Eileen gently patted him on his hand playfully, and he took it in his own and kissed it. This was a very strange little group.

"I come to a workshop once a year to work on my body confidence," Tony admitted.

"That's great," I said. "I mean they're all great." I was being honest. I respected that these were things they wanted to work on in their middle-age and beyond, and I particularly admired their lack of embarrassment.

"Wait a minute, we haven't got to me yet," the man opposite me said. "And I'm Louis by the way."

"We call him Lord Louis," Eileen said to me in a fake whisper so that Louis could hear, and he rolled his eyes. "On account of the fact that he's something like the king's cousin three times removed or something."

"I'm his third cousin, four times removed. It's barely a connection at all," Louis said, leaning forward to me again. "These two like to make a fuss about it, though. Anyway, I'm here to work on intimacy and connection."

"That's interesting too," I said. I hadn't realized how many aspects there were to tantra and what it could help with.

"And you?" Eileen asked. "You can tell us. It helps to share your intentions, after all."

"Yeah, it does," I said, and took a deep breath. "I'm here to learn how not to be afraid of sexual intimacy."

All four of them began nodding and I felt my shoulders drop and the tightness in my chest loosen. There was not a single iota of judgment. But that chimed with what Lanni had been saying in the initial gathering.

Effectively the first workshop was stripping us back to the basics, to the evolution of our sexual energy in order for us to remove the baggage that we had attached to it along the way.

I paused for a moment considering this, letting my eyes glaze over as the others continued talking to me about their various experiences with the workshops to come. Eileen was particularly reassuring when it came to discussing nudity and how entirely optional it was—but how freeing it was when you feel able to do it.

By the afternoon, when we all returned to the sunroom for the second half of Lanni's Walk the Earth workshop, I felt my hips naturally swaying with confidence. I felt energized, like I had just had a sugary drink, and I was eager to consume more. This was more than just enlightenment, this was relief that this experience might actually produce results or at the very least some understanding of my sexuality and boundaries. Suddenly just being here and communicating with others about my sexuality and desires already made me feel lighter about my virginity status.

"What did I miss?" Serena said, rushing into the room last, yawning from her nap.

"Nothing yet," I told her, trying to keep in the zone I had entered the room in.

"Oh goody," she said mockingly.

"Welcome back, everyone," Lanni said from the front of the room. "I would just like to take a moment to return us back to the place we previously were before the break. Please walk around the room at your own pace, but this time reach out and touch your fellow neighbors. Place your hands on their shoulders, their arms, and their hands. No need to grip or pat, simply graze and stroke and feel. Feel the heat of their skin, their vitality, and their essence pouring out of them. Release the tensions of your body wherever you feel someone touch you, inhale and exhale. Take your time."

I jumped into action immediately, allowing my arms to fall where they may, feeling the soft supple skin of the younger patrons, and the moisturized wrinkles of the older ones. Heat trailed and perfume dragged on my fingertips, and I felt the fine edges of others' skin pass my shoulder blade, the exposed skin of my neck and my waist.

Nothing was sexual in this movement—nothing obvious anyway. I was giving them permission, but no one was truly touching me. Not in the way that the man had during the speed-dating fiasco, not in the way that even Guy—or *Rupert*—had tried to when I straddled him. This was an innocent touch.

I caught Serena's eyes briefly through the crowd and I could see that she was biting her bottom lip so as not to giggle. She just hadn't got it.

Surprising, really, for someone so sexually in tune.

I wondered what she had said was her intention for the uni-

verse that morning? To have fun? To experience a new form of
orgasm? Honestly, I hoped she might have spoken something
similar to my own intention: not to fear intimacy.

"Lovely, well done. Well done," Lanni said soothingly.

Our next instruction was slightly more intense, and I could
see what Eileen and the others had meant when they said that
each workshop escalates through your comfort levels.

Lanni instructed us to find a partner within the room, someone we were drawn to for whatever reason, sexually, aestheti-
cally, or even by smell. Before I even had a chance to consider
my options, Serena had grabbed my wrist and was standing so
close to me our hip bones were grinding together.

I was hoping to experiment a little, maybe work with one
of the seasoned attendees I had spoken with at lunch time. But
instead I licked my lips and just accepted that this was the way
it was going to be. Me and Serena, as always.

"Now, the smaller of the two partners should lie on the floor."

Well, that was me, so I did as Lanni said.

"Shut your eyes and place your hands palm down to the
floor. Just relax. Sink into the floor. Feel your energy filling
every cavern of your body from the very tips of your toes to the
follicles of your head. It's spreading and spreading."

I found myself wanting to drift off.

"Those standing, please kneel beside your partners." I felt
Serena's knees at the side of my rib cage. "Place one hand
central on their belly, and the other on their chest." This was
where I sensed, rather than saw, Serena's hesitation. No touch
came initially and when it did, I heard her giggle. One hand
rested on my stomach but the other wasn't on my chest, it was
nearer my neck.

This should have been easy for us. We weren't fussed about

nakedness, and we were very tactile. Yet something was clearly off.

"It's fine," I whispered to her, not opening my eyes as I wanted to capture the bubble of energy I had found myself in earlier. But with each of Serena's giggles I was slipping further and further away from what Lanni was trying to help us connect to. Soon I began to feel inhibitions creeping in, and that wasn't what I wanted at all.

"I can't believe people believe this shit," Serena said quietly, although it sounded loud enough to me that I wondered if others around us could hear.

"Shh!" I twitched and readjusted my shoulders, trying to reenter the calm space Lanni was trying to create.

I thought Serena was here to help me. Yet her being there was just making this more difficult. It was like I had an audience, someone judging my performance.

"Channel their energy," Lanni was saying to the kneeling partners. "Feel their breath and their spirits rising to your touch. The beat of their heart and soul against your twinning skins. They are alive. They are alive."

"I now understand the frustration women experience when their midwives keep reminding them to breathe during labor," Serena said out of the corner of her mouth. "I've been breathing my whole life; I don't need you to remind me." I refused to react. It wasn't funny and I was trying to concentrate.

I am alive, I thought. *I am alive.*

"Softly, whisper their name to them. Remind them who they are, how powerful they are. Just say their name over and over again. Whisper it into their ear, say it to their heart. Just their name."

Serena did nothing. I could imagine her opening and closing

her mouth, faking that she was saying my name, but she never actually did it.

And within a few minutes of hearing other names being spoken round the room—Beryl, Tony, Grace, Achmed, Sam—I lost all hope of Serena taking this seriously and broke out of my bubble. The day's growth was lost.

CHAPTER 33
SERENA

BETH HARDLY SPOKE to me over the next few days. After the first workshop she had blanked me when I tried to debrief with her, and instead she chose to go to dinner with a group of older patrons. I joined them in the canteen and introduced myself but didn't partake in much of their conversation, which seemed to involve the different types of tantra. (We were doing white tantra, a spiritual approach, apparently.)

I hadn't even realized there were types of tantra before, and I doubted white tantra would have been the one I would have selected if I had known or done my research before booking. I was more likely to have gone with red tantra, which focused more on sexuality and sensuality, since that was what Beth needed to work on more than anything. At least in my opinion.

After I finished my meal, I excused myself and went upstairs to the bedroom, where I sat on my phone, emailing Arnold's wedding coordinators and calligraphists, organizing the little elements I had promised to help him with. Beth didn't seem to care, or rather notice, when I left. She didn't even come looking for me when it was time for the evening socials.

She was obviously frustrated that I hadn't taken the initial workshop so seriously, but honestly there is only so much chanting I can take.

The second day's workshop was a lot like the first, except we were outdoors and focusing on movement. Doug ran this session, shirtless and with his hat on backwards like a wannabe skateboarder. His stomach wobbled as he demonstrated the positions he wanted us to get into using one another to balance ourselves.

I berated myself for focusing on his paunch during a workshop where body weight, age, and beauty shouldn't matter, but he lost me when he described our joint pose as the giant centipede. Beth didn't laugh.

Once again Beth had hastened to sit with her new tantra pals at dinner before I had even got my cutlery. It didn't feel great to be avoided, but I didn't feel I was missing much. The conversation was hardly the most riveting I had ever heard. Sitting on my bed sorting out the small amount of wedding tasks I had taken on for Arnold, as a good friend—and glutton for punishment—was preferable to listening to inane conversations about tantric experiences.

But on that third evening, waiting for Beth to come up from dinner, I broke my own cardinal workshop rule: not to message Zoey.

She had texted *again*, after four unreplied messages, to ask how the workshop was going, and I crumbled.

> Hey. Sorry for not replying, I can hardly get any signal out here! It's gorgeous though, a very idyllic countryside manor. I feel like I'm in a Jane Austen novel.

> The workshop itself is not-Austen though. There are about twenty of us and we spend most of our time breathing and chanting in carpeted rooms like school children. It's supposed to return us to a childlike innocence and reboot our sexual evolution or some shit.

> I say "some shit" as honestly, I don't think it's working for me. Although Beth seems into it. How about you?

> How's London life–the early days?

I watched the *typing* . . . button at the top of my screen until the message came through.

> Oh good! I'm so glad it's going well for Beth; I can't wait to hear about the later stages. I hear it can get pretty hot at those kinds of gatherings. Jane Austen certainly would not approve. London's fine–it misses you!–can't wait to meet up when you're back. X

London misses me? She can't wait to meet up?

This was not our usual way of speaking. It felt almost juvenile, like we were teenagers dabbling in dating for the first time.

I climbed out of bed to get one of Beth's remaining gin cans and sipped it gingerly while thinking of a reply. I was miles away in Devon, so surely a little flirtation over text wouldn't be a bad thing.

> I miss you too. Particularly your body.
> One thing is for sure, tantra workshops
> make me horny. And there's not a single
> bangable person here!

I deleted the last line, not wanting to suggest I would have sex with just anyone.

> Pick up some tips for when you get back
> then, you can give me a tantra lesson.

And from there the sexting began. It was nothing I needed to go get the complimentary lubrication for, but still fun. It certainly released some of the sexual tension I was holding inside me, and I felt much more relaxed as I fell asleep that evening—well before Beth returned to the room.

"TANTRIC TOUCH IS incredibly powerful," Beatrice was explaining from her kneeling position on the floor.

For the first time clothes had come off some of the patrons. Beth's two older pals were both topless but still wearing lacy see-through bras. Another guy was sitting crossed legged in just his underwear. One woman was completely naked on top; she'd kept her jeans on, but her bulbous breasts hung out, free from boob-jail. Her boyfriend's hands rested on her stomach from where he sat behind her in a straddle.

Beth and I remained clothed, although we had both opted to take off our jumpers. I didn't want to be too overdressed.

We were sitting in a circle on cushions, while Beatrice knelt in the center next to a naked woman who lay face down, her bottom half covered by a fake-fur blanket.

"It is not a form of massage used to instigate an orgasm,

but a form of massage that uses a partner's natural energy and chakras to relax them into a place beyond the physical."

She was rubbing her hands with heavily scented oils, letting the liquid run past her wrists and down her exposed arms, her chains and elbow bangles jangling.

"Tantric massage should be performed over a long period of time, to truly allow your partner to find peace and pleasure." Beatrice leaned over the naked woman, brought in especially for this presentation of tantric massage and thanked with gentle applause for her courageousness at sharing her body in a public forum. She had shed her dressing gown like it was nothing upon entering the room and lay down in the middle of the circle of cushions, as we all put our mugs and breakfast snacks to one side like a group of elderly pensioners gathering in a care home for a magic show.

"Tantric touch is far gentler than other massage," Beatrice said, smoothing the woman's body with the oils. "It should be done with care and a deep sense of love." Moving away from the woman's back she rubbed the oil all the way down her arm and began by massaging each finger. "Every place on the body should be touched, from the webbing between the fingers to the creases behind the knees. You are spreading your love with every moment of skin on skin, and you don't want to miss an inch."

While watching Beatrice massage the naked woman, I was struggling to stifle a yawn. This was a show I had seen too many times before, although usually in fast-forward and without sitting cross-legged on the floor. Already my legs had gone numb twice. Luckily I could hide my groans of pain in time with the naked woman's groans of pleasure, so all the other patrons just seemed to think I was enjoying the performance. This was what all the workshops felt like to me: a performance.

"A crucial part of a tantric massage is the touching of genitalia," Beatrice explained, smiling simperingly. "For women this is called a yoni massage and for men a lingam massage. It may sound intimidating at first, but it is a transcendent experience for your partner, and their pleasure will make any discomfort you initially feel dissipate like a rain cloud."

I highly doubted that. I looked at Beth, who was flushed and breathing a little quickly. This was exactly the sort of thing that would set her anxiety soaring.

All around us patrons had begun to shed more clothing as Beatrice continued to explain the art of a good yoni massage. The naked woman turned over for the full effect to be seen around the room. She was clearly high on oxytocin already—I would know that look anywhere—but strangely, without being involved in the moment, I didn't find myself caring much about how the woman was feeling or how Beatrice was pleasuring her. I had never been into voyeurism, and strangely I felt tense sitting next to Beth, who was stock still but had the nervousness of a chihuahua at the vet.

"I'm surprised you don't need to lie down after that," I said stretching my arm above my head after we were released for our lunch and afternoon walk. Beth ignored me.

"We should have just watched some feminist porn, saved us the whole afternoon," I joked, trying to get her on board, yet someone tutted at me as they left. As if they weren't all thinking the same thing.

"I thought it was helpful," Beth remarked tonelessly, her eyes skirting around the others exiting the room. She leaned over and quietly said: "You did promise to take it seriously."

"And I am!" I swore, frustrated that she felt the need to remind me, like a child on a school trip testing the boundaries. "It was just a joke."

Beth smiled and followed the crowd. It made me anxious; it was the kind of forced smile you give someone on the tube when you accidentally make eye contact after you've been secretly thinking what a dickhead they were for having their bag on a seat. It wasn't Beth's smile.

But I brushed it off and went to look at the workshop schedule on the bulletin board. The afternoon session was going to be about giving and receiving tantric massages from our fellow patrons—but only so far as we wanted to go. Honestly, I wanted to go the whole way—my body was stiff with disuse. What was the point of going to a sex workshop and not having sex? Okay a *tantra* workshop, but still, it's about sex.

"If I'm receiving," Beth whispered over my shoulder, "I'm only doing the neck, head, and shoulders version of that massage."

"It's not a facial." I laughed. "And besides, aren't you here for the full bodily experience? It's time to strip off, lie back, and think of England."

"It's not *that* kind of experience." Beth blushed horribly.

"Well," I began, pinching at her shoulder blades and she flinched. "I'm an excellent masseuse either way," I said confidently, believing that Beth would be my partner for the session.

After we returned that afternoon, I realized quickly that that wasn't the case. As soon as Beatrice instructed us to find a partner we were drawn to, Beth took off in the direction of one of the women (Eileen) and asked if she would be hers. I was left with a thirtysomething man called Sam, who was good enough for me, but still I was hurt that Beth didn't want me to work with her seeing as nudity was nothing between us. Dick-stick, anyone?

Regardless, I let the moment pass and ignored her for the rest of the session choosing—or demanding, really—to receive the tantric massage rather than give and happily shed my top, leggings, and my bra in order to have a full-on tantric experience. We started on our fronts, and I found Sam to be a very adept masseuse. He knew all the erogenous zones on which to pay particular attention. This didn't appear to be his first tantra rodeo.

I was a little hesitant to turn over and let him play with my tits, but *play* would be the wrong word. He caressed them, and I—with my eyes firmly shut—was able to leave the space mentally, as Beatrice said we would, and returned to my bedroom and my last evening with Zoey.

It was just as I was feeling comfortable enough to take Sam's hand from where it resided rubbing oil into my ribs, down to the edge of my knickers when Beatrice called time on our tantric touching and instructed our partners to cover us with the allotted fur blankets and leave us for several minutes to lie in peace.

Like any good dream, we awoke just before we got to the satisfying ending.

"With tantric touch, it's not all about receiving the massage, it's also about giving. Some people need to learn how to give as much as receive to truly experience the transcendentalist nature of pleasure. Like yin and yang, you need balance, you need sun and moon energy, you need sexuality and sensuality."

And back to the mumbo jumbo we returned.

I looked over at Beth, looking remarkably relaxed as she hugged her fur blanket to her chest, wearing only her bra and jogging bottoms. Clearly, she had embraced her discomfort and was feeling the delights of it.

Would she have looked so relaxed if I had been her partner? I like to think so. After all, we were well acquainted with each other's bodies. If anything, Beth should have been *more* relaxed if I had been her partner as she wouldn't have needed to worry about a stranger judging her body. And they must have been judging her—we all do it, even when we tell ourselves we don't.

But, I thought, banishing my intrusive thoughts, at least the tantra workshop was working for her. That was the aim of us being here after all.

Or Beth thought it was.

She glanced over and smiled at me. I looked away guiltily.

CHAPTER 34
BETH

I HAD NEVER been so exhausted by focusing. While I couldn't say I was much further ahead in my tantric *journey*, as Lanni would say, I was definitely closer than I had been when I first arrived at the workshop.

Serena, however, seemed as blasé as ever. And she was continuing to embarrass me despite promising she'd get involved and take it seriously. A promise I kept reminding her of.

"You said you'd support me through this," I whispered as we ascended the stairs to our bedroom.

"You went with someone else," she remarked, seemingly annoyed. "How can I support you if you're on the other side of the room."

"I meant you said you'd take it seriously."

"I am!" she scoffed. "I let my partner go to town on me. If only they had held off for five more minutes—we were just getting to the good part." She skulked off after that, to the bathroom to finish what her partner had started, while I returned to our bedroom and screamed into my pillow.

Once again she had not asked me what I had felt. Clearly, my feelings were not going to feature in her bloody article.

Excluding the massage Serena didn't seem to care or even try in any of the workshops, despite her promise and my frequent reminders. It was almost as if she thought the workshops were beneath her because she had been confidently having sex for years. But that wasn't the point of tantra, at least not this kind. For me, all the teachings about the way to connect through touch and feeling was kind of leading me to have a demisexual epiphany. If I was able to receive a tantric massage, I would be able to give one. (Though maybe I wouldn't be able to give a lingam massage straight off the bat.)

There was no pressure at the workshop, not from the leaders or the other patrons. The only person who was making me feel awkward was Serena, and, ironically, she was the one that was supposed to be here to support *me*.

After introducing Serena to the other patrons and trying to include her in more of our conversations, she didn't engage. Instead she just focused on making fun of the fact that we were at a sex workshop with the cousin of the king.

"Maybe I'll write about it!"

"He's his third cousin, something removed, and I doubt he would want to be mentioned in *any* magazine story," I said sternly.

"I wouldn't write about him without his permission," Serena laughed. "But imagine that clickbait headline. 'I went to a sex workshop with the king's cousin.'"

"It's a tantra workshop," I said calmly, crawling into bed and turning off my light immediately. I wasn't going to give her a chance to rebut me as she made a childish "okay!" noise and turned off her own light.

In the night I woke up desperate for the loo.

I blindly reached for my phone so I had some entertainment while I did my business—and light as I walked down the corridor.

In the bathroom, I realized I had picked up Serena's phone by mistake. There was no point turning back just to get mine, not when I was bursting. I knew Serena's password. I settled down and opened her phone to play a round of *Candy Crush*.

But the first thing that came up wasn't her home page but her WhatsApp.

She had been texting Zoey before we went to sleep, and Zoey had sent her a load of photos. I knew I shouldn't have read the messages, but I was curious. So I did.

Zoey had been sending pictures of flats in London. A few studio flats, a house-share or two. Zoey seemed to be finalizing her decision to go with a studio flat in West Croydon.

Serena had been playfully arguing with her that that wasn't anywhere near a tube or train line that would take her to Euston, which seemed to have been her original desire for a flat, but Zoey just shrugged that off by saying it was near to Serena.

They were flirting. Even I could see it clearly. And Serena was obviously into it otherwise she wouldn't be replying.

She hadn't even told me that Zoey was moving to London.

The last I knew of the Zoey and Serena drama was that Serena had fucked that Tinder bloke and was feeling guilty.

I hadn't even realized she and Zoey were back to talking again. I thought Serena was still avoiding her. But now here was the evidence that that was not the case.

I scrolled up the messages, confused as to when Zoey and Serena had started talking again, and why Serena wasn't responding to Zoey's clear hints that she wanted more than just a London fuck buddy.

A week or so beforehand Zoey had been confirming the dates she would be down in London. Immediately after receiving them Serena had said that she and I were off to the tantra work-shop together and wouldn't be there.

Hmm.

I checked the date of the messages. The day Serena told me about the workshop.

Then it clicked.

She hadn't booked and paid for the tantra workshop to help me with my sexual odyssey as she still referred to it, she had booked us a trip to avoid Zoey and avoid dealing with her feel-ings for her.

I knew Serena could be tactless and ignorant to what others wanted, even herself, but I had never thought she would use my feelings to run away from her own. She wasn't helping me with my experiment simply to help me. She didn't care about *me*, or my sexual confidence, at all. I was just her decoy. She just wanted to *use* me.

THE NEXT MORNING I acted as if nothing had happened, unsure how to address it without exploding. Yet even before breakfast the blister of hurt underneath my skin was growing to an un-comfortable size. Serena, in classic style, didn't sense anything was wrong.

"Eggs and ham?" She began to pile up my plate before I could say yes or no. Helping herself to the last pain au chocolat on offer, she complained after one bite that it was stale.

I said nothing.

The fourth day's session was all about yoni and vajra. Alice was running this session and told us all about the power of the yoni: the place we all began.

It was almost a feminist seminar, except with more medita-tion and conversations with our yonis.

I tried to clear my head enough to actively participate and focus on me for an hour.

Alice instructed us to ask questions to our genitalia aloud, going around the room so that each person got the chance to ask their yoni or their vajra one question. The questions ranged from queries about *why do you grow so much gray hair*, to *why do you contract so much during my period* and *is it possible for you not to be so lubricated that it sounds like my yoni is farting during sex*.

When it came to my turn my mind froze, just like it did when I was at the hen do. Did I ask it why it—*I*—was so afraid of intimacy? Did I ask why I had a sudden interest in sex? Did I ask why Serena thought she could use my yoni as her excuse for her commitment issues? Instead, I stuttered, *why does my cervix have to be so shy?*

Serena, sitting on my left and stifling giggles throughout the whole session already, instantly burst out laughing and she didn't even attempt to hide it this time.

What might have been a genuinely funny moment had it happened between the two of us in our flat before this whole experiment began, was the breaking of a cardinal rule during a tantra workshop. She was laughing *at* me, not with me.

And worse, she was laughing at me after making me come to this retreat I didn't even plan on going to. After I decided to make the best of it. After I explicitly asked her to support me and help me be comfortable.

She had disregarded me entirely.

Alice said nothing, but the whole room stared at Serena.

The workshop was a sacred space, built on respect and compassion. And she'd wrecked it.

I got up from my seat and left without even pausing to look at her.

She would follow. And I would be able to blink back the tears of fury in my eyes.

The rest of the group watched me as I grabbed my coat off the chair, and I heard the shuffling of feet as Serena followed.

Alice's voice carried out into the hall, attempting to take back control of the workshop as I stepped out onto the veranda and down the steps onto the grassy field. I waited until we were a good enough distance away from the house before I turned to see Serena awkwardly jogging to keep up with me, a smile still plastered on her face.

"I'm sorry, I'm so sorry," she said, her hands held up.

"What the hell are you doing?" I shouted. "That was so embarrassing!"

"You were the one asking your cervix questions."

"That's the whole point of the workshop! That's the whole point of this week! Why is that so funny to you?"

"I'm sorry, I know it is. I do. It's just—" She laughed again, accidentally spraying my face with spit. "It's just so stupid."

I turned around, unable to face her like this.

"You're being a total bitch," I whispered furiously, trying to contain myself but knowing the lid was close to flying off.

"Oh come on—"

"No!" I spun round again. "You said this whole week was supposed to be about me, about helping *me*, and you've done nothing to help. In fact, you've made it worse! You won't participate, though you promised me you would. I told you I didn't want to be uncomfortable and the *only* person making me uncomfortable is *you*." I poked her hard in the shoulder, unable to contain myself. She stumbled and the smile dropped from her face. "I started to feel like I was getting somewhere with this whole journey, no matter how ridiculous it all seems to you. I started to feel comfortable in my own body, but you're completely *fucking* it up!"

"Well, I'm *sorry*!" she said. "I'm just the one who booked and paid for it."

"And I thank you for that, truly! Because I *am* learning things, and I wouldn't have ever thought to go to one of these workshops if you didn't book it. But you didn't *ask* me." I began to jot off my grievances with her from my fingers. "You didn't give me a choice of dates, you didn't think about my mental health, you didn't even consider my work!"

"Oh, *what* work?" she said harshly.

"My work with WOW! The brand-new project that I have been working my arse off on for weeks! My job may not be as *fancy* as yours, or as well paid or as reliable, but I am trying and I'm finally succeeding. Not that you care."

"That's not what I meant," Serena began.

"Oh, shut the fuck up," I said, unable to control my anger anymore and past caring. "I know you think my whole freelance thing is a joke, and guess what, so do I. I think it's a joke too, although I just got hired by Evan Cartwright—and yes, *that* Evan—and I didn't even want to tell you because what would it matter?"

"Wait. *Evan* Evan?" She looked stunned.

"Yes, Evan fucking Cartwright. He's the guy from WOW, and that's not all. We've actually been texting. Not that you've cared to ask about my personal life. He's the guy who's currently paying me enough money that I can finally pay my rent on time. But what does that matter, you don't give a shit if I pay my rent on time or not. You'll just bail me out—that is, when you're not paying for me to go to super-expensive tantra workshops."

"Wait, you're angry that I pay for things sometimes? That I help you out?"

"It's not that you pay for things, it that's you pay for them and then don't respect me when I try to get value out of them." I ran my fingers over my eyes viciously, trying to compose myself enough not to cry. "This may mean nothing to you, financially, but this workshop *is* valuable. And you could learn something from it if you were willing to put in the fucking work like I asked and you *promised* to do. But you never fulfill your promises, you don't even care what I want anymore. You just use me, I'm just the subject of your latest bloody article. I'm not even someone you care about!" I stopped sharply.

"What's that supposed to mean?"

"Zoey," I said simply and breathlessly, hands on my hips as I tried to inhale as Lanni had taught us in our first session. It wasn't so I could find my center though, it was so I could breathe like a normal human being.

"What's Zoey got to do with me not caring about you? Are you jealous of her?"

"No," I spat. "But she's in London, right now, isn't she?"

"What?" Serena said, feigning ignorance.

"She's flat hunting in London this week. The *week* that you chose to surprise me with a tantra workshop."

"Well, I had it booked."

I scoffed. "Oh, stop lying! I saw the messages between you and her. You didn't even tell me about the workshop until after she confirmed what dates she was coming down. I doubt you booked it until then."

Serena gasped. "You went on my phone!"

"It was an accident, I grabbed yours by mistake."

"And you just thought you would read my messages."

"Well, I'm sorry I'm such a bad person. Honestly, *my bad*. But you went and used me and my anxieties to avoid telling the woman you're in love with that you're in love with her!"

"I am not in—"

"Just admit it! Stop lying to yourself, and me!" Our voices were getting louder and louder. They echoed across the field.

"You're fucking mental."

"And you're a shit friend who's afraid of commitment and completely unfixable!" I barged past her toward the house.

"What did you say?"

"You heard me." I didn't look back. I felt the strong urge to cry, and I refused to let her see me do that.

"I'm unfixable? You're the one who's too scared to have sex at twenty-fucking-eight."

I stopped then because that was the lowest she could get. She was purposely trying to hurt me now. All rules were suspended.

Turning on the spot, tears forgotten in their entirety, I just stared at her. Nothing was spoken, nothing needed to be said, I just stared at her.

What had just happened was unfixable.

The one person I always thought had my back, that was my best friend and who loved me no matter what, had just brought up my biggest anxiety and used it as a cheap shot simply because I had called her out on her own cowardly behavior.

She opened her mouth, but I'd heard enough. I turned on the spot and walked inside. It was then I noticed that some of the patrons were watching. We had had an audience. Someone had even opened the window to hear.

Now everyone was scurrying away from the sunroom windows with wide-eyed expressions and "oh shit" mutterings.

CHAPTER 35
BETH

I DON'T REMEMBER climbing the stairs. Or pulling out my suitcase from under the bed. Or even packing it. The box with one brownie was coming with me, though. (The complimentary lubrication was not.) I needed to get the hell away from Serena. And fast.

I stumbled hurriedly down the stairs, dragging my not-so-heavy suitcase quickly, in case Serena decided to come in for a second shouting match, or the patrons escaped the sunroom to pity me.

"I want to check out," I told Beatrice on reception, glancing briefly around in case anyone else appeared. Just the thought of Serena returning made my heart start to pound against my sternum.

"If we could be quick. I have a taxi outside," I lied. Beatrice smiled nervously.

"Well, you've already paid so there's nothing more to clear. But the workshop isn't over for a few more days. Are you sure you want to . . . ?"

I didn't let her finish. "Thanks for everything."

Before she could respond, I rushed out of the front doors and into the empty car park. I could call a taxi from the main road. I wasn't waiting anywhere near the house in case Serena found me and tried to persuade me to stay. And she would. She had that special knack for knowing everything I wanted to hear, or felt guilty hearing. Not today, Satan!

Inhaling deeply, I shook out my head, trying to rid myself of the guilt that was beginning to rise up like bile. I thought about Mr. Bates and how proud he would be of me for standing up for myself. About how Delphi would punch the ceiling for my finally saying my piece. And Penny . . .

Penny! That's where I could go.

I had to go somewhere that wasn't here, and I couldn't go home. But I could go to Penny's. She would listen to me. And, importantly, she would take my side.

I stopped as I reached the end of the drive.

I was hyperventilating from the speed of my walk. My lungs were on fire.

Dropping my suitcase and the brownie box, I lifted my hands to my eyes. Why was I even crying? Why did I feel like my heart was breaking?

I snottily breathed in and forced myself to gulp down some air.

"I'm not doing this," I said to myself angrily. Pulling my phone from my pocket and slamming my fingers on my phone screen, I hastily found a taxi service online and called them to book a car to the station.

I was going to Penny's in the Cotswolds, screw the cost, I was getting out of here.

CHAPTER 36
SERENA

I SAT ON the grass, with my back to the house, and sobbed.

I always described Beth as the friend I could give my soul to, and she would take care of it. But I had now discovered she could also destroy it. In this case by being honest.

When I told Zoey about the then make-believe tantra workshop, I was being a terrible friend. But at the time I was just looking for an escape, and Beth happened to be the perfect excuse. Something I knew a friend should never be. But I couldn't help myself.

Zoey blindsided me by being everything I wanted and was afraid of. If I told her that I had feelings, *strong* feelings for her and she rejected me, I didn't think I'd ever be able to stand up again.

And though I knew she has feelings for me—*everyone* told me she did, and Zoey tried to show it—what would happen if she saw me for what I truly was? Damaged, heartless, impulsive.

Beth saw it, and she left.

Relationships weren't in my DNA. I had never had a successful one, not until Beth, and look how badly I messed that up.

Sex was easy, it was swift and in the moment. Spontaneity was my calling card—not long-term emotions.

I had only ever fucked and been fucked. And now I was just fucking everyone over, from my best friend to the girl she said I was in love with. And she was right, I was in love with Zoey.

I sat and sobbed.

The sun had reached its peak long before I felt able to go back inside, and the patrons of the workshop had been released for their lunches and daily walks.

None of them approached me on the green, though they'd clearly heard and seen everything. No one tried to comfort me or stop me crying. They either respected my need for a moment of emotion, or they were simply too embarrassed to interrupt. Considering I'd seen most of them undressed, that felt ironic.

Either way when I stood up and went back inside, wiping my face constantly with my hands and sleeves. I didn't look at any of them and none of them looked at me.

When I reached our room, the door was open and all of Beth's things were gone. She had left, and I doubted she had just got another room. I knew what Beth was like in a fury. There was no way she would stay.

I shut the door, placing the do not disturb sign on the handle, and got into my bed fully clothed.

I didn't emerge until the following morning, and that was just because my stomach was aching for food. I had searched for the remaining brownie, but it was gone.

In the canteen, I tried my hardest to not let any tears fall.

I loaded up on all the good stuff that Beth and I usually missed out on from being late risers, and I hid myself at a table in the farthest corner away from the food and the doors.

Though I tried to distract myself, my mind continued to race with retorts and apologies as I thought of all the painful words that Beth and I had exchanged the day before. But mostly I just thought about her calling me unfixable. I certainly felt that way.

Why had I treated my friend so badly when I knew she was going through an already delicate experience? Beth may have appeared confident and up for anything when it came to her sexual odyssey, but she was saying yes just so she didn't give herself the opportunity to say no. Everything she had done, from having a smear test to going to see a sex therapist and using a dilator was her form of conversion therapy. She was trying to "fix" a problem that wasn't even there, rather than embracing her sexuality with confidence and accepting her position as a virgin without fear.

She didn't need to do all these things, but she had done so because they made a good story for me. I'd been chasing that story, rather than genuinely helping her explore.

I placed my head in my hands, unable to stomach my food after all.

Footsteps came and stopped in front of me. Hesitantly, I looked up and saw Lanni peering down at me.

She was smiling rather than scowling.

"Mind if I join you?"

I shook my head, and she sat. But she didn't say anything at first.

She looked at me, or rather stared. But somehow *stared* seems like too harsh a word. She was simply *seeing* me. It was a very pointed, emotional observation and one that I think we were meant to have performed during our first session. I realized now that I had only ever stared at my partner, Beth, and I'd never really seen her.

Leaning forward gently, she placed her hands on my arms, forcing them down away from where they hovered from holding my head. She clasped them and continued to look deep into my eyes.

Two days ago I would have been thinking about how ridiculous this all was. But now I realized that I wasn't feeling ridiculous or awkward at all. I was feeling an unusual kind of release, like something internally—a voice separate from my own—was saying that it was okay, that I had done things wrong but nothing was unfixable. Not even me.

I began to cry again, softly at first and then racking sobs once more. I didn't want to believe in all this spiritual bullshit, it went against everything in me and everything I had ever experienced when it came to connecting with other people. From Tinder dates to journalistic projects to my parents.

During my childhood—even my adulthood—I threw everything of me into trying to make my parents love me, or at least see me. From school grades to back-and-forth trips, beauty, and success. But nothing ever worked. Beth wanted to be seen herself, so we connected on that level, though it did grow over time into something uniquely ours. I didn't realize how much I depended on it, let alone appreciated it. And Zoey saw something of me that no one else had ever taken the time to find.

Lanni's gaze was similar to Zoey's, so piercing yet kind, and her energy so free of judgement yet full of care, and I understood what she wanted me to take from it.

"You should come to the initiation today," she told me finally. "Even if only to experience your own initiation. There is no need to prepare, you can do what you need to do. What you feel able to do."

"I don't think I should do that," I said, removing my arm from one of her grasps so that I could wipe away the tears. "I've not exactly been doing great in the workshops."

Lanni shrugged and released my other arm as well, leaning

back in her chair and stretching. Returning to being a typical middle-aged woman in a caftan.

"And you think I understood the whole concept of tantra when I first started? No, no, no, it took years. Many years of self-discovery, understanding, and emotional review. I don't think it has quite caught you the way it caught your friend, as you were not willing to let go or share your real intention with the universe." She stood to get her food, placing a hand gently on my shoulder before she did so. "Use the initiation to do that. Share your intention with the universe and release your beliefs. Then you can go after your friend and fix things."

"You think so?" I sniffed loudly. She smiled softly.

"I know so."

THE INITIATION WAS done in the sunroom, but after the moon had risen and the room was cool. Thick velvet curtains had been hung across every window and the room was plush and cozy, with extra throw pillows, fur blankets, and candles everywhere.

In the center of the room was an altar of the thickest blankets and pillows, ready for the first initiation. (Lanni reassured everyone that blankets and pillows would be changed between initiations if we so wished.)

Lanni and the other workshop leaders were all in the room, stationed at each corner like chess pieces. As soon as everyone was in the room, the leaders shut the doors and extinguished a candle or two.

I missed Beth.

"Who would like to go first?" Lanni asked, looking around the room expectantly.

I imagined that people would be nervous to kick-off the show, but then I realized that this wasn't a show, and this wasn't a place of nervousness either. Not if you had done the workshop correctly over the last week.

One of the couples chose to go first, with her giving him a tantric massage. She took her time, but not as much as Beatrice had with the model when she was showing us the various techniques. The woman teased her partner's genitalia, rather than massage it ferociously, but the result was still exceedingly pleasurable for him.

I was surprised when she said that that was both of their initiations, and not just his since he had been the one to receive pleasure. But the woman clarified that she had got what she wanted out of the workshop by learning how to give as well as receive.

One by one initiations took place, some explicit and others simple. Eileen asked Sam, my massage partner, if she could touch him for her initiation and he agreed. It wasn't a tantric massage, but neither was it unsexual. It led to Eileen and Sam kissing each other very actively. Eileen thanked him when she was finished.

Louis asked one of the women if she would mind sitting with him naked from the waist up. She agreed and the two of them sat opposite each other cross-legged, each with one hand placed on the other's chest just above their hearts. They stared into each other's eyes.

Hardly anyone was left now. I realized I hadn't even considered what my initiation would be. It hadn't crossed my mind the sort of things that would happen at a workshop like this. I hardly thought I would be watching people masturbate or communicate through silence.

My mind was rampant with suggestions, as if I were coming up with a theme for a talent show. I could sit naked in front of them I supposed, but that wasn't something I particularly felt like doing right now. I could ask Sam to give me another tantric massage, that was nice. But surely, I had already done that, and it had not been particularly tantric for me, just relaxing. Maybe relaxation was what I needed?

I glanced at Lanni and reminded myself of what she had said about letting go, setting my intention. But what was my intention? I had no sexual intentions; I didn't even have a five-year plan!

Lanni said my name when all the others had completed their initiations.

"Serena, would you like to have an initiation?"

I could have very easily said no, but she looked at me again and I felt her gaze and the power it held from before.

"Yes, please," I said softly.

I stood, removing my cardigan and dropping it on the floor so that I was only in my jogging bottoms and top, improvising. I took off my shoes and stepped onto the altar.

I took a deep breath, faced the crowd of patrons and sat cross-legged with a quiet grunt. The others were barely visible in the candlelight, only their eyes really proved that they were there. I inhaled a few times, feeling nerves climbing up my throat and developing into a tight knot at my collarbone.

Unconsciously I closed my eyes and placed my hands on my knees, feeling that this was a safe and comfortable position for me to be in.

"Could . . ." I began but stopped and inhaled again. A minute passed and then I tried again. "Could a . . . woman please come and touch me. On my arms, on my neck. On any exposed skin," I said, still with my eyes shut and without any preference for who did it.

There were shuffling sounds and then I felt the weight of another person on the blankets around me. From the left-hand side I felt the soft brush of knuckles go over my arm, and I inhaled deeply again. The touch continued across my top half, up and down my exposed arms, across my knuckles through to the webbing between my fingers. I felt a woman's warm breath fall across the back of my spine and I leaned into it, instructing her to do that again.

A mix of touch, breath, and scent filled me up and I felt comfortable, but also aroused.

"Zoey," I said, letting whatever instinct took hold of me do its thing. "Zoey."

The touching continued and so did the light touch of breath on my skin. She moved my hair away from my shoulder, holding it up as she breathed gently on my neck. I could almost feel her lips touch my radiating skin and I rose to meet them, but they fell away. She moved from one side of my neck to the other and back again.

In the space, with the woman behind me, I felt like I could have stayed there forever. It was safe, loving, and sensual, not full of energy that filled you with adrenaline but with an energy that was like a power source. My thoughts quieted and my breath slowed, and although tears did fall from beneath my eyelids and I felt the familiar lump rise in my throat, it was because I was relieved and I couldn't contain the emotion anymore.

I was fixable. I was capable of love and, most importantly, I would be able to admit both to anyone already in, and soon to be in, my life.

Instinctively I placed my hand between my thighs and started to rub. Softly, slowly, and then fast. I followed the woman's breath, turning my head each time I felt her. She was my magnet, my lighthouse.

I was touching myself over my clothes, but I was so sensitive and entirely focused on the woman, Zoey, that it wasn't long before I felt every nerve in my body tense and liquefy within me. I shuddered with the force, unable to hear the room for the blood rushing through my head like a dam had broken within my skull.

I exhaled and shuddered again, leaning forward into my lap into an almost mock bow, as the woman's hand pressed lightly on the small of my back.

I opened my eyes after a bell rang softly to signal the end of the initiation, and I turned to Lanni, who had been the volunteer to touch me, and breathlessly said, "Thank you."

CHAPTER 37
BETH

I CAN'T BELIEVE you had the money to get here," Penny said, sliding over a coaster to me as I cradled a coffee at her kitchen table.

"I do have a job, you know; it does pay." I placed my mug on the coaster.

(Patrick, wisely, had taken himself off to give us some privacy and was in the living room, playing *Call of Duty* with his bulky headphones on.)

Getting a last-minute train from Devon to the Cotswolds had not been easy. Three changes later I had finally made it to Penny's local station, and I called another taxi to take me to her house. Being a village stuck in the 1950s, the driver only took cash. I explained this to my sister at her front door—shouting "I need a tenner" over her "fuck me" reaction to seeing me standing there.

Now it was the next day. Penny paused and then asked, "So are you ready to explain now? You weren't exactly talkative last night."

I shrugged. "I was tired from the train—or rather *trains*—from Devon. It was kind of spur of the moment."

"Why were you in Devon?"

"You'll laugh."

"Try me."

So I did.

I explained about the tantra workshop with Serena and that I had found myself really enjoying it, and even connecting with the idea of tantric energy, leaving my head and entering my heart. "It's beyond hippie, I know, but I got it."

Penny was rolling her lips together in a clear attempt to stop herself giggling, but I knew her too well.

"It is a little funny."

"Well, if that's your thing, who am I to judge?"

"How very big-sister of you. And I wouldn't call it my *thing*," I said. "I don't see myself becoming a regular attendee. But it was a refreshing take on sex and intimacy that I haven't experienced before. It felt safe. Even if I was a virgin in the middle of a sex workshop."

"It sounds like the sort of thing you'd do." Penny took a drink of her coffee.

"Does it?"

"Yes," she said. "The fact that it is so the opposite of you. It shouldn't work but it does. Honestly, Mum and I have always said that you're like a magnet, always attracted to the opposite of what you are. Look at you and Serena!"

Urgh, Serena.

"Not anymore, we've had a cataclysmic falling out."

"Oh crikey, what happened?" Penny settled herself back in her chair, even lifting a leg to rest on the chair opposite.

"You comfy?" I teased. She nodded and gestured for me to continue. So I told her everything. Well, nearly everything. The whole Rupert fiasco is not something I wanted to get into with my sister.

"So, wait a minute, she's in love with Zoey but can't admit it—to herself or to Zoey?" Penny asked.

"Both."

"And so the whole thing was for her to have an excuse not to be in town while Zoey was there? But she didn't tell you any of that?"

I pursed my lips and sat back as if to say, "I told you it was bad."

My rage wasn't as bad as it had been when I had first had it out with Serena on the green, but I could still feel the aura of it sitting on my chest like an irritating cat that wants to be fed but strikes you in the face with its claws when you try to move it.

All the calm and self-confidence I had felt pouring into me at the workshop had dissipated over the course of the train journey. Had I really thought it was working for me? But what if it was and by interrupting it, I had lost it all, like a download with a disrupted internet connection? Would I find it again? Or was the whole experience a laughable anecdote to share with Delphi in a few weeks?

Mostly: Why did Serena have to go and ruin everything? Why did I let her?

"She had been acting weird and childish all week. I know that tantra is quite silly when you look at it on the surface, but she didn't even try to embrace it. Not even for my sake when I started to enjoy it."

"For someone so sexual I'm surprised that she didn't enjoy it," Penny said softly.

"I kind of wish you wouldn't describe her as 'so sexual,' Pen," I said, rubbing the spot between my eyes. Serena *was* sexual— her sex positivity was one of the most refreshing things about her, but still it seemed like a derogatory identifier used on its own now that I'd done all this self-love and tantric workshopping myself. Being called "so sexual" was just the opposite of my fear of being called out for being a virgin.

"Sorry," Penny said sincerely. "I wasn't trying to be mean."

"I know, and I hate that I'm defending her when I'm so mad, but she's other things too. She's funny, honest, a great writer. She's a bloody mess and a right idiot sometimes. She can make anyone her friend but just as easily her enemy. She's difficult, sure." I pinched the bridge of my nose and felt the stress wrinkles across my forehead. Serena was going to prematurely age me at this rate. "She's fucking annoying, either overthinking or barely thinking or never *actually* thinking and she makes *so many* bad decisions, but she's . . ." I exhaled loudly and groaned. "She's just so complicated."

"Aren't we all? I think all anyone thinks of me these days is 'the one who can't get pregnant,'" Penny said.

"Come on, that's not true." I reached for her hand across the table.

"Isn't it?" She looked me dead in the eye and then toward Patrick, just to check that he wasn't listening. "I have a business that I built from scratch, I have a loving husband—even if it's not always perfect. I have a first-class degree in architecture and have won awards for my drawings. I like woodwork and Duolingo, and I'm part of the freaking Women's Institute in my midthirties. And I'd like to think I am a good person with a good sense of humor."

"Yeah, you're funny. Most of the time." I grinned.

"Well, there then! Why is my identifier not one of those?"

I didn't have an answer to that.

That's just life, I suppose, others judge you by what they see or hear that's the most scandalous. No one ever describes a person as "that really selfless lady next door" or "that generous child." They describe you by your most outrageous or impressive story.

You're either the slut who has a new conquest every weekend, or you're that failing freelancer with no money. Or the virgin scared of sex. Or the emotionally stunted woman who runs away from her feelings.

No one would ever describe me and Serena as two successful young women living their lives solely as they want to without self-judgement or fear. I'm always the virgin, and she's always the sexual one. Those are our two identifiers.

"I'm sorry if I've been tactless," I admitted guiltily.

"It's okay," she reassured me. "The world is sometimes cruel and that's just the way it is." She pushed back her chair, letting her legs fall to the floor with a thump. Penny took her empty cup of coffee into the kitchen, and I followed with my own.

"Don't get me wrong when I say this," Penny began with her back to me as she washed out her mug. "I think Serena's made a mistake and you need to confront her for it—but it's not the mistake you think."

"What do you mean?"

She gestured for my cup; I drained the dregs and handed it over.

"She clearly has feelings for this other girl, Zoey, and she's screwed it all up, screwing you over in the process. I bet that she feels like crap right now. Especially since you figured it out, confronted her, and then left."

I didn't say anything. I could feel an angry retort rising in my throat. I was still furious with Serena for using me, and then lying to my face.

"What she did to you was wrong," Penny continued. "But I don't think she's a bad person, I just think she made a big mistake. Aaand . . ." She turned to face me. "I think you want to forgive her. If you didn't, you wouldn't have just defended her right now. You would have called her a bitch, or a slut at the very least."

"Slut is way too harsh," I said, recoiling at the term.

"You're a good friend," Penny said, smiling at me from the sink, the suds still slipping down her arm.

"I'm allowed to be angry, though." I wasn't forgiving Serena just yet. "It's one thing to be *overly* helpful—actually a bit pressuring—about my newfound desire to learn about sex and stuff. But it's a whole other thing to use my anxieties as a way to cover for her own."

"I agree," Penny said. "And you've never really explained this whole *sexual odyssey* thing to me either? I mean, fair do." She held up her hands placatingly. "But still. It's a little . . . *unusual*." She picked her words carefully, and I could only laugh.

"It's ridiculous," I told her, giving her permission to tease me and question me as much as she liked. She only did so out of love, and Penny knew exactly where the line was.

There was something about being in her presence that was instantly calming and reassuring. I knew I wasn't going to be coddled by her, but I was going to get some solid advice without any bullshit, and so far she had delivered.

"I've missed you," I said, holding out my hand.

She took it and smiled. "You can come and see me anytime. Not that there's much to see, beyond my puffy face." She pinched her cheeks disparagingly.

"Your face is not puffy."

"I've been eating way too much brie and drinking too much red wine lately. That's why I didn't offer you anything stronger than coffee; we don't have any wine left."

I laughed and put my arm around Penny's shoulder as she began wiping down the sink.

"It's your house, here you're the boss, you drink what you like."

"Thank you for your blessing," Penny said, before turning to me in all seriousness and with a pause that suggested she was about to say something superior or incredibly wise. "When was the last time you and Serena talked? And I mean *really* talked, not just danced around a subject."

Urgh, wise.

I shrugged. Honestly? "Not for a while."

"Patrick and I make a point of checking in with each other at least once a week—as woo-woo as that sounds—one of the counselors at the IVF clinic suggested it when we started trying, and it really helped."

"Therapy has helped me too."

"I wouldn't call it therapy. It's honesty," Penny said.

I inhaled deeply. "What's the latest on everything with you? If you don't mind . . ."

"I wish people wouldn't pussy-foot around it," Penny said, suddenly harsh. "I can't carry a child to term, that's it. It's crap and I hate my body for it, but it's the truth and I'm done with feeling like I must protect everyone else's feelings when really it only concerns me. And Patrick. And we're happy as we are. I promise. I swear it. We're happy being together."

"Okay. Good for you. But Mum's going to never get off your case about grandkids, particularly with me on the market."

"I think we should buy Mum a puppy and be done with it," Penny suggested dryly.

"Do you know, that's not a bad idea." I laughed as she handed me another dish to dry.

"I'm full of good ideas," she teased. "And my next one is for you to go back to London and have it out with Serena. But listen, don't just shout. You both need to say your piece. And be honest, because once you admit what you actually want and are afraid of it's so much easier to face it."

CHAPTER 38
SERENA

I WASN'T SURPRISED to find our flat empty. There was no evidence that Beth had ever come home, and I hadn't expected her to.

She was too angry with me, and rightly so to be honest. But I was glad to get a little down time to really process everything that happened at the workshop.

My initiation had moved me in a way that I hadn't expected.

There had been no judgement. And crucially, no one mentioned Zoey or Beth afterward.

Lanni was particularly praiseworthy of what she called my "bravery" and "acceptance" into the tantra lifestyle. Clearly, she hadn't realized how little effort I had made during the previous workshops. But I didn't correct her. It was nice to be praised. I was still only human, however guilty I felt.

It was now Friday night, and I didn't know what to do with myself.

Dropping my bags on my bedroom floor, I returned to the kitchen and began tidying. Usually Beth did the cleaning—she was home all the time. But in the last few weeks, when she had kept herself to herself in her bedroom, she had barely done any. I guess she had had other things to focus on.

And I, as the other housemate, and friend, should have pulled my share. But I hadn't.

Beth wasn't my maid, she was my best friend. The least I could do to show her how bad I felt was spruce up our space.

Not to mention, cleaning is a great distraction when you want to stop thinking.

First, I tidied the kitchen, filling the sink with extra-hot soapy water and breaking out a fresh pair of rubber gloves to scrub every surface I could get my hands on. From the counters to the plates, everything sparkled by the time I was done.

My knees protested painfully when I got down to the floor to wash the baseboards, but I couldn't remember whether we'd ever cleaned those before. (The hardened splash marks and dusty cobwebs confirmed that we hadn't.)

From the now-spotless kitchen I moved into the living room.

I folded the many blankets we had draped over our cozy sofa, plumped up the cushions, and sprayed down the coffee table with some funky-smelling wood polish I found in the back of the cupboard under the sink.

By the time I had cleaned all the surfaces, straightened every piece of furniture, corrected the placement of every knickknack we owned, I finally wiped down the mold-ridden windowsill and opened it to let in some air.

The sun was beginning to rise; I had spent the whole night cleaning.

The light cast a gorgeous golden glow about the room and made it seem much homelier than I had ever seen it before. At least not since we had first moved in. It finally looked like the living room of two grown-ups and not two students. Two women with interests and passions, with a clear workspace and a comfortable living area to lounge.

So, what next? I hadn't set out to Marie Kondo the flat, I just wanted to distract myself and make the flat a nice place for Beth to come home to. But standing there, inspecting my hard work, I realized something.

She might not want to come back.

Was I being dramatic? This was just one fight and could easily be remedied with an apology and an explanation. But I had treated Beth badly in the last few weeks—and even before.

Had I shown her as much support as I could have done when it came to her freelancing, or had I merely showered her with platitudes that only meant something to thirteen-year-olds on Instagram? Had I tried to understand her anxieties about her sexuality or her body, or had I merely been chasing a story?

Beth hadn't said anything, but I hadn't asked her either.

Beth could read me like a book and called me out when she saw me making the wrong decisions or struggling in silence. She had done it with my feelings for Zoey, and when I struggled, but pretended not to, with regard to my family situation. Yet when I had sensed her insecurity and the change in her attitude over the last few weeks, I hadn't done anything about it. I had simply left her to her own devices and waited for her to come to me. But Beth never came to me.

I had told her that she had a bad habit of making a decision and then sticking by it. It was true, but I realized now just how stupid that must have made her feel; like she was a self-saboteur. She wasn't that in the slightest—she was merely stubborn and determined and those were two traits I really respected in her. She knew what she wanted, and she went for it, even when things got tough or seemed impossible. But some-times it hurt her.

She had decided to work on her sexuality and her relation-ship with sex, and that was that. She hadn't asked for help from me. I forced myself into her plans. From that moment on she was stuck with me, and would never say no, even when it began to screw up our relationship. Although truly it was me who had screwed it up. Beth was trying, legitimately trying. I was the one who ended up using her for my own good. It turned out in the end to be nothing but to my detriment.

I threw my head back against the sofa and tried to stop the tears that began to flow down my hairline. No amount of wip-ing or pinching would stop them. They were flowing out of me as steadily as the guilt I couldn't silence.

My phone buzzed.

And then again.

Someone was ringing me.

Beth!

I sat up quickly, hunting around my trouser pockets to find my battered phone before the call went to voicemail. I didn't even read the caller ID.

"Beth!"

"Hello?"

My breathing stopped.

"Mum?"

"Oh." She sounded surprised. "Serena." Had she thought I wouldn't answer her?

"Mum?" I repeated. Why was my mum calling me?

I hadn't meant to, but I had asked the question out loud.

"Can't a mother call her child?" She laughed, but it wasn't confident. "How are you?"

"You never ask me how I am," I said, unable to stop the bitterness seeping through my voice.

"Well." She laughed nervously again. "Honestly Serena, I hadn't meant to call you."

Wait, what?

"I made a new friend when I saw some Kabuki theater this week. Her name's Seren; she told me to give her a buzz when I was going into town, so I thought I was calling her. Oopsie!"

Oopsie.

"Right," I said. Same story, then. Forget my mother trying to be a parent. She'd given that up after I could walk, talk, and go to the toilet by myself. Self-sufficiency was key in our family—I use the term lightly—you always look out for number one and don't depend on others. That was one of the few life lessons my mum bestowed on me after she and Dad had finalized their divorce.

Dad certainly put himself first, practically from the moment Mum got pregnant—at least according to the gossip I got from being a wallflower at my mum's birthday parties growing up—and Mum did the same after I was born. It was a miracle that their marriage lasted as long as it did. But divorce proceedings are expensive and drawn out, especially when you have a child who can't look after herself yet.

As soon as I was able to travel unchaperoned on airplanes it was a lot easier. But by then, the resentment of my being around, delaying my parents' happiness and freedom, had set in and my parents' narcissistic personalities took over. At least, that's what my school counselors wrote in my notes at school. Notes I happened to steal during the final week of term.

I wish I could say it was a surprise. But it wasn't. Just like this call.

Mum continued to laugh oddly but didn't hang up. Was this guilt? You would think I'd recognize the symptoms, but I couldn't sense it. I don't think my mother, or my father, ever felt guilty about me, certainly not now that I was older. After all, they had done the bare minimum to keep me alive until I was eighteen, and as such their obligation to me had been fulfilled. They were done and had been done for years, I just hadn't wanted to accept it, because who wants—or can—accept that their parents never wanted them and were indifferent to them? It's unthinkable, and yet here I was realizing it. I was a mistake carried over, like an algebra equation—I was never going to be right. The best way to correct a wrong equation is to erase it and start again.

"Do you know what? I'm finished with this. You can go ahead and delete my number; I don't think you need it anymore. I don't think you even want it."

"Oh Serena, don't be dramatic," she said. Ironic, as I got that from her. It was about the only thing, apart from money, that I ever got from her.

"You can stop the allowance as well. I don't want anything from you anymore. Not you or your money."

"Serena, darling."

"Don't call me darling," I whispered. "Just don't call me. That's easy enough for you, Mum, just do what you've always done and forget about me. I don't need you. I need . . ." I knew who I needed, and she wasn't speaking to me. "Just fuck off."

I hung up and dropped my phone on the sofa cushions next to me and placed my head in my hands.

Beth was right. I was broken.

But I didn't need to be.

Taking up my phone again I texted my dad.

> Just a PSA from your daughter—Serena, FYI—you can stop the allowance. I've decided I don't want it anymore, and you can delete my number as well. I won't be coming to Dubai again and I won't ask you for anything. I don't want you or Mum in my life anymore, and I don't think either of you will care anyway.

It might seem cowardly to text, perhaps even a little ridiculous, but my dad wouldn't answer if I called—maybe his latest girlfriend would, though—and I couldn't chance that he wouldn't listen to a voicemail.

And then I deleted his number. And then my mum's.

"MY GOD," **ARNOLD** gasped, though his face was frozen in place by the clay mask he was currently wearing. "You have been through it."

The spa facilities at the hotel where Arnold and Gareth were getting married the following day were limited—but Arnold had come prepared with Elemis face masks, homemade exfoliators, cucumber slices in iceboxes, and an unseemly amount of prosecco. All of which he had planned on using solo while Gareth enjoyed his last day of freedom on his stag do.

My blubbering phone call had made Arnold so anxious he demanded I come be with him for an impromptu stag do. Involving, as mentioned, an inordinate amount of face products, day drinking, and *The Princess Diaries*.

"You needed this self-care sesh more than I did, darling," Arnold said, leaning over the bed to pat me on my robed shoulder.

"I've been so stupid, Arnold," I said, licking the homemade honey and oatmeal exfoliator I was wearing off my finger.

"You're not meant to eat it!"

"It's delicious."

"*You're* delicious, you sexy hunk of loveliness." He threw a damp flannel from the nearby icebox on the floor. "Next up, cleanser."

"You don't hate me, then?" I asked as I wiped my face with the flannel. I avoided his eyes.

"Why would I hate you? You've done nothing to *me*."

"I crashed your spa day."

"I invited you; there's a big difference," he laughed. "Also, how sad would it have been if I had just stayed in on my own with a face mask, eating room service, and watching Disney Plus? I'm over forty."

"You're fifty-two." Though he did look in his forties. The face masks were clearly working.

"Precisely!" Arnold shouted. "Serena, baby, I want you here. I want my best woman here with me, safe and sound while I get ready to marry the man I love—who she introduced me to! This is perfect, this is how it should be."

I said nothing but blushed as I wiped off the last of the exfoliator.

Arnold sighed, the type with a thousand meanings.

"Right, I feel like I need to say this plainly, so you understand." He cleared his throat and moved to the edge of the bed so he was directly opposite me. "I love you. You are a brilliant friend, a fantastic coworker. You're funny, reliable, and loving and you put other people first—though you also fuck up, can be incredibly ignorant and self-serving, and lack a lot of self-esteem."

I was unsure how to respond. "Thank . . . you?"

"You are a human. A beautiful, lovable human. You've made a few mistakes, and you know it. But you also know that you need to fix them."

I said nothing but exhaled quietly, as a single tear began to develop at the crease of my eye. Arnold wiped it away.

"You're a beautiful mess," he said. "But with a little acceptance, a few apologies, and explanations, you could just be beautiful."

"I don't know if I can," I admitted pathetically.

"I think you've already started," Arnold said, leaning back on his elbows. "You told your parents where to go. I think that was a long time coming."

I laughed bitterly. "I'm going to miss the money, though."

Arnold screwed his eyes up. "Are you, though? You seem to spend most of it on other people. The flat, the bills, the holidays? It's hardly like you're rolling in Louis Vuitton and Chanel."

"I've never had to be cautious about money before, though. Now I will."

"Oh *responsibility*," Arnold said, rolling his eyes. "What a hard life you lead."

I tutted. "Okay, I know I've had it easy my whole life."

"Babe, you've never had it *easy*, you've struggled with what your parents have done—or not done—your entire child- *and* adulthood. *Now* you've got it easy. You don't owe them anything. You're free. And you're free at a time when you have a solid income, a flat, and potentially a few other opportunities. You just need to take them."

My phone sat silent on the side table of Arnold's bed, and I was not without hope that it would ring. The Liverpudlian lilt of Zoey's voice would be so comforting right now, not to mention her humor and her patience. She would listen to me, I knew that, but I was also afraid of what she would think if she saw me as I was. At my worst. "Zoey? It's scary."

"Relationships often are." Arnold laughed. "They sometimes lead to this." Arnold lifted his hands to the decadent room. "Overpriced celebrations and familial ties."

"You sell it so well."

"I do it with love, though. I can't show it, mostly because this face mask is harder than Mount Everest. I now know how Madonna must feel after all that Botox. But honestly, I *love* love. I adore being in relationships, though they don't always work out. But I'm not afraid of relationships ending. Some would say I don't fight hard enough; I would say I'm a pragmatist. I'm also not afraid of making mistakes. Whereas you, my dearest darling, fear it."

"I do not!"

"Really," Arnold said. "Look at you."

I licked my newly hydrated lips and waited for him to continue, but he didn't need to, I knew what he wanted me to do. "You think I should call Zoey?"

"And Beth."

"Now?" My heart began to race.

Arnold paused. "When you're ready. But you need to get ready *soon*. Isn't Beth coming to the wedding tomorrow?"

I shrugged. "I invited her, but it was before the argument. I don't think she'll come."

"Well, text her to remind her! Offer her a plus-one! Just don't let it fester."

"Do you think a plus-one would help?"

"Otherwise you could guilt-trip her, reminding her how much I paid for each person to eat, but given the circumstances . . ."

I felt a nervousness in my stomach I hadn't had since waiting outside the nurse's office when I first got my period. I held my hand out for my phone. Arnold grabbed it and gently threw it to me. I had no messages, as expected, but phones work both ways. Taking a breath I started to type.

> Hey Beth, I'm so sorry for everything and I really want to fix this. I realize that I've made mistakes and I fucked up royally. I'm so sorry for hurting you, it was never my intention but I realize that that's what I've done. Please come to Arnold's wedding tomorrow, if you still can. It would be great to talk. And feel free to bring a plus-one if you'd like, for the evening (you're still invited for the whole day). The wedding's not until three p.m. but I'll be here all morning if you want to chat beforehand. I'm really, really sorry. Please come. Serena x

Without editing or rereading, I pressed send and threw the phone straight back to Arnold to avoid the temptation of watching and waiting for the "read" ticks.

"And Zoey?" Arnold asked softly.

I inhaled deeply.

"Tomorrow?" My heart was hammering just from texting Beth. I felt like I needed to fix that relationship before I fixed everything with Zoey. Technically we weren't even in a bad place, I just needed to admit the truth.

Arnold inclined his head.

"I never realized how much I relied on other people," I admitted. "My parents for money, Beth and her friendship—basically caretaking—even Zoey for that hit of love. And you." I smiled at Arnold. "My boss but also . . ."

"If you say father figure!" I couldn't tell if he was smiling or if he was horrified at being my surrogate parent.

"Never!"

"Right, we need a change of subject. I'm too young—looking, at least—to be a father figure." He shuffled off the bed. "Do you think that the ice sculptor is still here?"

"What? Why?"

"I think we'll need to borrow his chisel to get this mask off my face."

CHAPTER 39
BETH

EY UP!" DELPHI said when I entered Edith's café. "Unlike you to be here on a Saturday."

"I just got back from the tantra workshop," I replied. Delphi practically bounded over the counter.

"Tell me everything," she said, pulling me into a booth.

"Well . . ." I paused, placing my hands on my hips, unsure of where to begin. "There was drama."

"Michel!" Delphi shouted. "We need a pot of tea. Now," she grinned at me. "Spill it."

It took me nearly forty-five minutes to explain everything to Delphi.

The blow-up with Serena, going to my sister's, coming back to the flat to find it spotless to the point that there was nothing edible or drinkable in the whole flat. The only thing I found in the fridge, apart from the lingering scent of lemons, was our extraordinary collection of condiments.

One should always use a condiment.

It didn't take me long to dump my stuff and head to Edith's, but in that time I'd also received Serena's message about Arnold's wedding.

"So are you going to go?" Delphi asked, downing the dregs of the cold tea in her chipped cup.

"I don't know," I said. "I feel like I should, what with the money and all, but it's a bit weird going when Serena and I aren't exactly talking. And I barely know her boss."

"Well, you can go before the wedding to chat and if you're still not okay with each other afterward, then you go home."

"I'd still have to dress up, though. Make the effort."

Delphi rolled her eyes. "Oh, woe is you, having to do your lipstick and wear earrings. Suck it up: your friendship is at risk."

I raised my eyebrows. "I didn't even think you liked Serena."

"I hardly know her," Delphi pointed out. "But you are like sisters. And that relationship shouldn't fall to bits just because you had an argument."

"A very big argument."

Delphi grimaced as she tasted her cold tea. "We need another pot. Michel!"

"I don't even know how we'll fix things," I told her honestly, while she grabbed the teacup and saucer from my hands. "It wasn't like we were arguing over the chores or a bloke. We've got a lot of shit to sort."

"All the more reason to go tomorrow and get started," Delphi said. "You don't sound like you hate her guts."

"I don't," I said. "I'm just frustrated."

"Good, you should be."

"My sister said the same thing; she told me I should be angry with her."

"Yes, of course you should. Michel!" Delphi shouted again, slipping out of the booth to deposit the tray of tea on the side and to fetch the latest batch that Michel had brought out from behind the beaded kitchen curtain. "Fucking finally," Delphi muttered, sitting down again. "What was I saying?"

"That I should be angry with Serena?"

"Right, you should," she continued, sloshing milk into our fresh cups. "She betrayed your trust, which should never be taken lightly, but it seems like she's also having a crisis right now. And I'm not calling her a bully or anything but hurt people hurt people. She sounds like she needs to get her life in order and actually listen for once."

"Well, she never listens to *me*."

"She *only* listens to you. You're the only person whose opinion she really cares about. And you hers. It's slightly unhealthy, actually."

"That's not true," I said, lightly bashing her on the arm. "I care about your opinion too."

"Good." Delphi smiled. "Then listen to me and go. Sort this all out."

I paused, but Delphi had none of it.

"Nope! Stop it. Stop thinking of reasons not to go and instead just decide you're going and let's chat about what you're going to wear. You should wear green. You look great in green."

I shook my head with a defeatist grin. There was no stopping Delphi when she was sure she was right.

"I'm more concerned with my plus-one." I reached for the teapot.

"That's not brewed yet," Delphi complained.

"I'm not a builder or a Yorkshireman."

"No, you're sadist. Don't you pour that gray water anywhere near my cup. It needs at least another three minutes."

This could go on a while. "Do you want to be my plus-one?"

"I can't," she said. "I would, but I can't. Pete and I are going to a tattoo show at the ExCel London. It's official, Pete's taking his business mobile."

"Oh, that's cool. And are you still going to help?"

"I might." Delphi smirked. "Be his glamorous assistant. Or, more likely, his receptionist."

"Could you do that remotely?"

"Probably not, but it's not like I've got a career for life here."

"You would leave Edith's?"

"Shh!" she said hastily, dragging the teapot noisily across the table to cover my comment. "Not so loud. I don't want Michel to up and quit because I'm planning to."

"It won't be the same without you," I said seriously. "Who's going to talk to me during the day without you?"

"I don't know, Serena. Or maybe a new housemate?"

"What?"

Delphi sighed. "Look, I know I said you and Serena should make up—and you should—but maybe it's time you start to look for a new place. I mean, you can love your sister and not live with her. In fact, the less I see my sister the *more* I love her."

It was not a terrible idea. But . . . "I'm not sure I'd have the money to move out."

"Didn't you have a security deposit on this place?"

"Yeah, but I would only get that back if Serena moved out too. And I don't know how our friendship would recover if we made up and then I moved out? How would that work?"

"It's okay to need your own space."

"After ten years?"

"Especially after ten years!" Delphi argued. "A flatmate isn't for life—not unless you're secretly dating?"

"Serena and I have never dated."

"Fine. I ship you as friends. You should go tomorrow, fix things, and then seriously consider getting your own place. Maybe not immediately, but at the end of your tenancy. I've done this before with friends, you live together and then you run out of things to say and suddenly everything the other person does is irritating and everything they say is heartless as they're not respecting your boundaries. But you don't have boundaries in a flat share. You piss on the same pot. Get out! Get your own spaces, and you'll notice the improvement. After all, how many other thirtysomethings do you know who still live with their best friend from university?"

I didn't reply. There was no need. Delphi wasn't wrong.

"I'd have to move in with strangers . . ."

"Surely, you earn enough for a studio?"

"In London?"

"You're freelance, aren't you? Why do you need to live in London?"

She had a point.

"Since when did you become my life coach?"

"I should charge, but I'll give you mates-rates."

"How kind." I laughed. "Right, well, that's food for thought, but now I need to solve the plus-one issue. I might be able to ask my sister, though I'm not sure how she would feel dropping everything to come to London for a wedding."

"Oooooor . . . you could call Evan?"

I almost choked on my tea. "Absolutely not."

"Oh, come on! Why not?" Delphi grinned. "It's Sunday so he's not working, and it would be a great excuse for the two of you to spend time together. You've got the history."

"I regret telling you the history now," I said. "Why on earth would he want to come to a wedding with me?"

"Why would *I*?" Delphi reminded me. "We're not exactly *there* yet but you still invited me to your friend's boss's wedding, like that was normal."

"But it's Evan!" I said, weakly. "I wouldn't even know where to begin with inviting him."

"Well, first you dial his number . . ."

"I couldn't call him!"

"Don't give me that millennial shit," Delphi said, already reaching across the table for my phone. I dived to stop her but she got there first. "We are not twelve," she reminded me as she held up my screen to my face and unlocked it. "Just call him." She found his number in seconds and held the phone out for me. "Do it." She pressed dial.

"I'm going to kill you!" I whispered as the phone rang. It was late afternoon on a Saturday, what was the likelihood he would even answer? He was probably busy. A super social, popular guy like—

"Hi!"

"Hi!" I responded, shrill. Delphi raised her hand in a "softer" motion. "Hey Evan, it's Beth."

"Hey, I saw. How are you?"

"I'm really good actually, how are you?"

I pulled a face at Delphi that I hoped screamed "help me!" I was having flashbacks to when Serena tried to coach me. Oh god. I couldn't do this.

"You've got this," Delphi mouthed, and her calmness actually did help to calm me.

"I'm great," Evan said lightly. "Bit bored, though, had no plans so just been marathon-watching the latest Netflix shows."

"I wouldn't get attached; it will probably get canceled."

"I think it already has." He laughed knowingly, and I felt myself relax a little bit more.

"Look, I'm sorry for the call out of the blue—but I had a kind of time-sensitive request. And you're welcome to say no."

Delphi shook her head as if to say "don't let him say no!" but at the same time, gave me a thumbs-up. I barreled on.

"I'm going to a wedding tomorrow, and I got a plus-one. My, erm, friend is the Best Woman, so she's kind of taken, but I wondered if you were free and if you wanted to come? It's just for the evening, but it's at this fancy hotel in North London and there'll be free booze and dancing and lots of food. Kind of like a grown-up night out, but with less noise?" I finished weakly.

"Tomorrow?" Evan repeated, and I felt my stomach drop. He was going to be busy. "Sounds great. I'm free."

What the *fuck*!

My mouth had opened so far I felt like my chin was sitting on my chest. Delphi helpfully closed it for me with one hand while doing the "wrap it up" sign with the other.

"Amazing!" I said, my voice reaching a high pitch of excitement and relief. "It's a date."

Even more fuck!

Delphi's eyes widened. I automatically went to say "no, I mean, not a *date*" but something stopped me. I wanted this to be a date. I didn't want to lie.

I said nothing and waited. Half a beat later.

"Sounds like a perfect date," Evan said softly. "I'll wear my best suit and I'll see you there. Just send me the details."

"Of course, I'll text them to you in just a second." Was this adrenaline?

"Great! I'm . . ." He took a breath. "I'm really looking forward to it. Our date," he repeated. "It will be fun."

"Yeah, can't wait." There was another pause and both of us laughed. How old were we? "I'll see you tomorrow."

"Perfect, see you then."

"Bye." I hung up. Now it was my turn to shut Delphi's chin.

"You beauty!" she shouted moments later, arms outstretched victoriously, and I dived into her, lifting her in her seat in an all-encompassing bear hug. "Oh!" she said, surprised. "We are there then."

CHAPTER 40
SERENA

I SPENT THE morning dressing the hotel venue with the final accoutrements as Arnold prepared in the bedroom with his family for his big day. It took me all of thirty minutes to get dressed in my lavender taffeta dress and do my signature smoky eye and neat side bun. It's a life skill.

My outfit was simple but pretty, and it gave me plenty of time to sort out the last-minute panics that the wedding planner and Arnold seemed to discover every ten minutes.

"Where are the button-hole flowers?" Arnold had screamed.

"I've got them." I entered his bedroom with the tray of boutonnieres and began pinning them on him and his *many* groomsmen.

"And the . . ." Arnold began.

"If you're going to ask about the table display flowers, they're with the decorator."

"And the . . ."

"I'm going to help with the chair coverings."

"And the . . ."

"The swagging material just arrived."

"I love you." He fell into my arms in a sweaty, freaked-out mess.

"Don't let your fiancé hear you," I teased, kissing his clean-shaven face and depositing him into the hands of his mother and groomsmen.

If journalism didn't work out, then wedding organizer was clearly an option for me.

All the decorating, organizing, and planning only served as a distraction, though. The real task was yet to come.

After a long afternoon of anxious waiting, with frequent looks at my phone in between Disney originals and sequels, I finally got a text from Beth.

I'll be there at one tomorrow. No kiss, no "see you soon" or "let's talk." But it was something. I just had to fill my time until then and not panic about it.

We were going to talk. She was my best friend; we could sort this out. I just needed to be calm, listen, and not let my self-saboteur pay a visit.

Easier said than done.

It was nearly half past one, and I was separating clear pebbles from amethyst-colored ones into different bowls and chewing on my bottom lip nervously, when I heard a faint "hi" from behind me. My hands shook so suddenly in surprise I almost knocked the bowl of clear pebbles over. "Oh shit!"

"Steady," Beth said, appearing from behind my chair.

"Sorry, I was in my own world." I dumped the rest of the pebbles into the same bowl, regardless of their color and the hour I had spent separating them.

"I can see that. Charming decor," Beth said, looking around the room without irony. "Wish I had money for a party in a place like this."

"Same."

"Well, with your parents, you probably could afford this place," she said, and I bit my lip again. That story could come later.

Beth didn't seem angry or even upset, but she didn't seem like Beth either. There wasn't any warmth about her, just a simmering of anticipation. But maybe I was just projecting.

"Did you go to your parents?" I asked softly, unsure of how to start.

"Fuck no, my mother would never let me leave." She folded her arms. "I went to Penny's."

I glanced around the room again, trying to avoid the moment, looking at all the minor tasks I had yet to complete. The final chair covers, the neatening of serviettes on plates, and the straightening of cutlery. But those tasks were no reason to delay.

"I really fucked up," I said finally.

Beth nodded. I continued.

"I'm sorry I used you and didn't tell you what was really going on, and I'm sorry I wasn't more understanding about everything that's happening with your work and your . . ." I didn't want to call it her *sexual odyssey* anymore. "Your . . . research into your sexuality?"

Beth smiled.

"I'm a bitch?" I shot her a questioning look and she gestured for me to continue. "I used you like a friend never should and I will do anything to make it up to you. I'll . . . I'll do whatever you ask."

Beth pulled out one of the chairs that I had yet to cover and sat down heavily. I did the same, letting my knee gently graze against hers as we sat opposite each other.

She didn't move to hug me; she simply fell back against the table and began fiddling with the rogue pebbles on it.

"I'm still pissed," she said. "But I'm not the sort of person who rants and raves after *already* ranting and raving."

"I know."

Before this blow-up she had been almost a pushover, never really fighting for what she wanted, always avoiding a proper fall-out. But this time she wasn't. She was extremely calm—not from avoidance of a fallout, but in a way that was intimidating.

She scratched her top lip and took a breath. "What you did really hurt me."

Guilt flooded me.

"And I'm still really mad about it," she sighed. "But I also know that you didn't do it to purposely hurt me, because if you did, I wouldn't be here right now." She cleared her throat. "You and Zoey, this thing you have going on, you need to sort it the fuck out. It's all kinds of stupid." Her voice rose in pitch. "And this *discovery* that I'm on is now private. No article. I'm going to decide what I do and what I don't do and who I do those things with. With no input from you unless I invite it. Okay?"

"Of course," I said, holding her gaze. I would be lying if I said I wasn't struggling to hold back tears, but they were tears of relief. I was being reprimanded, but I probably deserved it, and it wasn't cruel. Beth was setting out the ground rules to forgiveness and that was the most important thing. Beth was my family, and I couldn't lose her. "I won't do the article for *The List*. In fact, I won't even mention sex again if you don't want me to. I'll even stop having sex at the flat."

She cocked her head at me, smirking. "Yeah right! What are you going to do, only sleep with Zoey at her place?" Then her smile faltered. "I'm going to look for another place to live, though."

What?! "You want to leave the flat?"

"Not immediately," she said. "But at the end of the tenancy

I think I should." She gulped. "It's been ten years. I think it's time. We could each do with the space, and with Zoey coming to London it might even be the perfect solution. She could even stay on in the flat with you and I can find my own place."

"But what about money?" Wasn't she broke? I always had to pay her rent. Not that I'd be able to do that for much longer.

She smiled again. "That's why I'm not leaving immediately— and I wouldn't anyway," she added. "I need to save, and I probably need to find another job."

"What about WOW? And Evan?" I pressed, leaning forward. This was a big decision for her. For both of us.

But an office job?

"WOW is just a freelance role." Beth smiled. "And besides, I'm not exactly cut out for this freelance lifestyle." She patted my hand.

"Okay." I laughed, wiping away the last of the almost-tears from my eye line. "We can't just return to normal, can we?"

"This is a new normal," Beth said. "New ground rules, a new understanding. I said my piece back on the field and I just gave my conclusion."

"Okay . . . I think." I paused. "Does this mean I can finally ask about Evan?"

"Perhaps." She grinned "If you don't tease me about it."

I held my hands up. "How did it happen?"

"His colleague found my details on LinkedIn and reached out about my rate card. Evan saw my email, realized it was me, and called."

"Oh like fuck that's what happened," I said without thinking. Her look of horror returned, and I shook my head. "No, I'm not saying *you're* lying, I'm saying I bet he was the one that found your details. It's too weird otherwise."

"Maybe it was fate?" Beth said coquettishly.

"Look, I get that you're more into the fated mindset these days, but that sounds like a setup to me. I bet you that he found your details and got his colleague to contact you because he was too shy. This is a guy who didn't make a move in the years you worked together. He wanted to get back in touch."

Beth returned to fiddling with the decorative pebbles, separating them back into the bowls as I was doing before, a slight smirk on her lips. "How much do you want to bet?"

"I bet you a month's worth of cooking dinners that *he* set this whole thing up."

"You're on," she said. "I'll ask him when he comes this evening."

I gasped and grabbed her wrist. "You invited him?"

Beth's face lit up and she nodded. "And he said yes!"

"Oh my god!" I screamed gleefully, throwing my arms up in the air as we both did an odd happy dance in our chairs in unison.

And just like that we returned to being the friends who could care for each other's souls.

If anyone were to look at us together in that moment, they would think we were sisters. And they would be right.

CHAPTER 41
BETH

FOR THE NEXT hour, as the decorators finished setting up around us, Serena gave me the quickest of run downs on all that had happened in the days after our argument.

"I don't think I'll be able to access the bank of Mum and Dad anymore," Serena admitted. "In fact," she laughed slightly forcefully. "I know I won't be able to because I cut them off. I blocked my parents."

"You what?" I almost fell off my chair. "You've blocked them?"

Serena gave me the update on her call with her mum and her dad's visit to London that he never mentioned.

"And you never told me?"

"We weren't really talking to each other, and I didn't want to tell anyone. It made it real. I just thought if I ignored it then the feelings would go away, but . . ." She cleared her throat.

"Oh honey," I said, squeezing her hands. "You are amazing."

"I don't think I'm amazing, I think I'm a fuckup. A newly broke fuckup!"

For a second, I wanted to tell her that I wouldn't leave, that we could still live together and save money.

But no, we needed our space.

Instead, I placed my hands on her shoulders in a steadying way.

"You'll be fine. You are a bad-ass journalist, you can earn money left, right, and center, you don't need them. I've got you, and so does Arnold."

Serena inhaled and shook out her head, deciding rather than telling me that I was right.

"I've got this." She winked and said, "Fuck them."

"Precisely. Fuck your parents," I repeated. "Not literally," I added, as Arnold's mother decided to walk past us at that moment, to chivy us out of the reception hall and into the foyer.

It was in the foyer that I properly had a chance to appreciate the beauty of the wedding. My entrance into the hotel had been marred by nerves and the quick downing of a complimentary bellini I stole from the bar. But now that my nerves had dissipated and my friendship with Serena had been given the lifeline it needed, I could enjoy the over-the-top elegance.

"Bloody hell, Serena," I said in awe, resting up against a vacant wall.

The foyer was colored in lilac, amethyst, and white, from the purple fairy lights to the mixed shades swagging up the grand staircase. There were petals cascading across the silver guest books, blown-up photos of Arnold and Gareth, tastefully done in black and white, at what was clearly their engagement photoshoot. It was cozy yet big at the same time.

"Is the swagging too much?" Serena asked, directing my gaze back to the staircase and what was clearly her handiwork, but I shook my head fervently.

"It's just the right amount of too much," I said, lifting my fingers in an "OK" symbol and she laughed. "And you . . ." I grabbed her arm and forced her to turn under it. The lavendar dress had a slit that reached her thigh and pulled in at the waist, so her curves were accentuated. It twirled elegantly against her skin, exposing her long legs in her four-inch heels, with the necessary blister plasters on her ankles. Even at a gay wedding I bet she could pull a bloke. In this dress, Serena could make a lazy eye straight.

"Phwoar!"

"I should get Arnold to hire you as a reviewer with all these 'phwoar' and 'A-OK' remarks," she teased, looping her arm around mine and directing me to the ceremonial room.

The doors to the ceremony room were opened by two ushers in white suits. They handed us each an order of service and a booklet of song lyrics; apparently the ceremony would involve elements of a sing-along.

"You can't have a gay wedding without someone singing Cher," Serena pointed out. It was hard to argue.

We took our seats in the second row, behind Arnold's immediate family.

"I need to fix my makeup before the ceremony starts," Serena said, wiping under her eyes as I pulled my clutch to my front. Inside I had all the necessary ephemera for a wedding: lipstick, concealer, a loose tissue, two paracetamols, plasters, a sample perfume spray, and my debit card and house key.

"Oh god," Serena said, looking at herself through her phone camera.

"You've just kind of made your eyes smokier," I told her. "How do you even cry perfectly?" I teased and Serena scoffed.

"Hardly, I'm pretty sure I was just all cried out," she laughed and then stopped suddenly. "But it was okay."

"Babe, it's fine," I reassured her, offering her my concealer. I knew she wasn't trying to make me feel guilty, and she hadn't. She needed to cry it out, she needed to feel again and stop keeping everything in. "I knew what you meant."

"Sorry," she said, smudging some of the concealer in her crease, as I offered her the tissue to wipe off the excess from the corner of her eyes. "How do I look?"

"Less like a badger."

"Just what I wanted to hear," she said jokily. "Right, I'm ready. I need to say a few hellos and get an update from the ushers. I'll be right back," she said, standing from her chair, giving me a chance to reapply my lipstick and check in with Evan over text. I had sent him all the details the night before and he had replied with a list of questions:

What should I wear?

What color are you wearing? Should I choose a matching tie?

Is a tie too formal?

It's too formal. I'm going no tie.

Is a bow tie more acceptable?

Ignore me. I don't own a bow tie.

He was clearly as nervous as I was.

Given the new "date" scenario, I had tried on nearly every outfit I owned searching for something sexy but suitable.

I decided on a string-tie black halter neck with a small slit in the cleavage that I accessorized with a loose French braid and some red fabric earrings that Penny told me looked like curtain pulls. The dress was racy and backless; it was something I had basically bought on a dare but never worn. The fact that it fit and I felt sexy was giving me the confidence boost I needed to not worry about my "date" with Evan.

Service is beginning soon, I texted him. Got some good seats. I'll save you a Bellini. Immediately I saw the text bubble from him appear.

Great! I'm heading for the train. I'll be there at five. Ooh! Delicious. And then almost immediately after, I can't wait to see you.

Oh my god. I could have melted in my seat.

> If you can't spot me, I'm the one in the backless black dress.

The eye-popping cartoon GIF that he sent in reply was the perfect response.

I was helplessly grinning from ear to ear when Serena returned to her seat. She didn't even need to ask why. Blithely she nudged me in the ribs just as "Chapel of Love" began to play and an officiant in a smart black suit and purple heels invited everyone to stand to welcome the grooms.

We all did as we were told and moments later the doors at the back of the hall opened and Gareth and Arnold appeared holding hands in their juxtaposing purple and white suits.

Tears began welling up almost immediately in Serena's eyes, ruining her newly applied concealer, while I put on my best "don't they look happy" face for the older relations. We all began to sing the lyrics of "Chapel of Love" as per our booklets, as the two grooms walked giggling, arm in arm down the aisle, mouthing, "Here we go!"

The vows were personalized by each groom, and the two of them sobbed delicately and wiped away each other's tears in between the singalong of Cher's "Believe" and Bruno Mars's "Marry You." Gareth stumbled over his words at one point and Arnold embraced him to give him the boost he needed to carry on. And then, all too soon, the ceremony was over. The rings were exchanged, the kiss was lingeringly passionate, and the two grooms held hands as they descended the aisle, now happily husbands for life. Or at least for as long as Arnold could resist filing for divorce again.

CHAPTER 42
BETH

THE CEREMONY WAS followed by a lukewarm three-course wedding lunch and speeches from the grooms only. Gareth shared a brief thank-you and then invited everyone to the dance floor.

At least when Evan arrived, shortly before five, I had an excuse for being a sweaty mess.

"He's here," I whispered to Serena on the dance floor, noticing that he hadn't yet spotted me. "What do I do?" I shouted, suddenly panicked.

She smiled confidently, grabbed my hand and danced me off the floor as Lady Gaga's "Born This Way" was belted on the floor by a gaggle of guests.

"Evan!" Serena called out as we reached the edge. He turned, looking bemused and out of place in his button-down white shirt, red tie, and navy trousers. He carried a blazer over his shoulder with two fingers. "Are you Evan?" Serena repeated and he nodded, immediately blushing I noticed. "I'm Serena."

She was drunk, but still appeared sober, and embraced him awkwardly.

"Oh, Beth's mentioned you," he said, placing a hand on her back until she finally released him. "It's nice to finally meet you."

"Likewise!" she shouted over the DJ. "I need a drink, but I brought you . . ." She left a pause as she pulled me into the front. "Beth. Enjoy."

"Thanks for that introduction, I feel like a dish." I laughed nervously.

"Well, she is very dishy," Serena scoffed. "Sorry, dad joke. I'm going to depart this hang. Find you on the dance floor later." She almost went to leave and then stopped and turned back. "Evan—"

"Yes," he said, smiling and clearly charmed by Serena despite her slightly messy appearance.

"Do you drink?"

"I do."

"Great." She beamed at him. "I'll grab you some drinks." She went to leave again and this time followed through, only stopping to turn and blow me a kiss and mouth along to the song.

"Sorry, she's had a few too many." I laughed, wiping the sweat off my top lip as Evan wrapped his blazer over his arm. I noticed he took a moment to look me over, his eyes traveling up and down my dress. And then again.

"You look . . . amazing," he said, blushing again. "Just . . . damn."

"Same." I smiled, feeling my confidence rising. "I see you went with a tie."

He picked it up and rolled his eyes, "Yeah," he said, slightly embarrassed. "I never know how to dress for weddings."

"Especially when you don't know either of the grooms," I remarked. "I don't often dress up so I thought I would make an effort for a change."

"You would look great in anything, even a bin bag," Evan said. "But I imagine that's not appropriate for a wedding?"

We smiled timidly in the brief pause. "I was going to get some air," I said as the music switched from Lady Gaga to Diana Ross in the background. "I've been dancing."

"Sure," Evan said, turning on his heel so I could walk beside him. There weren't many people in the smoking garden, only a few relatives—mostly teenagers—with vapes and a look of anticipatory guilt like they were waiting to be caught. Evan and I nodded in greeting as we took a seat on a nearby bench resting against the outer brick wall. It wasn't too chilly outside, but I wrapped my arms around my middle. Evan didn't say a word as he sat forward and wrapped the blazer over my back.

"Oh, thank you," I said, and he nodded again. "Thanks for coming, I know it was a bit of a random invite, but I thought . . ." I didn't know what I thought. I had a plus-one and I wanted him to come.

"I had nothing to do—not that that was the reason I said yes," he said suddenly, and I shook my head to show that I understood what he meant as he became slightly flustered. "I mean, I was just going to be watching TV or working, so it was really nice to be asked. And the fact it was you asking was really . . . well, I was pleased."

"We both kind of suck at this small talk thing," I blurted out, feeling that we needed to break out of the civilities and get back to being ourselves.

Immediately Evan relaxed, his shoulders sank and his smile went from nervous to playful. He gave me a pleased side eye as we both slumped against the wall.

"Would you really have been working on a Sunday?"

He nodded, sucking his teeth. "Entrepreneurial habit, I'm afraid. We're all workaholics. You should know that about me if tonight goes well."

"Oh, you're preempting a second date?" I bit my lip.

"I've cleared my diary, I've preempted several." He smirked. Chuckling, I reminded him he was supposedly a workaholic. "Well, I was hoping to invite you into the office next week actually, combine business with pleasure. Get a business meeting in with a lunch and then maybe dinner."

"Now would that count as one date or two?"

"I think two?" He laughed. "Pretty speedy work on our part."

"Well." I gestured between the two of us. "We've got to catch up a bit, I mean, how long have we known each other?"

"Three years?" Evan said gingerly, thinking back. "And I've been wanting to ask you out for at least two of those." His blush returned, but he pushed through.

"Same!" I said without hesitation, but then the age-old fears appeared in my train of thought. What stopped me? Sex. Sex stopped me. Would he understand? Could we make it work? Did he want to have sex? Is this the end, at the beginning?

I really liked Evan, but I couldn't just sleep with him off the bat. I knew enough from my experience with Rupert the escort that that wasn't possible.

I could feel myself beginning to freak out, my heart was hammering in my chest and my palms were clammy.

Oh screw it.

I pulled his blazer closer around my shoulders and turned so I was facing him more on the bench.

"There's always been a factor that's stopped me from reaching out, actually," I began, and I saw Evan's face expression drop a little in concern.

"Really? What was it?"

"Well, you know how I told you I went off to that tantra experience," I reminded him, "but it wasn't sex-based?" Evan nodded.

"Was it all crystals and meditation as you expected?"

"Sort of . . ." I lied, wincing. "I went because I was helping my friend with her article—though that's not happening anymore—but the article was actually meant to be about me and my sexuality." I inhaled again and forced a smile. It was okay to be uncomfortable, it was just Evan. His hand inched closer to mine on the bench and I felt the warmth of his fingertip against my thumb. He made no interruption, just gently pressed closer in a way that wasn't oppressive or invading; it was comforting. "I'm demisexual," I said finally and cleared my throat, not looking at him. "Do you know what that is?"

I looked up and could see that Evan was thinking.

"I've heard of demisexuality but don't know what the specificities are," he said, ever analytical in his speech. "Is it part of asexuality?"

Surprised, I nodded. The fact that he knew that was promising.

"It is. Where asexuality is when a person typically doesn't feel *any* sexual attraction for anybody, a demisexual—like me—can feel sexual attraction for a person but only after they develop a strong emotional connection with someone. And I don't mean they have a friendship or get on well, but a really strong connection like complete trust or a sense of absolute safety. At least for me. Everyone that's ace has unique feelings and different interpretations of a strong connection. But for me I think it comes down to a sense of safety. That no matter what that person will love me, even if I fuck things up or can't go through with something or I do something wrong."

I hadn't taken a breath and it showed. Sitting back against the wall I closed my eyes and exhaled harshly so a loose piece of my French braid flew across my face.

There was a pause and Evan said nothing, but then he moved the piece of hair back across my face for me.

Immediately the heat seemed to leave my cheeks and enter my chest instead. My ribcage was expanding from my inside, and I felt as if I had run a marathon.

"Thanks," I whispered. My tongue felt like it was swelling to the size of a sirloin steak, but I pushed on. I was feeling the beginnings of pure fear as I waited for the typical reaction I always got after telling men I was demisexual. That that was "fine" before they immediately started to make a move or quiz me further only with the aim of finding the flaws in the descriptors of asexuality. But Evan did none of that.

He sat back alongside me, and I heard him laugh quietly.

"Sex is something I've found so uninteresting my whole life, and I think for the first time I might know why."

I sat up like a bolt. "Wait, really?"

He nodded. "I mean, I've had sex a few times—at university, with a friend I thought was a girlfriend, and a one-night stand, but that was it. And, not to talk sexual history on a first date, but I didn't find any of those experiences particularly enjoyable. But that's probably because I wasn't sure I wanted to have sex. I kind of felt like I had to. But that's not to say it wasn't consensual," he added.

"I know what you mean. You kind of feel you can't say no in the moment." I nodded but then stopped. "Although, I've always said no, in fact . . ." I looked at the nearby group of vaping teenagers who were still enjoying their explicit freedom. "I've never actually had sex," I half-whispered, hoping it wouldn't carry. I didn't see Evan's reaction, but when I eventually faced him, he just continued to smile in his usual no-worries kind of way.

"I kind of wish I hadn't," he remarked eventually. "Although, I didn't know there was a name for that feeling. I just assumed my love language was words rather than touch."

"And yet here you are," I pointed out. "Touching my hand and wrapping your blazer over my shoulders."

He smirked again, fully taking my hand in his own. His palm practically enveloped mine, and he was so warm. There was nothing clammy or sticky about his skin, just warmth and comfort.

"I'm figuring things out, I guess," he said.

I laughed so hard it shocked him. "You have no idea how much I'm figuring things out at the moment."

"Really?" He was playfully intrigued, and I felt I had no choice but to fill him in on my recent sexual discovery. I told him about the sex therapist, the speed dating, even Rupert the escort. (I didn't mention the dilation kit; we certainly weren't *there* yet.)

"Did the tantra workshop enlighten you?" Evan asked. The teenagers had gone, they'd got bored of waiting to be caught and had made their way back inside to the warmth and joys of dancing the Macarena.

"In some ways," I admitted. "I mostly learned that there was more to pleasure and partnership than just sex. A lot of it is about trust."

"I'd agree with that," he said, still gently playing with the grip of my hand in his absent-mindedly. "I've never experienced tantra myself but I'm of the mind that for a relationship to work then there must be complete trust and honesty between the partners. Excluding the odd white lie about how much you like your girlfriend's new dress or how much you *love* watching *Bridgerton* with them."

In one laugh I seemed to release all the tension that I was holding in my body and for a moment I actually felt an odd stirring between my legs.

"What? Don't you enjoy *Bridgerton*?"

"Watching season one, episode sex—sorry *six*—with your three male housemates and one of their girlfriends kind of put me off for life," Evan admitted. "But, hey, if it made my girlfriend happy then I would do it for her. Small sacrifice."

"What about sex?" I blurted. "What if she asked not to have sex, at least for a while, is that a small sacrifice?"

"Yes. If she asked not to then we wouldn't have sex until she wanted to. And I'd hope she'd do the same for me if I asked not to."

"Sounds easy in theory," I pointed out, my mind slowly reminding me that I was having a sex talk with *Evan*! Wait until I told Serena, or Delphi, or Mr. Bates, or *anyone* for that matter!

He made a *pfft* sound. "It is easy. If a partner says *not tonight* then the other partner could always DIY or just go to sleep. I really don't get the fuss. But then I always thought I was odd for valuing emotional intimacy over physical. It's not that acceptable for guys."

I swallowed the huge amount of spit in my mouth and I crossed my legs as the stirring between them began to distract me. But crossing my legs only made it worse, in the best possible sense. Now I could feel a slight pulsing inside me.

"I feel like I've just converted you to demisexuality," I admitted, leaning into him so I almost rested against his shoulder.

"You make it sound like a religion. I just think sexuality is fluid."

"You should go to a tantra workshop one day, you'd fit right in."

"Why, thank you. I'll take that as a compliment."

"You should!" I said, laughing, my smile widening across

my face. Out of the corner of my eye I spotted Serena for the first time. She was standing in the doorway that led to the smoking garden. She was hard to miss in her sexy lavender dress, standing legs akimbo in an unflattering way as she blocked the exit so no one could come out and disturb us. Instead, she was mouthing the words to "Spice Up Your Life," using her dancing hips to block the would-be smokers. "Vaping's bad for you!" I heard her shout periodically. "Do you like breathing?"

"I think we need to rescue the pulmonary-challenged smokers," Evan whispered in my ear, having spotted her as well.

"They have a right, I suppose," I agreed. "But before we do, can I ask, how do you feel about kissing?"

"Kissing?" Evan repeated. Our faces were inches away from each other. He knew what I meant, there was no need to explain. "It's underrated."

"I agree," I said. "Kissing's fun, sex is messy."

"Interesting philosophy."

"I should put it on a T-shirt." I leaned closer and so did he. Our lips met and the only sound I could hear was Serena screaming. We didn't pull away. I felt like fist-pumping the air like a modern-day Judd Nelson, but I didn't. Instead I fell into him and he placed his hand across my bare back, under the blazer, and held me closer.

Kissing him was just like holding his hand. Warm, comforting, and long overdue. I've never understood why people say they see fireworks, I just felt like I was as safe as I could possibly be. I was with Evan.

Suddenly the excited, slightly buzzed woman inside me made a mental appearance and I reluctantly released myself, and Evan.

"One final thing," I said quickly. "Did David actually find my details on LinkedIn or was that a ruse just to contact me?"

His laugh gave it away. "I found your details and I asked David to contact you as I was too nervous . . ." he said, and I had no choice but to let my smile reform.

"You owe me a month of dinners!" Serena shouted from the doorway.

CHAPTER 43
SERENA

NOT ONLY DID I love this particular wedding for the fact that it was so beautiful to see my gorgeous friend Arnold marry the love of his life—for now, as he would say—I also loved it because you can always depend on the gay community to provide the best kind of entertainment—in this case an impromptu *Drag Race*–style Ball with categories including Virgin Voguing, Butch Queen in Pumps, and an Open to All category, which I had to participate in, of course.

Once Beth and Evan had separated themselves from each other in the smoking garden, Beth rejoined me on the dance floor with Evan politely requesting to stay on the sidelines. He needed to catch up, and since I had scored two bottles of prosecco, he had the means to do so.

Happily, I was being bought drinks left, right, and diagonally by Arnold's other besties, the fun aunts, and even the occasional teenager who seemed to be up to no good and thought they'd try to score. The effort was a ten, the execution was a three.

Beth left me on the dance floor periodically to have a drink with Evan at the bar or to rescue him from the throngs of single, drunken gays who tried to charm him into batting for their team.

"You look just like my ex-husband!" one had said.

"Hold me! I've done my arms in doing the worm." Was another's attempt at snuggling, impressive as it worked briefly.

"Be careful," I told Evan while Beth was in the toilets. I thought I would rescue him from the latest batch of men eyeing him like a snack. "That one," I said, pointing to one of Arnold's ushers, "is the only person I know who has ever turned down a proposal and posed with the ring on social media. The caption was *I said no*. You'd need a lifetime of Sudocrem for that burn."

Evan was laughing.

"I'm glad you came," I told him honestly. "To see Beth. And that the two of you finally made a fucking move."

"I know, I know." He rolled his eyes in jest. "We took the slow route."

"Slow route? Darling, you walked backwards."

"But it was worth the wait," he countered.

I patted his cheek. "Aww, you're so sweet," I sighed. "It sickens me."

He blushed. "You did all this?" He gestured to what remained of my decorations.

"I'm multi-talented," I laughed. "Although Gareth did most of it; I just offered some leg work."

"I'm very impressed," Evan reiterated, beaming widely and sincerely.

"I like you!" I declared, slamming my hand against his shoulder so he went flying forward, almost spilling his drink over Beth. Miraculously she dodged just in time and draped herself over Evan's shoulder.

"I'm glad to hear it," she said. "But don't bruise him in the process."

"Sorry!" I shouted over the sound of "The Grease Mega-mix" beginning to blare from the DJ booth. "Ooh, my fave," I said, attempting to back it up onto the dance floor. But I noticed that Beth's facial expression had shifted into a look of pure dread. "What?" I asked, looking down at my front thinking that perhaps Evan's drink had gotten on me.

Beth lifted her hand and waved, offering a very tight smile. Evan stared at her oddly, that was not a smile for a first date.

"Are you okay?" he asked, and I stopped.

"Hi Zoey," Beth said, and my stomach dropped quicker than the beat to "Greased Lightnin'."

"Hey," came the reply from behind me. Her Liverpudlian lilt was more pronounced than ever.

I turned instantly; there was no stopping my body once Zoey appeared. We were like magnets.

She was smiling, fiddling with the chain of her clutch bag and correcting her navy mesh slit jumpsuit.

"Hi," I said, not knowing if my face was following my orders and beaming at her or if my insides and mind were melting and I looked completely panicked.

Her red hair was piled up in a purposefully messy updo and she wore blood-red lipstick to match, which accentuated her smile perfectly. I wanted to kiss her lips so badly.

Zoey's eyes flickered in Beth and Evan's direction over my shoulder, I could hear Beth's whispering. Evan had a lot to catch up on now that he and Beth were officially dating.

"We're going to grab another drink," Beth shouted pointedly, as "Greased Lightnin'" moved into "Summer Nights." "Evan spilled his," she explained unnecessarily to Zoey as she passed. "Can we get you anything?"

We, already.

"I'd love a vodka and orange," Zoey replied, and Beth nodded ferociously as if she had been handed a sacred task, before quickly dragging an enjoyably bemused Evan back to the bar.

Zoey and I were alone. Or as alone as you can be near the dance floor at a friend's wedding.

"Hi," Zoey repeated, not quite as brightly as me but still with her glorious smile. Her jasmine-scented perfume wafted in my direction and the moment I smelled it I felt my nerves from all the build-up around needing to admit my feelings begin to dissipate. It was just Zoey.

If Evan and Beth could tell each other how they felt with no issue, when they didn't even know how the other felt, then I could tell Zoey.

"I didn't know you were going to be here," I admitted. "But I'm glad you came, I wanted to talk to you."

Zoey stepped forward, warmly placing a hand on my arm and politely moving me away from the dance floor and a group of great-aunts who were arguing about the choice of cake. I noticed one of them looked like they had been stabbed in the neck when a nearby relative defended Arnold's choice to have a chocolate cake.

"What did you want to say?" Zoey said, when we were safely ensconced in the foyer outside of the reception hall, just far enough away from the wedding that we had privacy but not too far to look like we were hiding.

I shut my eyes momentarily and rolled my lips together in a nervous mix of anticipation and sudden fear.

"Zoey," I began weakly. "I've been a mess lately."

Zoey continued to fiddle with the gold chain of her bag and I pulled her hand into mine. I needed her for this, oddly. It used to be Beth I needed to bolster me up when admitting or doing things that frightened me, but now I realized it was Zoey. The woman who made me feel calm and excited all in the same moment. "I've also realized that I'm shit with feelings."

Zoey made a loud "ha" sound, although I don't think she meant to.

"I've never been any good at expressing how I feel, I keep it all bottled up and just hope that people either stick around long enough to break through or I just let them go. But with you . . . I've been so terrified that you wouldn't stick around that when you did, I freaked out and began to push you away."

Zoey didn't say anything, still. She wasn't usually this silent.

"But really . . ." I breathed in and noticed that I didn't feel drunk anymore. I felt in control. "Really I'm fucking falling in love with you."

It didn't take a second for Zoey's face to erupt into a wide smile.

"You knew?" I said accusatorily.

"Well," she began, but then she caught the giggles. A never-ending cascade of giggles that led me to start laughing and then to start crying with laughter, until the two of us were wrapped in each other's arms, holding each other up as we could barely breathe for laughter. "I've been waiting for you to realize it for ages!" Zoey managed to say, after several gulps of air, still holding me at the waist with one hand and pushing back the annoying loose piece of hair from my eyes with the other. "And Arnold may have called."

"He what?!" I flung my head back, looking into the reception hall in search of the romantic traitor, but he was too far gone doing the dance to "Tiger Feet" to notice either of us in the foyer. "He called you?" I questioned, and Zoey nodded, still beaming from ear to ear.

"Last night. He said I needed to get my arse to the wedding, to find you and not let you go as the two of us were made for each other and could we please just admit it so the world could move on."

"Oh, that little prick."

"He may have stolen your romantic moment," Zoey said, leaning in for the briefest of kisses, her hands on either side of my face. "But it was the best phone call of my life."

The kisses that followed were long and lingering and may have involved a dip or two on my part. I couldn't help it. The floodgates had opened, I was crying, laughing, and I wanted everyone to know that I was in love with Zoey.

"I want this to be more than just sex," I told her between kisses, feeling her breath on my chin, as her scent continued to drive me crazy.

"I should think so," she whispered teasingly, kissing one of my cheeks and then the other and then slowly drawing her lips over mine again.

"And I think you should move in with me."

She stopped, our lips just barely touching.

"What?" I felt her lips twitch into a smile.

"You need a place, I don't think I'll ever be able to be away from you for more than eight hours ever again, and I think that you should move in with me."

"Don't you need to check with Beth before you offer?" she suggested, still smiling.

"NO!" Beth shouted, suddenly appearing at our side. Clearly, she had been hovering by the doorway with Evan, listening in and celebrating for me just as much as I had celebrated for her. "Of course not! Move the fuck in. The more the merrier!" she said before turning on the spot and heading to the dance floor with Evan, making a large whooping sound that made the merrymakers cheer.

"She's amazing," Zoey said before we both burst into unstoppable laughter.

"It doesn't fully apply until she says it completely sober—but god I hope it's true." I chuckled.

"If that's good with both of you," Zoey said finally, placing one hand against my cheek, "I would love to move in with my girlfriend as well."

"Well, it's about time," I teased before we finally, desperately, kissed.

EPILOGUE
BETH

Six months later

TO BETH," DELPHI said, lifting her mug of warm white wine. I hadn't realized the fridge wasn't plugged in when they arrived, so our drinks were barely cool.

Serena sat panting, nursing an empty glass, having just slumped on the sofa after bringing up the last two boxes to my new flat.

"Never . . . again," she said between breaths, and Zoey sat next to her and swapped out Serena's empty glass with her full one.

"I got you, babe," she said, and Serena sat forward briefly to kiss her cheek.

"I love you," she said, leaning her head across Zoey's shoulder, and Zoey kissed her forehead.

My god. The image of the two of them in my flat loved up and perfectly in tune with each other was not something I could have even imagined a year ago. But then none of the scene I was currently sitting in had ever crossed my imagination.

On my left, sitting on the unmade mattress of my new bed were Pete and Delphi, the latter of whom was still gesturing for everyone to follow suit and lift their array of glasses in my honor.

And on my right was Evan.

My perfect—or near perfect—boyfriend, who was currently helping me organize my life, as he emptied the box of new crockery and kitchenware that Serena had just brought up three flights of stairs.

"To Beth," he said with his back to Delphi. Clearly he could feel her dark eyes baring into him when he hadn't raised a glass. He quickly pivoted on the spot to lean across the tiny dining room table I was currently sitting on to kiss me.

He went to return to the unboxing, but I placed my hand under his chin and drew him back to me for a further kiss, or three.

"We have company," he whispered cheekily, and I released him.

Although we may not have had *penetrative* sex in the six months we had been a couple, we had certainly explored other avenues of intimacy. From experimental touching in the shower—and the discovery that showerheads are much more affordable than vibrators—to hour-long kissing sessions when we were meant to be watching Netflix, which left us both in serious need of a lip balm.

I loved Evan, or at least I was getting to the point where I truly felt like I loved him and not just in a first-love infatuation kind of way. He was the first man I could see myself having sex with and not feeling repulsed by it; and though I hadn't shared it with him, there had been moments where I had been truly turned on by him. The eagerness was there but not the right timing—unless I'd wanted to make the mile-high club story from the hen do a reality.

He was more interested in me enjoying myself and *wanting* to try, than caring about whether we did try. To have someone like that on my side, who genuinely cared for me, and not just because of my body, was unbelievably reassuring. In fact, I'd go as far to say it was my biggest turn-on.

To the outside eye we were the Instagram ideal of a couple, though I would say we were a very pedestrian version.

While most Instagrammable couples were off galivanting in the Bahamas, making their friends jealous, Evan and I were happy going on trips to bargain home stores, having brunches with friends, and spending our nights in—with his three roommates or Serena and Zoey until recently—drinking beer and watching TV.

"You two are so loved up," Pete remarked about me and Evan, as Evan finally gave up on the unboxing and gestured for me to move over a little so he could join me on the dining table. He wrapped his arm around my waist and pulled me closer so my face was level with his shoulder. It was an awkward seat as space was so limited in my flat, but I didn't mind. He had worn his best cologne and was freshly shaved so his chin and neck were quite frankly the best place to be right now.

"Young love, ay." Pete laughed, following Evan's lead and pulling Delphi closer into him on the mattress. But Delphi wasn't having any of that and pushed straight back off him.

"I'm hot, babe," she complained, lifting her long hair and fanning the back of her neck with one of the many takeaway pamphlets that had been stacked on the floor of my flat when I arrived that morning with the keys. "Why would you move in during an unseasonal heatwave?" she remarked spikily, and I shrugged.

"The tenancy was up; it was the only day the movers could do it . . ." I looked around at my new studio flat with misplaced pride.

By some miracle I had found the money to rent a studio flat in Luton. (Although technically outside of London, it was still on Thameslink.)

It was tiny, with a one-size-fits-all bedroom, living room, and kitchenette, and a one-person bathroom so small that you'd be lucky not to graze your elbows against the walls when rinsing your shampoo.

It was going to cost me a little over six hundred pounds a month to rent, but it was just off the high street, close to the train station, and a short walk away from Evan's flat.

We had briefly discussed my moving in with him when I began flat hunting, but with his roommates and their many visiting partners, we agreed I was better off finding a place of my own. Evan moving in with me was not yet something we had discussed, even after the heavenly last few months. There was an unspoken understanding between us, as between me and Serena, that this was the time for me to have my own space. For the first time in my entire life.

"I feel betrayed, of course," Delphi added, sipping her warm wine. "That you would leave me alone in London with just Pete for company."

"Love you too, babe," he said.

"I'll visit, and you can come here whenever you want," I told her sincerely.

"I'll have to. Now that's Edith's closed"—the rundown little café had finally shut up shop—"where else would we meet?"

"We can make ourselves available, now that we're on the road," Pete reminded Delphi.

Ever since he had taken his tattoo business mobile, and Delphi had tagged along as his self-declared publicity manager—putting those Instagram skills to good use—our friendship had migrated to the natural next step of a WhatsApp chat. There was hardly a day that went past that we weren't swapping anecdotes of our daily routines or sharing GIFs for no reason.

Delphi was the friend who was determined to be my friend, and I had no choice in the matter. Not that I wouldn't want her to be; she was a refreshingly blunt addition to my growing circle of relationships. From the addition of Zoey, then Evan's mates and colleagues at WOW, to my new colleagues at my nine-to-five office job in St. Albans.

I had gone from struggling as a wannabe freelancer to working in an office with people I surprisingly could stand. Sure, the job—creating marketing campaigns to promote the nearby university—was often quite basic and a bit like talking to a room full of people with their backs to me, but it was nice to have a steady paycheck and not have to worry about adult things like my pension, paid leave, or office equipment.

The new job hadn't been celebrated, but my new flat was seen as a far more exciting life step. Penny had sent me some flowers and a card that read "Congratulations. I hope your new neighbors aren't pricks." My parents had given me a £300 Ikea voucher, which seemed like an unprecedented investment in my lifestyle, and of course I had mostly used it to buy decorative items and mason jars I had nothing to put inside.

"You can always come to ours," Zoey suggested to Delphi and me.

Ever since she had moved in with Serena and me a few months prior, Zoey had been the queen of the party. It hardly felt like a week went by without some visitors coming round for breakfast, lunch, or dinner. From Arnold and Gareth, post-honeymoon in Australia, both extremely sunburned and eager to discuss Zoey and Serena's massive PDA at their wedding, to Penny, who came down for a girl's weekend and for the first time in years seemed to relinquish some weight off her shoulders.

It had come as no surprise to me that once I had found a place of my own, Serena and Zoey followed suit and did the same.

Two things had become clear when Zoey had moved in with us. The first was that she needed more entertaining space. The second was that she and Serena needed to get a flat on the ground-floor. Mr. Kilmeckiz had punched a hole in his ceiling from complaining about the noise the two of them made within two weeks of Zoey moving in and had moved out fairly soon after. There are not enough brooms in the world to combat the gymnastics the two of them get up to.

But not only that, Serena admitted that the ghosts of the two of us, as we had been before my sexual odyssey—as I have become comfortable with referring to it again—were lingering in the old flat, and it no longer felt like her retreat.

She wanted a fresh start, just as much as I did.

The two of them had found a spacious one-bedroom flat just off Kentish Town with a massive kitchen for Zoey to cook in (Serena was still lacking in that department) and a living room that fit a dining table that the two of them could work at when working from home *and* use as a buffet and/or games table for when guests came by.

Their flat was on Thameslink, so Serena and I were only four stops away from each other. It was the space we needed, while still allowing us to stay close enough to see each other whenever we wanted.

"You know we'll be there," I told Zoey. "You have a forty-four-inch TV and a slushie machine. Try and keep me away."

"Do you have good Wi-Fi?" Delphi asked.

Serena had finally caught her breath after lugging all my belongings up the stairs.

"Wi-Fi is key, now that we're hybrid workers." *The List* had made a cost-cutting decision in the form of a new hot-desking office space that limited the days Serena, Zoey, and Arnold were in the office. "I wouldn't last without it."

"I'm there!" Delphi shouted and leaned over to high-five Zoey, who was thrilled to have inherited a new friend.

I laughed.

"I feel left out." Evan smirked as he rubbed his hand up and down my back.

"Maybe we'll leave them to it and just stay in," I teased, playing with the undone buttons of Evan's shirt. I heard Serena's gasp and turned to grin at her.

"You two!" she beamed at me, like a friend looking at their other friend's newborn baby. "I'm so proud of you."

"And look." I lifted my hair away from my ear. "No earphones telling me what to do."

We all laughed, except Pete. Delphi patted him on the chest in an "I'll tell you later" kind of way.

But I thought, *let me tell him now.*

"Pete," I began, still grinning as Serena and Zoey instinctively intertwined themselves on the sofa and Evan subtly moved his hand under my shirt onto my back. "Have you ever experienced a sexual odyssey?"

ACKNOWLEDGMENTS

If you're reading this because you've finished this book *or* you've jumped ahead to have a nosy look at my author life, then hello! Thank you for picking up this novel.

Acknowledgments, to me, are a lot like Oscar speeches. I'm always immeasurably surprised and overwhelmed that I get to write them. There are also always so many people to thank, and I'm terrified I'm going to forget someone.

The person I'm least likely to forget is my incredible agent, Hannah Schofield. I'll never say enough thank-yous, you have been my rock and my cheerleader throughout this whole process, and beyond, so thank you, thank you, thank you!

To Asanté Simons for acquiring my novel and to Shannon Plackis for editing it, you also enter into the above debt of thank-yous.

To everyone at Avon, I am eternally grateful for your support and your hard work. As a fellow publisher I know it takes a village so cheers to you all: Taylor Turkington in marketing, Camille Collins in publicity, Andrew Di Cecco in production, copyeditor Kim Daly, proofreader Nicole Celli, production editor Amanda Hong, interior designer Diahann Sturge-Campbell, cover designer Paul Miele-Herndon, illustrator Amber Day, Kelsey Heiss-O'Brien in content management,

Brittani DiMare in managing editorial, audio managing editor Kirsten Clawson, audio executive producer Abigal Marks, and audio production manager Peter Bobinski.

And not to forget the booksellers, reviewers, sales teams, and librarians, each and every one is a vertebra in the backbone of this industry and I'm grateful for every ounce of support offered. It really means the world.

Of course, I have to thank my family else they'll disinherit me . . . also I quite like them. To my parents for their endless supply of anecdotes, support, and laughter. To my sister and brother for firmly keeping my feet on the ground—but also secretly being quite proud of me—you can admit it!

And to my grandparents, who are sadly no longer with us. Whenever I write I can hear my grandma telling everyone about her granddaughter's erotic novels. (*face palm and smile*) And my granddad singing "Born Free" to annoy and distract Grandma. I miss them both.

To all the incredible friends for forgiving me when I don't make plans as I "have to write that weekend," and for always being my biggest supporters: Abi Walton, Angelize Williams, Clare Causley, Eleanor Stammeijer, Hannah Hawkins, Holly Domney-Ahearne, Kelly Smith, Sammy Luton, and Siân Heap.

And last but certainly not least, to Freyja Hides-Westwood, my best friend since school. Thank you for drinking cocktails out of a teapot with me and telling me that when you look for a man, you look for me with a penis. It is still the nicest thing anyone has ever said to me. And it inspired this very book.